H.M.S. SARACEN

The other officers had been quick to voice their opinions of the new captain, but he had been slower to make up his mind. He had served with too many eccentric or difficult skippers to do otherwise. This one was in a class apart, he thought. He actually *believed* in this ship. Whereas for some of the others she was a penance or a stepping-stone for something better, for Richard Chesnaye it was the ultimate reward. It was incredible, slightly unnerving. But as she watched Chesnaye's hand moving almost lovingly along the bridge screen, Fox knew he was right.

Also in Arrow by Douglas Reeman

Douglas Reeman

H.M.S. SARACEN

ARROW BOOKS

Arrow Books Limited
17-21 Conway Street, London W1P 6JD

An imprint of the Hutchinson Publishing Group

London Melbourne Sydney Auckland
Johannesburg and agencies throughout
the world

First published by Hutchinson 1965
Arrow edition 1966
Reprinted 1972, 1974, 1976, 1977, 1980, 1982, 1984 and 1985

Printed and bound in Great Britain by
Anchor Brendon Limited, Tiptree, Essex

ISBN 0 09 906260 7

I

The Ship

In fierce short gusts the bitter north wind swept across the wide confines of Portsmouth harbour, the ranks of wavelets made by the incoming tide crumbling into white confusion at each successive blast. In the narrow entrance to the harbour itself the sea boiled in a trapped maelstrom and leapt violently against the weathered stones at the foot of the old Fort Blockhouse before being shredded by the wind and flung back into the pressing tideway. It was as if winter was still unwilling to release its grip and accept that with the coming of March it too would have to relent.

The sky was high and without colour or warmth, yet its clear emptiness seemed to turn the water below to an angry pewter which reflected against the tall sides of the moored battleships, the pitching, uneasy trots of torpedo-boat destroyers and the countless grey craft which thronged the naval anchorage and waited for the gale to ease.

There was little movement of small craft, and apart from a fat paddle-wheeled tug, with its yawing tow of loaded coal-tenders, the normally busy concourse was deserted. For although Britain was at war, and had been for seven confused months, this was Sunday forenoon, and aboard every pitching ship the church pennant was hoisted, and somewhere within each glistening hull, or hidden below the spray-dappled superstructures, some thousands of men listened automatically to the words of Peace and Love.

Richard Chesnaye ducked his head into a sharp gust of wind and pushed his way gratefully into the small green-painted hut at the top of a flight of worn stone steps which ran down to the water's edge. The hut was empty, and smelled of damp and stale cigarette smoke. Through the stained windows he could see the distorted shapes of the ships, the streaming white ensigns and the vast grey panorama of power and lordly indifference.

He was tall for his seventeen years, yet his steady grey eyes reflected some of the growing apprehension he felt as he stared across the dancing whitecaps towards his first ship. Even his new midshipman's uniform seemed to scream a contrast with the flaked walls of the hut and the worn, scrubbed benches where generations of naval officers had waited for boats to ferry them back to their ships. After a thick night ashore, perhaps, dazed, irritable, but with the dulled satisfaction always enjoyed by an unfettered sailor. Or perhaps to face a court martial. Richard Chesnaye's mouth turned down slightly. Or, like himself, to join a new world. Across that strip of water anything might be waiting. It was 1915, and the war had *not* ended in six months as the newspapers had prophesied, and as far as he could understand it was only just beginning.

He took off his cap and shook the spray absently across the floor. His hair was dark and curled rebelliously across his left forehead, helping to defeat the sensitive gravity of his features.

It was still hard to believe he was actually here and that at any moment a boat would appear, presumably at the foot of these famous King's Stairs, and carry him forward into a new way of life.

After months of training, lectures, drills and frustration he was ready. He wondered briefly what had become of all the other cadets he had known, who, as midshipmen like himself, were even now spreading throughout the Grand Fleet and beyond. He thought too of the long battle he had fought to stay level with many of those contemporaries. Not with the mysteries of seamanship and navigation, nor with the complex cult of tradition and ceremonial—as the last of a long line of naval officers Chesnaye had hardly noticed the latter—but with a tiny allowance from home he had faced the daily, even hourly, problem of keeping pace with the financially blessed and more privileged young men who fretted to complete their training and get to sea before the war ended.

6

Some oilskinned seamen trudged past the window, their bearded faces bowed to the wind. All at once Chesnaye wanted to call out to them, to show them he was there. One of *them*. He smiled quickly at the impulse and watched the burly figures until they were lost amongst the maze of derricks and equipment which seemed to litter the whole of Portsmouth dockyard.

As he had followed the seaman who had carried his tin trunk, Chesnaye had stared at every ship, half expectantly, half fearfully, as he strode to meet his latest challenge. But H.M.S. *Saracen* was lying out in the stream, clean and untouched by the land, indifferent to the unimportant individuals who struggled to serve her.

At first Chesnaye had received his orders to join the *Saracen* with mixed feelings. As some of his friends had danced excitedly at the prospect of joining a dashing torpedo-boat destroyer or one of the hard-worked North Sea cruisers, he had stared at his appointment instructions with something like bewilderment. Unlike the bulk of the Fleet, the *Saracen* was very new, hardly older than the war itself. In addition, she was one of a fresh breed. A monitor. In every war hard experience and different conditions gave birth to new types of ships and strategies. From galleys and fire-ships to bombs and river gunboats. Wherever the tide of battle rose, so too did the requirements of the Royal Navy. After years of undisputed power and prosperity the challenge had come again, and like the waspish submarines which sheltered behind Fort Blockhouse so too the monitors were coming into their own. This war would be fought with great armies, perhaps the biggest land forces the world had ever known, but while they faced the field-grey masses on the Western Front the Navy would be stretched to the limit to sustain them. One of Chesnaye's instructors had received his questions with contempt.

'A monitor? A bastard-ship! Neither one thing nor the other!'

Chesnaye squinted his eyes to stare at the tall shape outlined against the dull slate-roofed shambles of Gosport town.

The *Saracen* was certainly an unusual-looking ship. Although she boasted nearly seven thousand tons, as much as

7

many a cruiser, her length was little more than one of the larger destroyers. Yet if her length was puny she gave the impression of tremendous strength, even belligerence. As the instructor had also pointed out, she had been designed primarily for giving artillery support to land forces. Even a landsman would appreciate this point after only one glance. Dominating all else, and behind which the towering bridge and sturdy tripod mast looked almost incidental, two enormous fifteen-inch guns, mounted in one raised turret, pointed across the harbour like the tusks of some armoured monster. To support these great weapons the ship's designers had substituted breadth for length, and the *Saracen*'s ninety-foot beam added to her appearance of ponderous indestructibility.

A small black shape detached itself from the monitor's side and began to curtsy across the disordered whitecaps. The bleak light reflected dully on the picket boat's brass funnel, and Chesnaye could see a seaman already in her bows with a boathook as the sturdy little craft turned in a wide arc towards King's Stairs. They were coming for him.

Chesnaye stepped out into the wind once more, suddenly aware of hunger pangs, a sure sign of growing nervousness. The boat surged alongside the piles, the boathook already pulling at the slime-coated chains. There was an alarming clamour of bells and the boat's propeller threw up a great froth under the stern as the engine went astern.

All at once the boat was secured and Chesnaye was aware that the small midshipman who had been at the wheel, and jerking violently at the telegraph, was staring up at him, his pale eyes strained and impatient.

'Chesnaye?' His voice was shrill and added to the impression of extreme youth. 'Well, get aboard, for God's sake! No use waiting for a damned fanfare!'

Chesnaye smothered a grin and felt his way down the steep steps, the tin box grinding down dangerously against his legs.

After the spartan precision of the training ship he was used to entering and leaving boats, nevertheless he felt slightly irritated that not even one of the boat's two seamen attempted to offer him a hand.

The midshipman nodded quickly. 'Right, Morrison, let

go forrard!' He jerked at the telegraph and glanced up at the dockyard clock. 'God, three minutes adrift already!' He shouted at the seaman in the bows : 'Bear off forrard! Watch that paintwork!' But already the boat was swinging away into the tide, the hull trembling and shaking as the engine turned at full power.

The midshipman swung the brass wheel and took a quick breath. 'Sorry about the rush. My name's Pickles.' His innocent features darkened into a scowl. 'And I don't want any funny remarks !'

Chesnaye grinned and gripped the rail by the small open cockpit. 'Why the rush? Are we putting to sea immediately?'

Pickles grimaced. 'Rush? *Everything* is done like this! Right now there'll be at least two telescopes trained on this boat, and all hell will explode if I take longer than the prescribed time!'

'But suppose I had been delayed, or late?' Chesnaye watched the short figure by the wheel shiver.

'The day *you're* late you'll know the answer to that one!' Pickles laughed nervously. 'I expect you think your training days are over, eh? Well, believe me, you haven't seen anything yet!'

Chesnaye shrugged his shoulders deeper into his greatcoat and decided not to speak further. Pickles had obviously not been aboard the *Saracen* much longer than his own appointment. It was the usual game which 'old hands' played with new arrivals. Or was it? Every move which the boy made seemed charged with urgency and anxiety.

Chesnaye turned his attention to the monitor, which had suddenly loomed from indistinct distance to stark and frightening reality.

She towered above the vibrating picket boat so that he could see the twin turret as well as the battery of small four-inch guns abaft the bridge structure and all the hundred and one other details which crowded the upper deck. There was only one funnel, just aft of the great tripod mast, and a certain nakedness towards the stern, as if to compensate for the ship's great weight of armament and equipment. No black smoke belched from the funnel, and Chesnaye remembered for the first time that this ship

9

would at least spare him the agony of coaling. The *Saracen* was modern to the last rivet, and she was oil-fired.

He glanced again at his companion. Pickles was without oilskin or bridgecoat, and the front of his shirt was grey with salt spray. Between his teeth he gripped the lanyard of a whistle which he wore about his neck, and he spoke through the cord in sharp staccato sentences as he mentally prejudged the business of getting the forty-foot steamboat alongside.

It would not be easy, either, Chesnaye decided. He had already noticed the curious way in which the monitor's hull bulged as it touched the water. All along the waterline it was swollen outwards like the ballast tanks of a submarine.

Pickles tore his eyes from the water for a moment and stared at him. 'Anti-torpedo bulges! They're an experiment!' He nodded towards the monitor's waterline. 'She's so damned slow we need 'em!' He started to smile and then checked himself. 'But you won't say I said that, will you?'

Before Chesnaye could answer he was already jerking at the bell, and the boat shuddered violently as the propeller went astern and slewed the boat dangerously into the lee of the monitor's tall side where a gleaming varnished gangway and grating hung suspended above the water. High above, silhouetted against the pale sky, a lieutenant in frock-coat and sword-belt peered down at them.

The bowman aimed at the chains and missed.

The bell jangled once more and the little boat surged ahead, the stem yawing violently in the racing tide.

Through the lanyard and his gritted teeth Pickles exclaimed, 'God Almighty!' Then in a louder voice, 'Morrison, hook on, for Pete's sake!'

The big seaman shrugged and took another swing. The hook connected, and seconds later a tugging bowline held the boat temporarily secured.

A thin voice floated from above. 'Tie up at the boom!' There was the briefest pause. 'Then report to me, *Mister* Pickles.' Another pause while Chesnaye stared at the anguish on the midshipman's face. 'A bloody *awful* exhibition!'

A seaman scurried down the gangway and picked the tin trunk from the cockpit. There was a silence but for the chafe of boat fenders and the unbroken ripple of water, and Chesnaye found himself on the great ladder and making his way upwards, towards the voice.

As his head drew level with the deck he braced himself once more, painfully aware of his heart pumping against his ribs. The quarter-deck seemed vast and vaguely hostile. In a quick glance he took in the gleaming expanse of scrubbed teak planking which curved inwards towards the rounded stern above which a giant ensign streamed stiffly in the wind. Everything looked new and perfect. Even the sideboys, whose wind-reddened faces were watching him without expression, wore white gloves, and the marine sentry, quarter-master and the rest of the gangway staff looked as if they had just been issued with fresh equipment and clothing.

Chesnaye saluted the quarterdeck and the tall, reed-thin figure of the Officer of the Day, the lieutenant whose querulous voice had already greeted his arrival.

Lieutenant Hogarth blinked his salt-reddened eyes and glared at the midshipman. 'So you're Chesnaye,' he said at length. As he spoke he opened and closed his long telescope with quick nervous jerks. 'I'll have you taken to your berth and then you can report to the Commander.' He craned his thin neck towards the silent group at the gangway. 'Bosun's Mate, have this officer's gear taken below and then show him to the wardroom!' His sharp voice followed the man along the immaculate deck. 'And tell Mister Pickles I want him at the double!' Half to himself he added: 'Damned snotties! Couldn't handle a damned boat to save his damned neck!'

Chesnaye thought of the frantic dash across the harbour. 'I thought he did it rather well, sir.'

Hogarth's jaw opened and shut in time to the telescope. 'You *what*? When I require the opinion of a bloody midshipman I'll ask for it!' In a more controlled tone he added: 'I am the Gunnery Officer here. *I* am the one man in this ship who is of supreme importance!' He gestured vaguely towards the hidden guns. 'They are my responsibility. Without them this ship might well not have been built!'

Chesnaye almost laughed aloud, but controlled the mad impulse as he saw the wild sincerity in the officer's eyes. 'I see, sir,' he said carefully.

'Yes indeed!' Hogarth spoke to the quarterdeck at large. 'The primary object of the vessel is to knock hell out of the enemy. With *my* guidance we have done and will do just that!'

Chesnaye saluted and turned to follow the fast disappearing shape of the Bosun's Mate.

Hogarth added sharply, 'Do you play bridge, by the way?'

Chesnaye could not hide his grin this time, but Hogarth was fortunately staring through the telescope at a passing sloop. 'No, sir.'

'Hmmm, just as I thought. The very *bottom* of the barrel!'

As he strode uncertainly along the maindeck beneath the slim barrels of the secondary armament Chesnaye almost collided with the returning Pickles. The latter skidded to a halt, his face glistening with sweat.

'Did you meet him?'

Chesnaye nodded. There was something both endearing and pathetic about this small midshipman. 'Yes. I did. I didn't know how I was expected to react!'

Pickles grinned nervously. 'Mad. Quite mad. But then they're all getting like that here!'

'He was saying something about his gunnery——'

Pickles waved his grubby hands. 'Hopeless! Apart from trials and a quick shot at the Belgian coast we've not done a thing yet. Even then we missed the target! The Captain's been giving Hogarth hell!'

'I've got to report to the Commander next.'

Pickles shrugged. 'He's all right. But the Captain's straight out of Dickens! Hates everybody, especially midshipmen!'

Hogarth's voice screeched along the deck with the wind. 'Mister Pickles! At the *double*, I said!'

Chesnaye found himself two decks down, breathless and

completely lost, and standing in semi-darkness beside an open steel door.

The Bosun's Mate gestured indifferently. 'Gunroom. All the young gentlemen mess in there.'

It was a small space with only one scuttle, which seemed so close to the tumbling water that it must be barely above the torpedo bulge. There was a long table with a soiled cloth, upon which two messmen were laying cutlery for the Sunday meal. Five other midshipmen's chests were stacked along one bulkhead, and there was a single piece of massive furniture which could be mistaken for either a sideboard or a bar. Apart from a few chairs and a large print of the King, the place was bare.

A messman showed his teeth. 'You'll be the new one, then, sir?' He pushed back a strand of hair from his narrow head. 'I'm Lukey, an' this 'ere is Betts. We looks after you all. Six young gentlemen, an' 'im!' He jerked his thumb towards a canvas partition which seemed to form one large tent-like cabin across the end of the mess. 'Yes, sir. Sub-Lieutenant bloody Pringle. 'E's in charge of all of you, and 'e enjoys it very much.'

Chesnaye kept his face blank. He knew it was wrong to stand and listen to a seaman openly criticising a senior officer, but he had already learned the hard way that a loyal messman was an ally indeed. So he coughed and said quickly, 'I am to report to the Commander.'

Lukey bobbed his head. 'Ah yes, sir. A real gennelman if ever there was. Commander Godden is a toff. You can't ask for 'igher than that, eh?'

'Er, quite. Where is the wardroom?'

'Right aft. All the other officers' accommodation is there. 'Cept for the warrant officers. They mess next to you.'

Chesnaye committed all these facts to memory. In a strange ship and once off the spartan lines of the upper deck it was not uncommon to get completely lost, knowing neither bows from stern, nor even which deck you were on.

Lukey rubbed his hands. 'Well, 'urry back, sir. Pork chops and roast spuds today! Nothing like Sundays on board. Bit of God, an' then a good tuck in!' He frowned unexpectedly. 'I'll bet those bloody Huns aren't gettin' grub like this!'

Chesnaye started with surprise. In the strangeness of the ship, surrounded by the unfamiliar grey paint, the whirr of fans and the gentle creak of the ship's six-thousand-odd tons of steel and machinery, he had all but forgotten the war. There just did not seem to be room for it. Pork chops, boats which ran by the clock and an Officer of the Day who looked more like a clergyman, it was all too remote for war and reality.

He turned towards the door where the seaman lounged with bored indifference. But Lukey crossed the mess in two quick steps.

'Oh, just a few things, sir.' He gave a conspiratorial wink. 'I 'ope you won't take any offence, but it's better to get off on the right foot, y'see?'

Chesnaye did not, but waited mystified as Lukey continued in his peculiar rasping voice.

'Firstly, sir, you never wears a greatcoat aboard without express orders. The Captain does not believe in 'em. Says they pamper the young gentlemen, like. Next, your tin box is an officer's pattern. The Sub won't like that. *Must* 'ave regulation midshipman's chest.'

Chesnaye heard himself say, 'It belonged to my father.'

'Ah yes, sir. Very nice, I'm sure, but it won't do. I'll see if I can fix something.' He looked directly into Chesnaye's eyes. 'In this ship everything is perfect. The Captain says that's 'ow it's got to be, so that's 'ow it is. Take my tip, sir. Tread carefully, and don't ask questions.'

The Bosun's Mate said: 'The Commander'll be waitin', sir. 'E's not used to that!'

Lukey grinned. 'Off you go, sir. An' remember what I said!'

*   *   *   *   *

The *Saracen*'s wardroom was situated beneath the port side of the quarterdeck, and just prior to this Sunday lunch presented a scene of detached opulence mixed with one of noisy excitement. The long business of Divisions and church was over, the tense moments of inspections and

14

cramped drills were behind for another week, and the ship's officers stood around the small oak bar, first and second drinks consumed, glasses shining in the cheerful flames from the ornamental fireplace. Large brass scuttles lined one side of the wardroom, and as the ship swung easily at her buoy the distant grey scene of Portsmouth dockyard drifted back and forth from one scuttle to the next. From the top of the tall signal tower the scarecrow arms of the semaphore wagged impatiently across the anchored warships, but these officers at least were free to ignore them.

Most of them stood in one group around the plump heavy figure of the Commander, while the remainder slumped in the well-fashioned red leather chairs, perhaps listening to the promising bustle of the stewards beyond the curtain which partly hid the long table, the shining silver and tall-backed teak chairs.

Commander Godden tilted his glass, allowing his eye to stray across the semicircle of faces around him. It was strange how no officer ever seemed to get used to the serious business of ship's ceremonial. The more senior the officer became, the more he seemed to take it to heart.

Now they were relaxed, yet at the same time excited. In their heavy dress-coats and glittering epaulettes they seemed like strangers to one another, so that their voices became louder, their gestures more extravagant.

Godden sniffed the faint aroma of roast beef and swallowed automatically. He nodded towards a hovering steward and said in his loud bass voice, 'Same again, gentlemen?' It was an invitation, and he allowed his wide mouth to lift in a grin as the glasses were raised and lowered as one.

He glanced around the spacious wardroom and felt pleased. There was something about a new ship. The fitted plum-coloured carpet, the shining gloss paint, the proud crest above the fire depicting a fierce Arab warrior with a raised scimitar; everything was glossy and full of well-being. There were only twelve wardroom officers, as some had already been taken to supplement the growing might of the Fleet, and this added little to the amount of work and increased greatly to their individual comfort aboard.

Lieutenant Travis, the Navigating Officer, watched the steward shaking angostura into some of the glasses and plucked thoughtfully at his neat black beard. 'We'll soon be away, I expect?' It was a question directed at large, but meant for the Commander.

Godden winked at the ramrod figure of Major De L'Isle, whose Royal Marine's uniform fitted his massive body like a silk glove, so that some wondered how he managed to bend, let alone sit at table. 'We shall see, gentlemen! I have invited the Captain here for a drink this forenoon, so we might be told!'

De L'Isle grunted and ran a finger around the top of his tight collar. 'All this damned excitement!' The marine glared at the opposite bulkhead, his small ginger moustache bright against his florid face, the whole of which was covered with a fine web of tiny broken veins, the mark of a heavy drinker. 'One would think this was the first war the Service had been in! Lot of damned rubbish!'

The Commander took his drink and initialled the steward's chit. 'Ah, but this might be a little different. Not like China, you know, Major. Germany's damned powerful and itching for a fight!'

Lieutenant Travis frowned. 'I wonder what our next job will be?'

'Always wondering, Pilot!' Godden beamed. 'Maybe we shall have another go at the Belgian coast, eh? Give poor old Hogarth another chance to prove his worth!'

There was a quick response of laughter. Even the Chief Engineer, a grizzled and grey-haired little man called Innes, who had been standing silently on the outside of the group, seemed to come alive. 'It's no job for a ship of war!'

They all looked at him with surprise. Godden watched him with silent amusement. 'Go on, Chief. Tell us what is wrong with a monitor.'

The engineer shrugged. 'Ships are for fighting ships. Get mixed up with the damned Army and anything might happen!'

De L'Isle nodded aggressively. 'Quite right! My marines can handle any of that nonsense!'

The Navigator swirled the gin round his glass and frowned. He was a quiet, deep-thinking man and un-

16

moved by the casual ease with which his betters were dismissing the efforts of another service. 'I think it may be a mistake to think that.' He kept his dark eyes lowered. 'Jerry can fight well enough, and our sea supremacy may have to take on a completely new challenge.'

Godden grinned. 'Of what, for instance?'

Travis shrugged. 'U-boats. Even their surface ships have done well so far.'

The marine major choked. 'Bloody rubbish, Pilot! We've beaten the Jerry in every combat so far! Whipped the hides off 'em!'

'What about Coronel?' Travis met his stare angrily.

'Well, what about Coronel?' De L'Isle seemed to bristle. 'And what about the Falklands last December, and the Dogger Bank battle a couple of months ago?' He turned to the group at large, his glowing face triumphant. 'We showed them well enough!'

Travis persisted doggedly. 'What I'm saying is that it will not be an easy victory!'

Godden licked his lips. The heat of the fire, the gin and the liveliness of the conversation were having their usual effects. 'I agree with the Chief. I don't much hold with inshore fighting. Shooting at some damned target ten miles or so inland, while some fool of a soldier signals his interpretation of what you are doing!' He groped for the words. 'It's not clean, not *naval* somehow!'

A steward glided closer. 'The Captain's coming, sir.'

Godden pulled down the front of his coat and turned to face the door.

Captain Lionel Royston-Jones was slight, and at first glance even frail. Yet his small body was trim and wiry against Godden's portliness, and the bright blue eyes which darted briefly around the waiting officers were completely steady and entirely lacking in warmth.

Godden cleared his throat. 'I am glad you could accept the invitation, sir.'

The customary remark seemed to fall short and left no impression on the Captain's neat, weather-browned features. Everyone knew that a captain only entered a wardroom by invitation. Yet one look at Royston-Jones' face shattered the illusion of a favour. Who, after all, would deny a man like the Captain entrance anywhere! Royston-Jones inclined his head slightly towards the Chaplain, whose dark garb, plus the outlandish habit of parting his hair dead in the centre, gave him the appearance of an anxious crow. 'Good sermon, Padre.'

The Chaplain, whose name was Nutting, rubbed his thin hands with agitation. 'Thank you, sir. Most gratifying!'

But Royston-Jones was already looking again at the Commander. 'Well, are you going to offer me a drink?' His voice was never raised, but it had a kind of crispness which made even a simple remark sound like a reprimand.

They all watched him sip his customary sherry, his pale eyes fixed on the nearest scuttle. His small figure seemed weighed down by the heavy frock-coat and gleaming epaulettes and gave him the added appearance of an officer from some bygone age. Even his hair was cut unfashionably long, with the sideburns reaching below his ears. On either cheek, too, there was a small tuft of brown hair, and these were said to have earned him the nick-name of 'Monkey' on the lower deck.

At length he said calmly: 'I have just received my orders. We sail tomorrow. Seven bells of the Morning Watch. After lunch, Commander, perhaps you will be good enough to see me about final arrangements.'

Only the Chaplain dared to ask the urgent question. 'And may I be bold enough to enquire our destination, sir?' He peered at the Captain as if to see the words emerge from his mouth.

'You may, Padre.' The cold eyes moved relentlessly over the tense faces. 'And, since no more shore leave will be granted, I can be sure of some sort of security!'

There was an uneasy ripple of laughter. It was never simple to determine the Captain's humour.

'The destination will be the Mediterranean. The orders specify Gibraltar, and thence to the Eastern Mediterranean for operations against the Turks.'

Godden whistled. 'Gallipoli, by God!'

Royston-Jones pursed his lips. 'As you put it, Commander. Gallipoli.'

Immediately everyone was speaking at once, while the

Captain stood like a small rock, unmoved and unmoving.

Innes ran his fingers through his grey hair. 'Well, the engine room is ready, sir.' He grinned wryly. 'No more coal to worry about!'

Royston-Jones touched one of the little hair tufts with a fore-finger. 'Fuel is the least of our problems.'

'But, sir, I thought the Gallipoli campaign was going to be allowed to fade out!' Travis spoke loudly in spite of the warning in Godden's eyes.

'Did you, Travis?' The blue eyes regarded him mildly. 'Perhaps their lordships have not had the benefit of your insight?'

Godden's huge bulk moved forward as if to shield the young officer's confusion. 'I think I know what Pilot meant, sir. We've been told that the squadron sent to bombard the Turkish forts along the Dardanelles and to force an entrance to the Straits was not powerful enough. There was some story too that our minesweepers were repulsed by gun-fire and the battleships have had to make do best they can against the enemy minefields. A sort of stalemate. A good idea gone wrong.'

The Captain laid his glass very carefully on a table. 'It is a campaign, Commander, not one Lilliputian skirmish.' He spoke without emotion, yet two spots of bright colour appeared on Godden's cheeks as if he had been faced with a stream of obscenities.

'Futhermore, the object of these operations is to *capture* the Straits, and not merely to give some apparently much-needed exercise to our gunnery officers!' He continued evenly : 'With the Straits captured, Turkey is cut in two. Our ally, Russia, will have her southern ports open once more, and we will then be able to assist her in an all-out assault on Constantinople. All Turkey's arms factories are situated there. Smash their capital and their production and they will soon collapse. Germany will be without an ally, and all neutrals tempted to throw in their lot with the Kaiser will think again. In addition, the back door to Europe will be open and in our hands.'

The marine major breathed out noisily. 'My God, what a scheme!'

Royston-Jones glanced sharply at the glass in De L'Isle's

hand. 'Quite so, Major. It will need *all* our attention. Also, it will mean a much greater campaign than first visualised by Mr. Churchill. Not just ships, but troops. Thousands of men and equipment must be landed and helped inland.'

Godden said quietly : 'But surely by now the Turks will have recovered from the first assaults? Won't they be dug in and ready for our troops?'

Royston-Jones smiled gently. 'I can see you have fully assessed the situation, Commander. That is where we come into the picture. A new weapon. A floating power of gunfire which can be brought almost to the beaches themselves. No more of this nonsense of battleships meandering back and forth under the muzzles of prepared shore-batteries. Ships too deep-hulled to get in close, or too puny to shoot more than a few miles. The *Saracen* will make history.' He looked sharply towards the shore. 'We will be well rid of the land. We will be able to concentrate on fulfilling our function before we become cluttered up with untrained men from the barracks or these wretched Reservists.' He moved towards the door. 'See that the ship is brought to security readiness immediately, Commander. You know the procedure.'

Godden nodded. 'Aye, aye, sir. We'll make a show all right!'

The slight figure stiffened. 'I am afraid that a "show", as you call it, would fall far short of what *I* have in mind!'

The door slid to and there was an empty silence.

Godden tried to grin at the others, but nothing happened. Viciously he slammed his glass on the bar and signalled for a steward.

'Bloody hell!' he said.

.   .   .   .   .

Richard Chesnaye settled his shoulders more comfortably within the tight confines of his hammock and stared upwards at the pipes which criss-crossed the shadowed deckhead barely inches from his face. The darkness in the stuffy gunroom was broken only by the shaded gleam of a blue police light, so that the strangeness and unfamiliarity of the place seemed to close in on him and add to his feeling of loneliness

His first half-day in the *Saracen* had been a long one, yet so crowded with events, faces and situations that only now, in the security of his hammock, could he piece them together in his mind and go over his own impressions and reactions.

He met the Commander as expected in the wardroom, or rather on the fringe of it. Listening to the babble of conversation and laughter beyond the curtain he had found it hard to picture himself as ever being one of them. He had stared at the table beside him, laden with caps, sword-belts, even swords, where they had been dropped by the officers as they had returned from Divisions. Caps exactly like his own, but for the Commander's with its leaf-encrusted peak, yet in a way so different. In the training ship there had been only two partitions. Cadets and instructors. Here in this strange ship everybody seemed slotted and packaged into divided messes, so that a sense of complete isolation existed between each one. The lieutenants and above had the wardroom, the sub-lieutenants their own mess. While the warrant officers and midshipmen, too, were subdivided again. Below them, the chief and petty officers and then the bulk of the ship's company were neatly stowed away in separate compartments, untouched by each other, yet constantly aware of status and authority.

Commander Godden had seemed pleasant enough. Jovial, full of vague encouragement, yet rather distant, as if his mind was elsewhere.

Chesnaye had returned to his own mess by a roundabout route, and met his own sort in the process of starting their Sunday meal. He had to sit on his tin chest because there were not enough chairs, but he had not minded. He had been too busy watching and listening.

There was Beaushears, who at this moment was snoring painfully just two feet away from him, his feet whitely protruding from the end of his hammock. A tall, deceptively languid young man, with the far-seeing eyes of an adventurer, he had casually introduced the others.

'This quiet one is Bob Maintland. Plays good squash, but if you've a sister you'd better watch him!'

With a fork he had pointed to the cheerful gnome sitting

opposite Chesnaye. 'Meet "Eggy" Bacon. Talks first, thinks later!'

The one addressed had merely grinned, showing a double rank of very small pointed teeth, and then turned his attention back to a tattered notebook which he was obviously studying.

Beaushears had observed : 'Better take the book off the table before the Master arrives. He can't bear anything which might distract from his fascinating conversation!' Then in his normal drawl, 'And this is "Ticky" White, so called because he is always scratching.'

White had been on duty on the quarterdeck when Chesnaye had arrived, and even now bore the red mark of his cap printed across his forehead. He was a pale uncertain-looking youth with jet-black hair and restless, very deep-set eyes. He shrugged and nodded to Chesnaye. 'I'm too tired to find a witty answer. A few hours with that maniac Hogarth drains me of human kindness!'

Beaushears smiled. 'And of course you have already met the genius of the *Saracen*, Keith Pickles.'

Chesnaye saw the small midshipman jerk out of his thoughts and look across with confusion. 'Oh, er, yes.' Pickles seemed at a loss. 'Hope you've settled in.' He had been about to add something more when the Sub-Lieutenant had entered.

Now, in the same gunroom, but in the unreal security of the hammock, Chesnaye tried to picture Pringle once more. He had the build and movement of a rugby player. Very big, glowing with health and surprisingly fast on his feet.

'Well, all sitting down!' Pringle had hurled himself into the big chair at the head of the table, his eyes already fixed on Chesnaye. 'Ah, the new boy. Good. Common practice to report to me immediately upon joining ship.' He spoke in sharp, almost breathless stacatto. 'Still, you're not to know. But in this ship ignorance is no excuse.' He snatched a spoon and dug into the soup even as the messman Lukey had placed it before him. Between noisy mouthfuls he continued in the same expressionless voice : 'Good, then let me see. What's next.' He lifted his pale eyebrows with theatrical concern. 'Ah, *yes*!' He turned to stare at Pickles.

'Another complaint about your boat-handling from

Lieutenant Hogarth!' He shook his head so that the over-head light glistened on his cropped blond hair. 'Tch, tch! The honour of the gunroom soiled again.'

Chesnaye was about to grin when he realised that the others were staring stonily in front of them or busily engaged with their soup. Except Pickles. He stared at Pringle with the look of a mesmerised rabbit.

Pringle added : 'You really are hopeless, you know. We can't have our new member getting the wrong idea, now can we?' Then in a matter-of-fact tone, as if the whole matter was of no importance, 'Now what's it to be this time?' He waited, and even Chesnaye was conscious of the silence. The clatter of dishes in the small pantry had ceased, and he could imagine Lukey and Betts listening to Pickles' answer.

Pringle threw back his head. 'Take this plate away!' His voice, too, was powerful.

As Lukey flitted across the gunroom he asked : 'Now, Pickles, you've not answered? D'you want to absolve your stupidity with gloves on? If so, we can settle it immediately after grub, eh?'

Chesnaye still hardly believed what he had witnessed. A great brute like Pringle offering to take on Pickles in combat. He could have killed him with one hand and blindfolded.

Pringle had eventually nodded with apparent satisfaction. 'Right. Punishment Number Two. Immediately after lunch.'

Chesnaye twisted on to his side, his eyes wide in the darkness. Punishment Number Two had entailed a cruel and systematic beating with the leather scabbard of a midshipman's dirk.

Pickles had bent across the table opposite Pringle before Chesnaye had realised the true meaning of the punishment. Each midshipman had taken the scabbard in turn and had given Pickles three strokes across the buttocks, a total of fifteen blows.

When it was Chesnaye's turn Pringle had said evenly : 'Lay it on hard, Chesnaye. If you don't we keep going round and round again until I am satisfied!'

Chesnaye still felt the nausea of those blows, as if he himself had been beaten.

Later he had tried to speak to Pickles, but even now he was out once more in his picket boat, no doubt ferrying some of the last-minute requirements before sailing.

The monitor had her orders. The Mediterranean. It should have been the moment for which he had waited so long. Away from the land, away from home and all that it had entailed.

He tried to exclude himself from what had happened, but he could not. He tried to tell himself that Pickles was inefficient, but inwardly he knew he was no different from any other midshipman suddenly pushed into the hard system of the Navy.

Beyond the steel hull the water rippled and surged against the tough plating while overhead the sentries paced the quarterdeck and peered into the darkness of the harbour.

Tomorrow was another start. It might all be different when the ship was at sea.

He thought of Pickles' face, and wondered.

2

No Survivors

Richard Chesnaye paused at the foot of the steel bridge ladder and stood momentarily looking up at the overcast sky. Six bells of the Morning Watch had just been struck, and already he could feel the tremor of excitement which seemed to run through the deck of the moored monitor itself. He began to climb, conscious of the darkness which still shrouded the harbour and the hard chill in the air. The wind had fallen away, and below him, just visible beyond the ship's side, he could see the flat oily current which surged into the harbour, now unbroken by whitecaps, but strong and threatening for all that.

The ship's bridge structure, pale grey against the dark clouds, seemed to overhang him like a cliff. As he climbed higher he saw the compartments and platforms alive with anonymous figures, busy and absorbed in the preparations for getting under way. Soon I will know all these faces, he thought.

The strident notes of a marine's bugle had urged the men to their stations. 'Special Sea Dutymen close up!' And now, like himself, the ship's company had fanned throughout the gently pulsating hull like small parts of a giant and intricate machine.

He reached the wide navigating bridge and slithered across the coaming into a small world of calm and orderly preparation.

From the moment the hands had been called from their hammocks Chesnaye had been on the move. In the black confusion of dawn he had followed Sub-Lieutenant Pringle's massive shape as he had strode the upper deck, pointing out all the various places of immediate importance to a new midshipman. There was so much to remember.

For entering and leaving harbour Chesnaye's place was on the navigating bridge. He had to study and assist the

Officer of the Watch and generally make himself useful. At Action Stations he was also on the bridge, but would attach himself to the Signals Department and the specialists who assisted the Gunnery Officer. For, unlike normal warships, additional signalmen were required to converse with forces ashore when a bombardment was being carried out.

In harbour, apart from his divisional duties, Chesnaye was to have charge of one of the oared whalers.

Pringle had pointed to the sleek boat high in its davits and said offhandedly : 'You should be able to manage that. But if Pickles does not improve you'll be getting his picket boat !'

A figure loomed out of the gloom. It was Midshipman Beaushears, who also had a station on the navigating bridge.

'You found your way, then, Dick?' His languid voice was hoarse, and Chesnaye could see his breath like steam in the damp air.

'What happens now?' Chesnaye found that he was whispering.

'Just keep quiet and get out of everyone's way !'

Chesnaye grinned and stood back from the quiet bustle of figures around him. As his eyes became more accustomed to the gloom he was able to watch every piece of the open bridge, which he knew he would soon recognise in complete darkness.

It was almost square in shape, with a raised compass platform dead in the centre. The front and sides were lined with voice-pipes which seemed to keep up an incessant chatter, and on either wing of the bridge was mounted a massive searchlight. Behind him the bridge opened into a dimly lighted charthouse where he could see Lieutenant Travis, the Navigator, leaning across a glass-topped table, a pair of brass dividers in his hands, his small beard almost skimming the chart itself.

Overhead, black and solid like an additional bridge, the great steel mass of the Upper Control Top was supported by all three legs of the tripod mast. From there Chesnaye knew that when *Saracen*'s turn came to fight the gunnery staff would plot and record every shot, every hit and miss, despite what carnage might be spread below them.

Commander Godden's bulky shape moved to the fore-part of the bridge. He stood on one of the newly scrubbed gratings and rested his hands on the bridge screen. His head and chest rose easily above the thin strip of canvas dodger which still glinted with a thin layer of frost, and he looked ponderously solid, like the ship beneath his straddled legs.

Without warning a sliver of grey light lanced across the harbour, a pathetic attempt to force the night to relinquish its hold. The ship's shape seemed to harden and faces took on personality and meaning.

Chesnaye ventured a glance over the screen. Below him, like its counterpart on the other side of the bridge, the signal platform was stark against the fast-moving water. He could see the watchful signalman and the neat racks of gaily coloured bunting. A tall Yeoman of Signals was peering through his telescope towards the dockyard.

It was surprising how much bigger the ship seemed from up here. The paleness of the freshly scrubbed decks seemed to sweep away far into the distance, so that he felt strangely secure. He watched the white blobs of the seamen's bare feet and wondered how they managed to ignore the bitter cold, and saw too the last boat being swung inboard by the big power hoist. The buoy-jumpers had been picked from the lurching buoy under the monitor's bows, the cable unshackled, and now only a thin wire remained reeved through the weed-encrusted ring. The last link with the land.

Far ahead beyond the tapering muzzles of the two great guns he could faintly make out the bustling activity of the cable party, and the stringy shape of Lieutenant Hogarth, who was silhouetted against the guard-rail, his pale face turned upwards towards the bridge.

A bell jangled with sudden urgency, and a seaman reported, 'Engine room standing by, sir!'

Godden nodded absently. 'Very good.'

Flat, disinterested voices, yet Chesnaye could feel the excitement running through him like wine.

Godden peered at his watch. 'Tell the Bosun to pipe all hands for leaving harbour.' A small pause. 'Mister Beaushears. My respects to the Captain. Tell him it is ten minutes off the time to slip.'

Chesnaye watched his companion slip away and be swallowed up in the grey steel.

Another voice said, 'All dutymen closed up for leaving harbour, sir.'

Godden shrugged and said testily, 'I should bloody well hope so!'

Chesnaye could feel the freshening quiver of the gratings under his feet, and turned to watch a thickening plume of smoke thrust itself over the rim of the funnel. A brief gust of wind plucked the smoke downwards so that he coughed and dabbed at his streaming eyes. Oil or coal, funnel smoke still tasted foul, he thought.

There was a brief rustle of excitement and then silence. Without looking Chesnaye knew that the Captain had arrived. Cautiously he watched the small figure move to the front of the bridge and place himself squarely in the centre.

'Ship ready to proceed, sir.' Godden's voice sounded different.

'Very well. Sound off.'

Chesnaye heard no order passed, but below him a bugle shrilled across the dark harbour, and he could hear the slap of bare feet as the men fell into ranks for leaving harbour.

'Signal from tower, sir!' The Yeoman's harsh voice lifted easily across the screen. 'Proceed!'

Godden coughed quietly. 'I have already signalled the two tugs, sir. They are standing by.'

Royston-Jones craned his head, first to peer at the two bulky shapes which idled in the froth of their own paddles, and then to stare at his commander.

'Tugs?' His voice was quiet, but sharp enough to reach even Chesnaye. 'Since when have I required *tugs*?'

Godden said at length: 'Strong tide this morning, sir. And very poor light.' He seemed to dry up.

'I am aware of that, thank you. The Coxswain is on the wheel. He knows what to do without a whole bombardment of orders and alterations of course!'

Chesnaye bit his lip. Another bad start.

The Captain adjusted the glasses about his neck. 'Stand

by!' He lifted the glasses to peer astern at the dockyard, which seemed to swing around a motionless ship. Irritably he added : 'One of the quarterdeck party is out of the rig of the day, Commander! Take his name, and deal with it!'

Chesnaye was almost fretting with suppressed excitement. How could this man bother his head with such trivial matters at a time like this? A petty officer scurried away in search of the culprit caught accidentally in the Captain's vision.

'Slow ahead together!' The bells jangled, and the bridge began to vibrate. 'Slip!'

There was a hoarse bark of orders from the fo'c'sle, and Chesnaye heard the rasp of wire as the last mooring flew through the buoy-ring and was hauled aboard by the madly running seamen.

Faintly but audibly Hogarth's voice came from the bows, 'All gone forrard, sir!'

Caught in the current, the wide-hulled monitor slewed untidily in the fast water, her stern already pointing towards Gosport, her bows swinging fast across the harbour entrance.

A messenger standing near Chesnaye sucked his teeth. 'Jesus Christ!'

Royston-Jones lowered his head to one of the voice-pipes. 'Watch her head, Coxswain!'

Chesnaye knew that the coxswain of a ship was always entrusted with handling the wheel at the most important and difficult moments. Without orders he was usually left to steer his ship straight for the harbour entrance, and thus avoid the delay of repeating and passing orders.

Godden shifted uneasily. 'Still paying off, sir.'

The Captain grunted. 'Half ahead port!'

The additional power sent a wake of white froth streaming after their unwieldy charge, no doubt followed with moments the blunt bows swung back towards the narrow harbour mouth.

'Slow ahead together!' Royston-Jones' right foot was tapping very quietly on the grating. 'Make a signal to our escorts to take up station in thirty minutes.'

Somewhere astern two destroyers would already be slinking after their unwieldy charge, no doubt followed with some ribald comment from their consorts.

Godden watched the pale walls of Fort Blockhouse sliding past. They looked near enough to touch, and he glanced quickly at the Captain's impassive face. It was as if he were steering close inshore deliberately. Any other warship of comparable tonnage would have scraped one of those vicious little black rocks by now. Godden watched the fast-rising tide as it surged through the glinting line of teeth below the fort.

'Fo'c'sle secured for sea, sir.'

'Very well. Fall out the hands, and stand by to exercise Action Stations. I want every man checked at his station.'

'That has been done, sir.' It was the Commander's responsibility, and Godden's voice was defiant.

'Well, do it *again*!' The Captain hoisted himself into the tall wooden chair which was bolted in the forepart of the bridge. 'And Commander, don't forget to signal to your tugs.' There was the briefest pause. 'Otherwise they might follow me to Gibraltar!'

. . . . .

The third day out from Portsmouth found the *Saracen* almost across the Bay of Biscay, with the westerly tip of Spain some hundred miles on the port bow. Crossing the Bay had been uncomfortable if not actually rough. With a following sea and a stiff wind, which veered from one northern point to another, the ungainly monitor made heavy going across the endless shoulders of white rollers, when even her ninety-foot beam seemed incapable of preventing a motion so violent that at times it felt as if the ship would never right herself. The following rollers would build up beneath the rounded stern so that the quarterdeck lifted until it appeared to be level with the corkscrewing bridge, then with a violent yawing heave the whole hull would lift its flat bottom stern first over the crest and sink heavily into the next glass-sided trough. Seamen dragged themselves round the upper deck checking and re-lashing the jerking equipment and boats, while the men off watch lay wretchedly in their hammocks, eyes closed so as not to see the oilskins and loose clothing as they swung away from bulkheads, hovered for endless seconds and then canted back through another impossible angle.

Richard Chesnaye braced his shoulders against a davit and allowed the cold spray to dash across his tingling cheeks. Astern the monitor's wake hardly made a ripple, a condemnation of the painful ten knots which had been their speed since leaving England. Zig-zagging astern he could see the solitary destroyer escort rising and falling across the broken water, its fragile hull often completely hidden by clouds of bursting spray. For them it must have been much worse, he thought. To retain station on their charge the two destroyers had been made to crawl at a painstaking speed, their narrow decks and low hulls open for anything the sea could throw in their direction. One minute Chesnaye could see down the three narrow funnels, the next instant he could watch the water streaming free from the actual bilge keel as the little ship rolled like a mad thing. The second destroyer had retired with engine trouble one day out of harbour, but this one seemed doggedly determined to keep with them at all costs.

Chesnaye shaded his eyes and looked upwards at the bridge which seemed black against the harsh grey light. He could see the pale blobs of faces where the lookouts peered through their glasses, and the machine-gunners who stood by their weapons in case a periscope should suddenly appear from the creaming wavecrests.

Chesnaye bit his lip. It sounded simple enough. If a U-boat showed its periscope even for a second a well-aimed burst of fire could blind it, and force the hidden boat to the surface where it could be finished by gunfire. He looked towards the horizon and shuddered. It was small consolation to know that even U-boats were said to find this sort of weather difficult.

Nearby he could hear his party of seamen talking quietly as they climbed in and out of the slung whaler, checking gear and killing time until the next 'stand-easy'. In three days he had hardly got to know them at all. Just faces that were free and open with each other, yet when he spoke to them they froze into attentive masks. When he had been watching the hands at work on the upper deck he had wanted to intervene, if only to show them he was alive. But there was always a seasoned petty officer in the way, with a gruff, 'Leave this to me, sir,' or 'We don't do it like that in *this* ship, sir!'

A big roller creamed broken and frustrated along the weather side, the spray sluicing across the bright planking itself. Droplets of spume clung to his trousers, and he was suddenly glad that he was not prone to seasickness like some of the others.

Sub-Lieutenant Pringle had been much in evidence during the slow journey from the English Channel. Bitter, sarcastic and ever watchful for a mistake, he had approached Chesnaye the first day out, his face solemn, even sad.

'That sea-chest of yours.' He had rolled back on his heels like a boxer. 'Not regulation, y'know?'

He had then launched into a long dissertation about the importance of uniformity and discipline, and the necessity of making an example. Chesnaye had been surprised, almost shocked, to find that this first clash left him feeling neither angry nor resentful. Pringle's attitude must be an act. Even his long speeches gave the impression of planning and careful rehearsing, so that Chesnaye felt vaguely embarrassed.

He had mentioned this fact to Beaushears when they had shared a Middle Watch together, but the seasoned midshipman had seemed disinterested.

'It's the system, Dick. As necessary as it is futile!' Then indifferently he had added, 'You just put up with it until it's your turn to be a Pringle!'

Chesnaye half smiled to himself. Heaven forbid!

A bugle shrilled, and as one of the seamen nearby stopped work and scampered towards the fo'c'sle for a quick smoke and a basin of tea, Chesnaye walked to the guard-rail and peered at the tilting horizon. Was it possible that they would ever reach the land mass of Europe again? It seemed impossible that hundreds of miles beyond that blue-grey line two giant armies were even now facing each other across the wire and sandbags of Flanders. Before the seamen returned to their half-hearted work hundreds of soldiers might be killed and wounded. Thousands more

32

would perish the moment a new attack was planned.

It was a good thing to be going to the Mediterranean. It was new, clean and fresh. At home even in England the excitement of war was stifled by the daily misery of casualty lists and scarecrow figures on crutches and sticks who thronged the railway stations or waited for ambulances. The men from the battlefront had all seemed cheerful enough. The worse the wounds, the higher the spirits.

Chesnaye had mentioned this point to a nervous-looking subaltern he had met at Waterloo station. The youngster had stared at Chesnaye and then smiled coldly. 'They know they can't be sent back!' With sudden fervour he had finished, '*They're* safe now!'

Out here it was different. The ship was uncomfortable at the moment, but soon that would change. His duties were arduous and complicated and it seemed impossible to please anyone, senior or junior, yet it felt good to belong, to be a part of this ponderous Goliath.

He wondered if his mother had already written to him, and how life was proceeding in the quiet Surrey home. He tried not to think of his father. The memory of their last meeting affected him like nausea.

Being away at training, he had seen little of Commander James Chesnaye. That last night at home, with the wind rattling the small latticed windows, he had forced himself to sit quite still, to watch and listen as his father rambled on about the Navy as it had been, as it should be. He lost count of the times the bottle had filled and refilled the glass at his father's elbow, but the record was stark in the man's slurred and aggrieved voice.

His father. To his wife, his son, anyone who would listen, he told the self-same story. It had been a mistake, but not his own. When his ship, the sloop *Kelpie*, had ripped open her hull on a shoal off the Chinese mainland he, Commander James Chesnaye, the vessel's captain, had been in his sea-cabin. The first lieutenant had been to blame. As the months and then years followed the court martial the blame spread. The helmsman had been unreliable, the navigating officer had borne a secret grudge, the charts had been incorrectly marked. And so it had

33

gone on. Each time Richard Chesnaye had returned home from his cadets' training ship he had found his mother older and more subdued, and his father more definite as to the root of the disaster which had cost the Navy a ship and him a career.

This last short leave, which should have brought such promise to the home, was no better. Chesnaye, in his new midshipman's uniform and his orders in his pocket, had been confronted with the final spectacle of misery and defeat. At the very commencement of war his father had gone to the Admiralty to accept even a small command without complaint. But the Admiralty had made no offer at all. There were no familiar faces to greet him, and the records when consulted were enough to finish his small spark of embittered confidence.

As he watched the slow, mesmerising pitch of water alongside, Chesnaye wondered about the truth of his own thoughts. He had wanted to believe his father, but all the time there had been the slow nagging pain of doubt in his mind. Was that why his father was so outspoken? Was it because the Admiralty had released him as painlessly as they knew how, when in fact the ill-fated *Kelpie*'s captain had been too drunk to cope with a situation for which he had been trained for twenty years?

Chesnaye thought of the tin chest which still stood in the gunroom. He had no intention of getting rid of it for Pringle or anyone else. As a boy he had watched that box arrive home from India, China, Malta and any one of the dozen stations where his father had served in the Navy. The scratched lid still bore the faint traces of the original owner's name and rank. The box had become a symbol of something he still wanted to believe.

His father had fallen silent towards the end of that last evening. His eyes had been red-rimmed as he had peered across the fire at his grave-faced son. Finally he had said, 'Never *trust* anyone, Dick!' For a moment he had been without anger, and as Chesnaye remembered that instant he could feel the emotion pricking at his eyes. 'Never trust anyone. Or you'll end up like me!'

He felt a step on the deck beside him and looked up to see Pickles watching him without expression.

Chesnaye shook the cloak of gloom from his shoulders and forced a smile. It had been pitiful to see Pickles being hounded and bullied by Sub-Lieutenant Pringle. It was equally dangerous to show such feelings. Any sign of disapproval or resentment seemed to drive Pringle to greater lengths, but always against the luckless Pickles.

'Hello, Keith, you look fed up?' Chesnaye saw Pickles' mouth turn down at the corners.

'Hell, yes. I tell you, Dick, I'm about sick of this ship, and the Navy too!'

Chesnaye looked back at the sea. Quietly he said : 'Your turn will come, Keith. Try and stick it a bit longer. Very soon the ship'll be too busy to allow Pringle much scope for his stupidity!'

Unconsciously he had spoken the last words with quiet venom, so that Pickles stared at him with surprise. 'I didn't know *you* felt like that!' His voice shook. 'He's made my life hell. I know I'm clumsy and not very good at my work, but I'm not the only one.' He glanced furtively along the spray-dappled deck. 'If you only knew the half of it.'

Chesnaye said carefully, 'If it were me I think I'd tell him to go to blazes!'

Pickles forced a grin. 'I believe you would too!' Impetuously he caught Chesnaye's sleeve. 'I'm damned glad you're aboard, Dick! You're different from the others. I'm a scholarship boy and I've not been used to their sort before. Some of them are so vain,' he floundered for the right words, 'so false. They seem to be playing some sort of game, whereas all this is terribly important to me.' He watched Chesnaye's face guardedly. 'My father has a shop in Bristol. It was hard to get me a cadetship.'

Chesnaye looked away. Hard? It must have been almost impossible.

Pickles continued, 'I'm the first in our family, but I expect you come from a long naval line?' When Chesnaye did not answer he added, 'And your father, is he still in the Service?'

'He's dead.'

The look of shock on Pickles' face matched the guilt which ran through Chesnaye's heart as the lie dropped so easily from him. He felt angry and ashamed with himself.

Why did I say that? Was it more honourable to have a dead father than a disgraced one?

They stood in silence for a while and watched the breakers with unseeing eyes.

Pickles said at length : 'March will be over by the time we reach our destination, and the Dardanelles affair will be over. So I suppose we shall just turn round and waddle back to Portsmouth!'

Chesnaye said quickly, 'What was the bombardment like along the Belgian coast?' Something had to be done to snap them both out of the feeling of depression which seemed to hang over them like a cloud.

'Noisy.' Pickles smiled at the simplicity of his answer. 'The big fifteen-inchers pounded away about three dozen shells, and all we saw was a cloud of brown smoke beyond the woods.' He shuddered. 'When we ceased firing we heard the soldiers having a go. It went on and on. Rifles, millions of them, rattling away as if they'd never stop!' He peered up at Chesnaye's thoughtful face. 'I don't think I could stand that sort of war. It's so personal, so filthy!'

A sharp clack, clack, clack made them look up at the bridge, and Chesnaye was surprised to see the nearest searchlight flashing urgently, its bright blue beam dazzling even in the harsh daylight.

'They're signalling the destroyer!' Pickles sounded mystified as he peered astern at the pitching escort. 'That's funny, we usually use semaphore for that sort of thing.'

But Chesnaye remained stockstill, his lips moving soundlessly as he spelt out the signal. As he read the stacatto flashes he could feel his body chilling as if running with ice-water.

'There is a mine drifting dead ahead of you!' He spoke the completed signal aloud and then swung to peer at the destroyer's distorted shape. Of course, from the *Saracen*'s high and reasonably steady bridge it would be possible to see a drifting mine. He stared until his eyes were running uncontrollably and he could only half see the other ship.

A brief light flashed from the distant bridge, but whether it was an acknowledgement or the beginning of a question Chesnaye never knew. There was a bright orange flash from somewhere beneath the little ship's pitching fo'c'sle and then a dull, flat explosion which rolled across the water like thunder. There was very little smoke, but in that instant the destroyer ploughed to a halt, paid off into a beam sea and began to capsize.

Chesnaye blinked and heard Pickles give a small sob. How long was it? Ten seconds? Already the frail stern was rising clear of the waves, the tiny bright screws spinning in the air like those on a toy boat.

The monitor seemed to shudder as the shock-wave punched her massive hull below the waterline, and then began to swing heavily towards the small, spray-dashed shape which rapidly grew smaller even as they watched. A bugle blared, and all at once the deserted decks were alive with running feet.

Bosun's mates urged the seamen along, their pipes twittering as they ran. 'Away first and second whalers!' The cry was taken up the full length of the ship before Chesnaye realised that he too was expected to act. His was the second whaler, and as he stumbled towards the quarter davits he could see the boat swinging clear over the water, while his five oarsmen and coxswain scrambled across the griping spar and fell into the narrow wooden hull. More cries and sharp orders, and he could see the whaler on the other side of the quarterdeck already starting to shoot down the ship's side, the rope falls screaming through the blocks like live things.

Rough hands pushed him up and over the spar, and as he fell at the coxswain's feet he heard the cry, 'Lower away!' and then the monitor's rail was above him, the waves suddenly near and frighteningly large. The boat hovered above the water while the *Saracen* still pushed herself ahead, then with the order 'Slip!' it was slipped from the falls and dropped with a sickening lurch on to the crest of a curling breaker, and immediately veered away from the parent ship on the end of its long boatrope.

Chesnaye fought to regain his breath as the hull leapt and soared beneath his feet, the first shock and panic replaced by a feeling of numbed desperation. He heard himself shout: 'Let go forrard! Out oars!' and then there seemed another agonising pause while the men thrust

37

their blades through the crutches and sat apparently glued in their places, their eyes fixed on his face. 'Give way together!' The men leaned towards him, the blades dipped, splashed at the uneven water and then sent the boat plunging into the next bank of whitecaps.

The coxswain, a leading seaman named Tobias, shouted, 'Head straight for the destroyer, sir?'

Chesnaye bit his lip hard and tried to control his shaking limbs. He had sent the whaler on a straight course to nowhere, and he glanced quickly at Tobias to see if the man was showing contempt for his stupidity. But the beetle-browed seaman's face was passive and grave.

'Yes. Thank you.'

The coxswain swung the tiller bar while Chesnaye regained his feet and tried to peer ahead across the tall, pointed white hoods. The wavecrests hid the horizon, and as the whaler dipped into each successive trough Chesnaye was conscious of the silence as the towering waves blotted out the other world, so that he was aware once more of panic, like a drowning man.

Once when he looked astern he saw only the monitor's tripod mast and upper bridge, as if the *Saracen* too was on her way to the bottom. It seemed impossible that this frail, madly pitching boat would ever regain the safety and security of its davits, or he the ordered world of the gunroom.

Tobias shouted, 'Put yer backs into it, you bastards!' He began to count, his hoarse voice carrying above the hiss and roar of the water. 'In-out! In-out!' But to Chesnaye's confused eyes it appeared as if the boat was motionless, no matter how much the men sweated and pulled on their oars. He could see the long tapering blades bending as they cut at the water, and felt the shiver and thrust of the boat's bows as each wall of spray bounded over the seamen's bent backs.

Tobias barked, 'Bows!' The man nearest the stem smartly heaved his oar inside the boat and swung himself right into the bows, his shoulders hunched as if to take on the sea itself.

Tobias said quietly, 'We're there, sir.'

The oars moved more slowly as Tobias's spatulate fingers beat their time on the tiller bar.

Chesnaye did not know how the man knew they had arrived at the place where the destroyer had been mortally struck, but he felt no doubt. Instead he was conscious of a sense of horror and of loss.

Cutting through the glassy side of a wave like a torpedo, a broken spar, its severed wood gleaming white in the grey water, loomed dangerously towards the wallowing boat. The bowman cursed, but with a deft thrust of his boathook pushed it clear. It drifted past, a tattered ensign, waterlogged like a shroud, trailing behind it.

The men rowed carefully, their eyes unmoving as they waited for some sign or sound, but still nothing happened.

Tobias spat suddenly over the gunwhale. 'Must 'ave gone straight down. Them destroyers is pretty poor stuff. Tin an' paint. Not much more!'

Chesnaye swallowed hard. Like the bowman he had seen a single spread-eagled figure, its face and hands incredibly white, outlined momentarily against the tumbling water.

Tobias said : 'Leave 'im, sir. Let 'im be!'

The sodden corpse was already sinking, dragged down by heavy sea-boots which such a short time ago had kept their owner warm. Chesnaye staggered and would have fallen but for Tobias's grip on his arm. It had to happen sooner or later in war, but this had been quite different. A silent, faceless nobody, drifting and already forgotten.

Tobias's face was very close. 'Take it easy, sir. There'll be worse before this lot's over!'

In spite of the nausea which threatened to make him vomit Chesnaye peered at the burly coxswain. But again there was neither contempt nor anger on his face, and Chesnaye realised that in that brief instant he was seeing Tobias for the first time. Not as a competent, bitter-tongued subordinate, but as a man.

The bowman said wearily : '*Saracen*'s signalling, sir! "Recall".'

Chesnaye glanced at Tobias, who merely shrugged. 'They kin see better'n us, sir. There'll be nothing left now!'

In silence the men pulled at the oars, but this time their eyes were facing the stern, where across Tobias's shoulders they could see, or imagined they could see, the frothing whirlpool which marked the destroyer's grave.

. . . . .

Commander Godden strode to the front of the bridge, his features strained. 'Both whalers hoisted and secured, sir.'

The Captain sat straight-backed in his chair, his eyes fixed on some point along the horizon. 'Very well. Resume course and speed, and instruct all lookouts of their double importance.'

'Shall I make out a signal, sir?' Godden saw the Captain's neat hands stiffen. He added carefully, 'Another escort can be sent from Gibraltar.'

Royston-Jones turned his head, his eyes momentarily distant. 'I knew that destroyer captain well. A very promising fellow. Great pity.' Then in a sharper tone : 'No, we'll make no signals as yet. By breaking wireless silence we will invite more unwelcome attention than by continuing alone.'

'It's a risk, sir.' Godden tried to shut his mind to the sinking destroyer.

Royston-Jones shrugged irritably. 'So is polo! In any case, the responsibility rests with me, doesn't it?'

'Yes, sir.' Godden bit his lip and started to move away. 'The whalers took far too long to get away, Commander.' The voice halted him in his tracks. 'The second whaler took six minutes to clear the falls. Should be three minutes at the most. See to it!'

Hogarth, the Officer of the Watch, called, 'Resumed course and speed, sir!'

'Very well.' Royston-Jones seemed to have dismissed them.

Godden said heavily, 'Pass the word for the midshipman of the second whaler!'

Lieutenant Travis walked from the charthouse and crossed to his side. 'Pretty sudden, wasn't it?'

'Bloody mines!' Godden felt the anger boiling up inside him.

'Probably very old.' Travis sounded thoughtful. 'Maybe dropped months ago by the raider *Kap Trafalgar* on her way south.'

'Poor devils.' Godden thrust his hands deep into his pockets. 'I knew every officer in that destroyer.' He glared quickly at Royston-Jones' back. '*Not* just her captain either!'

Travis shrugged. 'That's the trouble with this regiment. Just one great family!' He glanced to the sky and moved towards the bridge ladder as Chesnaye's head appeared over the screen. 'Never mind. Here's the most junior officer aboard. He should be good enough to carry *our* burdens!'

Godden opened his mouth, and then stifled the angry retort. Travis was a queer bird. You never knew whether he was making fun of his superiors. But his casual comment had struck home, and Godden was almost grateful. The Captain was always goading him, always finding fault. Travis had been right. Chesnaye had been about to take the weight of Godden's resentment.

He stared at Chesnaye's wind-reddened face. 'You were too slow,' he said at length. 'You'll have to halve the time it takes to get that boat away.'

'I see, sir.' Chesnaye looked upset.

'The power launches are useless in this weather. In any case it takes too long for the main derrick to swing 'em into the water. Whalers are best.' Godden sighed. 'But nothing would have saved those fellows, I'm afraid.'

Royston-Jones said sharply, 'Come over here!'

Chesnaye crossed to the tall chair and saluted. 'Sir?'

For a moment the Captain stared at the Midshipman, his eyes bleak and expressionless. 'Chesnaye?' The small head nodded slowly. 'Knew your father in China.' The cold eyes darted sharply at Chesnaye's. 'Commanded the *Kelpie*, eh?'

'Yes, sir.' Chesnaye could feel the bridge spinning beneath his feet.

Royston-Jones resumed staring at the horizon. 'The China Station. Now there was a place.' Some of the sharpness had gone from his tone, so that Chesnaye darted a closer look at him. 'Fleet regattas, or chasing Chinese pirates, it made no difference. No room for mistakes there, boy. A crack squadron!' The Captain's head nodded vigorously. 'A pity we're not going out there now!'

He turned in his chair, his eyes sharp and alive again. 'Well, don't stand there! Go and chase that fool Tobias and his men! Tell them you'll have their hides if they don't improve their timing!' One hand slapped sharply against the chair. '*Timing* is the thing!'

Chesnaye saluted and stepped back, conscious of the eyes all round him. 'Very good, sir!'

Royston-Jones yawned. '*Naturally*, Chesnaye!'

As Chesnaye stepped on to the top of the ladder Commander Godden patted his arm. 'Well done, lad. I think he likes you.'

His smile faded as a voice rapped: 'Too much talking on my bridge! We'll have an extra action drill before lunch to wake everyone up a bit!'

.   .   .   .   .   .

When Chesnaye reached the maindeck Sub-Lieutenant Pringle was waiting for him.

'Well, where the hell have *you* been?' Pringle had his big hands on his hips, and his chin was jutting with belligerence.

'To the bridge.' Chesnaye tried not to watch Pringle's eyes. Behind them it was almost possible to see the man's mind working.

'Bridge? Bloody crawling, I suppose! By God, you mids make me spew! Did a little bit of boatwork upset you?' Pringle's voice became a sneering lisp. 'Perhaps you thought you might see a bit of blood!'

Chesnaye felt the weariness soaking into his limbs. It was a game. But how sickening it was becoming! He thought of the faded corpse and gritted his teeth.

'Wait until you've seen a bit of service!' Pringle's face was getting flushed. 'You'll have something to weep about then!'

Chesnaye released his breath slowly. 'How much service have *you* seen?'

'*What* did you say?' Pringle stared at him with disbelief. 'By God, you've really asked for it now!'

Chesnaye licked his dry lips. He had committed himself. Over and over again he had warned himself about this, but it had come at the wrong time.

'Sub-Lieutenant Pringle,' he kept his voice level, 'I am not going to fight you, but if you threaten me again I am going straight to the Commander!'

Pringle's mouth opened and stayed open.

'You are my superior and I have to obey you. But as we are alone I can cheerfully tell you that in *my* opinion you are a cheat, a liar and a bully!' He stepped back, half expecting Pringle to smash him down with one of his doubled fists.

Pringle seemed unable to breathe. He spoke between short gasps, his cheeks mottled and shining. 'You'll see, Chesnaye! By God, you'll be sorry for this!'

Some seamen tramped along the nearby deck, and Pringle seemed to recover himself. 'Now get about your duties, and quick about it!'

Chesnaye touched his cap and smiled coldly. 'Yes, sir.'

Later, as he watched Tobias and his men scrubbing off the whaler's keel, he thought of the clash with Pringle and cursed himself. It would be as well to warn Pickles, just in case.

Automatically he looked astern, as if expecting to see the small, faithful destroyer. The empty sea seemed to be dancing, as if to mock him.

Suddenly, in spite of Pringle and the Captain's casual remarks about his father, the *Saracen* seemed very solid and safe.

He walked towards the slung whaler and said quickly, 'D'you need any help, Tobias?'

The unnatural brightness in his tone made the leading seaman glance at him with surprise. Then Tobias gave a slow smile. Sometimes when new midshipmen found their feet they could go either way. All being well, this one might be just tolerable.

'Always do with an extra 'and, sir!'

By nightfall the *Saracen* was steaming down the Portuguese coast, and somewhere at the bottom of the Atlantic the destroyer's hull had settled for the last time and was at peace.

3

A Girl called Helen

The sky above Gibraltar was a pale transparent blue,
whilst the craggy crown of the Rock itself remained
shrouded in a fine afternoon haze. A steady Atlantic
breeze prevented much warmth from reaching the
sheltered anchorage, but the sun was nevertheless welcome, and cast a sheen of grandeur across the straight
lines of moored warships. Sheltered and dwarfed by the
towering rock fortress, the town itself glittered and
sparkled in countless colours which again acted as a backcloth for the grey symbols of power and reliability.

Slightly apart from the other vessels, the flagship lay in
solitary splendour, the flag of Vice-Admiral fluttering
cheerfully in the breeze. Across the harbour entrance the
last traces of brown smoke hovered around the one moving
warship, and to onlookers the last detonation of a
nineteen-gun salute still seemed to echo against the
weatherworn walls of the Rock.

The Vice-Admiral stepped from the small sternwalk of
the battleship and entered a well-furnished stateroom. His
flag-captain remained momentarily in the sunlight, his
raised glasses following the slow-moving ship.

'Ugly-looking ship, sir?' The Captain reluctantly followed his superior.

The Vice-Admiral tore his eyes from the pile of signals
and reference books which littered his table and looked at
the other officer. 'The *Saracen* could be very useful, however.' His eyes flitted to a well-polished scuttle as the
monitor's blunt bow slowly moved into view once more.
On her distant fo'c'sle he could see the hands fallen in and
the small cluster of figures around the bows. In spite of
her unwieldy appearance there was something defiant
about the *Saracen,* he thought.

'What is her captain like, sir?'

The Vice-Admiral shrugged, watching the monitor's broad hull as it glided very slowly across the glittering water. 'Royston-Jones? An able man, to all accounts.' A small frown crossed his face. 'But *stubborn*. Damned stubborn!'

'All captains are made that way, surely, sir? The climb up the ladder is too long for a man who loses sight of his objective!'

'Maybe so. That gun salute, for instance. Did you notice?'

'Well, yes. But perhaps he overlooked the new orders about that. No salutes for the duration, that's what their lordships implied, but I daresay Royston-Jones had other things on his mind. The loss of the escort, for instance?'

The Vice-Admiral smiled wryly. 'He knew, all right. That is what worries me about him. He's one of the old school. He's always fired a salute to the Governor of the Rock in the past, and he does not see why he should alter now!'

The Captain craned his head. 'She's dropped anchor, sir.'

There was a faint splash of white beneath the monitor's fo'c'sle, and simultaneously the Jack broke out from the short staff in the bows and a new ensign appeared as if by magic from the quarterdeck.

It was as if the ship itself was alive and the tiny ant-like figures which scurried across the pale decks were superfluous. The big power derrick came to life, and almost before the vessel's bow wave had died away a launch was lowered alongside and another was being swung out ready to follow it.

The Vice-Admiral grimaced. 'He's a good captain. I'm not denying that. I imagine that by now the whole ship is working like a new clock!'

'You mean that may not be enough, sir?'

'You've seen the reports?' He gestured towards the table. 'The Dardanelles project is swelling out of all proportion. To think that a week or so ago our sailors were actually *ashore* on Turkish soil, blowing up gunsites as calm as you please!' He began to pace. 'Nothing but delays and more delays! And now they want a full-scale combined operation. Troops, landings and all the rest of it, while Johnny Turk digs himself in and prepares! By heaven, it'll be a bloody affair before we're done!'

'And now the poor *Inflexible*'s been put out of action too, sir.'

The Vice-Admiral walked to the scuttle and watched the neat launch curving towards the flagship. 'Yes. A good new battlecruiser thrown away in a bombardment, such a damned waste! After she did such fine work in the Falklands battle too. It'll take months to do the repairs!' With sudden anger he added, 'These damned stay-at-home strategists make me sick!'

An immaculate midshipman appeared in the doorway. 'The Commander's respects, sir. The captain of *Saracen* is coming aboard.' He spoke to his captain, his over-steady eyes adding to his appearance of nervousness provoked by the other officer whose flag flew high overhead.

The Vice-Admiral waited until the young man had departed. 'Do not mention the saluting business to Royston-Jones just yet.'

'Very well, sir.' The Captain looked puzzled.

The flag-officer made up his mind. 'No. I must have his full attention. You see, it's all part of what I was saying just now. The Royal Navy is our way of life. In addition it has always been in the background of the whole Empire. Since Trafalgar we have hardly been challenged. We are accepted as the greatest sea power, the most powerful force in the world.'

The Captain tucked his cap beneath his arm and waited. 'Well, yes, sir.'

'Exactly! Now we are at war. Real war, and some of us have been on top for so long we've forgotten what it is all about. We've been *too* rich, too damned confident!' He glared at the table. 'And now we've got to face it, to pay the price. A stupid, straightforward operation which has gone to blazes and all because our top people can't agree!'

The Captain was half listening for the sound of the launch alongside, but his superior's sudden show of angry confidence in him was not to be ignored.

'Winston Churchill himself said the Fleet could "take" the Dardanelles. A good sharp knock and we could force the Straits without too much fuss, eh? Some smart chart work and quick thinking, a useful bombardment and some new spotting aircraft,' the Vice-Admiral waved his hands, 'and the whole thing would be finished!'

'Well, sir, there is still time.'

He ignored the Captain's guarded words. 'And what did we get? A handful of obsolete battleships from the Channel Fleet and a couple of old aircraft which could hardly get off the ground! That fool Kitchener got cold feet in France and said he could not spare any troops to follow up our attack, and the government actually *believed* him!'

'The casualties have been very severe on the Western Front, sir.'

'And so they will continue to be while we've got stupid old men in charge of them! That is why we must watch ourselves too!' He looked towards the *Saracen*, which now swung easily at her cable. 'New thinking is what we want. My God, in some ways I wish we had not been so strong in the Navy.' He turned towards his captain. 'A starving man always hunts for food better than one who has been pampered and overfed!'

Later, as the pipes twittered and the marines presented arms, the Flag-Captain found a few seconds to reflect on the Vice-Admiral's words. He watched Royston-Jones' neat head lift above the rail, the hand raised to his cap, beneath which the pale, cold eyes flitted briefly across the flagship's reception party in sharp appraisal.

The Flag-Captain dropped his hand and stepped forward to welcome his opposite number. He thought irritably that it was as if Royston-Jones had come to inspect the flagship rather than receive his orders.

Royston-Jones looked along the vast decks and towering superstructure. Framed beneath the quarterdeck guns the *Saracen* looked small and deformed.

The Flag-Captain's mouth softened. It would be no joke for a senior captain to be given command of a monitor. Following the other man's gaze he said, 'Looks aren't everything, you know.'

Royston-Jones nodded vigorously. 'Quite so! Couldn't agree more!' He faced the Flag-Captain, his eyes hidden beneath his peak. 'Still, she could blow *this* relic out of the water any day, I shouldn't wonder!'

. . . . .

Richard Chesnaye allowed himself to be pushed along in the continuous, aimless throng which seemed to fill each and every narrow street. Although the afternoon had almost gone, it still felt warm, almost oppressive after England and the Atlantic. He had come ashore alone, and told himself it was because he wanted it this way. In fact, he knew that it was because Gibraltar was new and unfamiliar, and, as in the past, he wanted to feel his way, to hide any weakness. Pickles was on duty in his picket boat and most of the other midshipmen had headed ashore in one group to some prearranged party.

Chesnaye stared at the strange shops overloaded with garish rugs and countless ornaments and souvenirs. Already beneath his arm he was carrying a bright shawl which a beady-eyed merchant had thrust into his hands within minutes of landing. He did not care. He wanted something to send to his mother, and she would like it even though she might never wear it.

Chesnaye did not know where he was walking, and every street seemed exactly like another. All were crammed with sailors, and occasionally he caught sight of a familiar face from the *Saracen*, some already flushed with drink and full of that strange anticipation which every sailor seemed to wear like a mask when ashore.

Wearily he turned into a small, low-ceilinged café and ordered coffee. Things seemed cheap here, but all the same he would have to be careful. The café was perched on a shoulder of rock, so that he could still see part of the harbour. He toyed with the coffee and watched the moored ships and the colourful bustle below the window. There were big ugly troopships too. Their decks alive with khaki figures, the upperworks untidy with newly washed shirts and underwear. All at once he became aware of two voices behind him. The room was half empty and very carefully he turned to look at the girl whose voice broke into his tired thoughts and reminded him how few

48

women he had seen on the Rock.

She was about his own age, suntanned, and with hair so dark that for a moment he wondered if she were Spanish. She was speaking to a young army second lieutenant, and as Chesnaye watched them he knew that they were brother and sister. The soldier wore the badges of the Royal Engineers and from his creased uniform Chesnaye guessed that he was from one of the troopships and not a garrison officer.

Once the girl looked across at Chesnaye, apparently conscious of his gaze. Her eyes were dark and very wide, and she stared at Chesnaye for several seconds. Then she spoke quietly to the soldier, who turned to look also.

Chesnaye pushed his cup aside and groped quickly for his parcel. He felt confused and furious with himself, and half expected that the others in the room would all turn to watch him leave.

The subaltern called across, 'Why don't you join us?'

It was so unexpected that Chesnaye found himself thinking of several excuses for leaving rather than accepting the invitation. Stupidly he sat down at their table and said : 'I'm sorry. It's my first visit to Gibraltar. I'm almost a tourist!'

The soldier laughed. 'We'd never have guessed!'

The girl frowned as Chesnaye's face showed his mounting confusion. 'Don't take any notice of my brother.' She held out a small, well-shaped hand. 'I'm Helen Driscoll, and this is Bob.'

Chesnaye tried to relax the stiffness in his body. Her handshake was warm and strong like a boy's, the skin very smooth. He said quickly, 'Do you live here?'

She smiled. 'For another few days. Our father is the Army Victualling Agent here, and we are returning to England shortly.'

'Careful, Helen, careless talk, y'know!' Her brother grinned at Chesnaye. 'This chap could be a spy!'

'Nonsense! He's far too English!' She tossed her head so that the hair which hung down her neck glimmered in the filtered sunlight. The movement reacted like pain, and Chesnaye could feel his heart beginning to pump noisily. He cursed himself for his stupidity. Tonight he would be

49

back aboard the *Saracen* and in minutes this girl would get up and leave.

Almost too casually he asked, 'Are you under orders?' He saw the cheerful light fade in the soldier's eyes and added hastily, 'I suppose everyone who comes here is *en route* to somewhere else!'

The girl had stopped smiling, and all at once Chesnaye knew well enough why they had called him over. The soldier was from one of those troopers, and Chesnaye had already heard Commander Godden discussing their departure with the Navigator with a view to changing the *Saracen*'s anchorage. They were sailing at midnight. Eastward. That meant only one thing. The Dardanelles.

Chesnaye said awkwardly: 'Look, if you'd rather I went I'll take myself off now. I'm sorry if I was staring.' They were both looking at him. 'I suppose I'm a bit like a monk, not used to a girl like . . .' he faltered. 'Anyway, I'm sorry!'

He saw her hand on his sleeve. 'Please don't go. It was Bob's idea to call you over just to stop my worrying about him. He thought you would keep me quiet.'

Her brother did not answer but stared past Chesnaye at the darkening harbour. 'Listen!' He cocked his head as the sounds of distant bugles floated across the water.

Chesnaye nodded. 'Sunset,' he said. Somewhere out there the *Saracen*'s ensign would be slowly dipping down the staff in perfect time with all the others. It was strange, he thought. Sunset never failed to move him. The slow strains of the bugle. The sense of peace of a ship at anchor.

The soldier said suddenly: 'Yes, I'm under orders. It's no secret. I suspect we are both going to the same destination?' He smiled wryly. 'Although I also suspect that you will be travelling in rather more comfort!'

The girl stood up. 'Let's get away from here.' She gestured vaguely. 'Will you come back to the house, Richard?'

The use of his name made Chesnaye start. He knew she would only be asking him to speed the agonising hours remaining before her brother had to leave, but it would be enough. It would have to be. Chesnaye reached for his cap. 'Thank you. I would like that very much.'

Outside the sky was suddenly dark, but necklaces of lights sparkled about the base of the Rock and across the harbour the moored ships shone invitingly beneath riding lamps which reflected and multiplied in the black water.

Groups of seamen pushed their way past, faces turned to watch the young dark-haired girl and to envy the two officers whose arms she linked.

Chesnaye felt like singing. Yet the sense of sadness which his companions seemed to convey should have acted as a brake, and he knew he ought to feel ashamed of himself.

It was a short, priceless evening, the quiet house brought alive with gay, brittle conversation and laughter.

Then Chesnaye and the young subaltern took their leave, each to his separate ship.

As they stood in the doorway the girl hugged her brother and pulled his crumpled uniform into shape. Chesnaye could see her eyes shining in the lamplight and wanted to turn away.

Then she crossed to him and laid her hands on his shoulders. 'Thank you, Dick.' That was all she had said. She pulled herself up and kissed him very lightly on the mouth, and then in one movement turned away and was gone.

As the liberty boat bounced over the darkened water Chesnaye sat silent and thoughtful in the cockpit, his ears deaf to the drunken singing of the returning seamen. He tried to see the moored troopers, but it was too dark.

Next morning, when he stood quietly watching the deck parties busy with hoses and scrubbers, their feet pale in the early light, he looked again. But the moorings were empty.

He thought of the girl and touched his mouth with his fingers. He would never hear Sunset played again without remembering.

. . . . .

'Another boat approaching, sir!' The quartermaster spoke over his shoulder with bored resignation as a small bobbing light wound its way across the dark harbour towards the anchored monitor.

Chesnaye jerked himself from his thoughts and took a quick look around him. The gangway staff were all present, and like himself were made painfully conspicuous beneath the glaring overhead lamp and the long garlands of coloured fairy-lights which had transformed the ship into a floating carnival.

The wide quarterdeck was almost completely enclosed in immaculate awnings so that the packed crowd of officers and their guests should not be bothered by the cool evening breezes, and the small orchestra which was comprised of marines from the ship's band made a bright and colourful centrepiece to the noisy, moving throng. Long tables had been rigged on either side of the deck, and a small army of stewards and marine messmen offered drinks and a wide assortment of food to the ever-changing faces before them.

Chesnaye readjusted his unfamiliar dress-jacket as the latest arrivals drew near the gangway. He had tried hard to immerse himself completely in the business of entertaining, but he was unable to fight down the strange feeling of bitterness, almost disgust. There was an air of mad gaiety, something like pagan excitement, in the ship which affected him deeply. Everything had changed yet again, even the faces which had started to become familiar seemed like strangers once more. The bright glitter of full mess dress, dazzling white shirts and bow ties, gold lace and gleaming decorations, and, above all, the alien presence of the women who prowled the quarterdeck in such noisy profusion. He had never seen women like these before. They too seemed infected by the general excitement, and as he had waited on the gangway with his weary staff he had become dazed by the profusion of bright, laughing mouths, low-cut dresses, the bold, daring eyes. The gangway quivered and another group of officers stepped into the light, casual salutes followed by noisy anticipation as they saw the crowd already assembled beyond the awnings. Like most of the other guests, the officers wore long boatcloaks lined with white silk, which for Chesnaye only added to the sense of unreality he already felt.

Two women paused laughing at the top of the gangway. Chesnaye watched them warily, his face impassive as they stared round them with bright, shining eyes. One had beautiful breasts only just concealed by her flame-coloured dress, and from the corner of his eye Chesnaye could see the corporal of the gangway as he ran a hot, appraising glance over her slim body.

It seemed as if these women, like many of the others, were acting this way deliberately. They must have known the effect they were having on the stiff-backed, regimented seamen and marines around them. The sure knowledge that they were equally beyond these men's reach must have given them added confidence, he thought.

The arrival of Lieutenant Travis, the Officer of the Day, broke into his thoughts.

Travis, his neat beard making him look almost Elizabethan, swept the women before him, his words flattering, even insolent, as he piloted them into the noisy crowd which already had started to overflow from the quarter-deck.

Another boat, and yet another. Salutes, quick greetings, and then Chesnaye was alone again, immersed in his speculations. At length the flow ceased, and to Chesnaye's mind it was just as well. It seemed unlikely that the deck could hold any more. The ship's officers, once in the comfortable majority, were lost in the press. That too had been different, he thought. Usually the various grades of officer stayed apart except for matters of duty. This wild guest night had shown Chesnaye his superiors as something else again.

Commander Godden played his own part well, the busy, jovial host ably supported by the Chief Engineer, Innes, and several lieutenants.

The ship's warrant officers, hardy professional seamen, who for all their service were more strange to the ward-room and an officer's life than they were to the lower deck, kept mainly as one body, flushed, noisy, yet seemingly lacking in their younger superiors' confidence. There was Mr. Porteous, the Boatswain, his bald head crossed by one slicked wing of hair, which from a distance looked like a feather, flanked on either of his ample sides by Mr. Tweed, the Gunner, and Mr. Jay, the Gunner (T).

There was Holroyd, the pasty-faced Paymaster, and

53

Mildmay, the Surgeon. The latter was a fierce, nuggety little Welshman who rarely seemed to work. Chesnaye had often seen him sitting in his Sick Bay reading while his attendants dealt cheerfully with the waiting line of bruises, cuts and other afflictions.

Even Nutting, the Chaplain, looked different. Chesnaye could just see his narrow head with its ridiculous centre parting jerking and bobbing like a bird's as he shouted at someone across Major De L'Isle's broad shoulder.

The marine, of course, was already past the danger marks of discretion. He stood very stiffly, untroubled by the pushing bodies around him, his face getting more and more flushed, so that his neck seemed to merge with his scarlet jacket. Every so often he would drop a sharp, harsh insult into the throng and watch for results. It was a game he played very often. Women, he contended, enjoyed this form of approach. They admired his strength, his obvious virility, and they only needed that extra touch of his verbal brutality to find themselves completely defenceless. Unfortunately De L'Isle's conviction in this direction seemed to be shared by no one but himself. So he drank harder, if only to bolster his own belief.

"Evening, Dick!' Pickles stood blinking in the bright gangway light, his uniform sparkling with droplets of spray. 'I don't think my boat will be required again for a bit. Shall I send them below for a breather?'

Chesnaye grinned. Lieutenant Travis had instructed him to make all the necessary decisions should he not be present on the gangway; it was surprising how easy the role had become.

'You do that, Keith.' He waited as the small midshipman waved to an anonymous dark figure on the maindeck. 'Kept you busy, have they?'

Pickles puffed out his cheeks. 'Like wild beasts to the fray!' He gestured towards the dark shadow of the Rock. 'Not a woman under sixty ashore tonight!'

Chesnaye's nose twitched. Pickles was reeking of beer.

'Have you had the good fortune to booze yourself, Keith?' He frowned with mock disgust. 'Never a thought for the poor watchkeepers!'

Pickles smiled unmoved. 'There is a whole gang of petty

officers at the landing stage. Boat coxswains and various other skivers! They're not too proud to remember the poor snotties!' He winked. 'However, since you are my particular blood brother, I have brought you this.' From beneath his jacket he produced with a flourish a large bottle of port.

To the watching quartermaster he said, 'Any glasses?'

The quartermaster stared at the bottle, his eyes hungry. 'Only the gangway mugs, sir!'

Pickles belched. 'Can't have that. Must have proper glasses! This happens to be vintage port. The Vice-Admiral apparently left it in his pinnace this evening!' He looked sad. 'Very careless, you will agree?' Then, in a sharper voice: 'Right, Corporal! Double away smartly and explore the underside of the awning there! Some idle drinkers always put their empty glasses on the deck so as not to waste time!'

Chesnaye smiled. It was amazing what confidence Pickles exuded with the beer under his belt. It was obvious that the men liked him too. They liked him for himself, not out of respect or necessity. They were a little sorry for him as well. Pringle's bullying was well known on the lower deck. With other midshipmen they might have said the usual, 'Well, he shouldn't have joined if he can't take a joke!' or 'What the hell does it matter, they're *all* bloody officers!' But Pickles they accepted as they would a ship's mascot.

The corporal of the gangway eyed the bottle. 'How many glasses, sir?'

Pickles grinned. 'One each, of course!'

The gangway staff brightened visibly, although Chesnaye wondered what would happen if Travis returned unexpectedly. He felt naked beneath the glaring lights, but strangely reckless.

The marine returned with an assortment of glasses, and the Admiral's vintage port was slopped into them like so much cider.

Pickles lifted his glass with obvious relish. A thin trickle of red port ran down the corner of his mouth and splattered across his shirt like blood. He said, at length, 'At least I don't have to worry about bloody Pringle!'

It was strange the way Pickles was prepared to talk about Pringle, Chesnaye thought. Not as a person, but as a disease or a strange filthy circumstance which was unavoidable.

'Good.' Chesnaye gestured towards the quarterdeck awning. 'I suppose he's enjoying himself with the other sub-lieutenants?'

Pickles darted him a sharp glance. 'You might have thought so, yes.' He eyed the glass. 'However, for a change Mister bloody Pringle is attached to the most gorgeous little piece you have ever laid eyes on!' He bobbed his head forward and mimicked Lieutenant Hogarth's high voice. 'The most alluring, quite the *most* alluring, creature aboard!'

'This I must see!' The port flowed like hot oil across Chesnaye's empty stomach. Followed by Pickles, he walked to a slit in the awning and peered across the swaying, sweating concourse.

The women looked wild and abandoned, their naked shoulders pale beneath the coloured lights and strings of gay bunting. Their escorts surged and jostled for position, but whereas Chesnaye could see Major De L'Isle's tall frame well enough, the Captain was invisible. His eye fell on Pringle's cropped blond head. He was endeavouring to dance to the muffled beat of the sweating orchestra, his broad shoulders acting like a battering ram for his partner.

Pickles grinned unfeelingly. 'That girl deserves a medal! She's keeping that ape off our backs for a bit yet!'

Chesnaye hardly heard him. As Pringle passed beneath a cluster of fairy-lights he saw the girl's upturned face. It was Helen Driscoll.

*   *   *   *   *

For the very first time since the *Saracen* had left home waters the sun was at last making itself felt. It seemed to enfold the ship and the water beyond, so that the air felt heavy and humid. Gone was the Atlantic grey and silver. Instead, from the clear water alongside the hull to the hazy bridge of the horizon, the sea shone in a mixture of

56

blues both dark and fragile, while every unbroken wave and roller reflected the sun in a million glittering mirrors.

The monitor leaned slightly, as if putting her shoulder into the inviting water to test its warmth, whilst from beneath her stern the wake curved and continued to curve until the ship had altered course yet again, the other vessels astern following suit in a slow and ponderous 'follow my leader'.

Richard Chesnaye stood on one of the bridge gratings and levelled his telescope astern. He imagined he could still see the Rock's brooding outline, but could no longer be sure. There, the horizon was lost in a mirage of vapour and reflections, so that it appeared to be shrouded in steam. He steadied the glass with his elbow resting on the screen and allowing it to swing slowly over the assorted craft which had followed the monitor from Gibraltar while the town had still slept and the stars had not yet begun to fade. Like two white ghosts the tall hulls of the hospital ships cut through the water with all the elegance and grace which had made them famous less than a year ago as crack Atlantic liners, whilst astern of them three bulky colliers and an ammunition ship plodded heavily in their wake, their ugliness made apparent by the competition. On either wing of the assorted convoy a sloop moved watchfully and with the patience of a sheepdog, and far astern, her outline merely a masthead above an indistinct shadow, another sloop maintained a wary eye on the stragglers.

Chesnaye blinked as a shaft of reflected sunlight lanced up the telescope. Through the screen beneath his arm he could feel the steady, pulsating beat of the monitor's engines as the power transmitted itself to every corner and rivet of the hull. He lowered the glass and looked quickly around the upper bridge. It looked different in the bright sunlight, and the officers and ratings in their white uniforms seemed by their contrast to have severed the last link with the other world of damp and cold.

Royston-Jones was sitting in his tall chair, his head turned to watch the manœuvring ships. His cap was low across his forehead, but Chesnaye could see the glitter in the Captain's eyes as he followed each movement.

'Make a signal to sloop *Mystic*.' Royston-Jones' voice was sharp and seemingly out of place in the warm enclosure of the bridge. 'Maintain position four miles astern of convoy. Report presence of any other ships immediately.'

The Yeoman of Signals wrote quickly on his slate, the pencil squeaking viciously and reminding Chesnaye briefly of a far-off schoolroom.

Lieutenant Travis looked down from the compass platform and rubbed his eyes. He looked pale and tired against the clear sky, and Chessaye wondered if he was still recovering from the week in Gibraltar.

'Course south seventy east, sir!' Travis waited, watching the Captain's foot as it tapped gently on the grating.

'Very well.' Royston-Jones did not sound very interested.

'Speed of convoy is steady at eight knots, sir.' Travis added bitterly, 'No wonder the Admiral delegated us to this lot!'

Chesnaye knew that the bulk of warships had gone on ahead, a fine picture, even without the blessing of daylight. The remaining battleships from Gibraltar, a rakish cruiser squadron and three flotillas of destroyers, their hulls almost hidden in eager bow waves, had steamed into the darkness and vanished as if wiped from a slate. The monitor was too slow to work with the Fleet, so Royston-Jones had been ordered to make his way eastwards with this small convoy. Although senior officer present, he was probably being cursed by the three sloop commanders, who must know that he was as much their responsibility as the colliers and the others. For the hospital ships, too, the slow progress must be infuriating, Chesnaye thought. They could manage twenty-three knots without too much effort, yet at eight knots they had to take their time from the slowest ships present.

Commander Godden removed his cap and wiped the band with his handkerchief. 'The hospital ships are a waste of time in my opinion. With all the troops we're mustering it will all be over in a day or two.' He looked at the Captain's shoulders. 'Before *we* get there, I shouldn't wonder!'

Royston-Jones crossed his legs and settled back in his chair. 'We will spend the forenoon at gun drills and damage control, Commander. All heads of departments will stand fast and their subordinates will take over.' He added sharply, 'Even if we are too late this time it may prove to be a long war!'

As the sun climbed higher the monitor's guns crews were led through one crisis after another. While Hogarth looked on, edgy and helpless to intervene, his assistant, a baby-faced lieutenant named Yates, sent the men sweating and cursing to obey the situations which Royston-Jones seemed to conjure up without effort. The secondary armament were divided to track and carry out mock attacks on the other ships in convoy, while the giant turret endeavoured to follow the tiny shape of the escort astern. The sloop only appeared occasionally, as it was usually hidden by the *Saracen*'s own bridge. This meant that one minute the twin fifteen-inch guns were swung round one side of the monitor's superstructure, and the next, almost before the ranges and deflections could be checked, the sloop had sidestepped daintily to the other quarter, so that the great turret had to swing through an angle of nearly two hundred and eighty degrees.

Once Hogarth, all but wringing his hands, had voiced a short protest. 'They're not *meant* for this, sir! The sort of targets they are designed for are stationary!'

Royston-Jones was unimpressed. 'Suppose the Turkish Fleet breaks out of the Straits, eh?' His eye was pitiless. 'What am I expected to do then? Send the Major and his marines to board 'em, I suppose!'

Once the training mechanism had failed in the turret, so that it stayed pointing impotently at an empty horizon while Royston-Jones barked a series of orders and complaints which became more savage as the minutes passed.

Godden, who was supposed to be 'dead' for the exercise, said in a strangled voice, 'Shall I order Secure, sir?'

'No, of *course* not! Mister Chesnaye, get forrard and check what is wrong!'

Chesnaye was glad to get away even for a few moments. He had grown to hate the constant battle between the Captain and Godden, although no actual argument ever seemed to show itself. The Commander was his usual self when Royston-Jones was away, but together they seemed unable to agree about anything. Chesnaye had often imagined Godden in command, and wondered how his more humane influence and understanding would affect the ship.

Panting, he climbed the straight ladder which ran up the side of the tall circular barbette upon which the turret revolved. He could feel the sweat running down his skin and clinging to his drill tunic, and wondered if he was getting out of condition. In the training ship they had always allowed for this and had exercised the cadets without let up. Here, in spite of the complex organisation, he felt restricted and cramped. The inside of the turret was like a scene from another world. He had not entered it before, and as he blinked to accustom his eyes to the harsh glare of electric lighting he realised for the first time the ship's tremendous hitting power.

The turret was bigger than the monitor's bridge and funnel combined, and was dominated by the two giant polished breeches which gaped open and allowed the distant sunlight to reflect down the rifled perfection of the twin barrels. The white painted turret was crammed with gleaming equipment. Brass wheels, dials, voice-pipes and hoisting tackles which snaked away through circular hatches towards the bowels of the ship and the magazines. Stripped and sweating, their shining skins making them look like slaves before a mechanical altar, the gunners leaned and panted by the unmoving breeches. The gunlayers and trainers, breech operators and loaders, all waited and watched the Quarters Officer, a Sub-Lieutenant Lucas, whose narrow frame was hung about with gleaming instruments like a pantomime surgeon.

He glared down from his tall stool as Chesnaye paused below him. 'Well, what the hell do you want?'

Chesnaye smiled. 'The Captain wants to know——' He never finished.

'Mother of God! What does he *expect*?' The officer peered down at his men. 'They'll all be dead before we reach Gallipoli if we keep up this pace!'

An oil-smeared petty officer appeared from nowhere.

'Fault discovered, sir.' He stared at Chesnaye as if he had come from another planet. 'Mister Tweed is fixing it now.' He added vaguely : 'A pawl in the training clutch has sheared.'

The Quarters Officer said severely, 'Mister Tweed is supposed to be "dead".' He sighed with relief. 'Still, there's no need for anyone to know !'

'What shall I tell the Captain?' Chesnaye waited, conscious of the gunners' grinning faces.

The Quarters Officer, whose father owned half of Cornwall, said stiffly : 'Report that the target returned our fire and we have sustained a direct hit. The turret is out of action !'

Chesnaye found his way back to the sunlit arena of the upper bridge and dutifully repeated the insolent message. He heard Godden catch his breath, while Hogarth looked as if he was going to be sick.

Royston-Jones nodded and rubbed his hands. 'Very well. Excellent !' He gave a sudden chuckle. 'A bright young man, that one ! Uses his imagination !'

The bridge relaxed slightly. The Captain added after a moment : 'Pass the word to the Surgeon about casualties. I would like to see the Quarters Officer splinted and bandaged for, er, let me see, multiple fractures. When that has been done he can be carried to his quarters while his men are sent to Stand Easy.' He grinned with sudden delight. 'How does that suit, eh ?'

Chesnaye turned away. It seemed useless to try to better Royston-Jones.

.   .   ▪   .   .

The hammocks creaked gently with each roll of the hull, but because of the lack of cool air Chesnaye felt unable to sleep. About him the gunroom was in darkness, even the police light being partly obscured by a pair of underpants. He reached above his face and felt for the valve in the overhead ventilating pipe to make sure that it was directed towards him. But the air was without life and seemed to smell of oil and paint.

Chesnaye pushed his hands beneath his head and took deep breaths. He had thrown the blankets aside, and he

61

could feel the steady stream of air across his naked body. Nearby he heard 'Ticky' White chuckling, but as he listened he realised that the other midshipman was asleep. Two days out from Gibraltar and the pace was beginning to tell. Drills, exercises and practices of every sort on top of watchkeeping duties. At first the ship's company had turned to with a will, used and trained to every whim and will of their officers. But on a placid sea, with the following ships already like part of the scenery, the enthusiasm had waned into resentful clumsiness. Things went wrong, and the harder it became to bear, the more the Captain conjured out of his imagination to drive them to the limit of endurance.

Chesnaye thought of Gibraltar, and again the feeling of loss moved inside him. It would be another week before the *Saracen* crawled to her destination, which was apparently to be Mudros, a Greek island where some of the assault forces were being assembled, and he knew that with each turn of the screws he would be blaming himself for his own handling of those short, haunting moments in Gibraltar.

The night of the big reception aboard, for instance. When he had seen Helen with Pringle he had wanted to turn his back, to hide his resentment from Pickles and cross the girl from his mind. Instead he had waited morosely by the gangway until the time had come for Helen and her father to leave. It had been difficult with the milling crowds shouting and singing around the gangway, the boats jostling for position, the women shrieking and laughing. It had been more than difficult.

He had wanted to confront her, to ask her why she had not even visited him at his place of duty, but his pride had clashed with his disappointment. When he had eventually managed to reach her she had merely looked uneasy and said, 'A very gay evening!' Then she had glanced away, her eyes sad.

He had mumbled something, but could not remember what. In any case, it did not matter when he had met Pickles that same night. Chesnaye had stumbled into the gunroom and found Pickles pressing trousers beneath a bench cushion in readiness for the morning.

Tonelessly Pickles had said, 'So it was your girl, then?'

Chesnaye had not answered, angry with himself for showing his feelings.

'It's none of my business, Dick, but . . .' Pickles turned, his eyes shaded. 'Pringle was here just now, boasting about what he'd done . . .' He faltered.

Chesnaye punched his hammock savagely. 'He was talking rubbish! They did not leave the ship together!'

'I didn't mean that, Dick. Pringle said that she was asking where *you* were, you see . . .'

Chesnaye felt uneasy. 'Well, what of it?'

Pickles fidgeted. 'Pringle pretended to be friendly, you know how he is. Then he spun her some yarn about you.' He gulped. 'That's what he was bragging about!'

'For God's sake make sense! *What* did he tell her?'

'He warned her against you. Said that you'd been boasting about the things you'd done with her . . .'

The rest of his words had been lost in the wave of fury which had engulfed Chesnaye, which still haunted him like a nightmare. Pringle had had his revenge, as he had promised. He had even managed to prevent Chesnaye from going ashore on one pretext or another, and by making a point of being meticulously correct in his behaviour had nailed down the last point in his victory.

Even now, as he lay sweating in his hammock, he could feel the anger rising within him like a flood. What was it made men like Pringle what they were? He hoarded titbits of information and used them like a sadistic blackmailer. It was obvious that he was doing the same to Pickles, although the latter strenuously denied it when Chesnaye asked him. His round face had puckered into a frightened mask and he had said: 'It's nothing, Dick! For God's sake forget it!'

The fans whirred steadily, and two decks above his head the watchkeepers peered into the velvet darkness. Chesnaye forced his eyes shut and tried to sleep. Surely his father had been wrong in his philosophy? It was futile and stupid to trust nobody.

He thought, too, about Pringle, and discovered that he was actually beginning to know the meaning of hatred.

4

Gallipoli

The *Saracen's* broad wardroom seemed unusually crowded as the ship's officers arranged themselves in the carefully placed chairs which faced the table at the far end. The evening air was warm and heavy, and the fans which whirred from the deckhead did little to ease the drowsy stuffiness, but instead kept the infiltrating flies constantly on the move to the annoyance of the seated officers.

Outside, the darkening anchorage of Mudros was alive with launches and small craft which prowled and fluttered around the moored warships and troopers like insects, and over the whole assembly of shipping there seemed to hang an air of excited tension and eagerness.

Richard Chesnaye craned his neck to pick out each officer in turn, aware that only a chief petty officer guarded the gangway and every officer, high or low, had been assembled for what must now be a final briefing. Like the others, he was relieved, almost glad that the waiting was over. Even if he had found the time to get ashore, and his increasing duties had prevented that, Mudros seemed a dull and unprepossessing island. Crammed with troops, tented camps, ammunition dumps and makeshift field hospitals, it had wilted beneath the crushing weight of the invasion force. For two weeks the *Saracen* had lain at anchor, the sun always making the preparations harder to bear, the ship's forced immobility adding to the sense of frustration and irritation. But now, as April moved nearer its close, it looked as if the great offensive was about to begin.

Chesnaye sat tautly in his chair, his limbs stiff with expectation as he listened to the loud, indifferent voices of his superiors and the excited whispers of the other midshipmen, who like himself had been seated at the very rear of the wardroom as if to doubly indicate their lack of seniority.

He could see Travis, the Navigating Officer, Hogarth and all the other lieutenants. Pringle's glossy head was prominent among the sub-lieutenants, while Major De L'Isle jutted like a glowing pinnacle above the packed ranks of experts and professionals who made up the ship's complement of officers. The engineers, warrant officers, Surgeon, Paymaster, even the Chaplain, were crammed into the well-lighted interior.

The Captain entered without fuss or announcement, followed by Commander Godden and an unfamiliar officer in army uniform.

Royston-Jones waited beside the table until the assembled officers, who had sprung noisily to their feet, had resettled themselves, and then laid his cap carefully on a nearby chair. His cold eyes flitted briefly across the watching faces, as if to make sure that there was neither an absentee nor an interloper, then he uncovered the tall chart which up to this moment had been hanging, shrouded, on the bulkhead.

The Captain glanced at Godden, who with the soldier had seated himself on the far side of the table. 'All present?'

'Yes, sir.' Godden looked meaningly towards the sealed pantry door. 'And I've sent the stewards forrard.'

Royston-Jones gave a wry smile. 'No doubt this meeting will be common knowledge between decks whatever action we take!'

A ripple of laughter transmitted itself around the wardroom. The lower deck's telegraph system was as reliable as it was uncanny.

'However . . .' the laughter died instantly, 'I shall expect each of you to bear the importance of security in mind. This whole operation could be jeopardised by rumour, equally it might be delayed by the inability of an officer to hold his tongue!'

The officers shuffled uneasily, and Chesnaye saw that some of them held unlit pipes and cigarettes concealed in their hands. They had apparently expected the Captain to permit smoking, but as yet there was no sign of any relaxation.

Chesnaye turned his attention to the chart as Royston-

Jones continued to speak. The chart showed clearly the long, sock-shaped peninsula of Gallipoli, and was dotted with small coloured counters and hostile-looking arrows.

'Gentlemen, the main Allied assault will take place forty-eight hours from tomorrow morning.' He allowed the murmurs to die. 'The main landings will be down here at the toe of the Peninsula at these three beaches, V, X and W. The Australian and New Zealand Forces are to make a separate landing to the north-west,' his brown hand moved slowly up the coastline, 'and thereby divide the enemy deployment.'

Beaushears spoke from the corner of his mouth, 'We hope!'

Royston-Jones' pale eyes flickered in the overhead lights. 'The *Saracen* will assist in the latter landings, and will provide artillery support both in the assault and after the Australians have crossed the beaches and captured the surrounding heights.'

Chesnaye stared hard at the passive chart and tried to see beyond the Captain's laconic words. For days they had listened to the rumours and stories from the men of patrolling destroyers, who day and night had watched the beaches and kept an eye on the Turkish preparations. The tales they told were not reassuring. Apparently the enemy had taken full advantage of the Allied delays and, as expected by everyone aboard, had poured in soldiers by the thousand, many of whom had actually been seen and reported as throwing up massive earthworks and gun batteries, and sowing the cliffs and beaches, even the water itself, with a tangled web of barbed wire. In addition, it was well known that the Straits and surrounding areas were littered with minefields, some of which had already taken a bitter toll. In the earlier March bombardments, while *Saracen* had languished at Gibraltar, the French battleship *Bouvet* had struck a mine and turned turtle in two minutes. Within two hours the battleship *Ocean* followed her to the bottom and the crack battle-cruiser *Inflexible* had been badly crippled.

Royston-Jones continued : 'The landings will be made early, but not in complete darkness, for obvious reasons. However, we must face the fact that the troops *will* in probability be advancing into point-blank fire from well-sited guns of every calibre.'

Involuntarily Chesnaye glanced at the army officer's face. It was an expressionless mask, as if he was aware that every man present was thinking the same thing.

'So our own importance, our *duty*, is plain. We must keep up a steady fire at pre-selected targets, so that the enemy is not only tied down but is also unable to harry our troops as they make their way inland.' The hand swept across the peninsula. 'This whole area is criss-crossed with gullies and ridges, any one of which could force a stalemate within days, even hours, of landing. We shall in all probability be firing at targets beyond these ridges which we cannot see. For this and other reasons I intend to land spotting teams as arranged, and in co-operation with the Royal Engineers Signal Branch I shall expect an unbroken stream of information to be fed to Lieutenant Hogarth's gunners!' He stared abruptly at the Commander. 'Check each landing party personally. They might be cut off from the ship for some time.'

Chesnaye shivered at the words. With Pickles and Beaushears he was already detailed for this work. For days they had exercised with boats and men, in pitch darkness and at the height of the sun, while telescopes and watches checked every phase of the operations.

But it was good that the waiting was over. Even being chased and harried through every phase of the preparations had failed to exclude Helen Driscoll from his mind, and his feeling of helplessness had prevailed rather than faded. He had tried to tell himself that their meeting was a mere incident, something he had had to feel for the first time, but not remember. It was all useless, and the more he relived those moments at Gibraltar, the stronger his emotions became, just as his contempt and anger for Pringle had hardened.

The confined stuffiness of the wardroom was making him drowsy and he had to consciously force himself to concentrate on what the army officer was saying about the dispersal of troops, landing marks and areas of bombardment. Heads of departments were writing in their notebooks, and Godden was nodding judiciously at various

67

points made by the tall soldier. The midshipmen had nothing to do but listen. Their work was prearranged. If the rehearsals proved to be faulty it would be too late to change anything, Chesnaye thought.

He shifted his gaze to the Captain. Even his impassive features could not hide completely the inner feelings of tension and anxiety. Royston-Jones was carefully seated, yet informal enough to create his own atmosphere of unusual excitement.

Chesnaye tried to comprehend what the Captain must be feeling. The whole ship, her company of two hundred officers and men and the mission prepared for those two massive guns, all that responsibility lay on his slight shoulders. Yet he showed little sign of true uncertainty.

Chesnaye thought, too, of his father. This might have been his command, and he wondered how he would have reacted at this moment. A pang of regret lanced through him as he recalled his father's flushed angry face.

Perhaps I should have tried to understand him more. Instead of worrying about the effect on my own career? He shifted in his chair as Royston-Jones stood up impatiently and faced the company.

'There is nothing else to say at this juncture, gentlemen. The cards are down. We are committed.' He allowed his words to sink in. 'From the moment the sun rises over those beaches we will all be paying our way.'

He stepped forward, an erect figure in white against the sombre chart. Then he pointed slowly towards the ship's crest above the empty fireplace, its garish warrior's face bright in the lamplight. 'Remember the ship's motto, gentlemen.' His voice was for once without an edge, almost sad, ' "With courage and integrity, press on!" One quality is useless without the other, either for this ship or the Navy itself!' With a curt nod to the Commander he was gone.

Some officers groped for their unlit pipes and then faltered, aware of the churchlike silence which seemed to have fallen around the glittering crest.

Beaushears said quietly, 'An altar of Mars!'

But across the wardroom Nutting, the Chaplain, was not so cynical. 'May God go with us,' he said.

68

The army officer had gone with Godden, and Major De L'Isle clapped his massive hands across his breast and glared at the black-coated Chaplain. 'Just contain yourself, Padre!' He glared at the wardroom at large. 'I think one last damned party is indicated, what? These bloody soldiers will need too much looking after for a bit to give us much time later on!'

Beaushears winked. 'This is *our* cue to leave, Dick.' He took a last glance at the chart. 'Let's hope the whole thing doesn't get bogged down like Flanders!'

Chesnaye had a brief vision of a vast army, stale and unmoving, with the sea at its back. 'It's going to be harder than I thought.'

Beaushears shrugged. 'A noble thought. You can put it on your tombstone!'

*   *   *   *   *

'Steady on north eighty-five east, sir!' Travis's voice was hushed, almost lost in the *Saracen*'s sea noises as the ship crept forward at six knots.

'Very well.' Royston-Jones moved from his chair, his figure a white shadow against the grey paintwork.

Although the sea and sky still merged in darkness, the stars were already pale and indistinct, and there was a faint but steady breeze as if the dawn had started to find breath.

Chesnaye shivered, but ignored the chill in his body as he peered over the port screen towards a long white line which lengthened and rippled in time to the monitor's own wash. A black, shapeless mass was moving in line abreast, and another beyond that, and another. Out there in the darkness he knew that an armada of steel was steering one fixed course, and somewhere ahead lay the barrier of the Peninsula itself. He remembered the previous afternoon and felt a lump in his throat. Because of her slow speed the monitor had sailed ahead of the main invasion fleet, and at one time had actually passed through two dawdling lines of troopships and their watchful escorts. Chesnaye knew that if he lived for ever he would never forget that moment. The sun high overhead, the clear blue sky and tall-funnelled troopers glittering above their own reflections. It had been very quiet but for the steady throb of the *Saracen*'s engines, an almost lazy, holiday atmosphere had cloaked the meaning of those double, treble rows of watching khaki figures who swarmed over every foot of the troopships' superstructures.

Something was lacking, and eventually Commander Godden had remarked : 'What a way to go to war! More like a Bank Holiday!'

Royston-Jones had been sitting in his chair, apparently dozing. His voice had been sharp and unexpected. 'Have the marine band mustered on the quarterdeck.'

Godden had stared at him. '*Now*, sir?'

'At the double, Commander! And tell the Bandmaster to go right through his repertoire until those ships are out of sight!'

It had been impressive and unreal. The fat, belligerent shape of the monitor, pale grey and shining in her new paint, with a giant ensign curling from the gaff, whilst on her scrubbed quarterdeck, paraded as if in Portsmouth barracks, the ship's band stood in a bright square, instruments glittering like jewels, sun-helmets gleaming white, watching the deft strokes of the Bandmaster's baton.

They had steamed past ship after ship, the slack, humid air suddenly coming to life with the strains of 'Hearts of Oak' and 'A Life on the Ocean Wave'.

Much later people might laugh at Royston-Jones, but Chesnaye knew in his heart that anyone who had been there would have known his decision to be right.

First one ship and then another had come alive, the upper decks transformed into rippling lines of waving hands and cheering faces. The cheering went on and on, until the sea itself seemed to vibrate.

That had been yesterday. Now those same soldiers were waiting out there in the darkness, fingering their rifles, pulling in their stomach muscles.

'Fifteen minutes, sir.' Travis was crouched above the compass.

'Very well.' The Captain sounded distant, as if thinking of something else.

Lieutenant Hogarth pushed his way across the crowded

bridge. He paused to peer at Chesnaye and the two other midshipmen, Beaushears and Pickles. 'Right. Nothing to do at the moment—for you that is!' He stood, his gaunt frame silhouetted against the charthouse. 'The first wave of troops is already moving up through the destroyer screen. You and your landing party will go with the second wave—got it?'

Chesnaye felt himself nodding. All at once his head seemed full of questions and doubts, his mind blank to everything he had been told.

Hogarth rubbed his hands. 'Right, then. We'll show 'em a thing or two!' But he was looking forward, as if speaking to his guns.

Even as he spoke, Chesnaye saw the tips of the two massive muzzles lift gently above the bridge screen until they were at a forty-five-degree angle. Hogarth muttered to himself and began to climb the ladder to the Upper Control Top. The ship was already at Action Stations, but the voice-pipes and handsets kept up their incessant chatter, adding to the feeling of nervous tension.

The Yeoman appeared. 'Commence general bombardment in eleven minutes, sir!'

'Very well.' The Captain climbed to his chair, his feet scraping on the grating. 'Ear-plugs, please.'

Chesnaye remembered just in time and groped for his own plugs. It would be terrible to start off with shattered eardrums.

There was a faint whirr of machinery and the great turret swivelled slightly to port. Criss-crossed along the monitor's decks the leaky hoses kept up their constant dampening, a final effort to save the planking from splintering to fragments when the bombardment started. For hours the shipwrights and stokers had been unscrewing doors, removing crockery and wooden panels, and preparing the ship for the one task for which she had been built.

'Five minutes, sir!'

Royston-Jones said: 'Let's hope the battleships know what they're doing. We don't want any of their salvoes falling short on to *us*!'

The monitor had previously passed a line of battleships

71

steaming parallel to the invisible coast, their long guns already trained abeam, their battle ensigns making faint white blobs against the towering bridges and turrets. They would be shooting at a range of some twenty thousand yards above and beyond the wide phalanx of the advancing troops in their boats.

'Dawn's comin' up, sir!' A signalman spoke involuntarily, as if to ease his own nerves.

Chesnaye watched the pale grey and silver line with awe and surprise. It was amazing how quickly the dawn came here. But at the bottom edge, where the horizon should have been, there was a black, uneven line. The coast.

It was impossible to see the hundreds of small boats which must already be streaming towards the hidden beaches, but Chesnaye knew that they were indeed there. Whalers, cutters, pinnaces, boats of every shape and kind. Power-launches towing clusters of troop-filled boats like pods, men crammed together, sweating and silent, smelling the fear and the danger yet eager to get started.

Even the *Saracen* had sent some of her boats to help, and at least three of her midshipmen, Bacon, Maintland and 'Ticky' White were out there with them.

Overhead the range-finders squeaked slightly as they revolved in their armoured turret, and Chesnaye heard a voice-pipe stutter : 'High explosive! Load . . . load . . , load!'

Godden said loudly, 'Leaving it to the last as usual!'

'One minute, sir!'

The young signalman by Chesnaye's side hugged his body with his arms. 'Jesus, this bloody waitin'!'

'Standing by, sir!'

'Very well.' Royston-Jones sounded calm. 'Starboard ten!'

The ship shivered and paid off into a moderate swell, her high bridge groaning. A pencil rolled from the chart table and clattered at their feet like a falling tree. Somewhere above a man coughed, and another could be heard whistling without tune.

'Zero, sir!'

'Open fire!'

Even as the order was passed, the horizon astern erupted

into a jagged pattern of red and orange flashes as the hidden battleships commenced their bombardment. Seconds dragged by, and then high overhead, with the ear-searing shriek of a regiment of express trains, the first salvoes sped on their way.

Chesnaye felt the signalman gripping his sleeve, and saw the man's mouth moving. 'Gawd, sir, what a way——' But his frightened words were lost as the monitor's main armament steadied and fired. There was less sound than Chesnaye had expected, yet he was rendered deaf and stunned, as if the guns had fired beside his head. The air was sucked across the upper bridge like hot sand, and as the twin barrels were hurled back on to their recoil springs he felt the whole ship shudder and buck. It was more like being struck by a salvo than firing one.

He coughed as a cloud of acrid cordite smoke drifted across the screen. In the space of seconds it had got lighter so that he could see the lean shape of a nearby destroyer and the harder outline of the coastline ahead.

The bombardment mounted and thickened in noise and power, so that the shells screamed overhead in an unending procession. Chesnaye understood little of their effect, and only occasionally could he see the angry flash of an explosion ashore. But beyond the cliffs and hills he knew that tons and tons of high explosive were deluging down, so that the waiting Turks, if waiting they were, must be in a living hell.

'Shoot!' Again the monitor's guns bellowed and lurched backwards, and Chesnaye could imagine the Quarters Officer yelling at his gunners and listening to Hogarth's urgent orders from the Control Top.

The noise was crushing, devastating and without pity. Chesnaye lost count of time as his body and mind shook to the voice of the monitor's bombardment. Occasionally Royston-Jones ordered an alteration of course, and Lieutenant Travis, strained and ill-looking, would crouch across the binnacle, his hands shaking to the thunder of the guns.

The sun peered across the land ridge, bright and curious, an onlooker without fear. The cliffs and the dirt-brown hills beyond looked suddenly close, the narrow

73

strips of beach white crescents beneath the high rock. Like beetles the small boats were already merged with the shoreline, the progress of the soldiers marked only with occasional flashes of fire. How small and ineffective those flashes seemed compared with the monitor's guns, Chesnaye thought.

Two waterspouts rose almost alongside the *Saracen*'s fo'c'sle, and Chesnaye ducked incredulously as something sped past the bridge with the sound of tearing silk.

'Enemy battery, bearing red four-five!' a lookout shouted between the gun-bursts.

Royston-Jones swung in his chair. 'Tell the Director to open fire with the secondary armament immediately!'

A rating with the handset said, 'Gunnery Officer has fixed the battery's position below the east pinnacle, sir.' Below the bridge the slim four-inch guns were already swinging shorewards.

'Very well.' The Captain seemed angry. 'Increase to half-speed, Pilot. We will close the coast and concentrate on the local batteries. That ridge is too high for the Turks to get at us once we are inshore.' He fidgeted with his glasses. 'We can hit *them*, however!'

Two more waterspouts rose alongside. Much closer.

Chesnaye flinched as the four-inch guns opened fire independently. Their voices were different. Sharp and ear-splitting, a savage whiplash.

Somehow he had not expected to be fired on himself. Up to now his thoughts had been mixed, filled with anxiety for the soldiers and uncertainty for himself. This was different. There was no sign that he could recognise along those craggy cliffs and hills, no opposite ship to plot and stalk. Merely the abbreviated scream of shells and the tall, deadly waterspouts.

The Yeoman tilted his cap as the sun lifted clear of the land and squinted at the curtain of spray as it fell abeam in the calm water. 'Quite big, too,' he said at length. 'Nine inch or bigger!' He grinned suddenly, his teeth filling his tanned face. 'Cheeky buggers!'

'Port ten!' The Captain sat hunched in his chair like a small gargoyle, his eyes following the white whirlpool which still showed the last fall of shot. The monitor swung awkwardly on her course and then steadied as another order brought her bows once more towards the beaches.

The hidden Turkish battery dropped two more shells simultaneously near the monitor's starboard beam—where the ship would have been but for Royston-Jones' sudden alteration of course.

Again the falling spray, the taste of cordite. Chesnaye stared fascinated at the leaping water, only to be knocked sideways as the *Saracen*'s big guns roared out once more. It was a wonder the turret did not tear itself clean off the ship, or that the *Saracen* remained in one piece.

Then there were no more Turkish shells, and Royston-Jones twisted round to stare up at the Control Top. Almost impishly he lifted his cap and smiled. Peering through his armoured slits, like a knight at Agincourt, Hogarth must have seen that impetuous gesture and felt a glow of satisfaction.

Royston-Jones glanced briefly at the three midshipmen. 'Away you go! Stand by to lower your boats and embark landing parties!'

Chesnaye shook himself and tore his eyes from the Captain's unblinking stare. All at once he realised that it was not over. For him it was just beginning.

*   *   *   *   *

A steam picket boat took the *Saracen*'s two whalers in tow until they were within half a mile of the beach and then cast them adrift. A sub-lieutenant in the power boat's sternsheets waved a megaphone and bellowed: 'Pull like hell for your landing point! It's a bit hot around here!'

As if to emphasise his words, a small shell exploded nearby and sent a wave of splinters whirring overhead.

Chesnaye gritted his teeth and peered over the oarsmen's heads. The nearest cliff, shaped like a miniature Rock of Gibraltar, hid the early sun from view and cast a deep black shadow across the two pitching whalers. 'Give way together!' His voice was surprisingly steady, and he forced himself to look at Tobias, who because of the extra passengers was squatting right aft, his legs over the tiller bar. He caught Chesnaye's eye and grinned. 'Just like a trip round Brighton pier, sir !'

Hunched in the sternsheets Lieutenant Thornton, selected by Hogarth as senior spotting officer, pawed over an assortment of leather cases which contained telescopes, handsets and other necessary gear, his face set in a scowl of concentration. Pickles was by his side, his gaze fixed on the dark shadowed cliff. The oarsmen pulled hard and rhythmically, half watching the other whaler which was barely yards away.

Beaushears stood in the other boat and occasionally glanced across, his features drawn and unusually determined.

I suppose I must look like that, Chesnaye thought. We are all playing a part. More afraid of showing fear than of fear itself.

He shaded his eyes, conscious of the cool depths of the cliff's shadow as it closed about him. 'Steer over there.' He felt the tiller creak obediently.

It was too quiet, he thought. Like the sea and the sky, everything seemed shadowed and guarded by the might of the land. Faint and muffled, he could occasionally hear the sporadic rattle of small-arms and the steel whiplash of machine-guns. But they were impersonal and did not appear to belong here. Once when he glanced astern he saw the *Saracen*, her shape deformed as she turned slightly towards the headland, the long guns still probing the air, as if sniffing out a new target. Many other ships were silhouetted against the horizon, but the barrage had paused, no doubt waiting to see the effect of the troops' progress ashore.

As if reading his thoughts Pickles said breathlessly, 'It looks as if it's all over already !'

Chesnaye nodded absently. 'Watch your steering, Tobias ! There are shoals of some sort ahead.' He had seen what appeared to be low, sandy rocks littered along the water's edge.

Tobias said tightly, 'Not *rocks*, sir.'

The whaler moved swiftly inshore, the last few yards vanishing in seconds. Chesnaye saw the oarsmen watching

76

him curiously, and held his breath in an endeavour to conceal the slow sickness which was squeezing his insides like a vice.

Nearer and nearer. He could see clearly now the shoals which were strewn across the whaler's path. They moved gently in the lapping wavelets, their khaki limbs swaying and jerking as if still alive.

He heard Pickles gasp, and then as the boat cut a passage between the first of the dead soldiers the oarsmen looked too at the tangle of corpses and discarded equipment at the water's edge.

The stroke was momentarily lost, and Chesnaye choked: 'Oars! Stand by to beach!' He did not know how he had managed to give the order, nor did he recognise his own voice. The boat ground into the sand and the second whaler hit the beach close by.

A few soldiers moved along the base of the cliff, and he saw several tiny tents marked with the Red Cross already erected. But again his eyes were drawn to the waterline of dead.

Australians, New Zealanders and a few British, their faces already pale and expressionless in the salt spray. He could see the gleaming teeth of barbed wire, sewn deep in the water itself, and upon which little clusters of corpses bobbed like obscene fruit. There was blood too on the sand and all the way up the trampled beach to the foot of the cliff. A sergeant lay on his back, his hands digging into his stomach, mouth wide in one last cry. His uniform was stitched from shoulder to groin with machine-gun bullets, yet equipment and bayonet were still smart and exactly in place.

Lieutenant Thornton leapt over the gunwale. 'At the double! Put out the boat anchors and run for cover!'

The men gaped from the corpses to him and then jerked into life as the sand jumped at their feet and the air echoed to the high-pitched whine of bullets.

A soldier yelled: 'Come up here, you stupid bastards! There are still snipers about!'

A bullet whacked into the boat's warm woodwork at Chesnaye's hip, and with a gasp he started up the beach. He turned to call to Lieutenant Thornton and was just in time to see him reel back, his hands clawing at his face. In fact his face had been torn away by a bullet, but blinded and screaming he staggered drunkenly in a circle while the sand spurted around him.

An Australian corporal emerged from some rocks, his bush hat tilted over his eyes. Unceremoniously he pushed Chesnaye against the cliff and threw down his rifle. In three bounds he reached the naval officer, but before he could seize him Thornton dropped and rolled on to his back, his face a glistening, bright scarlet against the pale sand.

Chesnaye retched as the seamen crowded around him, Tobias carrying Thornton's leather cases.

The corporal returned and picked up his rifle. 'Of all the stupid jokers!' He pulled a cigarette from his hat and squinted up at the cliff. 'Pretty quiet landing so far, but the boys is held up in a gully over yonder.' He gestured vaguely to a small cliff path.

Beaushears sidled along the cliff and peered at Chesnaye. 'All right, Dick?' He glanced at the spread-eagled lieutenant on the open beach. 'It's up to us, then?'

Chesnaye nodded dazedly. 'I suppose so.'

'I'll set up my signal party here as arranged, Dick,' Beaushears was speaking fast as if unable to stop. 'You must take Thornton's job with the Army until *Saracen* can send a replacement.' He looked grim. 'Or do you want me to take over?'

Chesnaye shook his head. 'No. I'll go!' He wanted to scream. These stupid, formal tones. A man he had known was still bleeding barely feet away, his face a bloody pulp. An Australian was smoking a cigarette, his eyes on the distant monitor. Nothing was real any more.

Tobias said carefully. 'We'd better be off, sir. It may take some time to contact the army signals blokes.'

'Er, yes.' Chesnaye looked at Pickles' stricken face. 'Can you make it to the top?'

Pickles seemed to pull himself together. 'I'll be all right with you, Dick!'

Then they were off up the path, the soldier still leaning against the cliff, his eyes slitted as if in deep thought.

It took Chesnaye more than an hour to lead his small party of seamen to the top of the cliff path. The sun was already high in the clear sky, and every step up the dry, crumbling track brought the sweat pouring down his body, so that he repeatedly had to stop and wipe his face with his sleeve. At last he turned sharply into a deep fold of rock, the sides of the cliff rising on either side of him sheer and smooth as if the very weight of stone and boulders had split the land in two. His eyes were dazzled by the heat haze which shimmered above the barren countryside and the sparse tangle of small trees which clung desperately to the ridges above the cliff path, and he almost stumbled on to a group of soldiers who were squatting comfortably outside what appeared to be a narrow cave.

A harrased-looking subaltern rose to his feet and stared at Chesnaye and his men. 'You'll be the gunnery experts, then?' He grinned companionably and eased the weight of his revolver at his belt. 'In the nick of time, too!'

Chesnaye looked around him. Just beyond the V-shaped end to the gap in the cliff he could see the rounded crest of a long ridge. It seemed quite near, yet he knew from his map that there was a deep gully between it and the coastline. And beyond that there was a higher ridge, and then another. They had cut the Peninsula into a mass of valleys and gullies like a bird's eye view of a badly ploughed field, each ridge dominating the next for a watchful friend or enemy.

Already the sea had vanished, the hiss and murmur of wavelets along the beaches lost in the boom of artillery and the vicious rattle of machine-guns. Yet the dust which hovered in the humid air like smoke was tinged with salt, and a handful of angry gulls still circled and screamed above the narrow path from the shore.

The subaltern pointed towards the gap in the cliffs. 'Our chaps have pushed forward quite well. Not much resistance on the beach either, thank God!'

Chesnaye thought of the nodding corpses in the stained water. 'It looked bad to me,' he said quietly.

'Hell, no!' The Australian accent seemed strange and casual. 'My signals outfit reported that the main landings down south have had a really bad time of it! Lost hundreds in the first minutes.' He grimaced. 'Cross-fire. The Turks had the whole damn' beach zeroed in!'

Chesnaye looked across Pickles' heaving shoulders at his silent seamen. In their dusty and crumpled uniforms they seemed out of place, lost and dispirited. Chesnaye bit his lip. They had not started yet. He wondered how the dead lieutenant would have dealt with the situation. No doubt as casually and as efficiently as this young soldier.

'Can we go forward now?' Chesnaye saw Pickles stiffen at his question.

The subaltern gestured towards the squatting soldiers. 'Here, runner! Take these jolly Jacks up to the observation post.' He grinned again. 'If it's still there!'

Chesnaye waved his arm. 'Come on, lads!' He was too tired to look at them again. 'We'll rest when we get there!'

The subaltern called after them: 'Keep your heads down when you cross the first gully. There's a goddamned sniper about somewhere!'

They reached the end of the path and Chesnaye stared mesmerised at the small pile of corpses which littered the saucer-shaped arena at the opening of the gully. Not people, he thought. Just things. Khaki uniforms and discarded rifles. Heavy boots still stained from the beach, and fingers digging into the stony path as if to mark that last second of agony. Dried blood and staring faces across which the flies busied themselves in their hundreds.

The runner gripped his rifle and pointed to a deep hole which had been cut into the sandy side of the rock, 'Watch,' he said shortly. 'There's a fixed rifle somewhere up in that hill. The sniper fires it every so often in the hope some poor joker'll be crossing this spot. He's on to a good thing, really. It's the only path from our beach!'

There was a whiplash crack, and the gravel around the hole jumped as if blasted from the inside. The bullet must have passed right through the piled corpses, for one of them turned on its side, like a sleeper who has been momentarily awakened by some unusual sound.

'Now!' The runner ducked his head and ran.

Chesnaye banged Pickles' arm. 'After him! Come on, the rest of you!'

Dazed and unsteady, the seamen scampered across the opening. Chesnaye watched them melt into the boulders beneath the rock shadow and then took a last look round. Nothing moved, yet he could feel the eyes of the nearest dead soldier watching him with fixed curiosity. Crack! The stones jumped again, and the runner called, 'Have a go for it, chum!'

Chesnaye wanted to walk calmly past the silent figures, to pass some confidence to his own small party, but as he stepped into the sun's glare he thought suddenly and clearly of that hidden marksman. Perhaps he was already shifting his rifle and even now had found Chesnaye's shoulders within his sights. He had another stark vision of his own body sprawled on top of the others, and he imagined that the corpse with the staring eyes would be glad. He ran.

Up and up they climbed, each step dislodging stones and stirring the dust. The *Saracen* seemed impossible to imagine, their mission merely a memory.

The observation post consisted only of a natural wall of boulders strewn deep into a long patch of the small, stunted trees which Chesnaye had seen from the cliff path. There was no shelter from the sun, and the stupendous view of a wide valley and the ridge beyond was swirling in a fantastic heat haze. The ridge flickered with scattered flashes as hidden marksmen crawled and out-manœuvred the enemy, whilst below him Chesnaye could see the clean scars in the hillside where soldiers had already dug their way into a quickly arranged defensive trench which curved out of sight around the foot of the nearest hill.

The runner mopped his face and crouched gratefully behind the rocks. 'This is the narrowest part of the peninsula,' he said solemnly. 'That big formation of ridges to the left is Sari Bair, and over the ridge the Straits are only four miles away.' He smiled sadly. 'If we can break across this lot we'll cut the bastards in half!' He ducked instinctively as a shell droned overhead. 'Got to watch that sort,' he explained. 'Johnny Turk has got a big gun somewhere over that brown hillock. It fires shrapnel mostly. Got a lot of good cobbers this morning!' He stiffened. 'Ah, here comes your mate! I'd better be off to the command post.' With a cheerful nod he was off, his long legs taking him down the slope like a goat.

Chesnaye turned to face the young army officer with the blue and white brassard on his arm. The soldier was walking stiffly as if only just holding himself together. He looked at Chesnaye and they both stared at one another with disbelief.

Some of Chesnaye's despair seemed to melt. 'Bob Driscoll!' For a few moments he forgot his loneliness, the helpless feeling of loss, as he saw the weariness lift from the young officer's face.

They clasped hands and Driscoll said: 'Good to see you. It's been bloody hell up here!'

Chesnaye crouched beside him as he told the seamen where to find some sort of shelter while he outlined his orders. Chesnaye felt a stab of uneasiness as he watched Driscoll's dust-stained face. The same mouth, the same grave eyes as Helen. It was unnerving.

Driscoll looked at Pickles. 'Right, then. My sappers have started to lay a wire to the beach. As soon as they've connected they'll send a morse signal to my chap here.' He gestured to a small soldier hunched over a jumble of wireless gear above which glittered a single transmitting key. 'You've got a range map of the area, but I expect we'll have to make a few alterations after the first shots.'

Chesnaye nodded, his mind clearing slightly as he collected his thoughts in time to Driscoll's calm voice. The monitor would fire from somewhere behind their spotting post, hidden by cliffs and hills, her presence only marked by the passage of her great fifteen-inch shells. It would be almost a blind shoot to start with, not much more than a compass bearing. Chesnaye and Pickles would watch and note the fall of shot and pass the alterations of range and deflection to the man with the morse key. The message would travel down the new, hastily laid wire to where Beaushears and his signalmen would be waiting at the foot of the cliffs to flag it to the watching *Saracen*.

Chesnaye swallowed hard. It sounded simple.

Driscoll was saying, 'You must be quite an important bloke, Dick!' His teeth shone in his grimed face. 'I'd have thought that your C.O.'d send someone a bit senior for this job!'

Pickles spoke for the first time. 'He was killed on the beach!' He still sounded shocked.

'Hmmm, I see.' Driscoll settled his elbow on the rocks and lifted his binoculars. 'Get your telescope rigged, Dick. You'll be able to see the Turkish battery if you watch long enough.' He winced as a shell passed overhead. 'That's a small chap. Mountain battery. The whole bloody place is alive with Turks, yet I've not seen one!' He laughed bitterly. 'Imagine that! Lost my sergeant this morning. Bang through the head. Yet we didn't see a bloody one!'

Chesnaye jammed the telescope carefully in position. In its enlarged eye the ridge seemed very near, and as he watched he saw the telltale drift of smoke as the hidden battery fired once again. On the hillside to his right the pale rocks leapt high into the air, and he imagined that he could feel the ground lurch against his crouching body.

Driscoll took off his cap and wiped his brow. 'Their shooting is improving, blast it!' He pointed at the hillside where some running soldiers had shown themselves for a few brief seconds. 'If the Turks can batter down our defences to the right of us we shall be in bad trouble. When night comes they'll try to cut down the valley and split this section in half.' He shook his head. 'You men'll have to act like infantrymen if that happens!'

The linesman reported : 'We're through, sir! Contact with the beach signal party!'

Driscoll put on his cap. 'Well, Dick, it's all yours! Let's see what the Navy can do!'

Chesnaye peered through the telescope and watched the distant ridge. One real error and the shells would fall right on to the Australian positions below.

He gritted his teeth. 'Very well. Make a signal to *Saracen*. Commence first salvo when ready!'

His limbs seemed to grow tighter. He was committed.

5

The Enemy

The *Saracen* shivered as the two big guns recoiled violently on their springs and the twin detonations blasted across the placid water as one. The sound was magnified and echoed by the craggy shoreline, so that the noise of the bombardment was constant and enfolded the quaking ship like a tropical storm. The two guns were angled at about forty-five degrees and pointed directly over the port rail. Already the smooth barrels were stained and blackened for several feet back from their muzzles, and the acrid cordite smoke hung over the monitor's bridge in an unmoving cloud.

Commander Godden coughed loudly into his handkerchief and then looked with distaste at the black stains on his uniform. 'How much longer, sir?'

Royston-Jones was squatting forward from his chair, elbows on the screen, his powerful glasses trained at some point along the coast. The light was beginning to fail, and there was a hint of purple shadowing across the jagged headland of Kaba Tepe. He shrugged and then jerked as the guns roared out once more.

The Yeoman moved dazedly across the bridge. His cap and shoulders were speckled with flaked paint brought down from the upper bridge by the constant gunfire and recoil. 'Signal from beach, sir. Cease fire. Turkish battery silenced and supporting infantry dispersed.'

Royston-Jones gestured impatiently. 'Very well. Cease firing and secure the guns.'

Muffled and indistinct within the great turret they could hear the tinny rattle of the 'Cease Fire' gong. The sweating, near-demented gunners would be almost too dazed to leave their stations after a day of continuous bombardment. The Quarters Officer, too, would have his work cut out to prepare the turret for immediate action if required.

Godden sighed with relief as the turret squeaked round until it was trained fore and aft, while the two guns drooped wearily to a horizontal position, their dark muzzles still smoking angrily.

'Signal from Flag, sir.' The Yeoman watched his captain warily. 'The bombarding squadron will withdraw at dusk to reinforce the southern landings. *Saracen* will maintain position in this sector until relieved or reinforced, with two destroyers in attendance. Every available effort to be made to evacuate wounded under cover of darkness.' The Yeoman looked up from his slate. 'End of signal, sir.'

Godden groaned. 'Left alone again! God, what do they think we are?' He glared round the bridge. 'What the hell are we going to do with a lot of wounded soldiers?'

Royston-Jones said flatly: 'We have a surgeon, I believe? Right, assemble all boats and prepare to carry out instructions.'

Lieutenant Travis climbed down from the compass platform and tested his legs. Gingerly he removed his earplugs and peered through the smoke. 'We *are* a bit vulnerable here, sir?'

Royston-Jones levered himself from the chair. 'Anchored fore and aft, you mean?'

'Well, yes, sir.'

'Quite so, Pilot.'

The ship had been virtually stationary during the bombardment, a sitting target had the Turks been able to bring a gun to bear. But protected by her own heavy fire and the close proximity of the high cliff she had remained undisturbed and wreathed in the smoke and fumes of her bombardment.

Royston-Jones shrugged. 'Nothing I can do about that. Must maintain a good position for Hogarth's sake. He did very well to all accounts.'

Travis smiled. 'So did the young snotties, sir.'

'Yes.' The Captain stretched like a small bird. 'Pity about Lieutenant Thornton. Good officer. Must write to his father. Such a waste.'

Hogarth appeared, gaunt but grinning. 'Guns secured, sir. Permission to fall out crews?'

Godden nodded, his eye on Royston-Jones. 'Very well.' 'Ah, Hogarth.' The Captain turned slowly. 'Quite a good shoot, I thought.'

Hogarth beamed. 'Eighty rounds of fifteen-inch.' He turned down his mouth. 'Mostly shrapnel, of course, but you can't have everything!'

Royston-Jones nodded gravely. 'I am sorry we hadn't enough time to get you a more experienced spotting officer, but we were rather pressed!'

Hogarth smiled in spite of his weariness. While the whole ship had waited with frustration and anxiety for the landing party to get into position an unexpected Turkish battery had started to drop shells in the small bay, some very close to the monitor. The battery was shooting blind, but they must have known what they were after. A cheer had rippled throughout the ship when a signalman had excitedly reported contact with Midshipman Beaushears on the beach. Within a quarter of an hour the Turkish guns had fallen silent beneath a hailstorm of shrapnel and a few high-explosive shells for good measure. From that moment the *Saracen* had obediently hurled her shells inland, each salvo within minutes of the urgent signals from the beach.

Godden pulled at his lower lip. So Thornton was dead. But he was not the first casualty. Midshipman Maintland and his pinnace had been blasted to fragments by one stray shell from the shore even as he was returning to the ship. His crew of three had vanished also, and like a memorial the severed stem of the boat still drifted near the anchored monitor.

Pipes twittered below decks and within seconds the ship blossomed with seamen. Men who had stayed hidden and watchful behind guns and steel shutters, their ears deafened by the bombardment, scampered like children with a new-found freedom.

Royston-Jones frowned. 'Turn to both watches, Commander. Rig tackles for hoisting the wounded inboard, and have a constant guard rowed round the ship.' He

86

yawned elaborately. 'Send for my steward. I'm going to my sea-cabin for a few moments.'

Godden fumed inwardly. That meant that he would have to stay on the bridge himself. He desperately needed to sit down, to have a drink, to think. The fierce and sudden events had left him feeling old and helpless, and the knowledge had almost unnerved him.

Hogarth was about to leave the bridge. 'Shall I signal for the shore party to return for the night?'

Godden tore his mind from his wave of self-pity. 'No. Let them bloody well stay there! It'll do 'em good!'

Hogarth showed his long teeth. 'I *say*, sir, bit savage, isn't it?'

But Godden had turned away, tired and fuddled like an elephant at the end of a long charge. Already the voice-pipes were at it again, and far below the bridge the impatient, cutting voices of the petty officers could be heard mustering their men.

Hogarth shrugged and lowered himself over the screen. He paused for a moment and stared at the silent turret. It had been a triumph. From start to finish it had been a copybook bombardment. He thought of Godden's brooding face and wondered. Perhaps that generation were already too staid and steeped in peacetime routine to be able to accept this sort of warfare. Except the Captain, of course. Hogarth shook himself and continued his passage to the deck. That would be unthinkable.

The Quarters Officer, his round face blackened with powder, waited for him on the deck where seamen with hoses and scrubbers were at work removing the dirt of war. His teeth shone. 'Pretty good, eh, Guns?'

Hogarth smothered his sense of well-being and satisfaction and frowned. 'Bloody *awful*, Lucas!' He watched the other man's face lengthen. 'You'll have to do better tomorrow!'

Hogarth strode along the deck, his lips pursed in a silent whistle. It did not do to share one's laurels, he thought happily.

•   • • •

The tiny dugout was almost airless, so that Chesnaye awoke with the suddenness of a man suffocating in his sleep. For a few wild seconds he blinked at Robert Driscoll's bowed figure as he sat awkwardly beside a crude table of ammunition boxes, and saw that although the young soldier was staring fixedly at a worn map his eyes were empty and unfocused. The dugout measured less than eight feet by six, and the low roof, crudely supported by duckboards and wooden props, sloped steeply at the rear, where Pickles lay in a restless bundle, his head on his cap. A blanket covered the narrow entrance, and two candles, their air-starved flames short and guttering, cast weird and unnatural shadows around the hastily hewn walls. The place was crowded with ammunition cases, signals equipment and a pile of entrenching tools, and Chesnaye stared dazedly at each article in turn as understanding and memory returned to his sleep-fuddled brain.

Driscoll turned his head, his eyes in shadow. 'You've been snoring for a good three hours,' he said quietly.

Chesnaye sat up, every bone protesting violently. The earth was cool and damp yet his face still tingled from the blazing sunlight, and his eyes felt raw as if he had only just discarded the long spotting telescope.

He licked his dry lips. 'Have you just come in?'

Driscoll shrugged. 'An hour ago.' He fished in an open box at his feet. 'Have a drink?' He did not wait for an answer but carefully poured something into two enamel mugs. The liquid shone like amber in the candlelight. 'Brandy,' Driscoll said shortly. 'The last. From tomorrow we'll have rum like the lads. If we're lucky!'

Chesnaye swallowed a mouthful and felt the heat coursing through him. 'It's good,' he said.

'Carried it all the way from Gib.' Driscoll toyed with the empty bottle. 'God, what a long way off it seems!'

'Anything happening outside?' Chesnaye gestured with the mug towards the curtain.

'Quiet. A bloody wilderness!' He stood up, his shadow leaping across the dugout like a phantom. 'Come and take a look. I can't sleep.'

Together they ducked through the low entrance and stared up at the black hillside behind the makeshift trench. Somewhere up there the spotting post and its big boulders would be cool and deserted. But tomorrow . . . Chesnaye shuddered involuntarily.

Their feet scraped the pebbles as they walked, and occasionally Chesnaye caught sight of a dark figure huddled on the firing step, his shoulders and naked bayonet outlined against the stars. Other men lay unmoving like the dead, wrapped in greatcoats or blankets, their rifles nearby, but the war momentarily excluded from their minds.

Chesnaye had seen the stretchers going down the cliff path in the heat of the afternoon when there had been an ordered lull in the *Saracen*'s fire. Stretchers carried casually and clumsily by the Red Cross orderlies on their journey back from the vague front line. For the occupants of the stretchers were past care and beyond caring. So the living stayed in the trench and slept. Tomorrow the stretchers would take more of them away. For ever.

Chesnaye followed Driscoll as he climbed up on to the firing step near one of the sentries.

Chesnaye spoke quietly. 'There's a wiring party out tonight.' His arm moved like a shadow. 'Somewhere in front of us. Nasty job. The ground's too hard for staples or digging——'

Chesnaye gasped as a bright blue flare erupted slightly to his left and hung in the air apparently unmoving.

'Turkish flare,' said Driscoll calmly.

The unearthly light turned the night to day, yet gave the surrounding landscape the colour and texture of something illusory. Small objects stood out starkly, whilst the hillside and the black gaping slit of trench mingled and joined as if covered by vapour.

Chesnaye felt naked and exposed as he stood on the firing step, the thin layer of sandbags barely reaching his chest. The flare glistened along the teeth of the wire and the blackened mounds which marked the edges of the day's shell craters. Out there, Chesnaye thought, men are crouching or standing, caught and mesmerised in the unblinking glare. Even the smallest movement could be fatal. The slightest moment of fear might bring instant attention from the enemy line. The flare dipped and died. Far to the right the dark sky flickered sullenly and then blossomed

89

into a red glow. A rumble like thunder rolled around the gully and down into the deserted valley. It went on and on, so that Chesnaye found himself staring not at the glow but at the stars themselves, as if he expected to find the answer there.

'Somebody's getting it down south,' Driscoll commented. 'Night attack. It'll be our turn soon.' He stepped down into the trench and the rumble seemed to fade. 'How these Aussies can sleep!' His teeth gleamed faintly. 'They think it's a real joke to have the Navy *and* me here!'

Chesnaye smiled. 'What is your job exactly?'

'Well, apart from looking after you, I'm a jack of all trades. Communications, bit of sapping, all the usual stuff.' He sighed. 'It's a man's life in the modern Army!'

They re-entered the dugout, and Chesnaye lowered himself gingerly on to his pile of empty sandbags. 'A few more hours yet,' he said.

As he turned on to his side he heard Driscoll's voice, brittle and sharp. 'Are you in love with my sister, Dick?' Then, as Chesnaye tried to turn : 'No, don't look. Just answer.'

Chesnaye stared at the earth wall by his face. All at once he felt very calm. A girl he hardly knew, but remembered so clearly—'Yes, Bob.'

There was a silence. The dugout vanished into darkness as the candles were extinguished, and Driscoll added quietly : 'Good. I just wanted to know.'

Chesnaye tried to laugh. 'Why did you ask?'

He heard the other man sliding into a corner of the dugout. 'I just wanted to know. Out here you need something to hold on to.'

Chesnaye lay for long afterwards, his eyes wide in the darkness, half listening to Driscoll's breathing and half to the sullen mutter of gunfire.

■　　　·　　　■　　　·　　　■　　　·

The first shell landed on the hillside above the trench even as the first light of dawn felt its way across the floor of the valley. Richard Chesnaye felt the dugout's floor buck beneath his back so that real pain shot through his limbs which seconds before had been relaxed in sleep. He awoke coughing and choking in a thick vapour of dust and smoke, his head reeling from the shattering explosion, as the blanket curtain across the entrance was ripped from its frame as if by an invisible hand.

The narrow confines of the trench were alive to running feet and loud cries, and even as Chesnaye struggled to his feet a second shell exploded somewhere overhead. His shocked hearing returned with startling suddenness so that he was all at once aware of a sharp, intermittent sobbing. He turned blinking in the dust to see Pickles on his hands and knees like a blinded animal, his round face wrinkled with shock and stark terror. For an instant he imagined that somehow Pickles had been hit by a splinter, but as he moved towards the scrabbling figure he heard Pickles scream: 'God, help me! I must get away!'

Chesnaye gripped his tunic and dragged him to his feet so that their faces were almost pressed together. They swayed in a struggling embrace as the dugout rocked and shivered and more explosions thundered along the side of the hill. Chesnaye felt suddenly calm and ice-cold. The sickness of fear and despair which had held him in the shock-wave of the first detonation had gone with the quickness of night, and in its place he could feel only a quiet desperation and an urgent need to get out of the quivering dugout.

A harsh Australian voice yelled above the bombardment: 'Keep down, you lot! They'll be comin' over after this!'

Pickles whimpered and pressed his head into Chesnaye's shoulder. 'I can't go on, Dick! *Please* don't make me!'

Chesnaye peered down at him, his racing thoughts torn between disgust and pity. He prised Pickles' fingers from his arm. 'Snap out of it, for heaven's sake! It's a bombardment. The Turks'll be coming over as soon as it drops!' He thought of Driscoll's calm words the night before. It'll be our turn next. Attack and counter-attack. The probe and the follow-up. Generals of both armies had tried it so often on the Western Front where a glut of manpower made up for their own lack of knowledge.

Pickles shrank back, small and shivering. 'I *won't* go.

It's not fair!' He peered round the dust-covered floor. 'We shouldn't be here!' He stared fixedly at Chesnaye with something like hatred. 'We don't belong here at all!'

Chesnaye had a brief picture of the monitor, clean and untouched by all this disorder and sudden danger. Her guns would be helpless and impotent. Incapable of firing a single shot without the signals from the shore. From him.

He groped for his cap and then slung his telescope and leather case over his shoulder. 'We're going now, Keith,' he said quietly. 'They're depending on us.'

Without another word Pickles allowed himself to be led out into the distorted light of the trench. Dust and smoke were everywhere, and the narrow, crudely hacked defences were filled with crouching khaki figures, their bodies and weapons cluttering the bottom of the trench in a dust-covered tangle. It seemed impossible to believe that only hours before this same place had been quiet and deserted, the only furtive movement being that of a hidden wiring party.

A tall Australian lieutenant, wild-eyed and unshaven, cannoned into Chesnaye as he peered up and behind the stone-strewn defences to the high rounded shoulder of the hill. Somewhere up there was the abandoned spotting post. Chesnaye felt his arm seized and watched the angry snapping movements of the soldier's mouth.

'You'd better get the hell out of it, sailor!' The lieutenant glanced briefly at Pickles' stricken face. 'The bastards will be having a go in a moment!' He held his breath and ducked as a shell screamed overhead and burst on the hillside.

The air seemed thick with whimpering, hissing splinters, and somewhere beyond the black smoke Chesnaye heard a chorus of unearthly screams. A loud, urgent voice called, 'Stretcher bearers!' And the cry was carried on and away by other unknown, unseen men along the battered trench.

Chesnaye started as he felt sand running across his hand, and looked up to see a smoking slit in a nearby sandbag. The splinter must have missed him by inches.

He heard himself say: 'I must get up there! We're the only artillery support you've got in this sector!'

The lieutenant wiped his mouth with his hand. 'What about the rest of the Fleet?'

Chesnaye shrugged. 'Withdrawn. To support the other landing areas.'

The Australian laughed bitterly. 'Jesus, what a bloody mess!'

Nearby, a soldier was being sick while his comrades stared at him with empty, glassy eyes. They all seemed shocked and dazed by the shellfire, their faces devoid of expression.

'You'll never make it, sailor!' The Australian peered upwards, his eyes following Chesnaye's gaze. 'Johnny Turk knows what we're about. He's spraying the whole damned area with shrapnel and anything else he can get!' Angrily he added, 'I thought the Navy was supposed to have knocked out all their batteries?'

Chesnaye caught sight of Leading Seaman Tobias's tanned features at a bend in the trench and he beckoned him with sudden urgency. It was all quite clear what had to be done. In a strange voice he said: 'We're going up, Tobias. The second the barrage lifts we'll make a run for it!' He watched for some sign, but Tobias merely grunted. Chesnaye added, 'Get the rest of our men and check their rifles.'

Tobias pressed himself against the firing step as two shells tore into the hillside and sent a cascade of loose boulders clattering into the trench. A man cried out sharply, like an animal, and then fell silent. Tobias said thickly: 'Our lads won't like it, Mister Chesnaye. They're not soldiers.'

Chesnaye said savagely: 'They don't have to like it! Now go and tell them!'

He watched Tobias go, and then turned back to the lieutenant, who was crouching down and reading a signal pad which a panting runner had just delivered.

He looked up at Chesnaye's grim features. 'Worse than I thought. The Turks have overrun Hill Seventy-Five. The whole of the right flank is a bloody shambles.'

Chesnaye started to grope for his range map and then remembered. Hill Seventy-Five was directly on their right, the end-piece of a long ridge of narrow hills. The hill above this trench was the only one left in a commanding position now. If that fell, the way to the beach would be cut, and the enemy might roll up the flimsy defences like a carpet. He swallowed hard. 'It's as I said, then?'

The Australian eyed him with surprise. 'Well, it's been nice knowing you, kid!' He broke off, choking as an impenetrable cloud of smoke billowed round the curve in the trench. 'What th' hell?'

A brown-faced sergeant pushed his way through the crouching soldiers. His angry eyes swept across the two midshipmen and settled on his own officer. 'Bastards 'ave set the bloody gorse on fire, sir!' He waved his rifle as if it were a mere toy. 'The whole hillside is alight!'

The lieutenant shrugged. 'Accident or design, it's a cunning move. Our lads will be half blind in a second!'

Tobias appeared, followed by a bearded A.B. called Wellard. 'Ready, sir.' As if in response to his words, the barrage dropped, the echoes passing down the valley like a receding typhoon.

All at once it was very still, and Chesnaye could feel his legs quivering violently. He was almost afraid to move lest they collapsed under him. He looked at Pickles, and when he saw the naked fear on his face he felt suddenly unsure and alone.

Wellard spat into the sand at his feet. 'Not our bloody job!' He jerked his head at the rising pall of black smoke. 'Let's make for the beach now!'

Chesnaye knew that the other seamen were behind Wellard, hidden by the curve in the trench. They would be listening. Waiting. Pickles was useless, and Tobias was an impassive neutral. Either way it did not seem to matter to him.

Chesnaye felt let down and vaguely betrayed. He heard himself say sharply, 'Say "sir" when you address me, Wellard!'

The seaman plucked at his black beard and squinted at the midshipman. 'Aye, aye, *sir*!' He looked sideways at Tobias. 'Well, Hookey, don't you think it's bloody daft?'

Tobias picked up his rifle and stared at it as if for the first time. He glanced up quickly at Chesnaye's desperate face. 'Everythin' is daft 'ere, Wellard!' He gave a brief

94

grin. 'Now do as you're bloody well told and get ready for the off!'

Chesnaye opened his mouth to speak but was almost deafened by a shrill whistle blast at his side. The Australian officer seemed suddenly tall and remote, his features a mask of fierce determination. A bright whistle gleamed in one hand, while with the other the man groped at the flap of his holster. 'Come on, you Aussie bastards!' His voice cut across the encroaching rattle of small-arms like a saw. 'Stand to! Face your *front*!'

Obediently and dazedly, like animals, the soldiers came alive and began to scramble on to the crudely hewn firing step.

The lieutenant stood down in the trench for a while longer, his eyes darting along the bowed soldiers, the levelled rifles. 'Right, fix bayonets!' A hissing, metallic rattle rippled along the thin khaki barrier, and Chesnaye watched fascinated as the long blades were snapped into position and then vanished over the sandbagged barrier.

The lieutenant coughed in the smoke and then spun the chamber of his revolver. 'Best get going, sport. Up the hill like a Queensland rabbit, and the best of luck!'

A great sullen bellow of sound, like nothing Chesnaye had heard, echoed over the crouching heads on the firing step. He tried to place it. The baying of hounds, the thunder of surf. It was impossible to describe it.

The soldier said sharply: 'Here they come! Calling on their god to protect 'em!' He pushed his way up beside his men, the sailors already forgotten.

Chesnaye ran quickly to the rear of the trench and vaulted over the loose stones. It was now or never. A second longer and that dreadful, booming storm of voices would have held him powerless to move. As if from miles away he heard the lieutenant shout: 'One hundred yards, five rounds rapid . . . *Fire!*' The air jumped again to the savage bark of rifles, whilst from somewhere on each flank came the searching, vicious rattle of machine-guns.

Chesnaye found his feet and began to run. Behind him he sensed rather than heard the thudding footfalls of his small party. The summit of the hill seemed far away, and as he ducked behind a natural wall of boulders Chesnaye could see the advancing barrier of short angry flames where the gorse had been set alight.

The valley was hidden in smoke, yet Chesnaye could imagine the enemy already within a hundred yards of the defence line. They must be up to the wire, even across it! He heard himself cry, 'We must get there in time!'

A seaman started to overtake, his boots and gaiters scything through the sparse stubble with all the power he could muster. The machine-guns chattered louder, and with sudden panic Chesnaye realised that the new sounds were coming from the flank, from the other hill. Hoarsely he yelled: 'Down! Get *down*!'

The seaman who had passed him peered back, his teeth bared with the determination of his own efforts to reach shelter. 'Get down yerself!' He turned to run on, but was plucked from his feet as the machine-gun found him. The corpse rolled down the hillside, followed and flayed by the hidden gun. The running man changed to a corpse even as the others watched. From a man to a rolling thing. From a recognisable, breathing companion to a tattered, scarlet bundle.

Tobias wriggled to Chesnaye's side. 'They've got us pinned down, sir.'

Chesnaye shut his ears to the sounds behind him, the bark and rattle of guns, the harsh, desperate voices and the clatter of rifle bolts. He must think. He had to decide. Like a wind the machine-gun fanned the air above his head, and he heard his men cursing and praying as they dug their fingers into the hillside.

Chesnaye could feel the early sunlight already warm against his neck, and saw a small beetle scurrying across the ground near his cheek.

He looked at the dirt on his hands and the scratches on the skin where he had torn at the loose stones to get clear of the trench. Perhaps the others were right. It was a futile gesture which had already cost a seaman's life. But he remembered the soldiers who were fighting for their lives with the blind desperation of all front-line troops. Not knowing what was happening or even why they were there. For all they knew, the whole front might have collapsed, with the enemy already encircling them for final destruction. He shook his head as if to clear his tortured mind.

Eventually he said : 'We'll work our way round the side of that small rise in the ground, Tobias. Once there we'll be under cover for a bit. Then we'll take the last hundred yards in short stages.' He gripped the other man's sleeve. 'But we can't hang about !'

The journey to the top was a nightmare. By a twist of fate it was the smoke from the burning hillside which saved them. The enemy machine-gunners fired long bursts through the drifting black cloud, but it was difficult for them to range their sights on the long slope, and so, gasping and sweating, the two midshipmen and five seamen found themselves once again in the spotting post. The cleft in the rock was scarred and disfigured by shellfire, and the wall of boulders was scattered amidst the black score marks of the Turkish barrage.

There were three soldiers waiting by the sandbagged wireless position. One was dead, one was white-faced and wounded in both legs, whilst the third sat by the wireless smoking a cigarette. The latter nodded companionably. ' 'Mornin', gentlemen ! I suppose you're ready to start?'

It was nearly half an hour before Chesnaye could plot some idea of the change in the enemy positions and from which direction the main assault was being directed. The smoke eddied and swam across the valley, trapped and demented, its colours changing to the flicker of countless rifles, and later to the brightly flashing grenades. Once there was a brief gap in the smoke, and Chesnaye lost valuable seconds as he stared mesmerised at the battle which raged below.

For the first time he saw the enemy. Not as individuals, but as a vast surging throng, colourless and without apparent shape. It broke across the narrow strip of wire, while the chattering machine-guns mowed down rank after rank, and left the scattered remnants hanging on the gleaming barbs, twisting and kicking. Still they came on, until the soldiers below could no longer fire, but leapt from their trenches to meet them on the parapets face to face. Chesnaye saw the madly struggling throng sway back and forth, while the flash of bayonets brought colour to the shrill cries and desperate movements of the battle.

Chesnaye caught his breath as a body of Turkish infantry overflowed the trench and began to run madly up the side of the hill itself. Another machine-gun came into play, and with systematic care cut the small figures to shreds and left them scattered around the body of the dead seaman. Chesnaye also saw the Australian lieutenant, hatless and with his revolver held like a club, fighting astride a pile of corpses, while dark-faced Turks closed in from every side. Even as reinforcements surged along the shattered trench Chesnaye saw the flash of yet another bayonet and watched sickened as the lieutenant screamed and fell clutching his stomach.

Behind him he heard the army wireless operator say, 'Contact with the beach party, sir!'

He had already scribbled the signal and range orders on his pad, and blindly he passed it to the man's eager hand.

How could he be sure he had done the right thing? There was no way of knowing in this confusion. Lieutenant Thornton would have known, but he was dead. Where was Robert Driscoll? He would have known too. Chesnaye peered through the smoke as the morse key began to stammer. Driscoll was probably down there, dead with the others in that bloody carnage, where terror was making men fight like wild beasts. It had all seemed so easy. An order. An alteration perhaps, but then the big guns would do the work cleanly and impartially. That was not war at all. *This* was real. Where you could see your enemy first as a living mass which came on in spite of everything until it was broken into individuals and flesh and blood. Until it was too close even for bullets, and you could feel his desperate breath on your face even as you twisted and struggled to drive home your bayonet.

The Turkish assault faltered and swayed back from the trench. In an instant the Australian infantry were at them once more. Down the slope from the parapet the battle-crazed Australians surged in pursuit, only to be met by a savage cross-fire of well-sited machine-guns. As officers fell they were replaced by sergeants. Within an hour the

98

sergeants were dead and junior corporals found themselves in command.

At the head of the valley, where Turkish reinforcements waited for the order to advance, the sky was bright and clear of smoke. It looked at peace and beyond reach through Chesnaye's telescope. Then a wind seemed to ruffle the hillsides and the end of the valley appeared to fade within a shadow. Chesnaye watched the sudden change with cold satisfaction. The *Saracen*'s first salvo had landed.

Tobias rolled on to his side and looked at the sky as the big shells sighed overhead. 'Just in time,' he said at length. He glanced quickly at Chesnaye's drawn face. 'You've done a nice job, sir.'

Chesnaye did not speak. He looked down at the shell-battered defences, the scattered corpses where here and there a hand or a foot still moved as if its owner believed in the right to survive. A bugle blared, and the Australians fell back, some still shooting, others dragging wounded comrades behind them. He could see the white brassards and red crosses moving up the line, the limp stretchers with their telltale scarlet stains. He saw it all with the patient horror of a man looking at some terrible panorama of death. Men without arms or faces, men who ran in circles blinded and lost, and others who whimpered like idiots until led away. Even the dead were without dignity, he thought. Ripped and torn, grinning and grimacing, broken and forgotten, their blood mingled with that of the enemy.

Chesnaye retched and leaned his head against a sun-warmed boulder.

A runner panted up the hill, his jacket soaked in sweat. 'Cease fire, sir!' He handed Chesnaye a grimy signal. 'Message from Brigade.' He glanced at the dead soldier without curiosity. 'This section will re-group and reinforcements are already movin' up!' He removed the bayonet from his rifle and stooped to wipe it on the gorse at Chesnaye's feet.

Chesnaye noticed for the first time that the blade was patterned with bright red droplets. He stared, fascinated at the soldier's lined face. 'How was it?'

The man took a cigarette gratefully from Tobias and sucked in slowly. As he breathed out his limbs began to quiver, and Tobias turned away as if ashamed to watch.

The soldier wiped his eyes with his cuff. 'Christ, it was awful. Lost me two mates, y'see.' He stared blindly at the bayonet. 'It was just a bloody slaughter!' He swallowed hard and then said harshly, 'Thanks fer the fag.'

They watched him go, loping down the hillside. A small individual who for a brief instant had detached himself from the mass.

The Australians counter-attacked in the late afternoon. The *Saracen*, this time supported by a far-off battleship and two destroyers, laid down a barrage which held the Turks in hiding until it was too late to stem their advance. By nightfall the enemy had lost Hill Seventy-Five and a mile and a half of the valley. Between dawn and sunset three thousand dead and wounded marked the rate of advance, but when the stars showed themselves above the highest ridge the new line was established.

Chesnaye followed his men down the hillside, his jacket open to the waist, the night air cold across his damp skin. He did not turn his head as he passed the shadowy shapes which littered the ground and lay inside the broken trench itself.

He was ordered to return to the beach and find his way back to the monitor. He still found it hard to believe that there was to be a break in this new world of noise and suffering.

A figure loomed from the darkness and a groping hand found his. Chesnaye swayed and heard Driscoll's voice say : 'I'm glad you made it, Dick! You did damned well!'

Even on the beach amongst the groaning lines of wounded which seemed to stretch into the infinity of the night Chesnaye could still feel the warmth of that hand-shake, and understood how the soldier with the reddened bayonet must have felt when he had lost his friends. His thoughts were becoming jumbled and confused, and he felt Tobias's hard hand at his elbow.

'You all right, sir?' The man's face seemed to swim against the stars.

Tobias added: 'I can see a boat comin', sir. That'll be fer us!'

He spoke with the fervent hope of a man lost in an unfamiliar world, but as the cutter moved smartly inshore and the rowers tossed their oars, Chesnaye was suddenly reluctant to leave.

He fell into the boat, and the last thing he heard before exhaustion claimed him was the voice of one of his remaining seamen.

'Move over there, lads! Let 'im sleep!' Then in a voice tinged with awe: 'Proper little tiger is Mister Chesnaye! You should 'ave *seen* 'im!'

6

Driftwood

Richard Chesnaye shielded his eyes from the sun's glare and peered astern. Like the purple back of a basking whale the island of Mudros was already merging with the shimmering horizon, its shape distorted by the heat haze. The sun was high overhead, and on the monitor's upper deck there seemed to be no cover at all in spite of the narrow awnings, so that Chesnaye's small working party toiled halfheartedly, their paint-brushes hardly moving across the shield of one of the small quick-firing guns below the tall funnel. Soon they would be released from the pretence of working and go below to their stuffy messdeck and the tempting tot of watered rum. Then, lunch over, they would once more be kept active for a few hours while the ship moved slowly and ponderously along her set course. Back to the Peninsula. Back to the bombardment and the mounting frustrations.

Chesnaye winced as a shaft of sunlight seared his neck like a flame. The ship was so slow, so completely airless that every movement was an effort. It seemed incredible to believe that it was less than three weeks since he had left the darkened beach and found his way back to the *Saracen*. They had weighed anchor almost at once and returned to Mudros, and there unloaded the wretched cargo of wounded soldiers. Some had died on the way, and the Captain had buried them at sea. April had given way to May, and the probing sun left no room for corpses in an overcrowded ship of war.

Chesnaye could not remember when he had enjoyed a full night's rest. There always seemed to be some crisis or other. Loading stores and ammunition from the ubiquitous lighters, the decks of which still bore the dark stains of wounded men, and then out again at dawn to take the monitor alongside the deep-bellied oiler to replenish the half-empty tanks.

Tempers became frayed, seamen overstayed their miserable shore-leaves, and were punished with the same weary resignation which had made them rebel in the first place.

The monitor had returned briefly to the Peninsula and had carried out two minor bombardments in conjunction with a battleship and some destroyers. No spotting party had been landed, but Chesnaye had stood on the upper bridge, his plugged ears conscious of the angry barrage, yet his mind constantly with the other world beyond the glittering shoreline and craggy hills. He imagined the tiny, antlike soldiers and the persistent probing and attacking which was going on beyond the range of his telescope. He remembered that last run up the hillside when the seaman had been cut down by the machine-gun. When he had pressed his face into the ground and seen the small beetle scurrying through the sand. Now distance had made the armies into insects, but this time he could understand their suffering.

The *Saracen* had waddled back to Mudros and disgorged another three hundred broken bodies, taken on more stores and was returning once more.

It seemed incredible to understand that the daring and desperate attack on the Dardanelles had been forced to a bloody stalemate. Day after day ships of the Fleet patrolled the slender Peninsula, like dogs worrying an aged deer, yet nothing happened to break the deadlock. Eighteen battleships, twelve cruisers, twenty destroyers and eight submarines, plus an armada of auxiliaries had pressed home attacks, blockaded, and covered innumerable landings, yet still the well-defended Turks held their own, and hit back again and again.

In the midst of it all the *Saracen*, unlovely and unloved, moved alone. Too slow to work with the destroyers, and too ungainly to keep with the battleships, she wandered from one allotted task to the next. Even the ship's company sensed their situation, and the Captain had ordered that no matter what else happened they were to be kept busy at all times and the ship maintained at a level of peacetime discipline.

There had been one break in the ship's misfortune, however. Mail had awaited the *Saracen* in Mudros, and Chesnaye had received two letters from his mother. His father was apparently ill, brought on by his mounting depression and his inability to return to active duty. Between the lighter comments his mother made about the weather and the state of the garden Chesnaye could sense her despair, and he was reminded of the great distance which separated him from his home. He had written a carefully worded reply, and even more thoughtfully had sent a letter to Helen. He had used the Gibraltar address, and wondered if it would ever reach her. Already he was regretting the impulse. Afraid she would not answer. More afraid of what her reply might be.

A bugle blared 'Up Spirits!' In a moment the sickly smell of rum would float along the spotless decks and the seamen would stir themselves like old cavalry horses at the sound of a trumpet.

Chesnaye yawned. 'Right, start securing that paint.'

The seamen did not even glance at him. They were lost in their own thoughts.

Soon it would be time, too, to return to the gunroom, to Lukey's rasping patter as he served another unsuitable meal of hot stew or leathery beef. Pringle would be sitting, glowing with health and vigour, at the head of the table, eating with obvious relish, while the midshipmen sat immersed in thought or hoping that their overlord would fall down dead. There was more room in the small mess now. With Maintland killed, and the overhanging threat of more action, the midshipmen seemed to draw further apart, a situation encouraged by Pringle, who took every opportunity to remark on Maintland's absence, as if to watch their reactions, or perhaps, as Chesnaye suspected, to show them how hardened and unmoved he was himself.

But the most changed member of the mess was Pickles. Morose and stiff-faced, he had borne Pringle's taunts without flinching, as if he had completely withdrawn into himself. Once Pringle had remarked loudly that he had heard some story that a certain snotty had lost his nerve ashore on the Peninsula and had broken down in front of the men. Pringle had yawned elaborately and added, 'Just the thing one might expect from a poor type with no breeding!'

Chesnaye had tried to ignore the constant friction in the gunroom, but it was beginning to wear him down. He noticed that Pringle was careful to be polite to him in front of the others, and had once seen the flash of anger in Pickles' eyes.

To Pringle it was just a game. But it could not last under these conditions.

Almost guiltily he heard Pringle's voice at his side. 'What the hell are these loafers doing? Who gave you permission to pack up your gear?' Pringle's question was directed at the bearded A.B. Wellard.

The seaman stiffened. 'Mister Chesnaye, sir.'

Pringle showed his teeth. 'Well?' He looked at Chesnaye without expression.

Chesnaye shrugged wearily. 'They were finished. There's only a minute or so to go.'

Pringle turned back to the watching men. 'Never take advantage of an inexperienced officer! Now take the lids off those paint tins and get back to work!'

'We've finished!' Wellard glared from beneath his shaggy brows.

A bugle blared sharply, but Pringle tapped the side of his nose with his finger and said pleasantly: 'Well you can do fifteen minutes' extra work to make up for your laziness. *Now get to it!*'

He stood aside and said quietly to Chesnaye: 'They're an idle lot of swine. You've got to keep them at it *all* the time.'

'I don't agree.' Chesnaye's cheeks were still smarting from Pringle's behaviour in front of his own men.

'Well, of course *you* wouldn't!' Pringle rocked back on his heels. 'You think that by being slack with 'em you'll win their hearts. Imagine you'll be their little idol, eh?' His face darkened. 'Remember what I said. They're the scum of the earth, and only understand firmness and discipline!'

Chesnaye felt the heat beating across his neck. 'I think I'll make up my own mind about that, if you don't object?'

Pringle paused as he turned to leave, his eyes red and angry. 'I *thought* so! Like father like son, eh? No wonder your old man got the bloody sack!'

The world seemed to explode around Chesnaye, and he was only half aware of the suddenly watchful seamen, the sun on his neck and the rasp of Pringle's words. He was conscious too of the pain in his knuckles and the jarring shock which travelled up his right arm.

His vision cleared just as quickly, and he found himself staring down at Pringle's upturned face. Pringle was holding his mouth, and his fingers were bright red with blood.

The seaman Wellard put down his brush and said flatly: 'Christ! 'E's 'it the sod!'

* ⸱ * ▪ ▪

Captain Lionel Royston-Jones bit his lower lip to control the rising irritation he always felt when watching Holroyd, the Paymaster, at work. The latter was perched on the edge of one of the Captain's pale green chairs in the spacious day-cabin below the monitor's quarterdeck, and as usual was nervously absorbed in the endless matter of ship's business. Royston-Jones stared slowly round his wide cabin, crossing his legs as he did so to force himself to relax. All forenoon he had made himself listen to Holroyd, the session interrupted at irregular intervals by the various heads of departments as the *Saracen* moved slowly towards the enemy coast. Soon it would be time to leave these comfortable quarters once more and return to the spartan restrictions of bridge and sea-cabin, but for the moment it was good to get away from the others and the pressing problems of command.

Here at least he felt almost remote from the rest of the ship, his comfortable chair placed barely feet from the ship's stern. The sea noises were indistinct and muffled, and even the regular bugle-calls were far off and impersonal. Royston-Jones scowled as if to dismiss the hint of sentiment, and Holroyd, a bald, worried little man, happening to glance at his captain at that particular moment, wilted accordingly.

Royston-Jones let his pale eyes drift towards one of the cabin's gleaming brass scuttles. The deep blue of the horizon line mounted the circular scuttle, paused, and then receded with the same patient slowness, while the hidden sun played across the sea's numberless mirrors and threw a dancing pattern across the cabin's low deckhead, where a wide-bladed fan revolved to give an impression of coolness.

An original oil-painting of King George made a tasteful patch of colour against the white bulkhead, and beyond a nearby door the Captain knew that MacKay, his personal steward, would be hovering and waiting for the bell. It was getting near time for a sherry. A quiet lunch, and then—Royston-Jones looked up irritated again as Holroyd gave his nervous cough and handed some papers across for signature.

'All complete, sir.' The little man blinked and watched anxiously as the Captain began to read. He never signed anything without reading it at least twice, and this fact did little to help the Paymaster's fading confidence.

'This war will be bogged down with paper before long!' Royston-Jones reached for his pen which stood exactly upright in a silver inkstand fashioned in the shape of a dolphin. On the stand's base a well-polished inscription stated: 'Presented to Sub-Lieutenant Lionel Royston-Jones, H.M.S. *Jury* 1893, Singapore Fleet Regatta.'

The private thoughts of sherry and seclusion vanished as Royston-Jones suddenly remembered that Commander Godden was waiting to see him. He toyed with the idea of keeping him waiting a little longer, but then decided against it. Almost savagely he wrote his signature on six documents and replaced the pen. Holroyd scrambled to his feet, his face filled with obvious relief. Royston-Jones almost smiled when he imagined what the Paymaster would think or say if he knew that his captain was so short-sighted that most of the documents were a meaningless blur. For reading Royston-Jones wore a pair of narrow, steel-rimmed glasses, but few had seen them. Mac-

Kay, his steward, was used to finding his master in the privacy of the day-cabin, glasses perched on nose, a favourite book of Shakespeare plays on his crossed legs. MacKay kept the secret well. For that reason he had been with the Captain for many years.

Royston-Jones jabbed the pantry bell, and added as an afterthought, 'Some of those victualling returns look a bit casual, Holroyd.' He watched the panic mounting with cold satisfaction. 'Check them again yourself.'

'Aye, aye, sir.' The wretched man almost bowed himself out of the cabin.

MacKay appeared with a tiny silver tray. On it was a decanter, one glass and a dog-like arrowroot biscuit.

Royston-Jones sighed. 'Get another glass, and ask the Commander to step in.'

What was wrong this time? he wondered. Some wretched nonsense about a split awning, or a petty officer sick with piles. What a small man Godden seemed to carry about inside that great body. Royston-Jones detested unnecessary size, and overweight officers were a particular hate of his. Perhaps that was why he never had got off to a good start with Godden. He knew it was more than that but even so . . .

Godden entered the cabin and waited in silence until MacKay had glided back to his pantry.

Royston-Jones felt his foot beginning to tap. Sharply he said, 'Put your cap down and have a sherry.'

'If you don't mind, sir,' Godden looked grim, 'this is rather serious.'

'Yes, I *do* mind.' Royston-Jones sipped at his sherry and then banged the glass down. It was all spoilt. 'Well, spit it out, man!'

'I think we have a court martial on our hands, sir.' He swallowed. 'Sub-Lieutenant Pringle has been assaulted!'

The Captain said slowly, 'And the rating responsible?'

'It was an officer, sir. Midshipman Chesnaye!'

Royston-Jones stood up and walked to the nearest scuttle. For a moment longer he watched the handful of white gulls which still followed the ship's slow course.

Wheeling and dipping they added to the impression that the *Saracen* was unmoving.

'I see.' Over his shoulder he asked, 'And what have you done about it, may I ask?'

'I have sent Chesnaye to his quarters. Pringle is outside. I would have brought him earlier, sir, but his lip was still bleeding.'

Half to himself Royston-Jones said coldly, 'I would have guessed that Pringle's mouth would be implicated!' He swung round. 'This is very serious, you realise that, don't you?' He waited, the absurdity and at the same time the danger of the situation making his cheeks burn with two small spots of colour. '*Well?*' He saw Godden jump as his voice echoed round the cabin. 'Is that all?'

'I thought you should know, sir——' Godden's face looked shiny with sweat.

'You did, did you?' The long-pent-up anger was coursing through Royston-Jones like fire. For a little while longer he would give way to it. 'If there had been no war, Commander, you would have been happier, I expect? The usual sickening round of events, regattas, fleet balls, admiral's inspections which end in a sea of gin and broken reputations. I can just imagine it!'

'That's not fair, sir!' Godden was quivering with sudden rage.

'Don't you dare to interrupt! It's a pity you can't show the same energy for your duty as you display in righteous indignation!' He took a few quick paces. 'The Commander's work in a ship is to present that ship as a working concern to his captain. You are not even near that standard. You are a passenger and almost a liability!'

Godden's face was white. 'Now look here, sir! How could I have prevented this trouble?'

The Captain's eyes glittered in a shaft of yellow sunlight. '*This* trouble! I have carried you through trouble of one sort or another since you came aboard! I have your measure now! You want *me* to act over this so-called assault so that you can sink back into your old role of jovial dependability, the friendly buffer between the downtrodden wardroom and the tyrannical captain, right?' He screwed up his face to watch Godden's reactions. 'I am telling you now, I am sick of your side-stepping! And I will not tolerate it!'

Godden did not speak, but looked as if he was going to be sick.

Almost as calmly Royston-Jones said: 'This is war. Nothing like it has ever struck the Royal Navy before. We have been unchallenged, untouched, for over a hundred years, and now the battle is joined. All of us have been trained for war by men who have known only peace and frivolous security.' He waved his hand with sudden bitterness. 'Take this ship, *my* ship. She is entirely new, a fresh weapon in a strange war. And why do you suppose I got command, eh? I will tell you. Because some pompous popinjays at the Admiralty are afraid that the *Saracen* will be a white elephant, a failure. So they must have a scapegoat, just in case!' He tapped his breast. 'Me! A good captain with a blameless record, so that the ship can be given every chance of success. But also a man without connections or influence, one who is expendable.' He gave a small smile. 'Your expression has changed, Commander! From guilt to anger, and from anger to shocked disbelief. Well, I'll not continue along these lines. There is work to be done.' He fixed Godden with a cold stare, unwinking and devoid of pity. 'But I can assure you that I intend this ship to succeed if I have to run her ashore to prove her worth!'

Weakly Godden said, 'And Chesnaye, sir?'

Completely controlled and calm, Royston-Jones turned the arrowroot biscuit between his neat fingers. 'Ah yes, Chesnaye.' Very quietly, 'What do you suggest?'

Shocked and miserable at the assault, Godden's words tumbled out in a confused heap. 'Well, sir, Pringle's a bit of a bully, I know that. But Chesnaye struck him, and there was one seaman at least who witnessed it!'

One word. 'Who?'

'Able Seaman Wellard.'

'Ah, that bearded oaf.' He nodded, the man's face registering like a faded photograph. 'Good boxer. Won a cup for the ship, I believe?'

'Yes, sir.'

'And you think that Pringle's majesty should be upheld?'

'Well, I'm sorry for the midshipman, sir, but we all had to go through it in our time.'

'That doesn't make it right, Commander. However, it must be stopped, you are correct there at least. Find out the reason for the assault——'

Godden interrupted quickly, 'Pringle made some remark about Chesnaye's father——'

'*What?*' Royston-Jones stared at Godden with amazement. 'Why didn't you say so?'

'Well, sir, I mean—it was true what he said——'

'I can imagine.' The Captain turned back to the quiet sea beyond the scuttle. 'I knew Chesnaye's father. He was a good officer. Perhaps *he* was a scapegoat too. But that does not alter the fact that young Chesnaye is now the only officer with battle experience of spotting ashore.' He laughed sharply and without humour. 'Laughable, isn't it? A young midshipman, a mere boy, and a valuable asset already!' He rubbed his palms together. 'And as for Wellard seeing the incident, I will leave him to you. But this war is getting to be a complex and serious affair. I will not jeopardise the use and safety of my ship because Able Seaman Wellard has had his illusions shattered. I doubt very much if he has *ever* respected a piece of gold lace!'

'I see, sir.' Godden's voice sounded strangled. 'And Chesnaye?'

'I will see both officers separately. In the Dog Watches sometime today. You arrange it. It will give them time to fret a little!'

'Anything more, sir?'

Royston-Jones picked up the glass and rolled its slender stem between his fingers. 'Oh, one thing, yes. We have been ordered to carry out a landing and a bombardment, south of the Anzac beaches.'

'Who are we supporting, sir?'

Royston-Jones waited a little longer. 'We will be alone, Commander!' He turned to watch the effect of his words. 'Quite alone. It seems that one or more U-boats have been making their way through the Mediterranean in this direction for some time. Their Lordships in all their wisdom have decided to withdraw the battleship *Queen*

Elizabeth and certain other units as soon as the Germans get too near.' He allowed the sherry to moisten his lower lip. 'So everybody else can apparently go hang!'

. . . . .

Lieutenant Hogarth, the Gunnery Officer, lifted his powerful night glasses and took a long look across the *Saracen*'s blunt bows. From the upper bridge he had an uninterrupted view of the whole ship, and although it was well past midnight, with the Middle Watch settled and composed at their stations, the sky seemed to lack depth, so that it merged with the sea in a transparent, vaporous obscurity. Untroubled by wind, the sea's surface around the labouring ship was flat and glittering in long oily swells, whilst around the monitor's rounded stern only a hint of froth broke the pattern and betrayed the power of the thrashing screws below.

Hogarth ran his eye quickly around the bridge to ensure that the lookouts were indeed doing their job. Somewhere on the maindeck Sub-Lieutenant Pringle, his assistant, was doing his rounds and would soon join him, his restlessness breaking the quiet of the watch.

He stiffened as a figure detached itself from the chartroom and glided to the front of the bridge. It was not the Captain, but Travis, the Navigator. Hogarth relaxed.

'Can't you sleep, Pilot?'

'Just checking my charts.'

They both spoke in a semi-whisper, their voices merging with the creaking of steel and spars. At night the ship always seemed to be more powerful, more overbearing.

Hogarth yawned elaborately. 'Ship's company all tucked up for the night. Just the poor bloody watchkeepers alive!' He peered at his companion. 'We'll be up to the coast before dawn then?'

'Running, or rather *crawling* to schedule!' Travis sounded bitter. 'I'll be glad when we get started.'

Hogarth nodded, and adjusted his meticulous mind to the problems the next day would offer him. 'A quick bombardment, rush in the landing parties, and then rapid fire on the enemy's flank. Sounds easy, eh?'

'I'm sick of it all!' Travis gripped the screen with frustration. 'The whole operation is going rotten on us!'

'Well, I would rather be in the old Keppel's Head in Pompey *naturally*, but as we are involved I don't see what we can do about it!' Hogarth shifted uneasily. Travis was too much of a thinker. That was bad.

Travis shrugged. 'It's better for you. You are so wrapped up with your damned gunnery you don't have time to contemplate the rest of the business. *I* on the other hand have had to sit and listen at every conference the Old Man has attended. God! The people at Whitehall must be raving mad!'

'How d'you mean?' Hogarth did not really care, but he was interested in Travis's sudden display of emotion.

'Well, you know that Fisher has resigned from First Sea Lord?' He did not wait for a reply. 'And Churchill is being hauled over the coals about the hold-ups and disasters out here?'

'What of it?'

'It means in simple language that the powers-that-be have lost interest in a quick victory. For all we know they may have written off the whole operation already!'

'Oh for God's sake!' Hogarth broke off as a telephone buzzed in the darkness by his elbow. In a strained voice he said into the mouthpiece, 'Upper bridge, Officer of the Watch speaking.'

Far below Pringle's voice replied : 'Rounds completed. All correct, sir.'

'Very well.' He dropped the handset and said absently, 'I think this assault business is much more serious.'

Travis turned away. 'You would!'

'There's no need to be like that, old man.'

Travis moved closer and tried again. 'Look, just think about what I've been saying. If the Gallipoli landings have been a waste of time, we should know about it. You can't just leave a whole army to rot away and do nothing!'

'I have always done my duty and nothing more,' Hogarth answered stiffly.

He sounded so hurt and pompous that Travis laughed, his teeth white against his beard. 'Well done, Guns! Spoken like a true gentleman!'

Hogarth did not smile. 'No, seriously, I feel very strongly about that. We must maintain our standards even in war. I think the Captain was wrong to ignore Chesnaye's behaviour, even if Pringle *is* a fool.'

'He's that, all right!'

'But he must be upheld. The Commander is quite right in his resentment.'

'Oh, has he spoken to you about it, then?' Travis sounded interested.

'A little He's pretty fed-up, actually.'

'Too bad. But in the meantime we've got a very nasty job on our hands at daybreak.'

'Oh *that*!' Hogarth sounded scornful. 'We'll manage the bloody Turks well enough, you see!'

Pringle appeared in the gloom and moved to one side of the bridge.

Travis said quietly but unfeelingly, 'How's your jaw, Sub?'

'I'd rather not talk about it.' Pringle sounded furious.

'Well, I think you asked for it!' Travis turned his back. 'I'm going to snatch an hour's sleep, Guns. Call me if the ship capsizes!'

He disappeared from the bridge and Hogarth was left with his thoughts. Travis was probably right, he thought. Few campaigns ever succeeded unless they got off to a good start. It was true that the more modern and useful ships were being withdrawn with unseemly haste, and even the *Saracen*'s future role was uncertain. Still, very soon they would be too occupied for conjecture. At first light his big guns would be needed again, and Major De L'Isle's mad marines would be hitting the shore for the first time. It would be quite a party. But suppose Travis was right too about Whitehall? To be killed in battle was one thing. To die for no purpose was another entirely.

Sub-Lieutenant Pringle, on the other hand, was not thinking of battle or the shortcomings of this campaign. He could still hardly believe the deliberate cruelty of the Captain's words when he had seen him in his cabin. Pringle had been so sure of his ground, so outraged at the deliberate affront to his position, that he had almost expected Royston-Jones to compliment him on his self-control. Instead, the Captain had gathered force and momentum like a small hurricane, his words stripping away Pringle's composure like the skin from his bones. He still felt the echoes of the little man's last words ringing in his ears.

'Remember this, Pringle! In war the demands will soon outgrow the supplies. Young and junior regular officers will be worth their weight in gold. Even this ship will have to take on Reserve officers and untrained ratings as soon as we return to Base, and every professional, no matter how inferior in rank and ability, will have his work cut out to make the simplest routine run smoothly!' The Captain had paused to run his cold eyes over the sweating officer. 'Even you will probably have a command of some sort within a couple of years, *if* you are careful! But I *will* not have you behaving is this irresponsible manner, do you hear? You insulted this midshipman and he reacted in the only way he knew at that time. He has lived under strain and in no little danger for some weeks, doing a job for which a much more responsible officer had been selected. I will not tolerate any such behaviour in future!'

Pringle still cursed himself for his own inability to justify himself. He had only managed a throaty and servile, 'I'm sorry, sir.'

The Captain had dismissed him with a few more terse sentences, ending with : 'I think you might have promise if only you can think a little less about yourself and a lot more of your duty. You will have that chance tomorrow when we reach the enemy coast. When the main landing is carried out you will take charge of the seamen employed ashore, is that understood?' The cold eyes flickered with something like menace. 'Be warned, Pringle. The light of forgiveness is short in its duration!'

He had not seen Chesnaye since his interview with Royston-Jones and he wondered how he had fared. The Captain had probably buttered him up instead of putting him under arrest, he thought savagely. They were all the same. All trying to get at him, just because he was better than they!

A voice shattered the silence. 'Driftwood on the starboard beam, sir!'

Hogarth strode to the screen and peered into the darkness. A few pieces of waterlogged timber bobbed down the monitor's bulging flank and vanished astern. It was odd how all sorts of driftwood and wreckage meandered around the coast, he thought. An endless journey in tideless waters.

He watched a faint red glow far on the monitor's beam where a momentary flash of sparks betrayed their escorting destroyer. No doubt her stokers were busy with the never-ending misery of fire-trimming. Thank God the *Saracen* was oil-burning. That at least was some comfort.

He said wearily : 'I'm just going to check our position, Sub. Take over.'

Pringle moved to the front of the bridge, his blood running hot as he relived each separate humiliation.

Almost bored, the port lookout's voice interrupted, 'Object fine on the port bow, sir !'

Pringle, caught off guard, snapped, 'Well, what is it, man ?'

A pause. 'A piece o' driftwood, I think, sir.' The lookout sounded aggrieved at being asked an unfair question.

'Well, keep your eyes open for important things, damn you ! *Not* this everlasting bloody driftwood !'

The man answered sulkily, 'Aye, aye, sir.'

Pringle breathed out hard and groped for his glasses. Damned useless fools, the lot of them. He trained his glasses across the port side of the gently corkscrewing bows. The white arrowhead of the bow wave, the undulating water, and then . . . he stared aghast at the shining black shape with its vicious horns which moved so calmly and deliberately towards the monitor's hull.

The frantic orders were torn from his throat. 'Hard a-starboard ! Mine dead on the port bow !'

He was almost knocked from his feet as Hogarth flung himself at the voice-pipe.

'Belay that order ! Port fifteen !' Viciously over his shoulder he added to Pringle : 'You'd swing the stern right across it, you idiot !' Then he ran to the screen, his lanky frame bowed to watch for the small deadly object. He punched at a gaping petty officer. 'Clear lower decks ! Jump to it !'

The mine curtsied past the bridge even as the monitor swung ponderously in response to the rudder. Once it seemed to brush against the massive anti-torpedo bulge, but a freak of current thrust it away, so that a watching seaman sobbed with relief.

A marine bugler sent the alarm call frantically across the sleeping ship, whilst messengers and bosun's mates scampered down ladders and hatches, pipes, shrilling, voices raised in hoarse urgency. 'Clear lower deck! Close all watertight doors and scuttles!'

Captain Royston-Jones was on the bridge even before the bugler had drawn breath, but as he crossed to Hogarth's side another freak current encircled the drifting mine and cradled it inwards towards the *Saracen's* stern. Another few feet and it would have vanished in the ship's white wake. Gently it bumped against the rough plating, the motion making the horns gyrate gaily . . . until one of them made contact and broke.

. . . . .

Richard Chesnaye could hardly remember how he came to be on the upper bridge. The previous minutes had been merged into a desperate scramble made worse by the blare of a bugle and the insane twittering of pipes. One second he had been lying in his hammock, the next he had been running barefoot for the nearest ladder, clad only in drill trousers with his jacket somehow wedged beneath his arm.

Then there had been the explosion. For one long moment the whole hull had quivered like an oil-drum struck with a massive hammer. Running men had faltered or fallen with the shock, that had been followed at once by a long-drawn-out shuddering which had seemingly gripped the ship from stem to stern. Every piece of loose gear had cascaded on to the dazed men, and as they had started running once more the hull had been plunged into darkness, so that Chesnaye was suddenly reminded of the two decks he must scale before he reached the open air.

On deck the packed ranks of stumbling figures had fanned out in every direction, while harsh voices called names and repeated orders, goading them on, stopping them from thinking. Chesnaye had been conscious of the smell of seared paintwork and the fact that the engines were stopped.

He reached the bridge, breathless, and suddenly cold. As he fumbled with his jacket he heard Royston-Jones say sharply, 'A complete muster of all hands, and then tell the Bosun to have the boats swung out and to check all rafts.'

A voice said, 'Port whaler destroyed, sir.'

'Very well.' The Captain added, 'Tell me the moment a report comes in from either the damage-control party or the engine room.'

Chesnaye was aware of the great pall of smoke which hovered over the after part of the ship and the sluggish movement of the hull itself.

Lieutenant Travis, who was by the wheelhouse voice-pipe, reported : 'Wheel not answering, sir. Way off ship.'

The Captain nodded. 'Hmm. Stopped engines in time, I think. You acted promptly, Guns.'

Another voice. 'Damage Control reporting from aft, sir !'

Royston-Jones walked quickly to the proffered hand-set. 'Well?'

Muffled by depth and distance, a voice he recognised as the Commander's reached his ear. 'After steering compartment and lower storeroom flooded, sir. Fire party dealing with outbreak in secondary paint store. All water-tight doors holding and secure.'

'Very good.'

Chesnaye strained his ear for some expression or hint in the Captain's tone, but there was nothing to show his inner thoughts.

There were said to be many hundreds of drifting mines in the area, but it seemed incredible, even impossible, that one had reached the *Saracen*.

A voice-pipe squeaked, and Royston-Jones bent his head to listen. 'Captain here !'

Far below, in the gleaming jungle of brass and powered steel, Innes, the Chief Engineer, adjusted his words for that other world of open sea and fresh air. 'The pumps are all working well, sir, but I'm afraid I can't let you use the port engine.'

Royston-Jones remained crouched by the speaking-tube, his eyes half closed as he translated Innes's brief words into their full meaning. 'The shaft tube is badly damaged, then?' He waited, forcing himself to keep his voice level.

'Can't tell for sure, sir. My lads are clearing away the mess, then they'll be able to get a better picture. My immediate guess is that the port screw is badly damaged too, might even have lost a blade.' Then, more firmly: 'Either way, it's a dockyard job, sir. We're lucky the mine didn't blow the guts out of the stern!'

'Lucky, Chief? It depends which way you look at it!' He snapped down the tube and stood up.

Travis, who had been waiting nearby, reported quietly: 'Damage Control have extinguished the fire, sir. And the intake of water has been contained.'

Chesnaye listened intently and tried to fit the terse pieces of information into the pattern of the ship. The monitor seemed too large, too vital, to be affected, yet she was noticeably heavier aft, and without power was yawing heavily in the small cross-swell.

When he had climbed wearily into his hammock Chesnaye had been unable to think of anything but his short interview with the Captain. His words had been harsh, cutting, but, Chesnaye knew, well chosen. Now all that was momentarily forgotten and the events which led to that interview made small and petty by comparison with this new disaster. He was more conscious of the weight of the Captain's immediate problems than he was of any sense of danger. The little man who now stood amidst chaos and disorder, whose mind was their only weapon, whose wrong word could only add to the ship's misfortune.

'Signal from escort, sir!'

'Well?' The Captain did not look up.

'Request instructions, sir. Will prepare to take you in tow at daybreak. Request permission to signal for further assistance. Signal ends, sir.'

Beaushears, who had appeared unseen at Chesnaye's elbow, whispered, 'That's the end of the landing, then!'

Chesnaye did not hear him, but watched fascinated as

the Captain turned yet again to speak to Mildmay, the Surgeon.

'Ten casualties, sir.' The Surgeon sounded brisk and fully awake. 'Also one man missing. Probably lost overboard.'

'Who was that?' Royston-Jones sounded distant.

'An Ordinary Seaman named Colt.'

'Hmm, yes. Fo'c'sleman. Bad luck.'

Chesnaye breathed out slowly. How in heaven's name did the Captain find time to remember a mere face at such a moment?

The Captain said sharply: 'Signal to escort to resume station. Negative her requests. I intend to continue at reduced speed on remaining screw.'

'But, sir——' Travis interrupted and then faltered.

The white figure moved slightly. 'Yes, Pilot?'

'Well, sir, I don't mean to question your judgment, but our orders are exact. We have to be in position before daylight, otherwise the enemy shore batteries will have our measure before we can cope with them! On one screw we can make a bare three knots!' His voice gained strength. 'We shall be a sitting target!'

'Quite so. Unfortunately we have no choice. Without us there is no support for the troops in that sector. They are relying on our attack on the enemy flank.'

Travis said tightly, 'We may not be in much shape to help anyone, sir!'

Royston-Jones seemed to have forgotten him. 'Pipe all hands to prepare ship for action. Then see that they have a good breakfast before dawn. I want the ship smart and efficient before that time!'

Commander Godden climbed into the bridge, his face streaked with smoke stains. 'She's two feet down by the stern, sir. It's not possible to rig collision mats, and in any case the frames are well buckled as far as I can make out in this light. When we get to the nearest dockyard we can assess the damage better.'

'I quite agree.' Royston-Jones sounded quite calm. 'However, we have this small operation to complete first. I shall want to speak to all heads of departments in one hour, particularly to the Major of Marines. We are one whaler short, I understand, so the boats will be hard-worked when the time comes. Perhaps you will arrange to have the larger rafts ready for lowering. I think they could be safely towed ashore under present conditions with some of the marines aboard?'

Godden sounded as if he had misunderstood. 'You are surely not suggesting that we go through with it, sir?'

'I will put your lack of respect down to strain, Commander. However, I should add that we are now committed. I have no intention of letting the disbelievers cast their scorn at this ship or her company. I thought I had already made that quite clear? If not, then let me only add that I expect every man aboard to, er . . .' He faltered, so that Chesnaye was conscious of the tension amongst the small group of officers. But the Captain smiled and continued, 'I *was* going to say "do his duty", but I realise that another distinguished officer has already said it rather better, and under more inspiring circumstances!'

Below in the shuttered wheelhouse Chief Petty Officer Ashburton, the Coxswain, leaned on the polished wheel and cocked his head as a gust of uncontrolled laughter swept down the bell-mouthed voice-pipe. The starboard telegraph swung to 'Slow-Ahead', but still the laughter persisted. The Coxswain turned his eyes to the binnacle and said just loud enough for the mystified telegraphs-men to hear: 'Listen to 'em! Bloody officers! All bloody mad!'

7

Pickles

Richard Chesnaye walked slowly forward along the monitor's broad fo'c'sle deck between the massive anchor cables and halted only when he stood hard against the jackstaff in the very bows of the ship. It was quiet, the sluggish bow wave hardly gurgling as the slow-moving hull thrust itself towards the long purple strip of land which lined the horizon. There was no warmth in the low sun, and although the clear bright sky hinted of the heat to come, Chesnaye's limbs felt stiff and weary from the night's exertions and his face a mask of tiredness. He looked back at the *Saracen's* bridge which seemed to hang between the two long guns, and up at the topmast which shimmered like burnished gold in the growing power of the sunlight. The bridge was faceless, yet he knew that many eyes were watching the gentle shore as it grew from the blue and silver sea and basked beneath the empty sky. From his lonely position Chesnaye could see that the ship leaned heavily to port, just as he could see the black smoke stains on her upperworks and bridge and the splintered deck planking which had been sandwiched by the mine's blast. The *Saracen* moved like an injured beast, almost crabwise, as her ungainly bulk fought against the thrust of one screw and the sweating exertions of the helmsman. He turned his back on the ship and leaned forward against the jackstaff. By so doing he could exclude the ship's indignity and pain, and as he watched the low-lying shapes of the two destroyer escorts which were already racing ahead of their charge he felt as if he alone was drifting towards that hateful strip of prized land.

He had been ordered to make a last check of the fo'c'sle, but a flint-eyed petty officer had made sure that there was nothing left for him to do. The ship was ready and waiting. It had received its first wound, but was already sniffing out the enemy in the manner of any injured beast.

Boats were slung out or ready and waiting beneath the big power derrick. Major De L'Isle's marines were, he knew, mustered in sections athwart the quarterdeck, their bodies, deformed by packs and rifles, entrenching tools and water-bottles. He peered at his watch. It was time to return to the others. To put on his mask and hide his apprehension.

Leading Seaman Tobias, hung about with webbing and bayonet, saluted him as he strode beneath the shadow of the bridge. 'Our party mustered, sir.'

'Good. See that they stay under cover until we leave the ship.'

Tobias squinted towards the bows. 'It's very quiet, sir.'

Chesnaye knew that he meant the shore, but his own thoughts returned to the feeling of loneliness and loss he had felt when the dawn had laid the sea bare.

Wiped away as if they had never been. The battleships and cruisers, the darting shapes of a hundred smaller craft. The majesty of the world's mightiest fleet gone in the twinkling of an eye.

What must the stranded troops be thinking? he wondered. Their ever-sure armada, the grey shield which every Briton had grown up to expect as a right had slunk away, vanished. Chesnaye tried to accept the reasons, but he could not swallow the feeling of hurt and loss. Of course, there were U-boats in the vicinity, but surely they must have been foreseen? Apparently not.

It was said that a battleship had already fallen to a U-boat's torpedoes off the very beaches which he had seen the Australians and New Zealanders take with his own eyes. Perhaps the Turks were unaware of the monitor's approach, or even indifferent. This part of the coast was separated from those other landings by that same jutting headland some miles to the north-east. The Allied forces in the south were even further away. A lonely, slab-sided coastline with a jumbled mass of hills and gullies beyond. No wonder the Turks were confident.

He imagined the thousands of soldiers to the north waiting for the *Saracen*'s bombardment of the enemy's flank. The relieving of the pressure just long enough for another small advance. He shut his eyes and saw again the wire and the minute running figures. Even in his nostrils he imagined he could scent the sickening smell of burned flesh and offal. The refuse of a battlefield.

Able Seaman Wellard slouched towards them and clumsily banged his rifle on the deck. He glanced at Chesnaye and then pursed his lips in a silent whistle.

Tobias tucked his thumbs in his belt and nodded towards the distant destroyers. 'They're getting pretty near, sir.'

Chesnaye did not answer. The monitor was about six miles from the land. The two escorts were getting dangerously close inshore.

As if in answer to his thoughts, two orange flashes glowed briefly against the purple hills, and seconds later the nearest destroyer was bracketed by twin waterspouts which seemed to hang for a long time before falling back as broken spray.

''Ere we go, then!' Wellard loosened his rifle-sling and glanced towards the bridge. 'I 'ope the Skipper knows what 'e's about!'

Chesnaye took a last searching look at Tobias's impassive features and then started to climb the long steel ladder to the upper bridge. Tobias would not break. He was no leader, but he was reliable.

The bridge was surprisingly calm and quiet. Each officer seemed to be looking through his binoculars, and every rating stood by voice-pipe and telephone.

The Captain was sitting in his chair, elbows on the screen, cap tilted against the slowly climbing sun. Over his shoulder he said, 'Hoist battle ensigns.'

Chesnaye felt a lump in his throat as he watched the giant ensigns mounting masts and ensign staff alike. The challenge was being accepted. It seemed wrong that the sea was so empty. No one to watch, to applaud. Even to pity.

He remembered the cheering troopships when they had first sailed for this place. The ranks of waving khaki. Now there was no one. Except the hidden enemy.

'The destroyers have opened fire, sir!' Travis looked

down at the Captain's slight shoulders. Across the still water they could all hear the sharp crack of the vicious four-inch guns, although the harsh sunlight and mounting haze hid the results of their work.

The big turret groaned slightly and the twin guns lifted a few inches. Behind that massive armour the Quarters Officer and his men would be straining every nerve and muscle, knowing that this time it was vital for everything to work like a precise clock. A misfire, an accident, and the monitor's role would be ended, and the men who served her wiped out.

A handset buzzed, 'Twelve thousand yards, sir!'

'Very good.' Nothing more.

Beaushears said thickly, 'They've started to make smoke!'

Sure enough the two small destroyers were weaving across the monitor's bows, parallel with the beachless coast, whilst from their squat funnels billowed a languid pall of black, greasy smoke. It hung across the water, shutting out the sun and darkening the smiling seascape like a curtain.

Chesnaye could feel his nails biting into his palms as he watched the destroyers' efforts and matched them against the *Saracen*'s slow and painful progress. They were nearer the coast now, but there was still a long way to go. He stiffened as he caught sight of more waterspouts beyond the smokescreen. More this time. Maybe six or seven.

Above the bridge the gunnery team would be watching too. Calculating and waiting. It could not be much longer.

The Captain spoke. 'Prepare to lower boats.'

The order was passed, and below the bridge Chesnaye could see the frantic efforts to get the big cumbersome launches slung out over the side.

Royston-Jones added testily : 'Pulling boats first. They can be taken in tow with the rafts.' He shifted briefly in his chair and glanced at the watching midshipmen. 'Well, off you go.' He waited as they saluted. 'And good luck.'

Chesnaye could feel his stomach muscles tight against his belt as he pushed his way through the marines who were milling excitedly around the davits. Half the night they had practised this manœuvre, but already the situation looked tangled and near disaster.

Commander Godden stood by the rail, his face grim as he watched the first boat squeaking down the falls. It hit the water and was soon drifting clear of the crawling monitor. Rafts, lowered over the side for once heedless of paintwork, were immediately taken in tow by the whaler, and as the power boats were lowered alongside, momentarily pinioned to allow more men to scramble aboard, Chesnaye suddenly realised the enormity of their task.

He caught sight of Tobias and then Pickles in their allotted places beside Major De L'Isle, and he felt himself scrambling with the desperation of the men he had just been watching like an onlooker.

The Major of Marines was standing up in the launch, his face scarlet as he yelled at his Colour Sergeant, who was in another boat. 'Keep those men quiet, d'you hear? God damn your eyes if I hear another word!' He flopped down on the thwart beside Chesnaye and banged his short leather-covered stick against his boot. 'Let them save their energy, that's what I say!'

Spouting smoke and fumes, the power boats gathered up the cutters and whalers with their attendant rafts into three separate tows. At a signal from De L'Isle they formed into lines and turned towards the shore, some of the men cheering and shouting in spite of the threats from the N.C.O.s.

The boats gathered way, so that the *Saracen*'s jagged shape seemed to grow small and indistinct in minutes. Only the three great ensigns stood out clear and bright, while the ragged hole left by the mine was already lost in the haze.

There was a great whistling roar, and for a few seconds Chesnaye thought that the *Saracen* had opened fire. As he twisted his head to watch he saw a blinding light burst alongside the monitor's low hull, so bright that he winced and shut his eyes. But not before he had seen the tall topmast quiver and then plunge over the side. The blast of the explosion fanned across the flat water and deluged the small boats in noise, so that most of the men could only gape as the falling mast slithered into the sea followed by its attendant tangle of rigging and men.

De L'Isle was the first to recover his wits. 'A big 'un, I should say. Fourteen-inch at least!'

Chesnaye's heart sank. No wonder the Turks were confident about this part of their coast. With a well-sited gun of that calibre, and with their target silhouetted against an empty sea, it was just a matter of time.

He dug his fingers into the boat's warm gunwale and gritted his teeth as another fountain of water burst abreast the monitor's bridge. Still she did not return fire, and Chesnaye could feel himself almost weeping at the ugly ship's slow progress.

De L'Isle sniffed and moved his holster on his belt. 'At least the bloody Turks won't be expecting us to arrive like this, what?'

Chesnaye turned with difficulty amidst the close press of bodies and looked at Pickles. He was surprised to see that the young midshipman was apparently calm, or was he resigned? He tried to grin at him, but his jaws felt stiff and enlarged.

Pickles moistened his lips and then reached across a seaman's bent shoulders to touch his hand. His lips moved very slowly, and Chesnaye realised he was trying to tell him something. The scream of the next shell made further words impossible, so he merely squeezed Pickles' hand and then turned back to watch the boats and the nearness of the smokescreen. But his hand, long after he had released Pickles', was still ice cold from the contact.

. . . . .

The beach at the foot of the tall brown cliffs was smaller than it had first appeared, and consisted not of sand but of broken stones and rubble washed or blown down over the centuries to form a narrow, treacherous slope. It shelved steeply and immediately into deep water which surged in the cliff's black shadow in a constant, angry maelstrom of short, steep waves. Singly and in pairs the boats staggered and lurched against the loose stones while the packed men leapt and stumbled ashore, their heavy packs and rifles adding to the confusion. All about them, wafted by a fresh off-shore breeze the remnants of the destroyers' smoke screen made some of them cough, others curse noisily as they peered anxiously for their comrades and correct positions on the beach. The sun was much higher, but beneath the tall, threatening cliff face the air seemed tinged with ice, so that some of the sweating marines were shivering and stamping their feet.

Keith Pickles felt the water draining from his trouser legs and stepped unsteadily towards the brown crumbling wall where Major De L'Isle and half of his men were already examining the means of reaching the top of this natural barrier. Pickles again tried to examine his inner feelings, to face some thought or idea which he could recognise, but nothing came. He felt light-headed, as if he was gliding from one phase to the next as in a dream. Time and distance had shortened, so that the long and agonising passage through the oily smoke to this shore now seemed the same length as climbing from the pitching launch or adjusting his belt and revolver.

He turned to watch as a section of marines led by Lieutenant Keats, De L'Isle's willowy second-in-command, moved briskly around a short spur of rock and began to scramble up the cliff face. Like mountaineers, they were silhouetted darkly against the pale colours and hues of the next bay, far beyond this overcast place, their bent bodies like bronze sculptures on a memorial.

He heard De L'Isle bark to no one in particular: 'Damn' fine landing! Not a man lost! Must have caught John Turk with his breeches dangling, what?'

Some of his men laughed shortly and nervously, as if they were out of breath. Pickles watched them narrowly and saw the way they were fingering their rifles and peering up at the moving section of marines. Nervous, afraid even.

Pringle's voice was here, too, loud and blustering as he yelled at the wallowing boats: 'Stand off the beach! Wait for further orders!' It was odd, but Pickles was able to listen and calculate Pringle's words without nervousness. The shouted orders seemed empty and meaningless, extra and unnecessary. It was strange he had never realised that so much of Pringle's world was pure show. Perhaps he was afraid too? He watched the man's flushed and angry face and wondered.

De L'Isle waved his leather stick. 'Close up! Lively there!'

Obediently the officers and N.C.O.s drew round him, their expressions mixed and cautious.

De L'Isle was speaking fast and sharply. 'Right. No time to lose. Second section move off to the left. Sergeant Barnes!'

The tall Colour Sergeant, who looked as if he had just prepared himself for an admiral's inspection, stiffened to attention on the loose stones. 'Sir?'

'You take 'em off at the trot right away. You know the picture, but things may be different once we get over this ridge. The Turks'll not be expecting our little lot, but it won't take 'em long to move up a force of some sort.' His bulbous eyes flashed meaningly. 'Your orders and *mine* are to hold off any local attack until the spotting team have homed the guns on the enemy's flank.' He spoke to the group at large. 'That fourteen-inch gun which is trying to knock hell out of the poor old ship is probably intended for our lads up the coast. That, and any other battery, must be wiped out, and quick.'

The Colour Sergeant was well over six feet tall and as broad as a door. His big-boned face was decorated with a ginger upturned moustache which gave him the appearance of one of Wellington's grenadiers, and he looked entirely calm and unmoved as he listened to his superior. At a nod from the Major he swung round and slung his rifle across his shoulder, his hard eyes already searching out his own particular section of marines. As they moved clear Pickles heard the sergeant say angrily : 'Keep your distances! Don't huddle together like a lot of bloody matelots!' Then they were gone.

The Major grunted approvingly. 'First things first. Don't fancy having some damned Turk bouncing grenades on us while we're chatting, what?'

Less laughter this time. Pickles realised that the beach already seemed larger, and the landing force which had been made important by its density now appeared small and insignificant as it broke up into little groups.

De L'Isle glanced at the officers. 'Ready, you three?'

Pringle cleared his throat. 'I'll stop here and supervise the shore party of seamen.'

The Major laughed unpleasantly. 'Like Jesus you will, boy! You get up to the ridge with the two snotties an' double quick!'

Pickles felt his heart thumping with sudden excitement. He turned to look at Chesnaye, but the latter's face was grave and expressionless.

Pringle seemed shocked. 'My orders are to stay here, sir!'

'Damn your orders! I'm in command here!' He leaned forward, his polished boots creaking. 'I've been in more campaigns and trouble spots than you've had pork chops! The men may think this is a picnic, but *I* don't. It may happen that once we top the cliff we'll be for it. If that happens, half our party might get wiped out, *see*?' He turned his heavy frame, his mind apparently busy on other things. 'In any case, you're more experienced. So do your job!'

Pringle did not look at the two midshipmen. Through his teeth he muttered, 'Come on, then, and no shirking, Pickles!' But there was no bite in his voice. It was as if he was someone else.

There was a sudden stammer of machine-gun fire from the extreme right, followed immediately by shouts and a ragged rifle volley.

De L'Isle was cursing quietly. He waved his stick and said, 'Corporal, get your men up this cliff, right here!' He stabbed angrily at the crumbling mound. 'Come on, lad! It won't bite you!' He waited impatiently as the first men began to climb, and then said to Pringle: 'You too. We might as well get started!'

Pickles felt the grit and stones falling on his shoulders as he followed the heavy-booted marines towards the pale bright sky, but he was entirely absorbed in his new thoughts. He felt hot and cold in turns, and once when he looked down at the handful of seamen left on the beach he felt like laughing aloud. It was as if every doubt and agony had left his mind at once. Just knowing that he was going to be killed seemed to make it much easier to bear.

Before, in that earlier landing, it had been different. There had been a small chance of survival, a tiny hope perhaps. It had made living and thinking a nightmare. Even his life aboard the *Saracen* had been a mere building up for this moment. Now there was no turning back, and the future was suddenly mercifully plain and exact.

Once when he rested in a hanging pattern of gorse he turned to look for the monitor. Small and pale, the ship was still shrouded in smoke. He could not tell what the smoke represented. Her own guns or the enemy's, or just the vapour from the screen left by the two small ships which darted along the coast. One of the destroyers appeared to be on fire, but her guns still flashed and her bow wave spoke of her tremendous speed and grace.

Pickles watched the *Saracen* as if seeing it for the first time. It could have been so different. Or could it? For once he could question his constant defence without a tremor. Pringle had brought an edge to his misery, but there had been his own stupid pride and ignorance too. It had all been so wonderful at first. Home on leave before joining the ship. The uniform, the admiring glances from all the girls he had once known and played with in the road outside his father's shop. He seemed to have grown to a man while they still appeared gawky and pigtailed. He remembered too the dark sweet-smelling parlour at the back of the shop where his early life had revolved. The mantelpiece crowded with silver-framed photographs of relatives, singly or in groups, of dogs and cats, and all the other faces which had made up the Pickles family past.

His father, short and fat, with a lick of hair plastered across his forehead. He had been proud, too, but more cautious. Perhaps he had known what lay ahead of his son in his new career.

'They might seem different to you, Keith,' he had said on more than one occasion. 'You know, posh homes and plenty of cash. I've had to work for what I've got here, and I was hopin' you'd join me one day in the shop.'

Pickles remembered now how he had felt embarrassment at the way his father had always dropped his g's. But he had been right. All the way. Try as he might, Pickles had met this strange barrier at every stage. He

had helped to make it worse by fighting back, by trying
to play a part he had never known. He had run short of
money two weeks after joining the *Saracen*, at a time
when the new ship was open for one party and celebration
after another. He had borrowed ten pounds from a tailor
in Portsmouth. Once in debt he had increased his misery
until the small tailor had come to the ship to press his
demands. It might have been better if the man had gone
to the Commander, but instead he had approached
Pringle, who with a show of hurt pride had paid the man
and sent him packing. From that moment he had made
Pickles' life a nightmare. He had piled one humiliation
after another on him, each time with some sneer or jibe at
his upbringing and background. The other midshipmen
in the gunroom stayed silent and watchful. Taking no
sides. They, too, obviously agreed with Pringle.

Then Chesnaye had joined the ship, and a small glimmer of hope had returned to Pickles' heart. It was
rumoured that Chesnaye was under a cloud because his
father had failed in some way, that he too was from a
poor family. He had felt something like love when the tall,
grave-faced Chesnaye had stood up for him against
Pringle, but even this had been soured by jealousy when
Pickles had seen that the other midshipmen had accepted
the newcomer in spite of his alleged faults. He was one of
them. He belonged whatever he did.

There was a sudden clatter of feet to his right, and he
craned his head to watch the first section of marines re-
appear on the top of a wedge-sided fall of rock. They
were already a hundred yards away, but he could detect
the sudden urgency and desperation in their movements.

A burst of machine-gun fire sent the pale dust dancing
once more, and three marines skidded down the rock face
their bodies torn and bloodied. The young marine lieutenant, Keats, seeing his men falter and hang back from
the sun-dappled ridge, leapt forward, waving his stick.
'Come on, lads! Forward, marines!' He staggered and
fell at once as the next burst smashed into his crouched
body.

De L'Isle raised his binoculars and dug his elbows into
the slope. 'God! What a mess!' In a louder voice he

shouted : 'Round to the left, men! Get that Lewis gun mounted and spray the slope!'

More marines ducked and ran forward. Some made it, others fell writhing before the unseen death which sang and whistled in the dusty air.

In twos and threes De L'Isle's party reached the top of the cliff and flopped down amongst a long line of smooth boulders. The Lewis gun began to chatter, and some of the men shouted encouragement to the section which was pinned down on the right.

De L'Isle was breathing heavily as he rested his binoculars on a piece of sun-warmed rock. To Pringle he said sharply : 'No need for you to bother about us. Get your party across this gully and up on to that ridge there.'

Pickles listened and moved up alongside the sweating marines to peer at the long, dark-sided ridge which lined the other side of a deep gully. It was slab-shaped with a tall pinnacle at one end, like the steeple of a petrified church. He saw too a small, stone-walled hut, roofless and deserted, at the foot of the pinnacle, perched on the ridge, as if forgotten for many years. He heard De L'Isle say : 'Make for that. Once up there you'll get a good view over the ridge and across the valley beyond.'

Pickles turned his head and looked at the rolling panorama of hills and cheerless ragged ridges which undulated away to the south where the high arrogant peak of Achi Baba still dominated the Peninsula. A barren, arid, unwanted place, he thought. Gorse, a few sparse trees and the ever-moving dust. Somewhere to the north the troops were waiting. But did it matter? Did anything count in this cruel land?

A bullet whimpered overhead and passed away over the sea behind him. He shivered and drew his head deeper into his shoulders. A sniper? They were said to be everywhere. On every hill and ridge. No man could move in the open and live. He stared at the dark ridge again. Yet we have to get there, he thought. Three officers and three seamen.

The Colour Sergeant called from what seemed a great distance, 'Ready, sir!'

Major De L'Isle wiped the sweat from his eyes. 'Must

clear those batteries before noon,' he said absently. Then, as if having come to a decision, he blew sharply on his whistle and lumbered to his feet. As the Lewis gun sprayed the slope beyond the cliff edge the ragged line of marines rose from cover and began to run forward. Slowly at first, and then when nothing happened faster and more wildly. There were a few unexpected rifle shots from the foot of the ridge, and three more marines cried out and fell face down in their own blood. Even more unexpectedly, as if from the rock itself, a handful of blue-grey figures rose directly in the centre of the small advance, their alien uniforms and dark faces suddenly very clear and close.

The marines faltered, but De L'Isle waved his stick and screamed: 'Get them! *Get them!*' The words seemed to be wrung from his very heart.

Two of the Turkish soldiers dropped to their knees and began to fire their long rifles as fast as they could reload.

Pickles realised that the strange real enemy was directly in his path, but he could not stop himself from running, nor could he draw his revolver. Faster, faster. The rifle muzzles spurted yellow flame directly in his eyes. A marine, yelling like a fiend, screamed and clutched his stomach as a bullet smashed him down, but another marine reached the seemingly paralysed Turk and drove his bayonet deep into his throat. The Turk gurgled and rolled on to his face. With a sob the frantic marine turned and swung the bayonet again, the full force of his body pinioning the writhing man on the ground like an insect.

From the flank Colour Sergeant Barnes bellowed: 'Just give 'im two inches! Don't make a bloody meal of it!'

The battle-crazed marine faltered as he withdrew the reddened bayonet and blinked dazedly towards the parade-ground voice, then obedient and happy he staggered after the rest, the Turk already forgotten beside the bodies of the others.

Like savage, desperate animals the marines fell into the position vacated by the small enemy outpost, fear temporarily forgotten as lust and hatred dispersed itself in a frenzy of preparations.

Grenades banged on the right, and another ragged

134

cheer announced the end of the hidden machine-gun. De L'Isle said unevenly, 'It's a start, anyway!'

A big shell sighed overhead, and then another. In the far distance beyond the ridge two green puffs of lyddite smoke blossomed and hung unmoving against the dull hills. The monitor had fired at last. Two vague, unchartered shots to give the enemy something to think about.

The marines settled down amongst the rocks and readjusted their sights. Sergeant Barnes strode briskly towards Major De L'Isle and saluted. 'Fifteen killed, sir. Ten wounded.' His pale eyes watched the Major's face with something like affection. 'I'm afraid one of the young gentlemen 'as bin 'it too, sir.'

Pickles, who had been fighting to regain his breath, jerked upright at the words. All the things Chesnaye had said and done, all the pent-up fears and wants of the past weeks roared into his brain as Barnes added sadly, 'Must 'ave got 'it just as we reached 'ere, sir.' Pickles stood up and began to run back across the open ground.

A wounded marine cried out: 'Help me, fer Christ's sake! Me eyes, I'm blind!' As Pickles dashed past he screamed again: 'Come 'ere, you bastards! Don't leave me!' Another marine, dead and cold-eyed, lay with his torn shoulder already alive with blue flies, his mouth half open as if in rebuke.

A bullet snickered past Pickles' head, but he ran on, deaf to it and the shouts of the marines. Perhaps this was how it was meant to end. He tucked in his head and ran even faster.

*　　*　　*　　*　　*

Richard Chesnaye forced himself to lie quite still until his mind was able to break through the enveloping pain, and only then did he try to move. Very gingerly he took his weight on his hands and pushed himself slowly into a sitting position. The sudden movement made him cry out, and with something like terror he forced himself to look at the long dark stain which was soaking his right thigh and staining the dry stones at his side. His throat felt raw with sudden thirst, and as he stared round the small, saucer-shaped depression into which he had fallen he was aware for the first time of the complete stillness and sense of loneliness. Gritting his teeth against the pain, he twisted his head to look around him, his eyes taking in the clear empty sky and the unmoving bent grass which crested the edges of the depression, and the clump of faded yellow balsam. He stared dazedly and uncomprehending for several seconds at the brown, claw-like hand which hung over the grass by his head, its wrist lined with dark dried blood upon which the flies were already at work.

He tried to concentrate, to recall the exact moment when he had been singled out from the frantic, noisy dash across that vague open ground and had been thrown down by the savage, white-hot blow. He lifted his wrist and then sighed with despair as he stared at his broken watch. Hours or minutes? The high unshielded sun gave him no clue. He stiffened as a distant rattle of machine-gun fire echoed through the dusty grass. They were not all dead, then. As if to settle his disordered thoughts a pain-racked voice, cracked and unrecognisable, cried out and then died before he could judge its distance. His ears began to pick out other sounds too. The far-off rumble of heavy guns, the background to some other battle.

He fell back again on the warm earth, his eyes closed against the glare. His brain told him to make just one more effort to move, but something else held him back. The pain washed over him, and in his mind he saw a sudden picture of his father framed against the deep green of the English lawn and the worn, leather-bound books along the wall of his room. He flinched as a spent bullet thudded into the ground by his side, and tried to think more clearly. Was the ship still off the coast or even afloat? With sudden clarity he remembered the small knot of Turkish soldiers and the flash of bayonets just before he had fallen. He recalled, too, that he had been keeping his mind blank when it had happened, yet unable to tear his eyes from the desperate, spurting rifles which blocked his way. Perhaps the dead hand which gripped so fervently at the grass by his head belonged to one of those soldiers? In any case it could not be long before others arrived. He felt his stomach muscles tighten as he imagined the figures tall against the sky on the edge of his hiding place, the agonising moment of discovery. And then the bayonets.

Another burst of firing cut through the lazy air, and it was followed immediately by distant shouts and more firing. Through the ground at his back he felt the sudden thud of running feet, and he imagined he could hear quick, desperate breathing as the running man drew nearer.

It was then that he realised just how desperately he wanted to live, and the approaching, hidden terror made him roll on to his side, his bloodied fingers groping frantically for his revolver. Whimpering and cursing, he tugged at the holster, the agony in his thigh adding to his sense of urgency. Just as he succeeded in freeing the flap a shadow blotted out the sun, and he tightened his body into one agonised ball, unable to look round, but waiting for the murderous thrust of steel.

As if in a dream he heard Pickles say: 'Thank God, Dick! Here, let me have a look!'

Chesnaye allowed himself to be rolled on his back, still only half believing what he saw. Pickles, breathless but engrossed, his round face screwed in set concentration as he tore open the side of the dripping trousers. More pain when his hands found the place, but a quick reassuring grin when the warm snugness of a bandage and dressing cut off the probing sun and the eager flies.

Pickles sat on his haunches. 'I don't know much about these things, Dick, but the bullet seems to have missed the bone.' He grinned widely, as if the realisation of what he had achieved had suddenly reached him. 'I *knew* I'd find you if I ran far enough!'

A shell passed overhead, and Pickles said: 'We must get out of here. The rest of our chaps are about a hundred yards further on, by the ridge.'

Chesnaye felt the relief coursing through him like brandy. 'I'm ready when you are!'

Pickles sat upright and wrinkled his nose like a dog. For a long moment he stared at the dead Turk and then said: 'Seems a bit quieter. We'll chance it.'

Together they crawled over the lip of the depression, their faces brushed by the grass and ageless gorse. Chesnaye kept his right arm across Pickles' shoulder, and dragging his damaged leg between them the two midshipmen pulled themselves towards the ridge which had now lost its shadow and shone in the sunlight like brown coral.

They paused for a brief rest and Chesnaye said slowly, 'There's a lot to do, Keith.'

Pickles grinned. 'You can say that again! We've not started yet, and, quite frankly, I think it'll be up to *us* again!'

Chesnaye stared at him with open wonder. Then he gave Pickles' shoulder a quick squeeze. 'Thank you, Keith. I'll not forget.'

Pickles sighed as three marines charged from cover and hauled them to safety behind a slab of broken rock. Dusting the grit from his trousers he said flatly, 'I'm not sure that *I* will either!'

Major De L'Isle greeted Chesnaye with a savage grin. 'Well done, lad. We'll be needing you as soon as my orderly can patch you up. Think you can make it up to the top?' He beamed as Chesnaye nodded vaguely, but then turned on a scowl for Pickles' benefit. 'By God, you should have been shot for what you did! You're raving bloody mad, did you know that?'

Pickles stood in the centre of an admiring circle of staring marines and felt the prickle of real happiness for the first time since he had stepped aboard the *Saracen*. He looked down at Chesnaye's drawn face and said, 'I suppose I've got used to running!'

8

The Pinnacle

The distant hills danced like a mirage in the twin lenses
of Chesnaye's field-glasses so that it took him precious
minutes to refocus them and assess what he saw. Each
second added to the pain in his leg, which in spite of the
dressing felt raw and torn, and the more he looked
through his glasses, the more hopeless seemed the task. It
was quiet on top of the ridge. Quiet and with very little
cover. The three naval officers and three seamen had
crawled back and forth over an area which measured
about fifty yards by twenty and represented the highest
part of the ridge. Highest, that is, but for the tall, bleak
pinnacle.

It was funny how clearly he could think about the job
in hand. Chesnaye moved the glasses slightly and watched
two faint shell-bursts to the north. Perhaps the concentration was the only thing holding back the nausea and
agony, or the sense of defeat.

He tried again. Everything seemed to come back to the
pinnacle. The ridge was good enough to pinpoint the
enemy bombardment area, but then again was invisible to
the ship. The pinnacle was the monitor's aiming mark, a
known object on chart and gunnery grid-maps. It glimmered in the bright sunlight, smooth and unlovely. It was
about sixty feet high with a deep cleft just below the top.
His heart quickened and he looked sideways at Sub-
Lieutenant Pringle, who was squatting tensely behind
some boulders his back against the wall of the derelict
hut. His sun-reddened face was worried and brooding.

Chesnaye cleared his throat . 'We'd better send a runner
back to the beach with the first signal.' He spoke through
tight lips, intolerant of Pringle's silence, which was even
more unnerving than his noisy protests when the party
had landed. 'What d'you say?'

Pringle jerked himself from his thoughts. His eyes flashed with some of his old arrogance. 'What's the hurry? We're probably wasting our time, anyway!'

Pickles said quickly, 'Shall I go?'

Chesnaye wrote on his pad and handed the folded signal to one of the seamen. 'No, Keith. You and I are going up the old rock needle here.'

Pickles looked up and grimaced. 'Ouch!' Then with a look of concern. 'Can you make it? I would have thought *he* could go!' He spoke loudly enough for Pringle to hear.

'Now that's enough from you!' Pringle leapt to his feet, his face working furiously. 'Just because you've been doing some petty heroics you think you're something, eh?' His face twisted with anger. 'Well, *I* know a few things about you! By God, I'm sick of the lot of you!'

Chesnaye nodded to the gaping seaman, who tore his eyes from the gesticulating Pringle and began to climb over the side of the ridge. Below him the marines in their prepared positions watched him descend with interest.

With the whiplash crack Chesnaye had heard before, the sniper's rifle sent the birds wheeling from the ridge in screaming protest. The seaman hung for a moment longer, his eyes on the pinnacle above him, and then plummeted down the side of the ridge.

The hillsides re-echoed again to the rattle of the Lewis gun as the marines swept the silent rocks in a miniature dust-storm in a vain effort to find the hidden marksman. Then there was silence once more.

Chesnaye bit his lip with sudden determination. 'Here, give me a hand, Keith.' Slinging his glasses round his neck he walked to the foot of the pointing rock and began to climb up towards the small cleft. Each move was agony, but his mind was too occupied with the urgency of his task and the fact that he had just sent a man to his death for nothing.

Pringle's nerve snapped as the two midshipmen turned away from him. He shook his fists in the air and yelled: 'What the hell is happening? For God's sake let's get out of here!'

Pickles paused ahead of Chesnaye and held out his

hand to help him. 'I know how he feels,' he said hoarsely, 'and that makes a change!'

Chesnaye forced himself to grin, and dragged himself further up the steep edges of hot stone. Once there and I'm done for, he thought. He could feel the blood beginning to pump through the bandage, and his right foot seemed to be dead.

He heard another crack, and a bullet smacked hard against the pinnacle, hurling small splinters against his hands. With a sob Pickles pulled him unceremoniously into the cleft and a tiny, wonderful patch of shade.

Chesnaye had difficulty in controlling his mouth as Pickles upended his water-bottle to allow a little lukewarm water to moisten his parched lips. He nodded, grateful, not trusting words. He watched Pickles with something like apprehension as he stowed away the bottle and busied himself with making Chesnaye comfortable. How much longer could they both last? he wondered. If he died what would Pickles do? It was suddenly terribly important that Pickles should be spared any more of this nightmare.

Pickles pointed with surprise. 'Look, Dick! The ship!'

Sure enough, the *Saracen* was visible, listing and shrouded in smoke.

'She's in much closer.' Pickles leaned out to watch, but jerked back as another bullet whipped against the rock and ricocheted away over the ridge with an insane shriek. 'God, they're after *us*!'

Chesnaye twisted round on the tiny space and levelled his glasses.

Pickles tore his eyes from the ship and pulled the long Very pistol from his belt. 'Ready?'

Chesnaye nodded grimly. It had been arranged that if the exact bearings and ranges could not be sent by signal then a blind shoot would be carried out.

Pickles snapped a cartridge into the breech and then said quietly, 'God, there are Turks on that hill.'

Chesnaye turned in time to see sunlight flash momentarily on metal and the quick movement of men amongst the rocks on the nearest hillside. They're going to try and stop us, he thought dully.

141

The Very pistol coughed and sent its light soaring high over the ridge. Like a green eye it hung apparently motionless in the clear sky, and some of the marines cheered.

'Watch the ship!' Chesnaye rested on his elbows and concentrated on the brown elbow of hills some four miles distant where the main Turkish support lines were said to be.

Behind him Pickles said excitedly, 'Now!'

Subdued by the sea-cliff and the side of the ridge, the monitor's voice was none the less impressive. Chesnaye waited, the sweat running into his eyes as he counted away the seconds. His heart sank as twin clouds of white smoke erupted above the slumbering hills. The monitor was firing shrapnel first. It was easier to see. He groaned: 'God, they're miles out! They're almost firing on to our lines!'

Pickles leaned over the side of the cleft and shouted down to Pringle: 'You must get a runner back to the beach and send a signal! It's an overshoot!'

Pringle stared up at them, his eyes red. 'No one can get through! There are snipers all round us!'

From below came a sudden burst of firing from the marines and the sound of Major De L'Isle's whistle. Chesnaye closed his eyes and tried to clear his reeling mind. The monitor would wait for another flare and then open the real bombardment. Or would it wait? He tried to imagine the battered ship with the impatient, desperate gunners crouching beneath the sun-heated armour. They might not wait, and it was not unknown for ships to drop shells on their own men. But not a ship like the *Saracen*. Each of her giant shells weighed nearly a ton. He shook himself angrily. It did not bear thinking about. Tightly he said: 'Tell Pringle to get up here and have a look! He must be made to realise what's happening!'

Pringle did not even listen. He covered his head with his hands and ran into the roofless hut.

One of the seamen ran from cover on the far side of the ridge, his face angry. ''Ere, come back, sir!' But instead of an answer he received a bullet in the throat and fell back writing on the rocks, the dust around him brightly speckled with his blood.

Chesnaye felt sick. 'Here, give me a hand up.'

Pickles reached out, his face mystified, until he saw Chesnaye's leg buckled under him. Chesnaye lay on his back, his eyes still on his objective. Pickles followed his gaze and then stood up, his face suddenly white. 'I'm ready. I'll make that signal.'

Chesnaye wrote shakily on his pad, the figures and bearings dancing as if through a mist. It had to be done. It was the only way. He felt a wave of fury run through him as he thought of Pringle hiding below in the stone hut. 'Here, Keith.' He handed him the pad. 'Just semaphore the first four sets of figures. They will have to do!'

A voice called up from below : 'The Major's compliments, sir, but can you get a move on? The bastards are trying to get between us an' the cliffs!'

But Chesnaye did not answer. There was a lot he wanted to say, but nothing came. Instead he gripped Pickles' hand. 'Be careful, Keith!'

With a quick grin Pickles leapt from the cleft and began to climb with the ease and agility of a monkey. Pieces of rock splintered around him as snipers on the hillside became aware of the small dark figure that was making for the very top of the pinnacle.

Chesnaye lay back, his eyes fixed on Pickles' body as he reached the end of his climb. For a second he peered down at Chesnaye and then, turning his back on the enemy hills, he commenced to wave his arms towards the distant, toy-like ship.

Still the rifles cracked, but as the big searchlight on the *Saracen*'s bridge flashed an acknowledgement Pickles began to send his message. Chesnaye could picture the activity in the big turret, the gleaming shells being rammed home, the creak of elevating gear as the twin barrels lifted on to their target.

'Finished!' Pickles threw his cap in the air and yelled, 'They're going to open fire now!'

Then he fell. Without a cry or protest he rolled down the steep slope and crumpled across Chesnaye, who could only stare horrified at the widening patch of scarlet across his chest. Pickles' eyes were still wide from excitement, but without recognition or understanding. With a sob Chesnaye pulled him against his own body, aware again of the cold hands and that last insane eagerness.

Overhead, the great shells winged on their way to roar and thunder across the enemy lines, to destroy guns and stores, and the men who waited for the attack.

But Chesnaye did not notice. He watched his dead friend and the bright red stain which was still spreading. He remembered that night at Gibraltar, when it had all begun. Pickles with his shirt sprinkled with port. So eager to please.

It still seemed impossible to believe what had happened. Yet the sigh of the monitor's shells told him it was true. Once again Pickles had surprised them all.

.   ,   .   -   .

'Signal from tug *Crusader*, sir.' The Yeoman of Signals paused and coughed uneasily. For a moment he thought that the Captain was asleep in his chair on the deserted bridge, but even as he looked Royston-Jones turned his head very slightly and gave a faint gesture with his hand. 'Will be alongside in half an hour. Will you be ready to slip?' The Yeoman followed the Captain's gaze towards the tall-sided hospital ship which was anchored two cables away. White and graceful, she looked invulnerable against the low hills and straggling trees of the Mudros foreshore. 'Signal ends, sir.'

'Thank you, Yeoman. Tell them affirmative.' Royston-Jones held himself stiffly in his chair until the Yeoman had clattered down the ladder to the signal bridge, and then allowed his narrow shoulders to sag. There was so much waiting to be done, yet his mind and brain rebelled against even leaving the bridge. The sun was harsh across his smoke-stained uniform, and the humid air was filled with the smells of scorched paintwork and burned cordite. It seemed impossible that the ship was so still, that the great guns, blackened and blistered with continuous firing, were silent in their turret. Without looking over the screen he knew the seamen were busy on the upper deck, still using their hoses and scrubbers to clean away the filth and dirt of the bombardment and the destruction. He stiffened as a string of bunting broke out from the hospital ship's main-yard. She was getting ready to sail. It did not take much imagination to picture the pain and misery which was outwardly hidden by that white hull, he thought.

Almost unwillingly he stood up and walked to the rear of the bridge. Very gently he ran his hand across the scarred teak rail and looked up at the tall funnel pitted with shell splinters, blackened by smoke. Down towards the maindeck where only hours before the hands had been busy removing the empty shell-cases from around the secondary armament and gathering the shattered remains of boats and hatches, and mopping away the dark stains from the once smooth deck planking. The ship still listed to port, but she was quite motionless, as if resting. Shortly they would be weighing anchor once more, but this time in the care of some grubby tug which would take them on the long haul to Alexandria. And then? Royston-Jones shook himself as the weariness and inner misery closed over him once again.

There was a quiet step on the gratings nearby, and he turned quickly as if to cover his thoughts.

Lieutenant Hogarth saluted and glanced momentarily towards the splintered topmast above the bridge. 'I have reorganised the watches, sir. The Bosun has given orders for the fo'c'sle party to fall in in fifteen minutes.'

Royston-Jones blinked. It seemed strange for Hogarth to be speaking about the ship's organisation instead of his beloved guns. It should have been Godden, but, of course, he was already in that hospital ship, a shattered arm his passport to another world. 'Very good.' He forced himself to look at Hogarth's concerned face. 'Anything else?'

Hogarth shut his mind to the scenes he had witnessed for so many long hours. The shell-holes and broken plates. Armour twisted into the fantastic shapes of wet cardboard, everything battered and smashed into a shambles. It did not seem as if the ship would ever be the same again.

He cleared his throat. 'I think you should go aft to your quarters for a while, sir,' he said carefully. 'I have instructed your steward to get a meal for you.' As the Captain did not reply he added more firmly, 'You have done more than enough, sir!'

Royston-Jones made a small sound. It could have been a laugh or a sob. 'You are talking like a commander already, Hogarth!' He placed his hands on the screen, as if to feel the reactions of his battle-torn ship. It was quite still. He sighed. 'There were moments when I thought we should never see Mudros again. Or anywhere else, for that matter!'

They stared in silence as the big hospital ship's anchor cable began to shorten and a small cloud of steam rose from her capstan.

If he closed his eyes for one moment he knew that he would not sleep. They were all worried about him, but he knew that food and rest were not the answer. If he faltered for an instant and allowed himself to relax he knew it would all come back. The bombardment and the havoc wrought by the Turkish guns would be a mere backcloth to what had happened later. The returning boats, barely half filled, and then mostly with wounded men.

He could torture himself by remembering Major De L'Isle's empty face as he had climbed to the bridge to make his report. The bridge, with its pitted plating and dead men, an unrecognisable place.

Royston-Jones had sat quite still in his chair, almost afraid to look at the marine's features as he retold the efforts and the final retreat of the landing party.

De L'Isle had said of Sub-Lieutenant Pringle, 'He was shot during the final Turkish attack.' Then, 'He was shot in the back, sir.'

Pringle's death had formed a background to the rest of that heartbreaking report. Somehow it seemed to sum up their brave but pathetic efforts, to mark the whole episode with shame.

Over half the landing force had been killed, and many of the remainder wounded. Some had died well, others had ended their moments in the madness and bitterness of men who had been cheated and betrayed.

Royston-Jones listened unmoving to De L'Isle's account of Pickles' death, and wondered how much more he could stand.

De L'Isle's harsh voice had been unsteady. 'Colour Sergeant Barnes had to go up for the two snotties in the end, sir. Chesnaye was in such a bad way we thought he was past hope. But even then he put up a fight.'

Royston-Jones' mind had been too dulled to realise what he meant. 'Fight?'

'He wouldn't leave young Pickles, sir. He hung on to his body and refused to leave without him!' De L'Isle's reserve had suddenly fallen away. 'My God, I was proud of them! *All* of them!'

Now it was over, and soon the *Saracen* would be crossing the open sea once more. Perhaps then he would be able to tell De L'Isle and the others. Tell them of the signal he had received to mark the end of what might now be classed as a mere episode.

So far only Godden knew, and he would no doubt make use of its contents once his own personal pain was sufficiently dimmed for him to remember beyond those moments of united suffering and valour.

The attack, the suffering, the slaughter, had been for nothing. At the very last moment the Army had not made its attack.

As Pickles died on a bare rock pinnacle, and Chesnaye fought his own battles against pain and grief, even while Pringle received a bullet from some unknown marksman as he ran terror-stricken from the enemy; while all these things and many more were happening, and the *Saracen* changed from a sparkling symbol to a battered and listing hulk as she pressed home her attack, the soldiers stood in their trenches and listened. Some were grateful, others were ashamed. All wondered at the circumstances which allowed such things to happen.

Royston-Jones had not left his bridge since the anchor had dropped. He knew he was afraid of what he might see and of what he might find in the eyes of his men. For nothing, he thought. It was all for nothing.

De L'Isle had faltered as he had been about to leave the bridge. 'What shall I say in my report about Pringle?' He had seemed at a loss. 'I don't see why the others should have their names slurred because of him!'

He had replied : 'Say that he died of his wounds. That is enough.'

Hogarth's voice cut into his wretchedness, 'The hospital ship has weighed, sir.'

Like a white ghost the ex-liner began to glide between the moored ships. Royston-Jones saw, too, the tug's ungainly shape hovering nearby. 'Tell Lieutenant Travis to come to the bridge,' he said to a messenger.

The young seaman only stared at him until Hogarth gestured quickly for him to leave. Quietly he said, 'Travis was killed, sir.'

The Captain rubbed his dry hands across his face. 'Oh yes. Thank you.' He turned, caught off guard again as a ripple of cheering floated across the glistening water. 'What is that?'

Hogarth said : 'The hospital ship, sir. The men on her upper deck are cheering the old *Saracen!*'

Royston-Jones blinked and rubbed his eyes. 'They are cheering *us?*'

'Yes, sir.' Hogarth watched sadly as the little figure in soiled uniform and scorched cap looked round him as if lost in bewilderment.

Then with something like his old vigour he climbed on to the screen and held his cap high above his head. As his arm tired he changed his cap from hand to hand, his eyes blinded by the sun.

Long after the hospital ship's wash had been smoothed from the quiet anchorage he still stood and saluted his men, and a memory.

.   .   .   .   .   .

Unlike the engines of a warship, those of the hospital ship seemed far away and remote, so that the gentle tremor which had started almost unnoticeably was more of a sensation, like something in the mind.

Chesnaye cursed the weakness in his body and tried once more to lift himself in the narrow, spotless-sheeted bunk. He had no idea what part of the ship he was in, nor did he care. From what he could see in the vast compartment he deduced that the whole vessel was crammed with wounded like himself, regimented and lined up in enamelled bunks, bandaged, splintered and drugged for the voyage to England. Above his head a large fan purred discreetly, and the long rectangular port which opened on to the sunlit anchorage seemed to accentuate his new status, his sense of not belonging. By straining every muscle and ignoring the fire in his thigh he could lift his head far enough to see the tapering topmasts of an anchored cruiser, her commissioning pennant limp in the scorching heat, her tall funnels devoid of smoke. And, beyond, the rounded hills which now seemed alien and hostile.

Another gentle vibration rattled the enamel dishes on his small bunk-side table, and very faintly he could hear the shout of orders and the brief scurry of feet on the big ship's spacious upper deck. Soon they would be leaving Mudros and the Mediterranean, perhaps for ever.

He fell back, biting his lip to stem the feeling of anguish and misery. Like unfinished pictures in his mind the memories of the Peninsula, with its record of pain and death, flooded through him. Those last moments were still hazy and obscure, and again he wondered if time would clear away the mist, or if in fact he would lose the reminders altogether.

He closed his eyes tightly as Pickles' face came back to him. The empty loneliness of that rock pinnacle and the triumphant crack of snipers' rifles. Nothing seemed to go beyond that, but for his own weak but desperate struggle with Sergeant Barnes, who had somehow climbed into that terrible place and had carried him to safety. There were a few madly distorted recollections of running marines, their mouths and eyes working in frenzy or fear, rifles glowing with heat as they fired and fired again at the invisible enemy. Then there was one final picture, stark and terribly clear.

He had seen Leading Seaman Tobias running towards him as he lay helpless in a tiny gully, the man's face suddenly alight with pleasure. Tobias's expression had changed to one of disbelief as Pringle had burst from cover and had run blindly towards the path to the beach. Chesnaye still wondered how many of the others who had lived had seen what he and Tobias had then witnessed. Able Seaman Wellard, bleeding from several wounds, had staggered to his feet from a small pile of rocks, his teeth bared in his beard from the agony that movement must have cost him. As more bullets whipped and cracked about him he lifted his rifle, the final effort making him cry out like some trapped animal, and then he had fired. As Pringle's running figure had fallen, Wellard had thrown down his rifle and stood quite still. Then, with a final glance towards the gentle sea he had limped away, back towards the enemy lines. He had not been seen again.

Chesnaye realised that morphia must have claimed his reeling mind for some long hours after that moment. When he had opened his eyes again he had been aboard the *Saracen*, and there was no more gunfire, no scent of smoke and scorched bracken in his nostrils; just the pain and the sense of near breakdown to keep the memories alive.

The Captain had visited him, but it now seemed like part of a dream, with Royston-Jones' figure hovering against a background of red mist. Beaushears, too, had found a moment, and had patiently answered Chesnaye's desperate, wandering questions.

Now, as some of the mist cleared, he could piece together what he had been told. Of the faces he had known in the *Saracen* who were now dead, or scattered somewhere in this ship like himself. Of Lieutenant Travis who had lost a leg but stayed on the bridge until he had died. Of Nutting, the Padre, who had gone mad as he had crawled from one corpse to the next, his gabbled prayers meaningless in a world for which he had never been trained. And of Commander Godden, who despite his wound seemed happier and more relaxed than he had ever been.

Beaushears had said bitterly : 'He's glad to be out of it! He must think the Captain acted wrongly.' He had shrugged, suddenly old and weary. 'To think I once thought him a better man than the Captain!'

Chesnaye remembered, too, what Major De L'Isle had said when he had paid one of his visits to his wounded marines. 'It could have been a great campaign, boy!' He had peered round the shell-scarred wardroom which was being used as an additional sick bay, his red face sad and disillusioned. 'It was devised by a genius, but it was left to bloody fools to carry out!'

Perhaps that was a suitable epitaph.

There was a step on the deck beside the bunk, and Chesnaye opened his eyes. For several moments he stared at the soldier who leaned on his stick and peered down at him.

Robert Driscoll took a deep breath and shifted his bandaged leg to a more careful position. Very carefully he said, 'I knew I'd find you if I looked long enough, Dick.'

They watched each other without speaking. Driscoll looked thin and much older, his uniform hanging on him like the rags on a scarecrow. After a while he added, 'We can go and see Helen together now, eh?'

As the hospital ship shortened her cable, Driscoll perched himself on Chesnaye's bunk, and each allowed his thoughts to drift back to the distant Peninsula and all that it would mean to them for as long as they lived.

Driscoll's sudden appearance had brought a faint warmth to Chesnaye's heart, but sadness too with the memory it had conjured up. Again it was of Pickles, when he had come to look for him. 'I knew I'd find you if I ran far enough!' Perhaps he was still up there in the cleft of rock, his eyes wide and empty of pain.

There was the sound of cheering, and Chesnaye roused himself from the drowsiness which always seemed to be ready to close in. With sudden desperation he gasped: 'Help me, Bob! Hold me up!'

His eyes eagerly sought the bottom edge of the big open port as Driscoll's arm lifted his shoulders from the bunk. For a moment he thought the other ship was moving, and then with something like numbness he realised that it was the hospital ship which was gathering way and already gliding towards the end of the anchorage.

He had to blink rapidly to clear his eyes so as not to miss even the smallest detail of that scarred but so familiar shape which passed slowly across his vision.

The high, ugly bridge and tripod mast, the big, ungainly turret, and those splintered decks which had once gleamed so white and new. In his mind's eye he could see the three battle ensigns, and hear the cheering soldiers on the laden troopships.

Driscoll said quietly, 'I've got my binoculars here, Dick?'

Chesnaye struggled upright and shook his head. The *Saracen* was already a world away, but the sudden pain of separation was almost too much. He wanted to find the strength to cheer with the others, but nothing came.

Almost to himself he replied : 'No, I want to see her just as she is. Or perhaps as she was.'

The hospital ship altered course, and the small picture of the blackened listing ship changed to one of the open sea.

Robert Driscoll stood up and glanced down the long lines of silent bunks. Perhaps, he thought, if someone like Chesnaye could feel as he did it had not all been a waste of time.

Limping heavily, he moved across to the open port, feeling as he did so the first easy pitch to the vessel's deck as she met the first swell of the open sea. He leaned out over the crisp water and drew several deep breaths.

He tried to sum it all up with a few thoughts, but he could only think of it as a farewell to something lost. The brooding shape of Achi Baba, the trenches and the wire. The true comradeship of fear and pride, the dirt and the ignorance of what lay in store.

He turned his back on the sea and looked towards Chesnaye's white face, and wondered.

I

The Captain

April in the Mediterranean, the month when Malta should have been at its best, with the night air cool and clear after the heat of the day. But this was April 1941, and the unusually low clouds which hung above the battered island and hid the stars were slashed and torn in a mad galaxy of colours as the nightly air raid got under way and mounted in steady force.

Occasionally above the crash of anti-aircraft fire and the rumble of collapsing buildings could be heard the steady, unbroken beat of aircraft engines. Dozens or hundreds, it was difficult to assess. The sound was without break, without change. It was a constant threat, a mockery against the blind barrage which seemed to rip the night apart.

From the naval anchorage the long streams of gay tracers crept away into the sky, whilst from inland the heavier guns hurled their shells to explode beyond the clouds so that their underbellies seemed to be alight.

Streets which had been clear and busy during the sunlight had become narrow valleys between walls of rubble and scorched timber, beneath which men and women cowered and waited, whilst in the chaos around them the despairing troops and workers searched out the feeble cries and felt for the imprisoned hands.

It was like a mad storm of forked lightning, every night a repetition, but for the fact that each one was just a little worse than the one which had preceded it.

The Night Operations Officer in one of the many naval underground strongpoints gritted his teeth as a fresh, muffled rumble made the naked light bulb dance on its flex and brought down another layer of dust to join that which already covered filing cabinets, desks and occupants in a grey film. The tarnished lace on his jacket proclaimed him to be a lieutenant-commander, but his tired and strained face, which twisted with each distant explosion, seemed too old for his rank.

Through a massive door he could hear the constant jingle of telephones and the clatter of a teleprinter. Signals, demands, orders and chaos. It never let up. His eye fell on a week-old paper from England. The headline referred proudly to Malta as 'the gallant island fortress'. 'The thorn in Italy's soft underbelly!' Another roar, and the lights flickered momentarily.

A petty officer crunched through the dust and placed a chipped cup and saucer on the officer's desk. 'Char, sir.' He glanced incuriously at the flaking walls and said, 'Good thing we're down here, sir?'

The Operations Officer picked up the cup and watched the tea's surface quivering in his hand. Bitterly he replied : 'Built by galley slaves hundreds of years ago. *They* at least had the right idea!'

A rating poked his head round the door. 'Stick of bombs across Parlatoria Wharf, sir.'

The officer looked at the floor. 'Again? I hope to God the destroyers there are all right.' Almost viciously he added, 'Let me know more as soon as you can !'

The petty officer walked to the operations board which covered one of the walls and ran his finger down the pencilled list of ships' names. 'With raids day *and* night it'll be hard for the ships to take on fuel, sir.'

'Unless we get some help and some fighter planes there won't be any damned fuel ! What the hell do they expect of us?' He glared at the man's worn features. 'Do they want us to go and fight them with pikes or something?' He broke off as the other door opened slightly. 'What th' hell d'you want?'

The petty officer stiffened and cleared his throat noisily, his eyes taking in the shadowy shape of the newcomer with both experience and immediate caution. He had seen the feeble light from the corridor shine briefly on the four gold stripes, and he tried to cover his superior's surprise by saying hastily, 'Can I get *you* a cup of tea, sir?'

Captain Richard Chesnaye limped into the centre of the room so that the naked bulb shone directly above his head and made his dark hair appear glossy and fresh, although in fact he had not slept for two days. He sat down in a vacant chair and looked calmly at the other officer's dazed face. He said : 'My name is Chesnaye. I believe I was expected yesterday, but the convoy was attacked.' He saw the man jump as the floor quivered to another explosion. 'So if possible I should like to join my ship at once.'

The Operations Officer passed his hand across his face and turned wearily to his desk. He forced himself to leaf through a pile of papers while he reassembled his thoughts. A year ago, perhaps even a month, and he would have jumped with horror at the thought of being caught off guard by a full captain. Now it did not seem to matter. The whole world was falling around them. It was just a matter of time. The enemy bombers which were destroying Malta and preventing sleep, or even rest, were flying from a mere fifty miles away. How could an island right on the enemy's door-step, with a mere handful of clapped-out fighters, expect to survive?

He glanced quickly across his desk at the newcomer. He noticed that one of the gold stripes was brighter than the other three and that he was wearing several decorations which he could not recognise in the poor light. His mind began to recover. This captain was yet another sign of what was happening to the country and the Royal Navy.

With Britain standing alone against the combined weight of Germany and Italy every experienced officer was seemingly being promoted overnight. At the other end of the scale even yachtsmen with brief weekend sailing their only background had been pitchforked into the battle as temporary Reserve Officers. There was no time for training now, and few with experience to pave the way. Yet from the look of this stranger's newly added gold stripe he guessed he had only just been promoted, and that pointed clearly enough to the fact that he was yet another officer who had been 'beached' between the wars and so lost way in the struggle for advancement and promotion. He noticed, too, the small tense lines at the corners of the captain's mouth. As if he was forcing himself to appear calm with constant effort. He had a grave, intelligent face, and his figure was slim, even youthful. And yet . . . he shook his head and tried to clear his starved mind. A month ago he would have had every appointment and fact at his fingertips. He groped through the pile of papers. 'Which ship, sir?'

Richard Chesnaye watched him without expression. He had seen that look on faces enough to know what the man was thinking. 'I am taking command of *Saracen*,' he said.

The Operations Officer sat down heavily and felt his inner resentment change to something like pity. It was slowly coming back to him now. In his mind's eye he could even see the signals which had referred to this man Chesnaye who was coming from England to assume command of the *Saracen*. He had seen the elderly monitor alongside the wharf only that forenoon. She must be over twenty-five years old, he thought. She was something of a joke at the Base, or had been until joking had gone out of fashion. She was an ugly, antiquated-looking ship, her disproportionate shape made even more peculiar by her garish dazzle paint which had been introduced to foil the prowling submarines. As a colleague had remarked at the time, 'Like a poor old spinster in a party frock!'

Her previous captain had just returned to England following a court martial. He had taken the old ship to the North African coast to lend support to the hard-pressed troops who, even now, were falling back across Libya, leaving positions and bases which they had won so bravely months before. The monitor had 'fired short', and several hundred British soldiers had been killed and wounded. On top of that the *Saracen* had run aground and had only been towed clear within minutes of the dive-bombers smelling her out. It might have been better if they had got to her first.

Too lightly he said, 'I expect you know all about her, sir?'

'My first ship.' He repeated the words in his mind. My first ship. What a lot they implied. But no one could understand what they meant to him at that moment.

Chesnaye added half to himself, 'Yes, I know a great deal about her.'

He shifted in his chair as the ache in his thigh returned.

156

A few more hours and he would be aboard. All the waiting and the yearning were nearly over.

What would she be like now? Perhaps like himself. Unsure, even unwanted.

Some of the old anger and defensive bitterness moved within him. Sharply he said, 'I should like to get to her at once.'

The Operations Officer nodded. 'I'll see what I can do. She's out on a buoy at the moment.' He smiled. 'I'm sorry I can't give you the full formality, sir. I expect you're thinking it's rather different from peacetime?' He bit his lip as the words dropped out. That was a stupid thing to say. This captain was like so many others. He must have spent many of the peacetime years lost and miserable without the Service which so unexpectedly had been denied them. He had seen them at Fleet Reviews and Open Days at the dockyards. Eager, keen-eyed, yet so pathetically on the outside.

He saw the shutters drop behind Chesnaye's grey eyes. Hastily he muttered, 'I'll put through a call, provided the line's still in place!'

Chesnaye forced himself to sit back in the chair, to ignore the officer's short, staccato words on the dusty telephone. The man was sorry for him, and confused too. It no longer mattered. It had hurt at first, but not any more. As if to reassure himself he touched the lace on his sleeve, and felt the excitement welling inside him.

The other officer dropped the telephone and looked uneasy. 'No boats running tonight, sir. Very heavy raid up top. It gets worse all the time.' As if to make the unwanted conversation last he added : 'They fly over in daylight and machine-gun the place too. St. Paul's Bay, the outlying villages, everywhere!'

'When can I get across, then?' Unwittingly Chesnaye dropped his guard and leaned forward.

'First light, sir.' He glanced at the petty officer. 'We could give you a bunk here if you'd prefer not to go over to the quarters? It's not much, but'll be on hand.' He dropped his eyes as Chesnaye's face flooded with obvious relief.

'Thank you. I'd like that.' Chesnaye stood up and grimaced.

The petty officer held open the door and reached for a torch. 'Hurt your leg, sir?'

Chesnaye paused in the doorway and regarded him slowly. 'A long time ago. But it helps to keep my memory intact!'

The door closed behind him and the Operations Officer stretched his arms above his head.

A rating called urgently, 'Number Seven fuel tank ablaze, sir!'

The officer shook himself. 'Bloody hell!' He reached for his telephone.

. . . . . .

Lieutenant-Commander John Erskine, the *Saracen's* First Lieutenant, ran his fingers through his long fair hair and sat back in his swivel chair. His tiny office was lined with shelves loaded with ledgers and files, and the hanging deck covered with signals awaiting his attention. It was early morning, and the sun which filtered through the one thick scuttle was as yet without warmth. Erksine had breakfasted alone in the still deserted wardroom which smelled of drink and tobacco from the previous night. He had persuaded himself that he wanted an early start to allow himself time to clear the mounting pile of paperwork, although he knew well enough that the real reason was quite different.

The other officers would be watching him, gauging his mood and reactions to the events which had so suddenly changed his small world. He was twenty-eight years old, with a clear-cut open face entirely devoid of pretension, but at this moment was filled with gloom. He had been in the old monitor for nine months, almost since the day Italy had cast caution to the wind and joined with Germany in a combined attack on Britain. During that time he had watched the change creep over the ships and men of the Mediterranean Fleet, once the most efficient and powerful force of its kind in the world, but now stretched to and beyond the limit even of safety. It had all been so clear cut at first. In peacetime they had exercised with extravagant enthusiasm under every condition conceived by an over-

158

confident Admiralty. Always with the knowledge that the other great navy, the French, was ready to close any gaps and make the Mediterranean the one sure buffer below Europe's long coastline.

Without apprehension they had watched the rebirth of Germany's sea-power and skill, and with amusement the preparations with which the Italians had followed their partner's every move. It was still hard to fathom what had gone wrong. The swift, lightning war in France, followed by Dunkirk and the complete collapse of England's European allies. Only the Greeks tagged along the end of the line now, and even then they were receiving the first probes from a confident Wehrmacht. In the Mediterranean the Navy had managed to retain its old appearances of calm superiority, up to the last few months, that is. Ships of the Fleet had followed the Army's triumphant advances along the North African coast, where one crushing defeat after another had scattered the Italian troops to the winds and filled the prison compounds to overflowing. Now the tide was turning even there. With Europe safely under lock-and-key and the remains of the British Expeditionary Force flung back across the English Channel, the German Army was able to look around, to estimate the extent of her enemy's remaining positions. Apparently disgusted with Italy's efforts, the Wehrmacht had joined the battle. In spite of the hard-pressed naval patrols, German troops were being ferried across to Africa, and aircraft of every kind were making their appearance in the clear and smiling skies.

In the *Saracen*, too, the new strain had shown itself very clearly. From a new complement of officers the strength had shrunk and changed. New, untrained faces appeared each month. The straight lace of the regulars was replaced by the wavy lace of the R.N.V.R. and the intertwined braid of the R.N.R. Erskine had been irritated by his appointment to such an ancient ship, although it was the rule rather than the exception now. The Mediterranean Fleet, once filled with the cream of the destroyer flotillas and the proudest cruisers, was now supported and reinforced with the strangest collection of craft ever assembled. Ex-China river gunboats, flat-bottomed and unsteady even in a slight breeze, cruised along the African coast and grimly exchanged shots with modern E-boats and screaming dive-bombers. Paddle steamers, once the joy of day-excursionists on their trips from Dover to Calais, swept mines, patrolled the boom-gates and tried to do the hundred and one tasks for which they had never been designed. So the old monitor was just another symbol of events.

Erskine was a calm, capable officer, and despite his lack of outward emotion looked forward to a command of his own. He knew his work in this worn-out old ship would serve him well when that time came. So too his contact with the new Navy, the reservists and the seamen who daily poured out from distant training barracks, would make him more confident when his chance came.

The previous captain had been too old, too long in retirement, for the breathtaking savagery of the Mediterranean war. But what he had lacked in foresight and preparedness he had made up in Erskine's estimation in his dignity and complete courage. He still remembered the look on the old man's face after the court martial. It was the expression of a dead man. In wartime anything could happen. Men died as easily from caution as from eagerness and as quickly from over-confidence as from cowardice.

The fact remained that the ship had disgraced herself, and not only the Captain would take the blame. Once it might have been different, but now with every ship and man stretched to the limit there were no acceptable excuses. Responsibility and personal liability grew as resources shrank, and in the cold, dispassionate arena of the court-martial room who could see beyond the bare facts?

There was a gentle tap at the door, and Erskine looked up to see Lieutenant McGowan, the Gunnery Officer, watching him with his sad, deepset eyes.

'Good morning, sir.' McGowan's voice was formal, but he gave a quick smile as Erskine waved him to a chair. He peered round at the piles of paper. 'What a war!'

Erskine tapped his pencil against his teeth and waited. McGowan was the only other regular officer aboard, apart from a midshipman and a couple of grizzled warrant officers, but apart from that fact he was also a close friend.

McGowan said slowly: 'Bad raid last night. A destroyer over in Sliema copped it, I believe. *And* the ruddy tanker they escorted all the way from Alex!'

Erskine watched the sun's rays strengthening against the sombre grey paint. 'We might get it again before we sail.' He frowned. 'When we've mustered the hands get the cable party to rig a slip wire to the buoy. If pushed we can break the cable and get away in a hurry.'

McGowan showed his teeth in a mock grin. 'Hurry? What, this ship?'

'Now look, James, let's not get started on your pet moan. This is our ship. We must do our best.' He cocked his head to listen to the sluice of water and brooms across the upper deck. 'It'll be Colours in ten minutes, so get cracking!' He forced a smile. 'You are O.O.D., I presume?'

McGowan stood up and reached for his cap. 'I wouldn't have stayed aboard otherwise, my friend! A nice booze-up followed by the exotic charm of a dusky filly, is more the way my mind is going these nights!' He suddenly became serious. 'I just wanted you to know I think it's a bloody shame about your getting saddled with this ship. First the bombardment going wrong, and then the old fool running her on the putty, that was all bad enough. I don't see why you should have to stagnate here when you're a natural for command of a destroyer!'

Erskine dropped his eyes. 'That will do, James.' His voice was flat.

McGowan snorted : 'I suppose the new skipper'll be even worse! One bloody deadbeat after another. Even a good ship couldn't be expected to survive this!'

Erskine looked up his eyes flashing. 'That will do! You know damn' well you shouldn't talk like this, and I won't have it!' He watched the surprise on his friend's face and added quietly : 'I depend on your support. Any sort of talk like that and there's no saying what might spread through the ship.'

McGowan adjusted his cap and said stubbornly, 'I still think it's a shame, even if I'm not allowed to say it!'

Erskine looked back at the signals as a bugle blared overhead. 'Go to hell!'

McGowan grinned wearily. 'Aye, *aye*, sir!'

Erskine threw down his pencil and stood up. As he leaned against the rough metal and idly watched the clear water below the scuttle he listened to the bugle as it sounded for morning Colours. Opposite the monitor's buoy he could see three destroyers and an anti-aircraft cruiser moored together. As he watched he saw their ensigns slowly mounting the staffs, as the *Saracen*'s was doing at that moment above the quarterdeck.

He looked past the other ships towards the unmoving pall of brown smoke which hovered across Valletta. Over there people had died in the twinkling of an eye. Women, children, it made no odds to death's impartiality. But so long as the White Ensign was hoisted every morning there was still a chance, a glimmer of hope. He smiled in spite of his complete weariness. I sound like a bloody politician, he thought.

He turned as a messenger tapped at the door. 'Yes?'

'Signal, sir.' He handed over a sealed envelope with the flimsy sheet of paper. 'And sailing orders, sir.'

Erskine darted a quick look at the man's wooden expression. On the lower deck sailing orders were a constant topic of conjecture. But today this rating had placed the signal in priority. It was unnatural. 'What does the signal say, Bunts?'

The man grimaced. 'New captain is comin' aboard in ten minutes, sir!'

Erskine stared at him, his normal reserve momentarily forgotten. 'What?'

'In fact, sir, there's a launch waitin' at the jetty *now*.' He spoke with the satisfaction of a man who has seen a superior caught off guard.

Erskine snatched his cap and jammed it on his head. One damned thing after another, he thought bitterly. McGowan was probably right. Troubles had a habit of breeding very rapidly.

'My compliments to the O.O.D. Tell him I require his presence on the quarterdeck immediately!' He took a last glance at the disordered office, his mouth curving with sudden resentment. 'And pass the word for the Chief Bosun's Mate.'

The man hurried away, and Erskine followed him more slowly. Of course, it would have to be like this. Night liberty-men not yet returned, the ship a shambles from the night's air raid and the Duty Watch only just recovering from a hurried breakfast.

On the broad quarterdeck he felt the first promise of the day's warmth, and unconsciously he ran his finger round the inside of his collar.

Chief Petty Officer Craig, a massive, wintry-eyed pensioner, saluted and tucked his list of working-parties beneath his arm. 'You want me, sir?'

'Yes, Chief Bosun's Mate. The new captain'll be aboard in a few moments.' He saw with faint satisfaction that the tanned face of the Chief Petty officer was unmoved by his terse announcement. 'Fall in the side party and stand by the gangway.' Erskine ran his eye quickly along the hose-littered deck. 'And for God's sake get this potmess cleared up!'

Craig saluted and marched purposefully away, his mouth snapping open and shut like a trap as he called out a string of names.

Gayler, one of the monitor's two midshipmen, saluted and cleared his throat. 'Boat shoving off from the jetty, sir!' He was fresh from Dartmouth and very conscious of himself. 'It looks like a fine day, sir.'

You don't know the half of it, thought Erskine. Aloud he snapped: 'Man the side! Stand by to receive the Captain!'

*   *   *   *   *

The pinnace squeaked gently against the jetty's rubber fenders, and as he looked down the flight of stone steps Chesnaye saw that his personal gear had already been stowed in the boat's cockpit. A seaman stood at the bow and stern, and the coxswain waited loosely beside the brass wheel.

As the boat pitched, a shaft of sunlight glanced off Chesnaye's metal trunk, and just for a brief instant he felt the old emotion touch his eyes. The years seemed to fall away. It could have been Portsmouth harbour with Pickles, a boy like himself, waiting impatiently to take him to the ship. So much had happened, yet so little. It was the same ship. As if she had waited all these years. Unfamiliar in her dazzle paint, but unmistakable. She had lost her tall top-mast, and her maindeck sprouted several Oerlikons and other automatic weapons instead of the old twelve-pounders. Yet she was the same. The ship which had stayed with his thoughts over time itself. Once or twice he had seen her since those terrible days at Gallipoli. At Portsmouth he had once watched her waddling out to sea past the misty outline of the Isle of Wight, and again in Rosyth, paid-off and neglected. She had steamed her way back to the Mediterranean, and on to China. From Hong Kong to Spain to evacuate refugees from the Civil War, and then across the endless water to Ceylon as a training ship for cadets. Back into Reserve again, and then called once more to serve, like himself.

Chesnaye shifted his weight to the other leg and cursed the pain in his thigh. Like his memory of the *Saracen*, the old wound had been his constant companion. He turned his head to look at the other warships moored nearby. Commanded by officers younger and junior to himself, they reminded him again that he had only held one command in his life. That had been a small sloop just after the Great War. A short, uneventful commission to break the endless monotony of shore appointments, junior posts in large ships and the final misery of his discharge from the Service.

Many others had been 'axed' from the reduced Navy, but each case was individual. Some had been grateful, after being entered into the Navy by their parents at the age of twelve, to a service they had always hated. Others had been defiant, unwilling to accept the injustice, and had wasted precious time and money in a flare of effort to prove their worth in other fields. Chicken farms, the Civil Service, even the Church, had received and rejected them. Men like Chesnaye had been too dazed, too shocked, to act foolishly. They readapted themselves more slowly, licked their wounds and tried again.

For nearly ten years he had wandered alone from one country to the next, working without complaint at whatever job took his eye. He had no ties. Both his parents were dead. His father during the final months of that first, far-off war, and his long-suffering mother in the influenza epidemic which followed it. Chesnaye first tried to return to the sea. He joined the Norwegian Antarctic whaling fleet, and for several years worked as a deck officer in the filth and noise of the factory-ship. His old wound reacted sharply, and he moved on to New Zealand, where with his carefully saved capital he bought a half-share in a farm-appliance firm. Business improved, but as world affairs deteriorated, and the clouds gathered above Munich, Chesnaye quietly said his goodbyes to his astonished partner and started back for home.

He was constantly dogged by the picture of his father as he had remembered him before the first war. He was determined that he would never lose his pride and suffer the final misery of complete rejection by the Service he had always loved. Chesnaye had never forgotten the Navy. He did not have to buy a bungalow in Southsea, to walk the promenade and watch the distant grey shapes slipping down-channel, and to stand moist-eyed at the sound of a barracks' bugle. The Service was part of him. It never left him, no matter what he attempted. And to symbolise that trust and understanding the memory of the ugly monitor had acted as a prop. He knew, too, that unlike his father, he would accept the position of Officer of the Watch on Southend pier if necessary; but he had accepted the post of Training Commander in one of the new intake establishments with equal calmness. It was a start.

But the waiting had been harder than he had anticipated. The first excitement of training and guiding the endless procession of civilian sailors—office boys, labourers, milkmen and others—wore off as he again felt the yearning and the want.

He had almost laughed when he had seen the expression on the face of his captain when that gentleman had told him of his new appointment. The old man had been apologetic and then angry. 'An old ship like that indeed! By God, Richard, you're more use to me here!' He had waved his veined hand across the expanse of the establishment, glittering with painted white stones, flagmast and immaculate sentries. Months before, it had been a holiday camp, but through the old captain's eyes it had shone like a battleship.

Now he was here. The waiting and the suspense forgotten. Like an unwanted burden the years seemed to slide from his shoulders.

A voice interrupted his thoughts. 'I say, any chance of a lift out to the *Saracen*?'

Chesnaye swung round, irritated at being caught dreaming as well as with the casual form of address. He saw a dishevelled officer, whose wide pale eyes were peering at him as if their owner were more used to hiding behind powerful spectacles. On his crumpled sleeve he wore two wavy stripes, between which ran a line of bright scarlet.

Chesnaye nodded. 'Yes, I am going in her direction.'

The officer beamed, his youthful face creasing with pleasure. 'Oh, jolly good!' He held out his hand. 'I'm Wickersley, the *Saracen*'s doctor, actually.' He chuckled disarmingly. 'I suppose I've got a cheek really. A tiny voice of caution warns me that you are *rather* senior!'

Chesnaye felt his taut muscles relaxing. 'Captain Chesnaye.'

'Oh, splendid.' Wickersley looked down at the waiting boat. 'I'm not really genned up on the ranks yet. I've only been in the Andrew a month. I was at St. Matthew's, y'know!' He gestured towards the smoke-covered houses behind him. 'Been over there all night keeping the jolly old hand in!'

They went down the steps, and Chesnaye automatically stepped aside to allow the junior officer to enter the boat first, as was customary.

But the Doctor shook his head cheerfully. 'Oh no, sir! After *you*!'

The coxswain dropped his salute and eyed the interloper balefully. He had expected the grave-eyed captain to blast the Doctor skywards as he bloody well deserved. Instead . . . ah well—he shook his head sadly. It was a different Navy now. 'Shove off, forrard!' he yelled. The little boat swung into the stream and turned towards the mass of shipping.

* * * * *

Spray danced across the pinnace's canopy as it lifted gaily on the sparkling water. Chesnaye staggered and put out his hand to steady himself against the motion. On the long voyage from England he had noticed how unprepared he had become for all the mannerisms and tests of seaboard life. The restless sea, the daily routine, all seemed vaguely strange and unnerving. The convoy had slipped through Gibraltar Straits and had been attacked soon afterwards. Appalled, Chesnaye had watched ship after ship blasted to fragments by the enemy bombers which appeared to fill the sky. The destroyer escort in which he had been a passenger was commanded by an Australian who had done little to hide his irritation at Chesnaye's constant presence on his bridge. Once he had snapped : 'Jesus, Captain, you'll get enough of this later on! Why don't you get your head down?' But Chesnaye had found the Australian accent somehow reassuring, as it reminded him of the life in New Zealand. He wondered how that captain had fared in the night's air raid.

He instantly dismissed the convoy and everything else from his thoughts as he watched the sharpening shape of the monitor. Eagerly, hungrily, his eyes darted up and down her length, as if afraid to miss some scar or mark, as a mother will look at a grown-up son. She was older, but the same. There were streaks of rust around her hawse-pipe and more than one dent along her bulging hull, but nothing that he could not put right.

The Doctor spoke from the cockpit. 'I'd like to ask you aboard for a noggin, but it's a bit early.'

The boat drew nearer, and Chesnaye saw the familiar scurry and frantic preparations which culminated in a rigid knot of figures at the head of the long varnished gangway.

His eyes misted, and over the years he heard Lieutenant Hogarth's high-pitched voice screaming down threats to the flustered Pickles. And later when Pickles had warned him of the Captain. 'He hates everybody, especially midshipmen!'

Is that how they are thinking of me? he wondered.

The boat lost way and idled towards the gangway, the polished boathook poised and ready.

Wickersley called, 'Jolly decent of you to drop me here!'

Chesnaye looked down at him, knowing that he was glad he had had company for those last few agonising yards. 'Actually, I'm coming aboard myself!'

The Doctor's eyes widened. 'Oh?' Then, as the realisation flooded his mind, '*Oh!*'

Chesnaye straightened his back and stepped on to the gangway. He tried not to count the wide, well-worn steps, his mind blank to all else but the whirl of events which had at last overtaken him. His head lifted above the deck, and his brain only half registered the line of tanned faces, the raised hands, and then the shrill twitter of pipes which washed across him like floodwater. A few mumbled words, more salutes, a guard presenting arms and the flash of a sword.

One face seemed to swim out of the mist. A calm, youthful voice said the words he had waited so long to hear.

'Welcome aboard, sir!' He was back.

Out of the Sun

Lieutenant Malcolm Norris, R.N.V.R., walked nervously
to the front of the bridge and stared for several seconds into
the darkness. The four hours of the Middle Watch had all
but dragged to their close, and now that it was almost time
to be relieved the same old feeling of nervous anticipation
was making his heart thump against his ribs.

It was still very dark, with the stars high and bright
against a cloudless sky and reflected in the black oily water
which slopped and gurgled against.the ship's labouring hull
as the monitor plodded slowly towards the invisible horizon.
A steady south-west breeze made the ship rock uncomfortably, so that every piece of metal in the bridge structure
groaned in regular protest, yet its clammy breath brought
no life to the men on watch, but made them move continuously as they peered into the darkness.

Norris cleared his throat and jumped at the noise the
sound brought to the silence around him. He still could not
believe that he was Officer of the Watch, for four hours in
sole charge of the ship and the safety of every man aboard.
For the four months he had been aboard he had been assistant to Lieutenant Fox, the Navigating Officer, and had
shared the Middle Watch without complaint. Fox was a
hard-bitten professional seaman from the Merchant Navy,
who until the outbreak of war had been First Mate of a
banana boat. He was an uncouth, outspoken man who fre-
quently gave vent to criticism of his straight-laced companions and all the Royal Navy stood for. As the months
passed and the ship took on more amateur officers like
Norris, Fox's criticism and complaints gave way to contempt and finally long periods of silence, broken only occasionally by a string of fierce swearing and rage when an
error of seamanship or navigation offended his watchful
attention. If nothing else, Norris conceded, Fox was a first-

rate seaman, and when you shared a watch with him you had nothing to worry about. Norris had been content to dream and dwell in the brave world of his imagination, and carry out the minor jobs of the night's most hated watch.

He realised now only too well that he should have made more use of his time. Overnight everything had altered. The watches had been changed around because Erskine, the senior watchkeeper, had been taken off the rota in order to assist the new captain during his takeover period. In a flash Norris found himself in charge of the watch, and, even worse, had been given Harbridge, the Gunner (T), as his assistant. Harbridge was a squat, vindictive little warrant officer of the old school. He had worked his way slowly and steadily from the spartan misery of an orphans' home to the undreamed power of his one thin stripe of gold lace. The journey had covered many years, through a boys' training ship, destroyers, cruisers, naval barracks and practically every other type of ship or establishment which flew the White Ensign. He had become used and hardened to harsh discipline, and had never expected anything else. Accordingly, he treated his subordinates with the same lack of feeling and understanding, and had never altered his own rigid standards of efficiency.

Norris knew all this about his companion, and had felt the man's bitter resentment the moment he had joined the wardroom. Norris had been a teacher in a London secondary school. Apart from a few evenings a week at lectures given by a fierce-eyed instructor at the local drill-ship, he knew little of the Navy. All he knew was that he loved and admired everything about it. The war had been the one final opening previously denied him. After an uneventful few months aboard an old cruiser which spent most of its time anchored in the Firth of Forth, Norris had been sent to a gunnery course at Whale Island. The shouting, noise and robot-like drill had appealed to him instantly, and although he had finished the course not far from the bottom of the list, the impression of the gunnery school had been marked on his mind like a battle honour. He had gone on leave and revisited the old school. How small and untidy it had seemed after Whale Island. The sticky paper across the windows as a safeguard against bomb-blast, the brown glazed tiles and the rain-dappled playground. Most of the children had been evacuated for the duration, but to the remainder, and the members of the dingy staff-room, Norris had tried to pass on the new-found glory and happiness which he had found in his new life.

When he had been appointed to the monitor Norris had outwardly expressed indignation and dismay. Inwardly, however, he was satisfied. The ship seemed big and safe. There always seemed to be another officer or a competent petty officer close by when a small crisis arose. In a destroyer it might have been different, but as it was Norris found himself in his present position with hardly an idea of how he got there.

Joyce, his wife, had been scornful whenever he had dared to mention his inner doubts to her. 'Don't you let them push you around, Malc!' He hated the way she abbreviated his name, just as he did her sharp South London accent. 'You're as good as they are, and don't you forget it!'

In his mind's eye Norris saw himself sitting in the ward-room as he had so often in the last four months. Outwardly attentive and bright-eyed, he had carefully watched and listened to the men who shared his steel world, and had tried to pick the ones he should follow, even copy, and those he should avoid.

John Erskine was his secret hero. Calm, handsome and so very sure of himself. The senior member of the mess, a Dartmouth officer, all the things which Joyce would have warned him about, yet the very accomplishments which would have made her purr should they have come in her direction. Norris liked the way the ratings respected Erskine yet never took advantage of his casual manner. He saw himself like that. Well, *one* day.

He disliked his immediate superior, the Gunnery Officer. McGowan always seemed to be watching him, just as Fox had once watched him on the bridge. It was more curiosity than concern, he thought, and this irritated him very much. He also avoided Tregarth, the Chief Engineer, and Robbins, his assistant. They were both ex-Merchant Navy like Fox, and kept very much to themselves. He quite liked Wickersley, the Doctor, but the man's cheerful indifference to ceremonial and tradition marked him as a man too dangerous to befriend seriously. The latest example of the Doctor's unreliability had caused a wave of laughter in the wardroom the previous day. He had actually come aboard with the new captain, apparently after cadging a ride in the boat, and even offering the Captain a drink in his own ship!

Harbridge's harsh voice cut into his thoughts. 'Watch yer course, Quartermaster! You're wandering about like a ruptured duck!'

Norris swallowed hard with disgust. He heard Harbridge slam down the mouth of the wheelhouse speaking-tube and stump to the rear of the bridge, the sound of his footsteps sounding like an additional rebuke. Norris knew that he should have checked the compass and warned the helmsman himself. On the other hand, Harbridge might have warned him.

A bosun's mate appeared in the gloom. 'Fifteen minutes to go, sir.'

'Very well. Call the Starboard Watch.' He tried to avoid listening to his own stiff, unnatural voice as he passed his orders. It was like Joyce, he thought. When she spoke to the headmaster, or met some of the awful school governors, Norris could hardly recognise her voice then. At home she changed back again, but in front of what she called 'our sort' she used her mock-B.B.C. accent.

Harbridge said suddenly, 'Bloody helmsman's half asleep again!'

'I shall deal with him later.' Then, in an effort to break the ice, 'Still, he's not been an A.B. long.'

Harbridge sniffed loudly. 'Not the only one either!'

Norris sighed and turned away. The watch was almost done. He had managed it on his own. After this he could meet Harbridge's eyes across the table without embarrassment.

The whirr of a telephone at his elbow made him start violently. He jammed it to his ear, his eyes screwed with concentration. 'Officer of the Watch.' He waited, his heart pounding once more. Probably some fool asking for a time check.

From the other end of the ship came a frantic voice: 'Man overboard, sir! Starboard side, aft!'

The handset dropped from Norris's fingers. For several more seconds he could only stare at the bridge screen, his mind blank, his eyes refusing to recognise even the familiar objects nearby. With each agonising second the monitor's big screws pushed her further and further away from that anonymous man who had brought Norris to the fringe of complete panic.

Harbridge said, 'What's up, then?'

'Man overboard.' Norris answered in a small voice, like a boy replying to his form master. Helplessly he twisted his head to stare at the swaying bridge, the great tower of steel which he suddenly did not know how to control.

'For Christ's sake!' Harbridge almost fell in his eagerness to reach the voice-pipe. 'Stop engines!' Then, as a bosun's mate scurried into view: 'Away seaboat's crew! Man overboard!' He then turned and stared fixedly at Norris's white face. 'You useless bastard!' He was shaking with sudden anger, but from across the darkened bridge Norris had the impression that he was grinning.

.   .   .   .   .   .

Richard Chesnaye rolled on to his side in the narrow bunk and turned his back on the glare from his desk lamp. He tried not to look at his watch, but knew nevertheless that he had been in the tiny sea-cabin for nearly three hours without once closing his eyes. Through the door and beyond the charthouse he could hear the faint shuffling footsteps of the watchkeepers on the upper bridge and the regular creak of the steering mechanism as the Quartermaster endeavoured to keep the slow-moving *Saracen* on her course away from Malta.

Chesnaye had had to force himself to leave the bridge. It had been almost a physical effort, but he knew that when daylight came the ship would still be less than a hundred miles from Malta, well within range of enemy aircraft as well as all the other menaces.

He rubbed his sore eyes and marvelled at the amount of ship's correspondence he had read and absorbed during the night watches. Piece by piece he had built up a picture of the men and equipment which filled the ship like machinery and made it work badly or well. During his one day in Malta he had toured every quarter of the monitor, and made a point of being seen by as many people as possible. He had spoken to all his senior ratings, and some of the new ones as well. Before lunch he had visited the wardroom and had confronted his officers. He was not sure what he had been expecting, but the meeting had left him feeling more than a little uneasy. He had known that the wardroom was comprised mainly of new and untried officers, but there was something more, an air of nervous cynicism, which seemed to border on contempt. Chesnaye did not care what they thought of him. Every captain had to prove himself. But much of their casual attitude seemed directed towards the ship. The respectful but distant interview had been interspersed with 'What does it matter?' and 'What can you expect in a ship like this?' When an air-raid warning had sounded it had come as something like a relief.

Erskine had followed him around the ship, full of information and quick suggestions which he was careful not to offer as advice. Chesnaye would have felt better if Erskine had been more outspoken, even critical, but he was careful not to commit himself. It was well known that any ship could be under a cloud after her captain's court martial, but with Erskine it seemed to go much deeper. The memory of Commander Godden kept returning like an old nightmare, and the way that he had secretly undermined the *Saracen*'s first captain. The monitor no longer even warranted a commander. There was this matter of the sailing orders, for instance. Chesnaye frowned as he remembered Erskine's reactions.

The ship was to proceed to Alexandria, escorted part of the way by one A/S trawler. It was incredible how short of minor war vessels the Fleet had become. In Alexandria she was to take on 'military stores' in accordance with so-and-so signals. When he had questioned Erskine about the stores he had replied with a shrug: 'Oh, we do any old thing! Hump stores, petrol, bully beef, anything the Senior Officer thinks fit!' He had spoken with such fierce bitterness that Chesnaye had looked at him with sudden anger.

'What do you mean by that?'

'Nobody cares about the *Saracen*, sir. She's old, clapped

out, like half the ships we've got here!' He had waved his arm vaguely. 'Now we're putting the Army into Greece to help out there. That'll mean ships to support them, and more work for the rest of us.'

'We shall just have to manage.'

Erskine had given a small smile. 'Yes, sir.'

'You don't like this ship, do you?' Chesnaye had felt the old agitation once more.

'I'm used to it. That's about all. She's slow, out-of-date, badly equipped and manned. Her main armament is so worn out by practice use in peacetime that the barrels are almost smooth-bores! No wonder we dropped shells on those poor pongoes!'

Chesnaye afterwards cursed himself for allowing himself to be drawn. He was tired and worn out after his journey and the excitement of joining the ship. Otherwise he might have been more guarded. 'When I first joined *Saracen* it was an honour to be selected. She was brand-new then, a different kind of weapon. But there were old ships in the Fleet as well, even older than she is now. The job had to be done. *Any* job.' He had regarded the other man coldly. 'And if our orders are to hump stores, then we will be better at it than any *other* ship, d'you understand?'

Erskine had stiffened, his face suddenly a mask. 'I think I do, sir.'

Chesnaye rolled on to his back and stared up at the deckhead. Of course he didn't understand. But I should have told him. *Made* him! A ship was what you made of her. It had always been true. It had not changed.

He thought again of his officers. Very mixed. Two or three strong characters who could make or break any ship. He started once more to mentally sort them into categories. Tregarth was a good man. Not much to say. But in his round Cornish voice, coupled with a hard handshake, he had told Chesnaye that when the time came he could rely on the engine room giving its best.

That's when Fox, the Navigator, had interrupted. 'We've got two speeds here. Dead slow and stop!'

Fox would have to be watched. Independent, and very stubborn. McGowan, the Gunnery Officer, seemed competent enough. A dead pattern of a regular officer. Like a hundred others, he thought. Reliable, but not much imagination. Then there was Norris, the officer on watch on the other side of the door at this moment. He could go either way. If only he could relax and concentrate on his job. Chesnaye had kept away from the bridge during the Middle Watch in order to give Norris a chance to assert himself The watch was quiet enough. It might be of some use.

The junior officers were all R.N.V.R., except Midshipman Gayler and the two warrant officers. They would behave and react according to the example set by their superiors. How *I* behave.

Of course, it was a disappointment to be relegated to a kind of store-ship. There was no hiding the bitterness and hurt he felt in his own heart. But, as Erskine had rightly pointed out, the line would be stretched even thinner, and there was no saying what might happen in the next months, even weeks.

The Fleet had scored a tremendous victory over the Italians off Cape Matapan only a fortnight earlier, when in a brilliant night action they had routed and decimated a force of powerful, modern cruisers without the loss of a single man.

But the land battle was something else. After a breathtaking advance along the North African coast they were now being forced to fall back. It was said that even Tobruk, the one hard-fought port of any true importance, was in danger of being retaken.

The Army, too, had problems, it seemed. With more and more troops and aircraft being withdrawn from the desert to help the beleaguered Greeks, and the Germans arriving daily to support the disgraced Italians, it would get a damned sight worse unless some sort of miracle happened.

Chesnaye thought of his officers' attentive faces and felt vaguely angry. They were amused, even scornful, he thought.

He sat up suddenly and stared round the little cabin. How many captains have sat here wondering about their officers? How many reputations have been formed or lost? Like Royston-Jones planning to hurl his untried ship into a battle already decided, or his most recent predecessor, out of touch but determined, who had ended his command in failure and disgrace.

He felt cold all over, and was conscious of the numbness in his leg. 'Not me,' he whispered. 'Not *me* !'

Outside a telephone buzzed impatiently. He peered at his watch. Ten minutes to eight bells. There was the sound of running feet, muffled shouts and the sudden jangle of engine-room telegraphs. With a shudder the engines' steady vibrations stopped, and as Chesnaye jumped to the deck and tugged on his leather wellingtons his mind began to click into place. He had wondered how he would react when the time came. It had been a long while since he had been tried. But the time was now. Perhaps they had overtaken the little trawler escort in the darkness and were about to run her down. He realised that his breathing was faster and his hand was shaking as he groped urgently for the door.

It was all over in minutes. He was grateful that he had been awake and that the darkness hid the anxiety on his face. He heard himself say : 'Resume course and speed. Secure the seaboat.'

And as Lieutenant Norris started again to stutter what had happened he barked : 'Make a signal to escorting trawler. Tell them to make a sweep astern for the missing man immediately!' Then to the bridge at large, 'Who was he, by the way?'

Harbridge answered. 'O'Leary, sir. One of the boat-lowerers. He was skylarkin' on watch and slipped on the guard-rail !'

'I see.' Chesnaye had a brief picture of a cheerful seaman suddenly thrown into nothingness. From a safe, well-worn deck to a nightmare of black water and cruel stars. 'He should be wearing a lifebelt and safety-light. The trawler might spot him.'

Erskine was suddenly at his side, his face made boyish by his dishevelled hair. 'Are you not waiting, sir ?'

Chesnaye shut out the intruding picture of the terrified drowning seaman, who could probably still see the monitor's fading shape above the water-crests. God ! 'We are not. I will not endanger the ship for one man.' He forced himself to look at Erskine's shocked face. 'I am far more

177

concerned about the apparent lack of control and discipline. I shall want a full report from the Officer of the Watch tomorrow morning.' He turned slightly. 'And, Norris?'

'Sir?' Small voice. Shaken. Unsure.

'Never stop the ship unless absolutely necessary. This area is alive with submarines and heaven knows what else. There are risks and *risks*.'

Harbridge said sullenly, 'Another minute an' I could've had the seaboat lowered, sir !'

'Then you can thank your stars you did not find that minute, Mr. Harbridge. I would have ensured it to be your last order !'

He forced himself to look across the screen as a dark shape with a towering white bow wave steamed down the *Saracen*'s beam. The trawler's signal lamp flashed briefly, and then she was gone. Below his feet Chesnaye felt the deck vibrating again. The monitor stopped her yawing and began to gather way.

Lieutenant McGowan appeared at the bridge ladder. His loud, cutting greeting, 'Morning Watchkeepers greet you all !' faded away as he assessed the grimness of the little group around the Captain.

Chesnaye nodded curtly. 'Carry on !' Then he walked slowly to the sea-cabin and closed the door behind him.

McGowan spread his hands and peered at Norris. 'What happened for God's sake?'

Norris half sobbed : 'Man overboard. The Captain left him to drown !'

Harbridge said, 'I can see we're going to get on fine, I *don't* think !'

The watch changed, and McGowan stood looking at Erskine, who had still not moved. 'Try to keep a sense of proportion, John.' McGowan resisted the temptation to peer astern for the searching trawler. 'It's hard luck, but we'll have to get over it.'

Erskine was staring at the closed door, his fists clenched. 'I've met some in my time. But, by God, this one is a callous bastard !'

Beyond the door the man who had so easily smashed the calm of the Middle Watch sat on the edge of his bunk, his hands clasped across his stomach as he fought back the wave of nausea which threatened to engulf him.

Ten minutes earlier he had been wondering what opportunity would offer itself to enable him to start the new pattern. Now he had made that start, but the cost was tearing him in two.

.   .   .   .   .

Lieutenant Roger Fox stood back from the chart table to allow the Captain more light. He waited in silence as Chesnaye pored over the worn chart and watched as he traced the faint pencilled lines of the ship's course, the neat cross bearings, times and distances which he knew were faultless.

Chesnaye straightened his back and stared thoughtfully across the open bridge to the straight silver line of the horizon. The first morning at sea was clear and bright, and the sun already hot across the steel plating and newly scrubbed gratings. The Forenoon Watch had just taken over, and he saw that Fox still had a trace of egg at the corner of his thin mouth.

'Another six and a half days to Alexandria.' Chesnaye was thinking aloud. He had been unable to sleep, and the hoped-for freshness of the new day still eluded him. 'It's a long way, Pilot.'

'Hmm. Six knots is about the best she can manage nowadays.' Fox shrugged. 'Poor old cow!'

Chesnaye eyed him sharply. 'You've not been used to slow passages?'

The Navigator grinned. 'Hell no, sir. Running fresh fruit to catch the market was a quick man's game!'

Chesnaye walked on to the bridge and immediately felt the sun across his shoulders. A round-faced sub-lieutenant was standing in the front of the bridge, his glasses trained straight across the bows. Chesnaye knew from the young man's stiff and alert stance that he was only bluffing and was very conscious of his captain's presence.

'Good morning, Sub. You are Bouverie, I take it?'

The officer lowered his glasses and saluted. 'Yes, sir.'

Chesnaye saw that upon closer inspection he was older than he had first appeared. That was the trouble with these

Reserve officers. You could never judge age by rank. Bouverie's boyish features were only a first impression. His eyes, squinting against the reflected glare, were steady and shrewd. His voice, too, was controlled and almost offhand.

Bouverie reported as an afterthought, 'Course oh-nine-five, sir.'

'Quite so.'

Chesnaye stepped on to the gratings and peered across the screen. On the port bow he could see the small trawler pushing through the flat water without effort, her spindly funnel trailing a fine wisp of greasy smoke.

Bouverie said quietly, 'They picked up the body of our chap, sir.'

Chesnaye stiffened. He had already been told about the dead seaman, but he was conscious of the casual way Bouverie was introducing the subject.

'Yes, I know.'

'No lifebelt, sir.' A small pause. 'Hell of a way to die.'

'It always is.'

Chesnaye walked to the tall wooden chair in the corner of the bridge. Ignoring Bouverie's curious glance, he ran his hand across the well-worn arms, remembering in an instant the small hunched figure of Royston-Jones with his cap tilted across his birdlike face. The same chair. Like the small sea-cabin, a place for thought and contemplation.

'I gather this is your first ship, sir?' Bouverie spoke respectfully, but as if expecting an answer.

Chesnaye ignored the question. 'How long have you been in the Service, Sub?'

'One year, almost to a day, sir.'

'And before that?'

'I am a barrister, sir.'

Chesnaye smiled to himself. Am a barrister, he thought. Not *was*. That accounted for much in the man's apparent ease and confidence. In the old Navy it had been so simple to get a man's measure. Rank and family background had usually sufficed to weigh a man's worth and prophesy his future. Provided there were no unfortunate interruptions, he added grimly.

'Do you like this life?'

Bouverie looked at him with open surprise. 'I really

hadn't thought, sir. But it is better than the Army, I suppose.'

Chesnaye sat down in the chair and took a deep breath. No, you could never tell from first appearances any more.

'Aircraft bearing Red one-one-oh! Angle of sight two-oh!'

Chesnaye swivelled in his chair as Fox bounded across the bridge and stabbed at the red button below the screen. The gurgling scream of klaxons echoed below decks, followed immediately by the rush of feet as the men poured through hatches into the sunlight. Chesnaye had to grip the arms of the chair to control the rising edge of excitement which was making his heart pound so painfully. He knew it had to come, but out here in the bright sunlight and placid sea it did not seem right or even real.

He lifted his glasses and moved them slowly across the port quarter. Once as he searched for the intruders his glasses moved across the *Saracen* herself, so that some of his men's faces sprang into gigantic focus, distorted and inhuman. He saw too the slim barrels of the Oerlikons already probing skywards and the short stubby ones of the two-pounder pompoms as the gunners whipped off the canvas screens.

Then he saw them. Tiny silver specks, apparently unmoving, like fragments of ice above the glittering water.

He heard Fox say, 'Ship at Action Stations, sir!'

'Very good, Pilot. Increase to maximum revolutions.'

The Yeoman of Signals, a bearded Scot named Laidlaw, peered round the steel lockers at the rear of the bridge. 'Escort requests instructions, sir?'

'Take up station in line ahead.'

He half listened to the clatter of the lamp as the signal flashed across the calm sea. There was no point in the trawler being impeded by the slower monitor. The enemy would be after the *Saracen*. The trawler could wait.

The mounting revolutions transmitted themselves through the tall chair, so that he imagined the ship was shivering. As he was doing. The sudden stark prospect of losing the *Saracen* had momentarily pushed everything else from his racing thoughts.

'Six aircraft, sir! Dive-bombers!'

Chesnaye gritted his teeth and turned to watch McGowan, who with handset in fist was watching the aircraft through his glasses. His voice was sharp, edgy. 'Stand by . . . short-range weapons!' He looked across at Chesnaye, but did not seem to see him. In his mind's eye he would be seeing his plan of anti-aircraft guns throughout the ship, each unit an individual weapon, every crew dependent upon its own ability and experience. In their huge turret the two big fifteen-inch guns still pointed imperiously across the blunt bows. They had no part in this type of warfare, and their size seemed to emphasise the ship's unnatural element.

Chesnaye watched the six small aircraft climbing higher and higher, their shapes drawing apart in the lenses of his glasses as they turned in a wide half-circle and swam across the pale blue sky. Higher and higher, and faster as they flashed along the monitor's beam. Well out of effective range. Marking their target. Drawing ahead, until in a moment of near panic Chesnaye imagined they were going for the trawler, after all. He blinked as the sunlight lanced down the glasses and made his eyes stream. Of course, they were getting the sun behind them to blind the gunners. Also, most of the monitor's A.A. guns were abaft the beam, they were taking the minimum risks.

'They're turning, sir!' A nearby bridge lookout was shouting at the top of his voice, although Chesnaye was almost touching him.

Chesnaye said sharply, 'Open fire when your guns bear!'

The first aircraft began to dive. Silhouetted against the sun like a black crucifix, it plunged steeply towards the labouring monitor. It seemed to be flying straight down the forestay, as if drawn inevitably to the bridge itself.

Again Chesnaye heard the unearthly scream as the bat-shaped bomber hurled itself into its dive. The sound he had heard in that Malta convoy. A prelude to death and destruction. But this time it was his ship. They were after Saracen!

In sudden anger he barked, 'Starboard twenty!'

Shaking at her full speed of seven knots, the monitor wheeled heavily in obedience to the repeated order. The ship's port side swung to face the screaming bomber, and in those frantic seconds opened up with everything she had. The bridge structure shook and vibrated as pompoms and Oerlikons and then the long four-inch guns joined in frantic chorus. All at once the narrowing distance between ship and bomber became pitted with brown shell-bursts, the empty sky savagely crossed with gay tracers.

Chesnaye forced himself to watch as the big bomb detached itself from the aircraft which now seemed to fill the sky itself.

He did not even recognise his own voice any more. 'Midships!'

The bomb seemed to be falling very slowly, so that he had time to notice that the small trawler had joined in the fray, her puny guns lost in the roar of the *Saracen*'s own defences.

The dive-bomber, having released its load, pulled out of its nerve-tearing plunge, the scream changing to a throbbing roar as the pilot pulled his plane out and over the swinging ship. For another moment Chesnaye saw the spread of wings, the black crosses, even the leather-helmeted head of a man who was trying to kill him.

The tracers whipped across the trailing wings, but the bomber was past and already turning away.

The monitor shuddered, and a few shreds of salt spray dropped into the bridge. Chesnaye swallowed hard, his mouth dry. The bomb had missed, he had not even heard it explode.

'Here comes the next one!'

Again the inferno of gunfire and savage bursts, the scream of that merciless siren, and then the roar of the bomb. Another miss. Chesnaye found that he was getting angrier with each attack.

'The bombers are splitting up, sir!' Bouverie sounded steady but different from the young man of ten minutes earlier.

'Three aside.' Chesnaye watched them with hatred. 'I am going to swing the ship . . . now!' In the same breath he barked. 'Hard a-port!'

Leaning heavily the old ship began to pivot, the distant trawler swinging across the bows as if airborne. Instead of a semi-defenceless wedge, the diving pilots saw the length-

183

ening shape of the *Saracen* swinging across their paths. As they dived she continued to swing, a wild surging froth beneath her fat stern as one engine was flung full astern to bring her about. Too late the airmen realised that their ponderous adversary was not just turning to avoid the next bomb. Before, she had side-stepped each attack and hit back as best she could. The airmen had split up to take care of this irritating manœuvre. One section to make the ship turn, the second section to catch her out. But this time the ship did not steady on course. With her protesting engines and rudder threatening to tear theselves adrift, and aided by her shallow draught, the *Saracen* curtsied round until every gun in the ship was brought to bear.

The first bomber staggered and fell sideways, its grace lost in an instant. Trailing black smoke, it dived over the heeling bridge and ricocheted across the water in a trail of fiery fragments. The leader of the second attack pressed on and down, he was committed, he could not reverse *his* engine. The tracers knitted and joined in a vortex of fire, so that the forepart of the aircraft seemed to disintegrate even as it plunged towards its target. With one blinding flash it vanished, while the clear water below was pockmarked with falling wreckage.

One bomb fell almost alongside the ship's anti-torpedo bulge, a shattering detonation which would have stove in the hull of a light cruiser with little effort. *Saracen* shook herself and steamed unscathed through the falling spray, her guns still chattering defiance.

Then the sky was empty. As suddenly as they had arrived the survivors of the would-be assassins planed towards the horizon, their engines fading and futile.

'Bring her round on course, Pilot!' Chesnaye kept his face towards the sea. 'Resume cruising speed, and fall out Action Stations.'

Fox's voice was husky. 'Aye, aye, sir!'

Chesnaye rubbed his palm along the screen. She had done it! Together they had shown them all, doubters and bloody Germans alike!

Erskine appeared at his elbow. His face was streaked with smoke from the guns he had been directing from aft. 'No damage or casualties, sir.'

184

'Good.' Chesnaye turned to see the watchful surprise on Erskine's features. 'I thought the port Oerlikons were a little slow in coming to grips. Have a word with Guns about it, will you?'

'I will, sir.' Erskine seemed at a loss for words.

Chesnaye rubbed his hands. Two bombers shot down. Not bad.

Below on the signal bridge he heard an anonymous voice say : 'Handled the old cow like a bleedin' destroyer! I thought we'd bloody well 'ad it!'

Another voice, loud with obvious relief : 'What's the use, Ginger? No bastard'll ever believe you when you tell 'em!'

Chesnaye smiled. His body felt weak and shaking, and he could taste the nearness of vomit at the back of his throat. But he smiled.

Fox stepped back from the voice-pipe and watched him narrowly. The other officers had been quick to voice their opinions of the new captain, but he had been slower to make up his mind. He had served with too many eccentric or difficult skippers to do otherwise. This one was in a class apart, he thought. He actually *believed* in this ship. Whereas for some of the others she was a penance or a stepping-stone for something better, for Richard Chesnaye it was the ultimate reward. It was incredible, slightly unnerving. But as he watched Chesnaye's hand moving almost lovingly along the bridge screen, Fox knew he was right.

.   .   .   .   .

John Erskine pushed the pile of opened letters away from him across the wardroom table and groped for a cigarette from the tin at his elbow. It was empty. He gave an exasperated sigh and looked over at Wickersley, who was apparently engrossed in one of the letters.

'Cigarette, Doc? My duty-frees have run out.'

Wickersley pushed an unopened tin towards him without taking his eyes from the letter. Eventually he said, 'Bloody amazing some of the things our people write to their wives.'

Erskine blew out a stream of smoke. 'You're supposed to be censoring those things, Doc. Not bloody well passing judgement!'

Wickersley looked up and grinned. 'All the same, they do make me feel as if I've been living a very sheltered life!'

Somewhere beyond the wardroom a tannoy speaker crackled. 'All the Starboard Watch! Starboard Watch to Defence Stations!'

Erskine glanced at the salt-streaked scuttle. Eight bells, evening drawing in, but still clear and bright. The horizon line mounted the scuttle, hovered motionless, and then receded with timeless conformity. The Port Watch would be coming from their stations to face greasy plates of bangers and beans, washed down with unspeakably sweetened tea. If they were very lucky the duty cooks would have skimmed the cockroaches off the surface beforehand.

In one corner of the wardroom Harbridge and Joslin, the Gunner, dozed in chairs like two Toby jugs, while at a writing desk Sub-Lieutenant Philpott, the Paymaster, was busy writing to his parents.

'How are you getting on with the Old Man?' Wickersley stamped the letter and reached for the cigarette tin.

'All right.' Erskine spoke guardedly. 'Why?'

'Oh, just wondered.' The Doctor waved the smoke away from his face. 'Seems quite a chap to me!'

Quite a chap. Erskine wondered how the Captain really did appear to one as uninvolved as the Doctor. 'Yes. But I don't feel I have his measure as yet.'

'He's got a lot on his mind.'

Haven't we all? Erskine thought of the three days which had dragged remorselessly after the monitor's wake. Two more bombing attacks. Constant vigilance, with the hands almost asleep at their posts. The ship's company was working watch and watch. Four hours on, and four off, not allowing for the constant calls to Action Stations and the normal work which had to be carried out no matter what happened. Painting, scraping, repairs and endless maintenance, with tempers and nerves becoming frayed and torn with each turn of the screws. All the time the Captain seemed to be watching him. He never actually complained about the way Erskine was running the ship, but a hint here, a suggestion there, made him wonder just what standard Chesnaye had in mind. He seemed to make no allowance for the ship's tiredness, her unsuitability, and the general pressures which were wearing down the whole Fleet, let alone this one old ship.

Wickersley was watching him. 'His leg seems to bother him. I might ask if I can have a look at it some time.'

Erskine smiled in spite of his preoccupied thoughts. 'You do that. He'll have you for breakfast!'

'He got it in the First World War, I gather. Odd really.'

'What is? Quite a few blokes got cut up then!'

'No, I mean it's strange the way he looks.' He eyed Erskine musingly. 'He's over ten years older than you, yet you look about the same age. Don't you think that's odd?'

Erskine laughed. 'It's a bloody wonder I don't look like his father, the things which I've got on *my* mind!'

Ballard, the senior steward, emerged from the pantry. 'We'd like to lay the table for dinner now, sir?' He eyed the letters bleakly. 'Er, could you . . .?'

Erskine nodded. 'I'll move.' He looked at his watch. 'I've lost my appetite.'

Wickersley rubbed his hands as some more figures drifted wearily into the wardroom. 'I think a noggin is indicated.'

Erskine shook his head. 'I never drink at sea, Doc.'

'Your loss, my friend!' Wickersley waved to a steward. 'Large pink Plymouth!' He beamed at Lieutenant Norris, who had just slumped down in one of the battered arm-chairs. 'What about you, old sport?'

Norris looked pasty-faced and crumpled from sleep. 'A large one, please.'

Erskine paused and looked down at him. 'Watch it, Malcolm,' he said quietly. 'You've got another Middle Watch in four hours.'

Norris flushed. 'I can manage, thank you.'

Erskine shrugged and walked to the scuttle. The sea was getting furrowed with deep shadows, and the sky lost its warmth. Three more days and they would be back in Alexandria. Then what? A place full of bustling activity alongside fear and indecision. Orders would be waiting for them, and then they would be off to sea once more.

And somewhere in the middle of all this there was Ann. Even now she might be in her tiny apartment above the harbour, watching the ships, and waiting for him. Or helping at the hospital. She might even be laughing over a drink with some other naval officer.

Ann Curzon, tall, slim, so completely desirable. Erskine remembered vividly that first night when they had had a little too much to drink, and they had made love with such fierceness in that same apartment.

Yet he knew so little about her, or what had made her leave England to join this mad world of uncertainty and chaos. She was only twenty-three, yet in so many ways seemed more mature than he. She always appeared to be laughing at him, thrusting away his caution and reserve with her own happiness. Yet he had the deeper feeling that she could be easily hurt.

How had it all started? He thought of her wide, clear eyes, and the way her short, sun-bleached hair tossed when she laughed at something he said. Now he would have to choose. Perhaps it would be easier than he imagined. He pressed his head against the cool glass to compose himself. The radio began to blare with another sentimental song. Vera Lynn. 'There'll be bluebirds over the white cliffs of Dover . . .' Somebody started to whistle. The clink of glasses. Small talk and age-worn jokes while the officers waited for dinner. Without looking round, Erskine knew what was happening. The exact picture, the exact moment.

The long tablecloth, now soiled and stained, the worn chairs, and the much-used wardroom silver. The officers sitting and standing around, legs straddled to the gentle heave of the deck, the eyes swinging occasionally to the pantry hatch. As if they did not know what was coming. As if some superb meal was to be expected, instead of tinned sausages and dehydrated potatoes.

He toyed with the idea of going to the bridge, and imagined Chesnaye sitting in the tall chair, his face in shadow. It was a strong face, he thought. But it was almost impossible to tell what he was thinking. Like Fox, Erskine was used to conforming to the ways of various captains. To all their little mannerisms and foibles. But Chesnaye gave away nothing. He seemed completely controlled, impassive. And yet there was so much more to him than Erskine could understand.

The way he handled the ship, for instance. Calmly

enough, and yet with a quiet desperation, as if he were afraid he was going to fail in some way. When the ship had left harbour Chesnaye had watched every detail, from the very moment the hands had been called for getting under way, from the second the slip-wire had been let go. He seemed to nurse the ship, as if at the slightest display of temperament from the old monitor he would feel that he and not this twenty-five-year-old relic had made a mistake.

At first Erskine had assumed it was because Chesnaye was unsure of his own ability after his enforced absence from active duty. After what he had seen when the bombers had made their attacks he knew differently. Even from aft he had seen the effort and cunning Chesnaye had used to elude the ruthless Stukas. Astern the ship's wake had curved and waved, and the deck beneath his feet had seemed to buck as the engines had been put this way and then that.

He shook his head. It can't go on. It can't last. Sooner or later Chesnaye was going to discover that he and the ship were only essential because of a general shortage. If he puts a foot wrong he'll be finished for good, he thought.

He looked again at the sea. Whatever else happens, I must not get involved again. He spoke the words inwardly like a prayer. Sentiment is one thing, but if I give way now I will never get another chance. He thought again of Chesnaye's face that first day when he had assumed command. Desperate, hungry, even grateful. *I* could be like him, he thought. When this war's over they'll soon forget. There'll be plenty of Chesnayes again. Thrown out, unwanted.

Ballard coughed at his elbow. 'Permission to lower dead-light, sir? We'd better darken the wardroom before we start dinner.'

Erskine turned away from the circle of sea and sky without comment. Yes, he thought savagely, let us get on with the game. Calm and cool. Cheerful and offhand about everything. Who the bloody hell are we fooling!

3

Face from the Past

John Erskine held up his hand to shield his eyes from the light which seemed to be burning into his brain. One moment he had been deep in an exhausted sleep, and the next he was struggling in his bunk, his body still shaking from the messenger's violent tugging.

'What is it, man?' Erskine peered beyond the torch at the seaman's shadowy shape. His brain still rebelled, and every muscle called out to him to fall back on the bunk. He was still partly under the impression that he was dreaming. His mind cleared with startling suddenness as he realised that the reassuring beat of the ship's full power was muted and feeble.

'Captain's compliments, sir. 'E wants you on the bridge at once.'

Erskine fell out of his bunk and switched on the small table lamp. No wonder he was tired. He had only been off his feet for a few hours. The Morning Watch had not even been called yet.

Being careful to keep his voice normal, he asked, 'What's happening up top?'

The seaman was looking round the cramped and untidy cabin with open interest. Perhaps he had expected something better for the ship's second-in-command. 'Stopped the port engine, sir. Trouble in the shaft, I think.'

Erskine's mind began to work again. That's all we need, he thought. One bloody engine. 'Tell the Captain I'm on my way.'

He followed the man briskly on to the upper deck, blinking his eyes in the deep darkness. By the time he had climbed to the upper bridge, past the dozing gunners and peering lookouts, his mind had been further cleared by the crisp night air, and only the soreness of his eyes and the kiln-dryness in his throat reminded him of his complete fatigue. He groped his way to the forepart of the bridge, where he could just discern the Captain's tall figure against the screen.

'Good morning, John.' Chesnaye's voice was calm enough, but more abrupt than usual. 'Bit of bother in the engine room.'

'Bad, sir?' Erskine tried to gauge Chesnaye's mood.

'More of a nuisance really. The Chief has been up to tell me that a bearing is running hot. Might be a blocked pipe.' He laughed shortly. 'He was very insistent that I stop that screw to give his men a chance to look round.' He added bitterly : 'It's an after bearing. A bit tricky to get at. Still, it might have been worse, I suppose.'

Erskine nodded. If they didn't stop the shaft it might seize up completely for lack of oil. There could be no dodging the bombers with only one screw, he thought. His tiredness made him suddenly angry and despairing. All Chesnaye's desperate manœuvring had done this. If only this was a thirty-knot destroyer, he thought. One screw or two, you always had a few thousand horsepower up your sleeve then !

He said, 'Shall I call the men to quarters, sir?'

'No, let half of 'em get their sleep. They need it.'

Chesnaye had spoken unconsciously, but his words brought the sudden realisation to Erskine that the Captain had been on the bridge almost continuously since the ship and slipped her buoy in Malta.

Erskine asked : 'Can I relieve you for a bit, sir? The ship'll hardly make headway in this sea.'

'I'm all right. I just wanted to put you in the picture.'

Erskine leaned against the cool plates and looked at the black sea. 'Very quiet, sir.' A slight breeze fanned his face and rattled the signal halyards overhead.

Chesnaye grunted. His arm moved like a dark shadow towards the starboard beam. 'Tobruk's over there. Less than a hundred miles away. I wonder how the Army are managing?'

Erskine stared at him. The Captain was concerned about his ship, yet he found time to worry about the nameless men in the desert. The ship trembled beneath his shoes, and he felt thankful that he were here and not lying out on the sand and rocks, waiting for the dawn to uncover the advancing enemy.

'You're not married, are you, John?'

The question was so sudden that Erskine was momentarily confused.

'No, sir. That is, not yet.'

'Thought about it?'

Erskine had a fleeting picture of Ann's face and felt even more unsure of himself. 'Not really, sir. In wartime it's hard to make such a decision.'

Chesnaye was tapping the stem of his unlit pipe against his teeth, and might have been studying him but for the darkness. 'You don't want to think like that, John.' Then with unexpected vehemence, 'No, it's a chance that does not come very often.'

There was a metallic clatter from aft, and Erskine heard Chesnaye curse under his breath.

Somewhere in the darkness Harbridge, the Gunner (T), said stiffly, 'The stokers are 'avin' a go, sir!'

'Bloody row!' Chesnaye took off his cap and ran his fingers across his hair.

'It's a big job. But Tregarth will be as quick as he can. He's a good Chief, sir.' Erskine waited for Chesnaye to answer and added: 'To go back to what we were saying, sir. About marriage. I was wondering why you haven't done so if what you say . . .' He faltered as Chesnaye took a step towards him.

'Let us keep our minds on the job in hand, eh?' Chesnaye's tone was cold, like a slap in the face. 'I suggest you take a turn around the decks to see that the men are aware of what is happening. We still have the A/S trawler with us, but I want a good lookout kept!'

Erskine stepped back, stifling his resentment and his surprise. 'Aye, aye, sir.'

As Erskine walked past the tall, warm shape of the funnel where the Morning Watch was being mustered, he bumped into the lanky figure of McGowan.

' 'Morning, John, is all well in the world?'

Erskine bit back the angry words which seemed to be bursting from his lips and replied shortly: 'Bit of a flap on.

Nothing the Captain can't handle, apparently.'

McGowan watched him go and wondered. He heard his petty officer say throatily : 'Two volunteers for a nice cushy job ! 'Oo are they ter be, then ?'

Two voices called assent from the anonymous swaying ranks of duffel-coated seamen.

'Right,' said the P.O. 'Bates an' Maddison. Get aft an' clear the blockage in the officers' 'eads.'

The men groaned, while their comrades sniggered with unsympathetic delight.

McGowan said severely, 'Now is that the way to get volunteers, P.O. ?'

The hardened regular rubbed his hands and grinned. 'A volunteer is a bloke wot's misunderstood the question, sir. Either that or 'e's as green as grass. But the officers' 'eads 'ave got to be cleaned afore you gentlemen gets up in the mornin' !'

'Er, quite. Carry on, P.O.'

The men shuffled away into the darkness, and McGowan started to climb towards the bridge.

.   .   .   .   .

For the rest of the night the ship pushed her way at a snail's pace, while down below, right aft and beneath the waterline, Tregarth and his mechanics worked and sweated to trace the one tiny injury which was making every man aboard apprehensive and irritable.

Morning passed, and with it came a stiff north-east wind which whipped the flat water first into a mass of dancing whitecaps and soon changed the whole sea to a pitching panorama of long, steep rollers. The *Saracen* slowed even more, until eventually it was only possible to retain steerage-way. The monitor took the mounting sea with obvious dis-like. The long diagonal swells cruised rapidly to hit her below the port bow, each jagged crest crumbling beneath the force of the wind, so that the men off watch felt the surging power of water thunder against the hull like a roll of drums, and then waited as the ship staggered and heaved herself bodily over and down into the waiting troughs, and so to the next onslaught. On watch it was even worse. The gunners, signalmen and lookouts were always in danger of losing their footing and handholds. Equipment and ammunition rattled and banged, men cursed as their boots skidded on the heaving decks, and their eyes and binoculars were blinded by the long streamers of shredded spray which seemed to cruise over the hull and superstructure like birds of prey.

In the near distance the trawler pitched and yawed, showing first her bilge and then her open bridge, upon which her watchkeepers in shining oilskins clung like seals on a rock.

Chesnaye forced himself to stay in his chair. Occasionally, when off guard, his eyes strayed to the engine-room telephone. The handset was temptingly near, but he knew it was futile and a waste of time to call Tregarth to speak to him. He was doing his best. That had to suffice.

'Your oilskin, sir!' A bosun's mate was holding it out to him, so that Chesnaye realised with sudden shock that his uniform was dripping from the spray and blown spume. He nodded with a brief smile and pulled it across his shoulders. As he leaned forward in his chair to tuck the coat behind him he caught a glimpse of Erskine and the Chief Bosun's Mate, followed somewhat reluctantly by a small party of seamen, making their rounds of the fo'c'sle and anchor cables. He noticed how the men's bodies stood at nearly a forty-five-degree angle as the wide deck canted against the weight of water which piled up beneath the bows. Spray burst across the guard-rail and drenched the groping men, and Chesnaye saw Erskine turn to shout something, his collar flapping in the vicious wind.

Chesnaye sat back and thought about his conversation with Erskine during the night. I was wrong to speak to him like that. Stupid, and cowardly.

He was glad he had been unable to see Erskine's face when it had happened. But even that was small comfort. How was he to know about Helen? Chesnaye cursed himself once more. By bringing up the subject of marriage in the first place, *he* and not Erskine was to blame.

He ducked his head as more water deluged across the screen and ran down his stubbled face and through the soggy protection of the towel he had wrapped around his neck.

The Mediterranean. Calm and inviting. Or wild and irresponsible. It had all happened here, he thought. Meeting Helen Driscoll in Gibraltar. The Dardanelles and the misery which followed. He remembered the long journey back to England in the hospital ship. So full of hope in spite of his feeling of loss and despair. Robert Driscoll had never left his side, and even afterwards in that Sussex hospital he had visited him often.

But the rest of the dream had never materialised. Helen Driscoll had stayed in Gibraltar, and had been there when the *Saracen* had eventually dropped anchor *en route* for home waters and the final battle for France.

Even now, after all these years, Chesnaye could not accept what had happened so easily. He knew he had no rights, no first call or demands over her. Nevertheless, he had felt real pain when Robert Driscoll had met him with the news.

Helen had become engaged to Mark Beaushears, once midshipman of the *Saracen*'s unhappy gunroom, then acting lieutenant and *en route* with the monitor for a new ship. An up-and-coming young officer, they had said, and Chesnaye had written to him to wish him luck. He had written the letter while the misery was fresh in his heart and the hatred very real in his mind.

In all parts of the world and on many occasions he had told himself : If only she had waited. Why Beaushears? But he had known well enough that it was just another delusion which, like the *Saracen*'s memory, never left him.

Lieutenant Fox lurched across the bridge and saluted. 'Signal, sir. Priority. Small convoy being attacked. Request immediate assistance !'

Chesnaye pushed himself off the chair and limped towards the charthouse. 'Is there more of it?'

'Yes, sir. Still coming in on W/T. Two Italian cruisers and some destroyers have dropped on the convoy from Piraeus. The bloody Eye-ties must have pushed down the Greek coast during the night.'

He watched Chesnaye's eyes flicker from the signal pad to the chart, and the almost desperate speed with which he moved the parallel rulers and dividers. He knew well enough what Chesnaye was thinking. Crete to the north, the Libyan coast to the south. The small convoy must have skirted the island of Crete on the mainland side to keep as covered as possible from surface attack. Then it had turned south with the intention of wheeling eastwards to Port Said. It was one of the many urgently needed convoys of supplies for the British troops in Greece. The enemy were obviously aware of the importance of every ship in the area. They intended to finish off this convoy, and only the *Saracen* by a stroke of fate was in a position to help them. That is, she *would* have been in a position to help them, thought Fox grimly as he watched the anguish on Chesnaye's face.

The dividers clicked across the chart once more, as if Chesnaye had not trusted his first impression. Slowly he said, 'But for this breakdown we would have been right amongst them.'

Fox glanced at his personal log. 'Yes, sir. We would probably have sighted the convoy wing escort at eleven hundred.' He sucked his teeth. 'Bloody bad luck!'

In a strange voice Chesnaye snapped: 'Bring her about, Pilot. Lay off a new course to intercept.' He hurried past the astonished Fox. 'Bosun's Mate! Get the First Lieutenant for me at once!' His mind was in a complete whirl as he picked up the engine-room handset. 'Captain speaking. Get me the Chief!'

At that moment Erskine pushed his way into the charthouse his eyebrows raised questioningly as he saw Fox's troubled face.

Fox shrugged and gestures towards the signal pad. 'Local convoy under cruiser attack. They're requesting assistance.'

Chesnaye's voice came from the bridge, sharp and urgent, 'Have you got that new course yet, Pilot?'

Fox picked up his logbook and looked hard at Erskine. 'I'm a seaman and that's all.' He turned slowly towards the open door. 'You tell the Skipper what it's all about. Frankly, I haven't got the heart!'

'What the hell are you saying?' Erskine rubbed his wind-reddened face. 'Why are we changing course?'

Fox sighed deeply. 'He thinks we should be there to give assistance. We would have been but for the bloody engines.

I must say *I'm* not sorry, I don't fancy mixing it with some brand-new cruisers, Wops or not!'

He walked briskly on to the bridge, his solid body swaying easily to the ship's heavy rolls. A moment later Erskine heard his voice, flat and calm once more. 'Port fifteen. Steady. Steer oh-four-five.'

Erskine swallowed hard and followed him into the wind. The ship was leaning heavily, her bows corkscrewing as she laboured round into the teeth of the gale.

Chesnaye looked past him, his eyes distant, as if his mind was somewhere else. 'Ah, John, here you are. The Chief has patched up the trouble at last. I am just ringing down for maximum revs.' Suddenly his grey eyes focused directly on Erskine's face. 'The W/T office are letting me have a regular report of the situation. I—I can't understand it. The convoy has called for air support, and nothing has happened!'

Erskine looked away. 'There isn't any, sir. It's been like that for months.' He turned slightly to watch the disbelief change to helpless anger.

Chesnaye waved his hand across the plunging white rollers. 'But good God, man! This is an emergency! There are valuable ships out there! Ships and *men*!'

You poor bastard, thought Erskine dully. 'Every available aircraft is in the desert, or Greece. If you're caught on your own, that's just too bad!'

'Signal, sir.' Laidlaw, the Yeoman, had appeared on the bridge, his beard glistening with diamonds of spray. He faced Erskine as Chesnaye read through the lines of neat, pencilled information.

Erskine watched Chesnaye's lips moving as he read in silence. He noticed that the Captain's hand was shaking. Erskine knew that this was a crucial moment, but for once he felt unable to cope with it. The shock and open despair on Chesnaye's face robbed him of controlled thought.

'They're relying on us.' The words were wrung from Chesnaye's mouth. 'The Second Inshore Squadron are on way to help the convoy. We are to engage the enemy until our cruisers arrive!'

A telegraph jangled, and moments later the bridge began to throb and quiver in response to the revived engines.

'We'll not be in time, sir.' Erskine hated himself as he saw the effect of his words. 'They've a head start on us.'

Fox called : 'Signal, sir. Convoy's scattering.'

Sub-Lieutenant Bouverie, who until this moment had been watching in silence, said : 'A bit too late, I imagine. These Italian cruisers are damn' fast.'

Chesnaye crumpled the signal flimsy into a ball, his eyes furious. 'Hold your tongue! What the hell do you know about it?'

'I beg your pardon, sir. I just thought——'

Chesnaye did not seem to hear him. 'You can't imagine what it's like. Waiting for help. Seeing your friends die around you and not able to do anything!'

'Maximum revolutions, sir !'

Chesnaye nodded. 'Have the main armament cleared for action.'

Erskine wanted to leave the bridge. To get away from the suspense and the feeling of helplessness. The Captain had proved himself so capable, so brilliant at handling the ship under the air attacks, that it had never occurred to him he was totally unaware of the true situation which faced every British ship in the Mediterranean.

He heard Chesnaye ask in a more controlled tone, 'What escorts do they have?'

'Two destroyers and an old sloop, sir.' Fox was holding his logbook like a bible. 'They can't spare much else at present.'

The big turret creaked slightly and the left gun dipped a few degrees. Within the massive steel hive the gunners were already testing the controls, preparing their cumbersome charges for battle. Not a stationary target ashore or a straggling collection of troops and installations, but the cream of the Duce's navy. Thirty-knot cruisers, most likely, each one a floating arsenal.

Chesnaye folded his hands across the screen and rested his chin on them. He could feel the hull's convulsions and hear the clatter of feet on bridge ladders as messengers raced to and fro and men hurried to their stations. Behind him nobody spoke but to relay an order or to answer one of the voice-pipes.

Damn them, he thought savagely. Bouverie with his immature and fatuous remarks. What did he know? They were not involved, so they did not care. One man was lost overboard because of his own carelessness and stupidity, and the ship almost went into mourning because their captain did not stop. In submarine-patrolled waters they had expected him to offer the ship as a sitting target. But now that hundreds of lives and precious ships were being smashed and killed beyond the horizon they just did not see reason for alarm or interest!

What was worse was the way Erskine accepted the Navy's new vulnerability. Chesnaye remembered his own feeling of loss and betrayal that morning off the Gallipoli Peninsula when the *Saracen* had moved in for her final bombardment. The supporting fleet gone. The sea empty. The men in the convoy must feel like that. Their only hope was the *Saracen*, and she was to be denied them.

He pounded the screen with slow, desperate beats. Come on, old lady! Give me all you've got. Faster . . . faster!

Only twenty miles to go, and but for the driving spray and gale they might even have been able to see something. But the sea was grey with anger, and the wind showed no sign of easing. Instead it hurled itself like a barricade across the ship's thrusting stem, cutting away the speed under remorseless pressure.

Fox looked across from the charthouse towards the Captain's stooped shoulders. 'No further signals, sir.' He caught Erskine's anxious stare. 'I guess it's all over,' he added quietly.

Erskine waited for Chesnaye to resume his old course and speed. There was nothing to be gained now. The small convoy must have been decimated, like others would be before this was all over. Chesnaye was only offering his own ship as a target and deck, nothing more.

Two more hours dragged by. Hardly a man moved on the upper deck, and the voices of the men on watch were hushed and rare.

The wind slackened, veered round and dropped away as if it had never been. The hazy clouds rolled aside and the sun moved in to greet them. Humid at first, and then with its old penetrating brilliance, so that the grey shadows fled from the sea and the wave crests gave way to deep swells of glittering blue and silver.

Once the engine room asked permission to reduce speed, but Chesnaye said shortly, 'Not yet.'

Erskine could not take his eyes off him. He is waiting for something to happen, he thought uneasily.

The watches changed. Men relieved went to their messes to eat, but without their usual noisy gaiety. Even the rum was issued without comment, and the men drank their watered tots with their eyes upwards towards the bridge, where the dark outline of the Captain's head and shoulders stayed rigidly like a carving on the front of a church.

'Smoke, sir ! Bearing Red two-zero !'

Every glass was swivelled and then steadied to watch.

Slowly, remorsefully, like a reaper in a field, the monitor pounded her way across the inviting water. Without a wind the sea parted to allow the *Saracen* easy access, as if eager for her to see the spoils.

Chesnaye said at last, 'Slow ahead.'

From the corner of his eye he saw the seamen off watch lining the guard-rails, their faces turned towards the smoke.

There was little of the ship to be seen. It had been a sizeable freighter, and it lay on its beam, only a fire-rusted shell to show where the hull had once been. The eddying bow wave from the monitor's blunt stem pushed gently against the dying ship and made the littered surface of the water between the two vessels surge with sudden life.

Chesnaye heard a man cry out, and saw a white flash as a hand pointed involuntarily at the flotsam of war.

Broken planks and blackened hatch covers. A headless corpse trailing scarlet weed in the clear water, an unused life-jacket found, too late.

The sinking freighter coughed deep in its shattered insides and plunged hissing into a maelstrom which mercifully sucked down some of the grisly relics also.

Far on the port beam the little trawler was picking her way through more wreckage, like a terrier in a slaughter-house.

A patch of oil a mile wide parted next across the monitor's bows. Then there was more debris, much of it human.

Erskine felt sick. When he looked sideways at Chesnaye's

face he saw that it was impassive, almost expressionless.

Chesnaye said quietly, 'If only we had been here in time.'

Then over his shoulder he said in a strange, cruel tone: 'Well, Sub, what do you think of all this, eh? We *were* too late for these chaps; you were right!'

A dead rating bobbed past the monitor's anti-torpedo bulge, and a seaman on lookout said in a strangled voice: 'God! One of *our* chaps!'

The guard-rail quivered as the lines of watching men leaned to look at the lonely, passing figure. At last the disaster was no longer anonymous and indistinct. The corpse was in naval uniform. Even the red badges on its sleeve were clear and mocking.

Chesnaye stood up, his feet thudding on the grating. 'Bring her back to her old course, Pilot!' He glanced only briefly at Erskine. 'Make a signal to C.-in-C., John. Repeated Second Inshore Squadron.' He looked up at the flapping commissioning pennant at the masthead. 'Convoy destroyed. No survivors.'

'Aye, aye, sir. Anything else?'

Chesnaye was filling his pipe with short, angry thrusts. 'There's a lot I'd like to tell them at the Admiralty. But it will keep for the moment!'

Erskine wanted to help, to make the Captain understand, and he tried to find the right words.

Before he could speak Chesnaye said: 'Get those gawping men off the upper deck, or find them something to do! Like a bloody circus!'

Erskine was suddenly grateful for the bite in Chesnaye's voice, even though they both knew it was merely acting.

.   .   .   .   .

Lieutenant Malcolm Norris stood high on the port gratings, his hands clasped tightly behind his back. From his lofty position he could just see over the Captain's shoulder and beyond the screen where, transfixed between the two big guns, the monitor's bows moved very slowly towards the long strip of land.

He could see Erskine and some of the fo'c'sle party already moving around the cables, making a last check before entering harbour.

He heard Fox say quietly: 'Starboard ten. Midships.'
The Navigating Officer's buttons rasped against metal as
he bent over the compass and swung the pelorus on to another fix. 'Steer one-seven-five.'

Norris bit his lip. Fox was so calm, so ice cold when he
was working. The halyards squeaked and a string of flags
soared upwards to the yard. Through the shore haze, beyond the long, low-lying breakwater, a signal lamp blinked
rapidly, and Norris heard Laidlaw goading his signalmen
into further action.

But as Officer of the Watch Norris had little to do. The
Saracen was at last arriving in Alexandria and the Captain
and Fox were conning the ship over the last half-mile.

Norris felt the sweat running down his spine, but did not
relax his vigilant position. It was like everything else he did.
He did not dare drop his guard for a second. Speaking,
thinking, passing orders, each action had to be vetted.

He watched the busy harbour life opening up across the
ship's bows. Nodding buoys, weird Arab sailing craft poised
like bats on their own reflections, an outward-bound sloop
gathering way as it passed the harbour limit.

As the sloop drew abeam the trill of pipes echoed across
the flat water.

The monitor's tannoy barked: 'Attention on the upper
deck! Face to starboard and salute!'

The bosun's mates, already in a small line on the *Saracen*'s upper bridge, raised their pipes. C.P.O. Craig
snapped, 'Sound!'

Again the twittering, shrill and ear-splitting as the senior
ship returned the sloop's mark of respect.

Craig watched the other ship with slitted, critical eyes.
'Carry on!'

The yeoman called hoarsely: 'Signal from Flag, sir!
Anchor as ordered!'

Chesnaye grunted, his eyes fixed on the shimmering anchorage. Like a pewter lake, he thought. Cruisers, destroyers and supply ships. Bobbing derricks, squealing
cranes, dust and busy preparation.

At the head of a line of moored cruisers was the *Aureus,*
the flagship. Every glass would be watching the monitor's
approach. Every eye critical, perhaps amused. He heard the

rasp in his voice as he ordered, 'Slow ahead both!'

He heard, too, Norris stammer as he repeated the order down the voice-pipe. He was obviously worried and strained. Like me, thought Chesnaye, with sudden bitterness. He wondered what Norris had thought about the shambles left by the Italian cruisers. Probably thinks I took the ship there just to frighten everybody.

Somewhere deep in his brain a voice persisted. Why did you go there? You knew it was too late! Was it to prove something to yourself?

'Time to take her round, sir!' Fox's voice startled him. A prickle of alarm made him stiffen in his chair.

Dreaming again. Too tired. Can't think clearly any more.

'Very good. Port fifteen.'

More shouted orders. 'Port Watch fall in for entering harbour! First part forrard! Second part aft!'

The decks blossomed with scampering figures, unfamiliar in correct uniform and without the well-used duffel-coats and balaclavas. Chesnaye's aching mind began to drift again. There should have been a marine guard and band on the quarterdeck. It would have made all the difference.

He gritted his teeth. Those days were gone. No marines. Just an old ship, with God-knows-what job ahead. 'Midships!'

'Coming on to bearing now, sir!' Fox sounded alert.

Chesnaye stood up and stepped on to the forward grating. The monitor moved slowly past a destroyer which glittered like a yacht from beneath its impeccable awnings. More piping, and tiny, antlike figures stiffening in salute.

'Half a cable, sir!'

'Stop engines!' Chesnaye shielded his eyes and peered down at the fo'c'sle. Erskine was standing right in the bows, his face towards him across the length of the foredeck. A signalman stood at his side ready to break out the Jack on the staff the moment the anchor went plummeting down. The cable party stood in various stances, like athletes waiting for the gun. Eyes on the massive, treacherous cable and the brake which would halt its welcome sound.

Still the monitor glided forward. Almost graceful in the clear water.

'Coming up now, sir!' Fox was busy checking bearings again.

Chesnaye lifted his arm, and saw the rating with the big hammer brace himself above the slip, the only force now holding the anchor. Chesnaye felt elated but unsteady. It was a combination of exhaustion and over-eagerness, so that he felt he had to speak, to break the unbearable waiting. 'The flagship looks smart enough.' He even forced himself to smile as he said it.

Fox grunted. 'The Flag Officer of the Second Inshore Squadron is rather particular!' The air on the bridge was light-hearted, even gay.

Suddenly Chesnaye realised that he had been so pre-occupied during the last harrowing days he did not even know who his new senior officer was to be. Not that it mattered now. The time he had been apart from the Navy had cut all his old connections. 'What is the Admiral's name, Pilot?'

Fox frowned, his gaze on the open water ahead of the bows. The Skipper was cutting it fine. From the corner of his eye he could see the empty tanker, high and ungainly, backing stern first across the narrowing anchorage. Absently he replied, 'Vice-Admiral Beaushears, sir.'

Chesnaye staggered as if struck a blow. It couldn't be! Not now, out here? He looked round like a trapped animal, his mind reeling.

Fox's voice, controlled but sharp, cut into his tortured thoughts. 'Let go, sir! Let *go*!'

Almost in a trance Chesnaye dropped his arm, and from forrard came the sharp click, followed immediately by the rumble of cable as the anchor roared from its rust-streaked hawsepipe.

Fox was now up on the grating, his eyes anxious. 'Are you all right, sir?'

Chesnaye swallowed hard and nodded. 'Yes!' Over his shoulder he called, 'Slow astern together!'

Norris, an imaginative man at any time, had watched the little drama mesmerised like a rabbit. He repeated the last order and heard the Coxswain's voice answer him up the voice-pipe. Slowly the monitor moved astern, paying out her cable along the bottom of the anchorage. But Norris was unable to take his eyes from Chesnaye's square shoulders and the anxious Fox at his side.

Later in his cabin he would be able to think about it more clearly. Norris knew that something really big had happened. With this vital knowledge, once he had unravelled it, he would make those smug bastards in the wardroom really sit up and notice him!

'Stop engines!'

Norris watched as the stern-moving tanker floundered across the bows, its half-bared screw thrashing the water into a snow-white froth. Norris held his breath. He was quite sure Chesnaye had not even seen the other ship. But for Fox's quick action there might even have been a collision.

Chesnaye turned towards him, so that with sudden terror Norris thought he had been thinking aloud. 'Ring off main engines!' He brushed past Norris and walked into his sea-cabin.

Norris was quivering with excitement, his past fears momentarily forgotten. 'Did you *see* that?' He waited impatiently as Fox stopped rolling a chart and peered across at the gleaming white buildings and tall minarets. 'Did you see the Captain's face?'

Fox cleared his throat and picked up the chart. For a moment he looked hard at Norris's flushed features. 'Nice place, Alex. Think I'll take a run ashore tomorrow!' Then he was gone.

Satisfied, the *Saracen* swung at her anchor while the cable and side parties dismissed and hurried below to escape the sun. On the maindeck Mr. Joslin, the Gunner, was supervising the rigging of an awning, while McGowan and Sub-Lieutenant Bouverie watched over the boats as they were dropped in the water alongside.

From the flagdeck the signalmen eyed the shore and the flagship, but in the wheelhouse the wheel and telegraphs stood unattended and already forgotten.

Norris still paced the empty upper bridge, ignoring the sun on his neck as he tried to fathom out the enormity of his knowledge. He felt a new man. The ship was safe in harbour, and there was the strength of other ships and men nearby. Already he had forgotten that but for the Captain the *Saracen* would be lying even more quietly on the bed of the Mediterranean, while on some distant airfield the Stuka pilots would be celebrating, instead of mourning their dead comrades.

Norris thought of his wife. 'You're as good as they are!' He grinned. For once she had been right.

．　　：　　•　　ɿ　　■

Chesnaye followed the flagship's captain down the quarterdeck ladder and into the cool shade below. His stomach felt uneasy, and he wished now he had made time to take a good meal before leaving the *Saracen* prior to attending for his interview with the man whose flag flew high on the *Aureus*'s tapering masthead.

The two captains passed down a narrow passageway, the sides of which were so well painted that they shone like polished glass. Chesnaye darted a quick glance at his opposite number and wondered how he got on with Vice-Admiral Sir Mark Beaushears. Captain Colquhoun had met him at the gangway, his tanned face set in an automatic smile of welcome. He was pleasant enough, but Chesnaye had the impression that he was a much-harassed man. It could not be pleasant to have a flag officer for ever breathing down your shoulder, he thought.

Chesnaye noted the smart marine sentry outside the the Admiral's quarters, and waited with mounting curiosity and apprehension as Colquhoun tucked his cap beneath his arm and stepped over the coaming. Chesnaye followed him, aware of the soft carpet beneath his shoes and the air of quiet well-being the stateroom seemed to exude.

There were two men present. A tall, languid flag-lieutenant rose slowly to his feet, glanced at Chesnaye and then turned to watch his superior.

Vice-Admiral Sir Mark Beaushears was only a year older then Chesnaye, but time and ambition had been hard on his outward appearance. He still appeared cool and relaxed, but his tall figure was markedly stooped, and his once-athletic body was marred by a definite paunch. His hair had receded, too, so that the high forehead gave him a new expression of watchful deliberation, and he appeared to be summing up Chesnaye from the moment he stepped into the cabin. Only his eyes were the same, Chesnaye thought. Veiled, giving nothing away.

Beaushears waved his hand to a chair in front of the well-turned desk. Again Chesnaye had the distinct impression that everything had been carefully planned beforehand and the chair had been placed in position like a stage prop.

He sat down and folded his hands in his lap. He ticked off each item in his mind. No handshake. Only the briefest hint of a smile.

Beaushears said evenly : 'It's been a long time. I watched you dropping anchor earlier and wondered if you had changed much.'

Chesnaye waited for him to dismiss the other officers. Colquhoun was looking stiff and uneasy, and the young flag-lieutenant faintly amused. He is going to keep them here, he thought. As a sort of barrier. He is afraid of old acquaintanceships and memories.

This new knowledge did nothing to comfort him, but instead made him vaguely angry. In a formal tone he began : 'I have submitted my report about the voyage from Malta. I was very sorry I was unable to help that convoy.' He toyed with the idea of mentioning the bombers *Saracen* had shot down, but he knew Beaushears was well aware of the facts. Let him bring it up first, he thought with irritation.

'Yes, a great pity. Still, if, as you say, you were unavoidably detained, there's nothing more to be said, is there?'

Chesnaye stiffened in his chair, his fingers laced together with painful fierceness. What did he mean?

Aloud he said, 'I did my best, sir.'

Beaushears leaned back in his chair. 'You lost a man overboard too?'

'It's all in the report.' Chesnaye could feel the colour rising to his cheeks. 'It was the only decision.'

'Yes.' Beaushears pressed a small button. 'The sun is well over the yardarm. A drink will do us good.' Almost casually he said, 'I thought for one small moment that you were going to overshoot the anchorage when you came into harbour.' He smiled for the first time. 'She's not a fleet destroyer, y'know !'

The flag-lieutenant showed his perfect teeth. Like a cat, Chesnaye thought.

A petty officer steward brought in a tray and glasses and busied himself pouring iced pink gins. No one was asked what he wanted, and Chesnaye had the idea that was the way the flagship was run under Beaushears. The gin was, however, a small but welcome distraction.

He drank deeply and signalled with sudden recklessness to the steward. 'Another!' He saw the man dart a brief glance at Beaushears and then pour the drink. Chesnaye smiled grimly to himself. A good master/servant atmosphere.

Beaushears cleared his throat impatiently. 'Well, now that you are here you'd better be put in the picture.' He turned to the lieutenant. 'Over to you, Harmsworth.'

The flag-lieutenant tapped a bulky envelope with his finger. 'It's all in here, Captain. You will be *attached* to this squadron until further notice.'

Chesnaye noticed the slight emphasis. *Saracen* was to be with but not *of* Beaushears' squadron.

Harmsworth continued in the same bored tones : 'You will find all the relevant information concerning the military situation in Libya up-to-date as far as it goes. You will start loading supplies and stores in the forenoon tomorrow. The Maintenance Commander has all the details ashore and will arrange for lighterage, etcetera. Your first destination will be west of Tobruk. The Army is getting in a bit of a flap down there.'

Chesnay looked at Beaushears. 'Will Tobruk be held?'

Beaushears shrugged. 'Unlikely, I should think. The enemy will probably bypass it and take it at leisure. We shall then have to evacuate the marooned troops with whatever we have available.' He gestured towards the open scuttle. 'Jerry has got his eye fixed on Alexandria. After all, he's less than three hundred miles away at this moment!'

Chesnaye twisted uneasily in his chair. My God, is it really as bad as that? He said, 'Can't they stop him?'

Beaushears glanced at his slim gold watch. 'They have a plan. But they intend to fall back and re-group. Present a fixed front outside the Alexandria perimeter. The Staff chaps say that with the sea on one side and the Qattara

Depression on the other the Army will be able to make a good show. It will make up in some ways for lack of air cover.'

Chesnaye remembered the mass of shipping in the harbour. 'And what of *our* support, sir?'

Harmsworth interrupted smoothly. 'Mostly for Greece. We're really giving a bit of weight in that direction!' He seemed pleased, as if personally responsible.

Chesnaye felt light-headed and suddenly reckless. He had been made to feel like a small boy by Beaushears in front of the others. He had expected it would be like that. He had thought about this meeting from the moment Fox had dropped his bombshell as the *Saracen* crossed the anchorage.

Beaushears had always been aloof and cool, even as a midshipman. Now he was something more, and although he acted in a detached and formal manner, Chesnaye thought he could detect a deeper meaning to his behaviour. His remarks had been double-edged, as if he had implied that Chesnaye could have done more.

Chesnaye felt the sweat forming on his forehead. Perhaps he had even suggested that the *Saracen* had deliberately held back from the convoy? That *he* had been afraid for the ship and himself! Even losing the man overboard could be misconstrued as an unwillingness to stop, even cowardice! He felt the glass shaking in his hand.

'I think Greece is a waste of time!' Chesnaye's voice was not loud, but from the other officers' expressions he got the impression he had just shouted an obscenity.

Beaushears controlled his features and said calmly, 'Please go on.'

Chesnaye shrugged. 'Have you forgotten the Dardanelles fiasco?' He saw Colquhoun and Harmsworth exchanging awkward glances, but he no longer cared. The fact was that behind Beaushears' manner, his ability to offend without the slightest trace of personal embarrassment, was something which had stayed with him over the years. He had probably wanted to meet Chesnaye, but for quite a different reason. He had no doubt expected a changed Chesnaye. Humble, even ashamed, of the circumstances which had parted him from the Navy and now given him com-

mand of the oldest ship in the Fleet. Then there was Helen
. . . Chesnaye checked his racing thought. 'Anyone can see
we can't hold Greece, let alone use it as a springboard into
Europe! If it's another proud gesture, then it's going to be
a damned costly one!'

Beaushears eyed him coldly. 'I think otherwise, Chesnaye.
However, it is hardly your concern. You are here to command your ship in the best way you know.' He was watching Chesnaye with sudden intentness. 'She's not much of a
catch, but we can't be choosers. I need every vessel I can
lay my hands on!' Carefully he added : 'When you reach
the Libyan destination you may find that the enemy has
overrun our people already. You'll get no support from
Tobruk, which is the nearest strongpoint. You will be on
your own.'

Chesnaye looked at the carpet. For a split second he had
a picture of the bullet-scarred pinnacle and Keith Pickles
dead in his arms. 'It won't be the first time!' He looked up
to see that the shot had gone home. Beaushears face was no
longer calm. He looked almost guilty.

Harmsworth said hurriedly, 'Another gin, sir?'

Chesnaye took the drink and touched his glass with the
tip of his tongue. If they expect me to crawl they are going
to get a surprise, he thought.

Beaushears had composed himself again. In a flat voice he
said, 'In your assignment you may have to sacrifice your
ship!'

Chesnaye started as if struck in the face. Lose *Saracen*?
He felt the cabin closing in on him. 'What do you mean?'

Beaushears stood up, the sunlight reflecting on his thick
gold lace. Without waiting further he attacked. 'She's an
old ship! Useful at the moment, but expendable! If you
are pinned down, and the enemy catch you inshore, you
must sink the *Saracen* before they get their hands on the
supplies!' His voice grew louder and sharper. 'This is a
mobile, fast-moving war! Tanks and armoured columns,
and *not* like the Dardanelles at all! No front line, poor
communications, with each day making the maps obsolete!'
He turned suddenly, his eyes flashing. 'Both sides need fuel
and supplies like life-blood!'

Chesnaye imagined the *Saracen* going down under his

own hand, and felt the pain in his heart like fire. 'I'll manage!' His voice was thick and unsteady.

'You *must*!' He eyed Chesnaye slowly, his face calm again. 'I know you of old. Sentimental and unrealistic.' He waved his hand. 'Don't bother to argue. I wasn't going to say this, but you opened the batting! The Navy's changed. You either keep up with events or you go to the wall! We've got amateurs, failures, has-beens and every sort of man who's ever breathed. There's no room for sentiment any more!'

'So I see, sir.' Chesnaye rose to his feet.

Beaushears forced a tight smile. 'Keep out of trouble, Chesnaye. Don't try to act as if your ship is a battlecruiser! Just do your job, and use discretion.'

Chesnaye turned to leave. Before he could stop himself he had asked, 'How is Helen?'

Beaushears dropped a hand to his desk as if to steady himself. He looked towards the scuttle, his face hidden. 'Lady Helen is well, thank you.'

Chesnaye felt the gin raw and hot in his throat. So he had been right. After all these years Beaushears was still jealous. It was incredible. He was successful, he had even stolen the girl Chesnaye had loved, yet he was still dissatisfied.

Harmsworth looked confused, the fierce exchange of words between his admiral and the tall, grave-eyed captain had been beyond his experience. He said, 'I—I'll see you over the side, sir.'

Chesnaye regarded him coldly. 'Captain Colquhoun can do that, thank you!'

On the sun-dried quarterdeck he looked down at the *Saracen*'s pinnace as it moved in towards the gangway. Beside the Admiral's barge and the cruiser's other smart boats it looked outdated and worn, but he noted with quiet satisfaction that the boat's crew were smart and alert, boathooks poised and ready. He felt a pang in his throat as he saw, too, the small midshipman who stood in the stern-sheets shading his eyes as he looked for his captain.

Damn Beaushears, he thought savagely. I did not want it this way, but if he expects me to grovel—he jerked from his thoughts as the flagship's captain held out his hand.

'Goodbye, Chesnaye. I hope we meet again soon.' He eyed Chesnaye with sudden warmth. 'A remarkable interview.'

Chesnaye grinned, feeling the recklessness once more.

Colquhoun looked up at the Vice-Admiral's flag, now limp in the dipping sun. 'I don't think that fool Harmsworth will sleep for a week!'

The two men separated, the pipes trilled, and then Chesnaye was in his pinnace, with *Saracen*'s outline ahead of him like a challenge.

4

Tobruk

The air in the small sea-cabin abaft the *Saracen*'s bridge was already thick and stifling, and the blue tobacco smoke hung in an unmoving cloud above the heads of the waiting officers. The door opened and Lieutenant McGowan forced himself round its edge and eased his shoulders against the steel bulkhead. Chesnaye sat on his bunk, his legs out straight beneath the littered table.

By his side Erskine was squatting on a chair, his eyes thoughtful as he checked each cramped figure. 'All present, sir.'

'Right.' Chesnaye eyed the others impassively, his features a mask for his inner thoughts. The head of every department was present, even Tregarth, his face pasty and moist from the engine room's humid breath, and Chesnaye could tell from their expressions that they were wondering at this unexpected summons.

He waited a while longer until McGowan had lighted a cigarette, and then tapped the chart which lay across the table. 'A change of plans, gentlemen.' Their eyes followed his hand across the straggling Libyan coastline. 'The enemy have pushed on rather faster than expected, and our proposed landing area has been overrun.' He had already explained this to Erskine before the others had arrived, and even now sensed the man's opposition to his words. 'Tobruk, on the other hand, has been bypassed by the Afrika Korps, so our people there will need everything they can get. Every sort of supply will have to be carried by sea. For that reason I intend to unload our stores there!'

It all sounded so cold, so easy, that he wanted to laugh. He remembered Beaushears' face when he had described the mission. He had known the impossibility of the task. He *must* have known.

Tregarth said imperturbably, 'Well, at least Tobruk's a tiny bit nearer!'

Erskine added half to himself, 'It's a damned long way back!'

Chesnaye scraped a match along a box and puffed at his pipe. It gave him time to think about the new developments. It had taken nearly two days to load these military stores in Alexandria. The Commander-in-Chief had made it clear that with Tobruk under constant pressure it was almost impossible to get into the port except with the cover of darkness. Now the place was bypassed, and no one seemed to know exactly where the nearest enemy units were. *Saracen* would be a sitting target the moment she was uncovered by daylight, and with her decks covered by drums of petrol and cases of ammunition.

It had taken three more days to make the trip from Alexandria, keeping well clear of the coast and skirting local convoy routes. By some miracle they had managed to avoid detection, and had only once sighted an enemy aircraft in the far distance. The aircrew must have been looking in the wrong direction, he thought.

But now—he looked up as Fox said thoughtfully : 'Is it really essential for us to go in, sir? I mean, according to the signals received, the Army is being supplied by smaller, faster ships than ours. A quick turn-round, and off to sea seems to be the order of the day.'

Chesnaye fought back the desire to yawn. The stuffy atmosphere and quiet watchfulness of his officers added to his feeling of complete weariness. Fox was right, of course. Beaushears had said, 'Use your discretion.' A trite, well-used phrase which had spelled disaster to many a captain. If you were right, others took the credit. But if you made the wrong decision you took the consequences alone.

Erskine seemed to make up his mind. 'I think it is a bad risk, sir.'

The others shifted uncomfortably. Fox, hard-faced and watchful, McGowan biting his lip and eyeing his friend with obvious agreement.

Chesnaye looked at Tregarth. Nothing there. The Chief would do as he was expected. In the engine room only the machinery meant anything to him. Above, in the clean open world of sea and sky, other decisions might be called for, but they did not affect him.

Wickersley, the Doctor, looked fresh-faced and bright, the only man present who never stood a watch or missed his sleep. He would be busy enough soon if things turned out badly.

Chesnaye said calmly, 'I don't see that we have any choice, Number One.'

Erskine tightened his jaw. 'We'll be close inshore for two or three days, sir. It could be fatal.'

Chesnaye shrugged lightly. 'It could.'

They all fell silent, so that the throb of engines intruded into the cramped cabin and they could hear the scrape of feet from the bridge and the creak of the steering gear.

A lonely, darkened ship, Chesnaye thought. Steering beneath an arch of bright stars which reflected so clearly on the flat sea.

He shifted irritably. 'Lay off the new course, Pilot. We'll close Tobruk tomorrow at dusk.' He eyed the Navigating Officer bleakly. 'Make a double check on recognition signals. I don't want a salvo from our own troops!'

Fox nodded. He at least did not appear surprised at Chesnaye's decision.

Erskine repeated, 'It's a bad risk, sir.'

'It's a bad piece of organisation, John. The men who should be in the desert are in Greece at this moment!'

Erskine looked at him with surprise. 'But, sir, surely that is entirely different? That risk is justified!'

Chesnaye heard an intake of breath from McGowan, but remained surprisingly calm. He tapped the sheaf of signals. 'The British forces in Greece are already falling back, John.' He remembered the smug confidence on Beaushears' face and felt suddenly sorry for Erskine and all those others who had never known the bitterness of defeat and betrayal. 'In a matter of weeks there'll be another Dunkirk in Greece.' He had almost said Gallipoli. The signals had briefly reported the quick change of strength, the savage enemy advance through Greece and Yugoslavia. The British Army was falling back so rapidly that already tons of arms and equipment had fallen into German hands.

Chesnaye shuddered when he imagined the waiting ships,

unprotected by air cover, which were expected to ferry the surviving forces to the island of Crete. And what then? How could they be expected even to hold that? What in God's name were the hare-brained strategists in Whitehall thinking when they ordered such a hopeless gesture? He could feel the old anger beginning to boil inside him.

'You have heard my decision.' He spoke to the group at large, but his words were directed at Erskine. 'In times like these morale is of the utmost importance. The men at Tobruk do not question their orders. It is our duty,' he faltered, 'no, our honour, to give them every support!'

Erskine stood up, his eyes dull. 'You can rely on the ship, sir.'

Chesnaye scraped his pipe, his features towards the chart. 'Good. For a small moment I was beginning to wonder!'

Wickersley stepped forward, darting a quick glance from Erskine to the seated captain. 'Perhaps I could be of some use to the army medical chaps, sir?'

His bright, eager voice seemed to break the tension, and Chesnaye looked up at him with a small, curious smile. 'Yes, Doc. We can take aboard as many wounded as we can, and then you can get some practice in!'

Tregarth laughed throatily. 'Better them than me!'

The officers collected their notebooks and caps and shuffled towards the door.

Erskine was the last to leave. 'If we fail, sir, you could lose the ship!' His eyes were hidden by shadow. 'It's happened to others.'

Chesnaye regarded him slowly. 'If I ran for home without trying, John, I should lose something more!'

Long after Erskine had departed Chesnaye sat staring emptily at the soiled chart. Everything was repeating itself. Only time had moved on. Like Tobruk, he had been by-passed and overlooked, but now the stage was set. He had committed himself, the ship and two hundred men to uncertainty, even disaster.

The ship wallowed heavily as the wheel was put over. Fox was already setting her on her new course. How did *Saracen* feel about it? he wondered. Right from birth she had never been offered a fair and balanced fight. Now he was doing this to her. Another uneven struggle. Another gesture.

Fox slid open the door and peered into the yellow lamplight. 'On course, sir. One-nine-five.'

Fox was looking at the pile of signals, and Chesnaye could imagine what was running through his mind. There was nothing to say that the *Saracen*'s stores were to be run into Tobruk. Not in so many words. Chesnaye was to use his discretion. He was to weigh up the situation as he found it. By which time, of course, it would be too late for alternatives. It was a heartless position for a man who commanded a ship too slow to run away.

'Very well, Pilot. Thank you.' Chesnaye looked up sharply, aware of the despair which had crept into his voice.

But Fox grinned, unperturbed by his captain's tired and strained features. 'It's a damned sight harder than running bananas, sir!'

　　　　ø　　　　　＼　　　　　ʒ　　　　　▪　　　　　▪

'Steady on course. Closing at two thousand yards.'

Erksine nodded. 'Very good.' Fox's voice was calm and unruffled, like a cricket commentator's, he thought. He wiped a drip of spray from his night-glasses and swung them once more across the screen. The monitor's fo'c'sle was like a pale wedge on the dark rippling water as the *Saracen* crawled at reduced speed towards the shoreline. Voices were hushed, and he was conscious of the metallic creaks around him and the distant ping of the echo-sounder. Across the bows lay the shore. With macabre regularity the night sky rippled with dull red and yellow flashes, like distant lightning, he thought. With each threatening glow he could see the undulating shoulders of the land mass below, where men and guns crouched and waited.

The ship trembled, and he heard a man curse as an ammunition belt jangled sharply against the steel plates. The monitor's crew was at Action Stations, and had been for several hours. During the Dog Watches they had first sighted the faint purple smudge along the horizon. As the daylight had faded, and the stars had picked out the clear sky, the ship had felt her way slowly and purposefully towards the coast, every man waiting for discovery and the touch of battle. Nothing happened, and the slow minutes dragged into hours. The same pace. The same sounds. But there was a new smell in the cool air. The scent of land. The smell of dust and smoke.

'Starboard ten. Steady. Steer one-seven-five.' A hushed order, and an uneasy movement of feet on the gratings.

Erskine tried to relax his taut stomach muscles. His whole body felt cramped and strained. Why was this time so different? he wondered.

He heard Chesnaye say evenly, 'Looks like a fair bit of activity in the desert tonight!'

Just words, thought Erskine. He's worried. He could find no consolation in the fact.

It was amazing the way things changed in war, even for individuals. In Alexandria Erskine had reported to the flagship to discuss some arrangements concerning the coming voyage. Quite by chance, it seemed, he had met the Vice-Admiral himself. Beaushears had insisted that he take drinks with him in his quarters, and, flattered, Erskine had accepted. Now, in the darkness, it all looked different. As he relived those friendly, casual moments it almost seemed as if Beaushears had been questioning him, as if the meeting had not been by chance at all. He had not asked direct questions about Chesnaye, yet he was rarely absent from the conversation. Beaushears had shattered Erskine's normal reserve and caution by announcing casually, 'You'll know in a few days' time, but I'd like to be the first to tell you the good news.' Beaushears had smiled, and waited for a few more seconds. 'I think you'll be getting a very pleasant surprise shortly. I happen to know that you are earmarked for a command in the very near future.' He had watched the surprise changing to pleasure on Erskine's face. 'A destroyer, as a matter of fact.'

There had been more drinks, which, added to the heat, had made Erskine dazed and openly overjoyed. He could not believe it was happening to him, after the confusion and slurs of *Saracen*'s behaviour and the threat to his own career.

Beaushears had chatted amiably and at great length. 'We

need your sort, Erskine. The Navy has got mixed up, slack. We have to put up with every sort of misfit imaginable, but, then, I don't have to tell you that, eh?' They had both laughed, although Erskine was only half listening.

Beaushears had continued : 'I wouldn't like to see your career damaged in any way because of a superior officer's ambition or pigheadedness. It would not be *right*. I can be blunt with you. I know your record and your family. There was a time when we didn't mention such things, but things have changed. One man's behaviour reflects on all those around him. Either way, as local commander I want to know what is happening in the ships under my control. Incidents, actions by my captains, can give me a clear-cut picture of the over-all efficiency, if you see what I mean?'

He had questioned Erskine about the *Saracen*'s inability to help the stricken convoy, even about the man lost overboard. Beaushears had ended by saying offhandedly, 'I daresay you might have acted differently were you in command, eh?'

Erskine had been confused, and tried to reassemble his thoughts. He still could not recall exactly if he had given the Vice-Admiral the impression that he disapproved of Chesnaye's actions or whether Beaushears had put the words into his mouth. In any case, he was glad to leave the flagship, to get back to his cabin and think about the piece of news Beaushears had given him. A command at last. The waiting and marking time were over. Soon the *Saracen* and all she represented would be a thing of the past. Like the disinterested wardroom and the endless, futile tasks the ship was called to perform.

A new ship would mean another change, too. He would have to return to England, and a new life which must exclude Ann. He stirred uneasily at the thought. Perhaps she would understand. Maybe she had guessed that their lightning affair would not last. In spite of his insistence, he could not console himself, or remove the vague feeling of guilt. Inwardly he knew that it had been his indecision and not duty which had stopped him going ashore to tell her the news.

'Ah, there is is !' He heard Chesnaye's voice very close. A faint blue lamp stabbed across the water.

'Make the reply, Yeoman!' Chesnaye turned in his chair. 'The M.L. is here to guide us in.' He sounded fully awake and relaxed, although Erskine knew how rarely he slept.

The motor launch's low shape cut across the bows and then straightened on course, a faint sternlamp glittering to guide the monitor's helmsman. From inland came the muted rumble of artillery, followed by tiny white peardrops in the sky. Very lights. Erskine shivered. This operation had to be all right. If anything went badly this time, Beaushears would be quick to change his mind about his appointment.

He heard Fox grunt with alarm as a bulky freighter loomed out of the darkness and seemed to hang over the monitor's port rail.

But Chesnaye said calmly : 'A wreck. That M.L. skipper certainly knows his harbour in the dark!'

Sure enough, the little launch glided between scattered wrecks, leading the cumbersome monitor like a dog with a blind man.

Chesnaye peered at the luminous dial of his watch. 'Right, John. Get forrard and prepare to let go. We'll be up to the anchorage in two minutes or so.' His teeth shone in the darkness. 'Probably find we're in the middle of a blasted sand-dune when the sun comes up!'

Erskine grunted and heaved himself over the side of the bridge. He's actually enjoying himself, he thought. Still doesn't realise what it's all about.

He reached the fo'c'sle breathless and nervous, and two minutes later the *Saracen*'s anchor crashed into the sand and shingle of Tobruk harbour.

* * * * *

Within half an hour of dropping the anchor *Saracen* was required to move again. Guided by briefly flashing handlamps and her own power boats, she sidled blindly and warily nearer the shattered remains of a crumbling stone jetty. Another listing wreck barred her passage, and with more hushed and urgent orders she moved alongside the broken ship and was secured for final unloading. Using the wreck as a quay, and aided by three battered landing craft as well as her own boats, the monitor began to unload.

Hours passed and the labour continued without pause. From nowhere, and with hardly a word being spoken, came a horde of unshaven, tattered soldiers, who handled the drums and cases with the practised ease of men who have become accustomed to anything. Occasionally their faces showed themselves in the cold glare of a drifting flare, but otherwise they remained a busy, desperate collection of shadows.

Lieutenant Norris was stationed aboard the wrecked ship with a working party of some thirty seamen. At first he tried to assist, even speed, the unloading, but his orders seemed superfluous, and he himself inevitably got entangled with a knot of scurrying figures.

Sub-Lieutenant Bouverie was with him, as well as the young midshipman Danebury. That suited Norris, they were both his juniors, and both were amateurs like himself.

Once he tried to start a conversation with an army lieutenant who appeared briefly on the wreck's listing foredeck. Norris said with elaborate coolness : 'Hell of a job getting here. Gets harder all the time !'

The soldier had stopped dead in his tracks. 'Hard? You must be bloody well joking ! Christ, I'd give my right arm to live your cushy life !' He had vanished before Norris could recover his dignity.

Out of curiosity he climbed a rusting ladder and found the comparatively undamaged charthouse. He lit a cigarette and was just settling himself on a small swivel chair when Bouverie clattered up the ladder and joined him.

Norris peered at him through the gloom. 'Everything all right, Sub?' He disliked Bouverie's casual manner, his complete ease with his betters. In his other life he had always feared men of Bouverie's calibre, their acceptance of things he was denied, the vague references to a world he could never join.

'Going like a bomb.' Bouverie squatted on a table and craned his neck to look through the shattered windows towards the *Saracen*'s dark outline. 'The Skipper seems to know what he's up to. I wouldn't care to con a ship alongside in pitch darkness !'

Norris forced a yawn. 'When you've had a bit more experience you'll get the hang of it.'

'Really?' Bouverie's voice gave nothing away. 'I would have thought otherwise.'

'What's the snotty doing?' Norris curbed his annoyance with an effort. He knew Bouverie was laughing at him again.

'Oh, just keeping an eye on things. He's got a good P.O. with him. He'll be better without us breathing down his neck.'

'Damned snotties!' Norris drew heavily on the cigarette so that his face glowed red in the darkness. 'Think they know it all!'

'He seems a nice enough lad to me. A bit quiet, but then he was at school only a few months ago.'

Norris grunted irritably. 'How some of these people get commissions I'll never know.'

'I've wondered about some.' Bouverie changed the subject as Norris peered at him more closely. 'Dawn'll be up soon. Things might get lively then.'

'Now don't get windy, Sub!' Norris sounded angry. 'It'll be the Captain's fault if anything goes wrong!'

'I'm not *windy*, as you put it. Not yet, anyway. I've not had a lot of experience of the Andrew as yet, but if I have to learn there's no captain I'd rather have as a teacher.'

'He choked *you* off a while back!' Norris felt that the conversation was getting out of hand. This knowledge only made him angrier. 'I suppose you think because you've had a soft upbringing he'll take you under his wing!'

Bouverie smiled. 'You really are being rather offensive, you know! Why the enormous chip on the shoulder?'

Norris choked. 'What the hell d'you mean?'

'Well, just that you seem to think the whole damned world owes you something. I'd have thought you'd have settled down very well in the Navy.'

'I will!' Norris was confused. 'I mean, I have! I didn't ask to be sent to this old relic. In fact, I think someone had it in for me. Some of these regulars can never forgive the fact that *we* can earn a better living outside!'

'Teaching, for instance?'

'Damn you!' Norris was standing. 'Yes, teaching, if you put it like that!'

Bouverie nodded solemnly. 'A very rewarding task, I should imagine. A kind of challenge.'

'You don't know what it's like!' Norris was completely lost now. 'You've had an easy life, and now that you've found your way here you seem to expect the rest of us to carry you!'

Bouverie laughed quietly. 'As a lowly sub what choice do I have?'

There was a scrape of feet, and Norris swung round to face Danebury, the midshipman. 'Well? What are you skulking up here for?'

Danebury was a slight, fragile-looking youth, with pale eyes and a wide, girlish mouth. Strangely enough, he was well liked by the ship's company, who seemed to think that he needed protecting rather than respecting.

'All the petrol is clear, sir.' He shifted from one foot to the other. 'The hands are starting on the ammunition now.'

'Well, what d'you expect me to do? Give you a bloody medal?' Norris was shouting. 'Get down to the foredeck and try to set an example!'

The boy fled, and Norris felt a little better.

Bouverie stood up and brushed at his jacket. 'You really are a little bastard, Norris!'

He turned to go, and Norris yelled: 'How dare you speak to me like that? Stand *still* when I'm addressing you!'

'There are no witnesses, Norris, so forget it!' Bouverie's drawling voice had gained a sudden edge. 'I've watched you for weeks. You don't seem to know what you want to get from life, and really it's rather sad. I don't know why you worry so much about your station in life, when in fact you don't seem to belong anywhere!'

Then he was gone, and for several minutes Norris could only choke and gasp for breath. He felt halfway to tears, yet his anger refused to be quenched. How dare that bloody ex-barrister, with his casual references to Eton, his maddeningly offhand treatment of superior officers, speak to him as he had just done? When we get out of this place I'll wipe that smirk off his stupid face!

He was still muttering to himself when hours later the first greyness of dawn touched the desert, and in their distant emplacements the German gunners rubbed the too-brief sleep from their eyes and turned their attention to the battered harbour.

．　　■　　■　　■　　ﾉﾉ

Chesnaye watched the paling edge of the eastern horizon and rubbed his face briskly with his palms. Sleep seemed to be dragging him down, and he knew that if he did not resist the temptation to sit on the bridge chair he was done for. He heard a petty officer reporting to Fox : 'The ammunition is unloaded, sir. We've got all hands on the other stores now.'

Fox sounded entirely spent. 'Very well. Get the Buffer's party to shift that tinned food from aft first. It'll give the stretcher bearers more room to breathe when they haul the wounded aboard.'

Chesnaye leaned against the cool plating. 'Has the Doc got everything sorted out down there?'

'Yes, sir. There are two hundred wounded expected, mostly stretcher cases. They're going in the wardroom, the petty officers' quarters and the forrard mess deck. We'll keep the lower decks clear of wounded for the moment. I imagine one lot of ladders is enough to navigate—if you've got a few splinters in your guts !'

Chesnaye smiled. 'I agree. I hope we can give them a quiet passage.'

'Me too.' Fox sniffed the air. 'Half an hour and we'll be kind of naked out here !'

Chesnaye rose on his toes and peered down at the wreck alongside. Already he could see the ship's outline more clearly, and the antlike activity back and forth across the upper deck. He felt the dryness in his throat and tried to control the urge to go below and hurry the men along.

It was not enough to get rid of the petrol and the ammunition. There was still the ship, and the real danger which lay beyond the dawn light.

'Have hands stationed at all wires and springs, Pilot. And make sure the Chief is kept informed of the exact position, so that he can crack on speed at short notice.'

'I've done that, sir.'

'Good. This must be a bloody awful place to defend.'

Fox grunted. 'Brings back a few memories does it, sir?'

'A few. I never expected I should see this sort of warfare again.'

'Too little too late.' Fox was yawning in spite of his efforts to stop himself. 'Always the bloody same!'

The hull shuddered slightly as a landing craft came along the unoccupied side. There was the clatter of a derrick and some fierce shouting.

White against the black water and dull steel Chesnaye could see the patchwork of bandages and could sense the suffering. With a sudden impulse he swung himself on to the ladder and began to descend. 'Take over, Pilot. I'll not be far away.'

He joined Erskine by the guard-rail and watched in silence as the wounded soldiers were swayed aboard. Many willing hands reached out to steady them, to ease the pain on the last journey.

A harassed medical orderly, his steel helmet dented and scarred, held up his hand. ' 'Ere, stop lowerin'. Let this one down 'ere!' Skilfully the seamen manipulated the guys so that the pinioned soldier could be laid on the deck. The orderly knelt down, his fingers busy with the bandages. Half to himself he said : 'Shouldn't 'ave sent 'im. 'E's done for.' He stood up as another batch of wounded were heaved over the rail, and then turned quickly towards Chesnaye. ' 'Ere, mate! Keep an eye on this bloke for a tick!'

Erskine stepped forward to speak, but Chesnaye shook his head. 'All right, John, you can forget the protocol!' Then he stooped down and peered at the soldier's face, which suddenly seemed so small and shrunken. The man stared with fixed glassy eyes at Chesnaye's oak-leaved cap, so that for a few seconds he appeared to be dead. Then his hand moved from the stretcher and reached out vaguely.

'Where am I?'

Chesnaye took the soldier's hand in his own. It was ice cold. Like Pickles' hand had been. 'It's all right. You're safe now.'

The soldier coughed weakly. 'The Navy. The bloody Navy. Never thought I'd see you lot again.'

Chesnaye watched the man's life ebbing away with each

feeble pump of his heart. Who was this anonymous man? What had his sacrifice meant?

The soldier spoke with sudden clarity, 'It'll be all green in Dorset now, I expect?'

Chesnaye nodded, unable to speak.

'A real picture. I wanted so much to . . .' Then his hand tightened on Chesnaye's and he was dead.

A petty officer said harshly, 'Two more boats comin' alongside, sir!'

Erskine looked swiftly at Chesnaye's kneeling figure. 'Shall we tell them to stand off, sir? We should give ourselves more sea room!'

'Carry on with the loading, John.' Chesnaye stood up and walked back towards the bridge. 'We'll slip when we've taken on the last available man!'

Erskine watched him go, his mind torn apart with emotions. All at once he felt that he hated the unsteady, groaning figures who were coming aboard with such maddening slowness. Each man represented precious minutes. Each minute brought more light to the harbour and the desert beyond.

He found, too, that he hated Chesnaye for refusing to listen. For that and many other reasons which he could no longer define. He had become a symbol, an outlet for all his pent-up anxieties. Yet he knew, too, that all this was inevitable, just as he understood with sudden clarity that he was afraid.

■　　　■　　　■　　　■　　　■

Daylight showed the vast undulating rollers of the desert and the pitiful shambles which had once been a dusty and untroubled town. The harbour itself was littered with wrecks, some only marked by a solitary masthead, others by listing bridges and bomb-scarred superstructures.

With the pale light came the first bombardment, probing and slow at first, and then with the fierceness of a tornado. There were few good houses left to fall, so that the screaming high-explosives ploughed into the rubble and churned the torn remains into a living ferment.

Alongside the wreck the *Saracen* still lay imprisoned by

her mooring wires, her decks littered with broken packing cases and discarded equipment. One landing craft was alongside, and the tired seamen worked in a living chain to carry or guide the last of the wounded aboard.

Erskine ducked involuntarily as a shell exploded in the centre of the harbour and sent a stream of splinters whining overhead. The landing craft sidled clear, her hold for once empty.

Erskine broke into a run, but skidded to a halt as the tannoy speaker blared, 'Clear the upper deck, stand by to slip!' He stared uncomprehendingly as the big turret began to swing slightly to starboard, the twin guns lifting with purposeful menace. Erskine could not believe his eyes. Surely Chesnaye was not going to open fire! The enemy did not know of the *Saracen*'s presence as yet, otherwise he would soon have called upon his dive-bombers. Yet Chesnaye intended to betray his presence, to throw away those last vital moments. He had ordered the upper deck cleared so that the guns could blast away the moment the monitor was under way. The last of the seamen were already leaping from the wreck alongside, and Erskine could see the men by the mooring wires already slackening off and getting ready to slip.

A trail of dark smoke blossomed from the funnel, and beneath his feet Erskine could feel the impatient rumble of engines. From the bridge a voice echoed through a megaphone. 'Get those men aboard!' The last of the seamen from the wreck looked up, startled, and then jumped for the guard-rails.

Erskine climbed rapidly to the bridge where Chesnaye was hanging impatiently over the screen, a megaphone in his hand. 'All working parties aboard, sir. Boats hoisted and secure. Ready to proceed.' The words dropped from Erskine's mouth as he watched Chesnaye signalling vigorously to the side party.

'Good. Let go aft. Slow ahead port!' Chesnaye walked briskly to the front of the bridge to watch as the monitor moved cautiously ahead and nudged her weight against the one spring which held her to the wreck. Using one engine the *Saracen* pushed until the wire was bar-taut, until her stern began to swing slowly away from the listing ship.

'Stop port! Let go forrard!' Chesnaye's red-rimmed eyes were feverishly bright.

A rating with a handset looked across at him. 'All gone forrard, sir!'

Chesnaye seemed to force himself to stand quietly in the forefront of the bridge, his shoulders squared against the bright blue sky. 'Slow astern together!'

Very slowly the monitor gathered way, her rounded stern pushing through the oil and scum which covered the harbour in a fine web. Overhead the director squeaked on its mounting as McGowan and his plotters adjusted their sights and weighed up their target.

Chesnaye said coldly, 'When we pass the last wreck we can open fire.'

Erskine felt unsteady. So that was why they were leaving sternfirst. Chesnaye had every intention of using the guns to best advantage. He seemed to have thrown reason to the winds.

Chesnaye peered astern, his cap tilted to shut out the mocking glare from the water. The turret was still swinging, the guns rising towards the sun. He forced himself to watch the ship's slow passage between two sunken ships, his mouth a tight line. 'Starboard ten. Midships!' He held his breath as the monitor's fat flank almost brushed a forlorn mast which still had a tattered flag trailing across the unmoving water. Soon now. He could still feel the soldier's cold hand and he moved his fingers with sudden anger.

A light stabbed from amongst the shattered town, like sunlight reflecting from a telescope. He heard a signalman spelling out the signal, and then Laidlaw called, 'They say "good luck", sir!' The light flashed again, even as a brown shell-burst exploded beneath a last defiant minaret. 'And "Many thanks"!'

Chesnaye kept his eyes on the stone breakwater. 'Tell them "It was all part of the service!"'

Surprisingly, a man laughed, and another lifted his cap to wave at the long line of sun-dappled ruins.

The breakwater sidled past, and a small wave-crest surged eagerly beneath the *Saracen*'s counter.

Chesnaye lifted his glasses and looked towards the shell-bursts and listened to the distant chatter of machine-guns.

Something stirred inside him like an old memory, and he found the he was momentarily able to forget the ship's nakedness and the open sea which awaited him.

He turned and met Erskine's stare and the watchful silence which seemed to hang over the bridge.

Almost challengingly he said, 'Stop engines.' And as the rumble died away, 'Open fire!'

5

Stuka

In spite of the steady breeze the air was without life, and
seemed almost too hot to breathe. The watchkeepers stood
listless and heavy, each man careful to keep his body clear
of the steel plates and shimmering guns as the sun ground
down on their solitary ship. A fine blue haze hid the horizon
and added to the sense of complete isolation, and a million
tiny mirrors danced on the flat water to add further to the
discomfort of the lookouts.

Chesnaye slumped in his chair, forcing himself to remain
still as a thin stream of sweat moved down his spine. His
clothes felt rough and sodden, so that even taking a breath
became sheer discomfort.

The bridge throbbed to the tune of the two engines
which in spite of all else maintained a steady six and a half
knots, and made the small bow wave gurgle cheerfully
around the ship's stem. On the decks nothing moved, although Chesnaye knew without looking that the ship's
company was at Action Stations. Men were relieved in
small batches to enjoy brief respite in the messdecks, or to
help tend the long lines of army wounded. Between decks
there was a smell of pain, so that the seamen were soon
back on deck, as if uneasy at what they had seen.

Chesnaye glanced at his watch. Five hours since the short
bombardment and their departure from Tobruk. It still
seemed incredible that nothing more had happened. The
shoreline had faded into the morning mist and the sun had
risen high as if to pin them down on this pitiless sea. But
nothing happened.

At first he had been almost unable to remain still under
the mounting tension. Now, with each cheerful turn of the
screws, he found a few moments to hope. In spite of
Erskine's doubt and open resentment, the watchful eyes of
the others and the very real fear of his own abilities, Chesnaye could feel a glimmer of pleasure, even pride.

A bosun's mate placed an enamel mug at his elbow. 'Lemon juice, sir.' Chesnaye nodded and sipped it gratefully. His eyes felt raw and gummed with fatigue, and any distraction, no matter how small, helped to hold him together.

As he sipped at the already warm liquid he glanced at the bridge party. The Officer of the Watch, Fox, and his assistant, Sub-Lieutenant Bouverie, were standing elbow to elbow on the central gratings, their reddened faces turned to either bow as they took occasional sweeps of the horizon with their glasses. Two bosun's mates and a messenger stood at the rear by the charthouse entrance, eyes heavy and listless, waiting like terriers to pass the word of their master. Just to the rear of the bridge Chesnaye could see the slim Oerlikon barrels pointing skywards, the gunners already strapped in position, their half-naked bodies deeply tanned and immune to the probing rays.

McGowan would be at his station, keeping a watchful eye on the ship's defences, while his mind was no doubt still thinking of the short attack on the German positions.

It had been quick, savage and breathtaking. While the *Saracen* pitched easily on the small harbour swell the calm morning air had been torn apart by her massive onslaught. To the German gunners beyond the battered town it must have been even more of a shock. Used to fighting artillery duels with guns of their own calibre, and confident that the Tobruk fortress was almost ready to capitulate, the sudden thunder from the harbour must have seemed unreal. Unreal perhaps until the great fifteen-inch shells had begun to fall around them. McGowan and his gunnery team had very little to go on, but with methodical determination he had laid down a barrage some five miles wide, his heart jumping as each gun hurled itself back on its worn springs.

Then, with smoke still streaming from the two long guns, the monitor had swung about and steamed towards the open sea.

That was five hours earlier. Five hours. Chesnaye rubbed his eyes and drained the last few drips from the enamel mug.

There was a rustle of movement behind him. Fox said, 'Signal, sir!'

Chesnaye felt his stomach muscles contract, but forced his voice to remain steady. 'Read it.'

'From C.-in-C. Italian minelayer reported in vicinity. Believed north of Bardia and heading west. Minelayer is damaged and will try to reach first available harbour. Must be sunk or held until other forces available. There are two escorts.' Fox took a breath. 'There are a few alleged positions, sir, but that is the crux of the signal.'

Chesnaye ran his tongue along the back of his teeth. Once again the *Saracen* was to forget her own immediate problems. By the moving of a small pin or flag on some distant chart she had been drawn into the over-all plan of campaign. A few seconds before he had been thinking only of getting back to Alexandria without loss. Now, in a stammer of morse, he had another picture in his aching mind.

A minelayer. No doubt one of those fast cruiser-type ships which had been playing havoc around Malta, Crete and every piece of British-held shoreline in the Mediterranean. In hours a ship like that could lay a deadly field which if undetected would send many good craft to the bottom. Even if discovered at once, a minefield was still a menace. It had to be swept, and during that slow and painful business nothing could be allowed to move in that area. This particular minelayer had apparently been caught, probably by one of the few aircraft available for coastal patrol. Damaged, her speed might be severely cut, and her captain would think only of getting back to safety.

Chesnaye stood up, and felt a shaft of pain lance through his cramped thigh. He tried not to limp as he led the way to the charthouse, and then he waited as Fox laid off the possible position and course of the enemy ships.

Chesnaye leaned forward and squinted at the converging lines. 'Not bad.' He prodded the chart with the dividers. 'If I were the Italian captain I would not keep too close to the coast. Yesterday *we* were none too sure of the enemy positions in the desert. If this minelayer has been in the Eastern Mediterranean on operations her captain'll be no better informed than we were!' He tapped the chart thoughtfully. 'Probably keep about twenty miles off. But will follow the coast just in case of surface attack.' He was thinking aloud, while Fox watched him with open interest.

'He'll know that Tobruk is closed as far as we are concerned. His only danger will be from behind him, from Alex, or from a patrol further north. The first is obviously the only likely one, as we'll not be able to spare anything from the Greek campaign.'

Fox said : 'That's what the signal meant, I expect? The "other forces available" must be pursuing him from Alex?'

Chesnaye tightened his jaw. The Second Inshore Squadron, no doubt. Beaushears so determined to catch this sly interloper in his own area that he had even called in the *Saracen*. He smiled, but added in a calm voice : 'Yes, Pilot, the Italian gentlemen will not expect a ship of our size right ahead of him ! Lay off course to intercept, and send for the First Lieutenant.' He walked back into the sunlight, his fingers tightly laced behind his back. This would make up for their inability to help the convoy, for the hints and sneers which he and the ship had been made to endure.

He turned to see Erskine's flushed face already on the bridge. In short, terse sentences he explained the position and what he intended to do. Erskine listened without speaking, his eyes fixed on some point above his Captain's right shoulder.

Chesnaye concluded : 'Two or three rounds from the main armament should do the trick, even at extreme range. If she's carrying mines she'll go up like a Brock's Benefit, but in any case she'll be no problem.'

Erskine asked quietly, 'And the escorts, sir?'

'Well, they say there are two. They can't amount to much, though.'

'Why do you say that, sir?' Erskine looked mystified.

'It's hardly likely we'd have been told about the damaged minelayer if the escorts were bigger and more important, is it?'

'Well, no, sir.' Erskine was dazed by the change of events. As his tired mind cleared, he found a growing excitement. This enemy ship coming out of the blue was a gift indeed. The monitor could pound it to pulp even if the other vessel was four times as fast and ten times as manœuvrable. It was as if Providence had decided to make an offering to relieve the fear and apprehension of Tobruk.

Erskine had hardly spoken to the Captain since the

233

monitor had left the smoking harbour. He had looked for some light of triumph or contempt on Chesnaye's face, but it was impassive as always, giving nothing of the inner man away.

But this new venture would make all the difference. Erskine could even feel the news transmitting itself through the ship as he stood on the bridge with Chesnaye. The infallible system which carried information from man to man faster than any telegraph.

There was a cheer from aft, and Chesnaye remarked, 'Our people want another crack at the enemy, it seems!' He spoke evenly, but for a few seconds Erskine saw through the mask to the almost boyish excitement beyond.

Erskine received his orders in silence, and then as Chesnaye began to move away he said quickly, 'I want to apologise, sir.'

Chesnaye turned, his eyes alert. 'For what?'

'Tobruk. I didn't think the risk was worth making.' He stumbled miserably over each word. 'I was wrong. This minelayer will put us one up again!'

He saw Chesnaye's mouth soften slightly. 'We've not sunk it yet, John!' But although Chesnaye's voice was gruff he was obviously pleased.

Erskine looked across at Fox. 'We'll be up to her in less than an hour, eh?'

The Navigator grinned and nodded towards the Captain's back. 'I hope so, for *my* sake!'

Erskine climbed on to the ladder. Chesnaye was right. This ship was alive. Nothing had changed, but for the vague news of an enemy ship and the consequences of possible danger. Yet the ship stirred and came to life in a way Erskine had never seen before.

As the hands of the bridge clock embraced for noon the minelayer was sighted. The powerful range-finder above the bridge fastened on the tiny speck which hovered just below the rim of the horizon, and McGowan informed the Captain.

Almost simultaneously, Able Seaman Rix, anti-aircraft lookout on the starboard wing of the bridge, yelled: 'Aircraft! Bearing Green four-five!'

The klaxons screamed their warnings, and once more the *Saracen*'s man faced outwards and waited.

.   .   .   .   .

Lieutenant Max Eucken licked his lips and tried to retain the taste of the coffee he had been drinking only half an hour earlier. In spite of the tremendous heat which glared through the long perspex cockpit cover Eucken was able to remain completely relaxed, and his eyes hardly wavered as he stared ahead through the silvery arc of the Stuka's propeller. Without looking he knew that the other six aircraft were formed on either flank in a tight arrow-head formation, just as he could picture the face of each pilot, as well as the exact capability of every man under his command.

Below him the sea shone like a sheet of bright blue glass, and around him the sky was clear and inviting. Eucken was twenty-two years old, and at that very moment extremely contented.

It was amazing what a difference it made to a man's life the moment he was airborne, he thought. All the irritating faults and stipulations of the dusty airstrip were forgotten as soon as the wheels left the makeshift runway. Up here a man was king. Master of his own and other's destinies.

Voices crackled in his earphones, but he was able to ignore them. The other pilots were like himself. Excited and eager. Discipline and instant obedience could be switched on at a second's notice with the precision of a bombsight. For the moment the pilots could be left alone, trusted to keep formation and good lookout.

Behind him, at the rear of the long cockpit, Steuer, the rear-gunner, hunched over his weapons like an untidy sack. A bovine, unimaginative man, but completely reliable. He did as he was told, and trusted his pilot. Those qualities were quite enough by Eucken's standards.

He pulled in his stomach muscles and felt the sweat trickling down beneath the waistband of his shorts. Apart from these he was clad only in flying helmet and sandals, and he flexed his arms with sensuous pleasure, pleased with his own reflection in the oil-smeared perspex. His body was an even golden-brown, and the hairs on his forearms were bleached almost silver from the strange hermit existence in the desert.

He twisted his head to look at the three Stukas on his port quarter. Rising and falling gently like leaves in the wind, they appeared to be hovering against the pale sky, their wide-straddled fixed undercarriages poised like the claws of hunting hawks, which indeed they were. The nearest pilot raised his hand, and Eucken acknowledged him with a brief wave. That was Bredt, the only man apart from Steuer who had been with him since France and the big break-through.

To Eucken each phase of his war was interesting, provided it did not remain the same. He needed excitement, and enjoyed each aspect of it as some men relished sexual pleasure. He had lived long enough and had taken too many risks to believe in fear. He had forgotten its meaning soon after the first solo flight, and almost certainly following his first individual action in France. He could still remember that first time, perhaps more clearly than some of the things which had happened quite recently. The long straight roads choked and overflowing with streaming French refugees. While the Wehrmacht battered its way through a crumbling and decadent French Army and the British Expeditionary Force scattered towards Dunkirk, Eucken and his squadron helped to sow the seeds of confusion and panic behind the front. Jammed roads meant chaos and a break in supplies. The Stukas dived and screamed on the terror-stricken columns, their bombs carving bloody craters in the helpless victims below. As each bomber whined out of its dive the rear-gunner would take his toll too, the stammering machine-guns mowing down the trapped people like corn. Men, women, children, horses and cattle swept across the windshield in a crazed panorama from hell.

And so it went on. Victory after victory, until France was contained and the Stukas were sent further afield in search of prey.

Eucken rarely thought of his comrades in the other services. He disliked the Navy for its hidebound and arrogant ways. The U-boat Service was the only real attack weapon they had. The rest of the Navy seemed badly organised and not used to its fullest advantage. Neither did the Army appeal to him. Their sort of warfare conjured up pictures of a bygone age, as told to him by his father. Squalor, lice, ignorance and stagnation.

No, the air was the thing. And of all the planes which flew for Germany, the Stuka had struck the greatest blow. He could almost sense the great armour-piercing bomb which was slung a few feet beneath him. Soon he would be rid of it, and another ship would be on the bottom of that glistening water.

He had been lounging in the mess-tent beside the desert airstrip when the news had been received. Army Intelligence had reported a sudden and devastating bombardment from the sea off Tobruk. The enemy ship had escaped it seemed, and now there were cries for recriminations.

How like the Army! he thought with contempt. Always wanted the Luftwaffe to do its dirty work. And then, of course, there was this Italian minelayer. That, too, was somehow typical. How much better it would have been if the British had been Germany's allies. Together they could have stamped on all these sub-standard nations. But as the Führer had already explained, the British had been misled by Jews and Communists. They would just have to pay for their mistakes.

His handsome features crinkled in a small frown as Bredt's sharp voice cut into his ears. 'There it is! Dead ahead!' Eucken gave himself a small rebuke for allowing his mind to wander and so allow another to make the first sighting report. He leaned forward, his clear eyes reaching out ahead of his formation.

At first he thought the ship was stationary, and then almost in the same second he imagined that the strange-looking vessel had already been attacked. She looked ungainly, her superstructure unevenly spaced, so that at first glance he thought she had lost part of her stern. But as he drew nearer, and the vessel's outline hardened through the haze, he realised that this was indeed the one they were looking for. From the approach angle the monitor's shape was not unlike a tailor's steam iron, and from her small wash he guessed that she was doing less than eight knots.

It would be a copybook attack. The one they had executed so often in these waters.

He felt quite happy at the prospect. Perhaps it was because this was to be another new experience. The monitor was quite big, although he had no way of gauging its actual potential and value in over-all strategy.

Calmly he gave his orders and settled himself more comfortably in his harness. It would soon be over. There would probably be more decorations after this. Personally he did not care very much, but he knew that his parents would be pleased. It would make up in some way for his two brothers who had already died for the Fatherland. One in France, on the flank of the Maginot Line, the other in Holland, when his scoutcar had run over a mine. Strangely enough, he could hardly remember what they looked like.

The Stuka wagged its wings as the air suddenly blossomed with brown shell-bursts. The Tommies were evidently awake. Eucken smiled gently. Let them make the most of it. It would be a long swim for the survivors. About forty miles, at a guess.

The joke amused him, and he was still smiling as the port wing of bombers, led by Lieutenant Bredt, curved away and plummeted down towards the toylike ship. More shell-bursts, but the three Stukas flashed through them unscathed.

The other three Stukas were climbing to the right for a cross-attack, while Eucken idled along the same course, his keen eyes on the drama below.

Another voice shouted, 'I can see the minelayer!'

Sure enough, the limping Italian ship was also appearing on the scene. Eucken grinned. The more, the merrier.

A nerve jumped in his cheek as the first Stuka exploded in direct line with the monitor. Impassively he watched as the remnants of Bredt's aircraft were scattered across the calm sea in little white feathers of spray. The second Stuka was diving. Tracers lifted to greet it. The plane quivered then dropped into a full dive. All at once smoke poured from its wings and it continued to dive straight for the water. Eucken imagined he could hear the thunderous explosion as the Stuka's bomb exploded on impact. Bomb, aircraft and crew vanished in a bright orange flash well clear of the defiant monitor.

Eucken could feel his hands shaking with sudden rage. It was *his* fault. He had been over-confident.

His voice grated over the stuttering intercom. 'Keep clear! This is Red Leader! I am attacking!'

He heard the engine swell into a ferocious roar as he gunned the Stuka into a sidestepping dive. He saw the third attacker falter and pull away, a thin smoke trail streaming behind it. Down, down, faster and faster; until it seemed as if the wings would tear themselves free. Aloud he said, 'Don't forget to give them a long burst as I pull out, Steuer!' Behind him he heard the gunner grunt assent. Steuer never saw anything until the aircraft was out of its dive. It was a lonely job.

Eucken forgot Steuer, the Squadron and everything else as he used every ounce of skill and cunning on his approach. Behind his goggles his eyes were slitted with concentration as he hurled the bomber towards the strange ship. Already it had grown in size. It filled the windshield, and he could see the white caps on its upper bridge like tiny flowers on a grey rock.

Steady now! Ach . . . here come the tracers. Deceptively lazy the red lines climbed to criss-cross over the bomber's path. He watched his sighting mark, his breath almost stopped. Now! The Stuka fell into its final dive, the unearthly scream enclosing Eucken's mind like a drug.

Faster and faster! The aircraft was rocking madly from side to side, and he felt the thud and rip of metal against the fuselage. Above in the clear sky his comrades would be watching and waiting their turn.

Everything seemed enclosed in those tiny final seconds of attack. Eucken could see himself in his mind's eye, the black aircraft almost vertical as it plunged down. Its proud yellow stripes and squadron badge below the cockpit, a wolf with a ship between its jaws.

Almost time. The moment! He pressed the release button and pulled the Stuka out of its headlong plunge even as the monitor's tapering topmast swept to meet him. The plane jumped as the bomb left its rack, and Eucken wished that he could watch it strike home, as he knew it would.

There was one abbreviated explosion, and the Stuka fell over on to its side. All at once the tense but orderly world of the cockpit had exploded about him.

There was fire all around him, and he could hear someone screaming like a tortured animal. Automatically he flexed his arms to adjust the controls, but dumbly realised that only his brain was working, his limbs were frozen and useless.

The bright sun—which should have been at his back—was suddenly below him. First there was the sky and then the sea. The aircraft was revolving with gathering force as it plunged towards the blue water.

The pain came simultaneously with the realisation. But it was all too late. With glazed eyes Max Eucken, aged twenty-two, watched the sea tearing upwards to meet him. He could see the windshield being sprayed with his own blood, just as he could hear himself screaming. But he felt completely detached, and was still staring when the black Stuka hit the water.

•   ▪   ▪   •   ▪

To drop the bomb which struck the *Saracen* the Stuka pilot had planned his approach with great care. With a slight curve he had dived across the ship's port quarter, almost brushing the main topmast, so that the few who saw him imagined for a moment that the screaming aircraft was going to plunge into the mouth of the funnel itself. While the bomber banked and began to haul itself out of its steep dive, the single, gleaming bomb detached itself and plummeted straight for the crowded bridge.

Then several things happened simultaneously. As the Stuka displayed its striped underbelly the monitor's Oerlikon gunners, who had been keeping up a steady fire since the first enemy attack, saw their opportunity. Even as the aircraft began to regain height the fuselage sparkled in a long, unbroken line of small shell-bursts. The Stuka staggered, picked up again, and then began to spin out of control while the Oerlikons still hammered home their deadly blows. No one saw the German actually hit the water, for in that tiny instant the ship seemed to jump bodily as the bomb exploded.

It was well aimed, and in the seconds which passed to the sounds of blast and destruction it should have sent the ship on its way to the bottom to join the remains of the shattered aircraft. With the speed of light the bomb struck the front of the bridge superstructure with the sound of a giant hammer and ricocheted forward and down until it sliced into the rear of the tall barbette upon which the ship's great gun-turret was mounted. That first change of direction saved the *Saracen* from the mortal blow. I. guided the bomb clear of the small area of thinly armoured deck between the turret and the bridge, and instead sent it smashing its way at a forty-five-degree angle towards the empty lower messdeck where it exploded. Had the bomb struck the area intended, it would have cleaved straight down through two decks and on to the keel itself. Fuel and ammunition would have made an inferno to cover the inrush of water, and would have made escape impossible for many of the ship's company. As it was, the bomb was turned aside, to spend itself like a crazed beast before exploding in the monitor's steel bowels.

But in those agonising seconds, and in the long minutes which followed, there were few who really knew what had happened. Each man wondered and feared for his own safety, and many verged on the edge of panic.

Tending to the army wounded in the forward messdeck, Surgeon Lieutenant Wickersley felt the bomb strike the ship, and sat frozen on the deck as he listened to the thing tearing its way through the toughened steel with the noise of a bandsaw. The explosion lifted him from his trance, and as the long space filled with dust and drifting smoke he found with sudden surprise that he was able to ignore the unknown danger and turn, instead, to the bandaged figures which lay trapped and helpless around him. His assistants, made up of cooks, stewards and writers, and many others of the men who were not actually employed in fighting the ship, were staring at him, suddenly dependent and waiting.

Wickersley stood up and brushed some flaked paintwork from his hair. He gave his orders in a calm voice, inwardly grateful that now the moment had arrived he had beaten his fear and was ready to cope with the work for which he had been trained.

High above the bridge in the encased world of the control tower Lieutenant Norris had been sitting hunched and fascinated beside McGowan, the Control Officer. The small armoured nerve-centre of the ship's gunpower had suddenly vibrated to the scream of the diving Stuka, so that even the stammer of Oerlikons and the deeper bark of pompoms seemed muted by comparison. Still Norris had been unable to accept that the moment had arrived. Not until the shadow of the screaming aircraft had enveloped the open bridge below him, and a dark streak had flashed down across his vision towards the figure of the Captain himself, did Norris fully realise his very real danger. He wanted to turn away, or bury his face in the back of the rating at the training mechanism, but he was quite unable to close his eyes to the impossible sight of the bomb grinding across the front of the bridge in a shower of sparks to disappear somewhere at the foot of the massive turret. The explosion came after what seemed an age of waiting, and then it was as if it had come from another bomb altogether. Far away, muffled and sullen, it seemed to be in the very bowels of the ship. The air was filled with black smoke which fanned by the breeze billowed back over the bridge until the lonely control tower was lost and isolated in an impenetrable cloud. McGowan's face looked grey, but his voice was toneless as he spoke quickly to his handset. The four ratings glanced quickly at their officers and then settled back again on their stools. If they were near terror they gave no sign as far as Norris could see, even though their small refuge and the tripod mast beneath still thrummed like some maniac instrument.

Until the bombers were sighted Norris had been watching the slow approach of the enemy minelayer. As Spotting Officer he had been mentally rehearsing his duties, even looking forward to the moment when the guns would begin to pound the injured enemy to fragments. His task would be to guide the groping guns directly on to their target, a feeling which at a safe range gave him the satisfaction of immeasurable power.

McGowan was saying sharply : 'Exploded in lower messdeck ! The damage control party is on its way !'

For something to say, Norris asked weakly, 'Is the turret safe?'

McGowan shrugged and looked at Norris for the first time. 'Quarters Officer reports several injuries. Concussion mostly!' He laughed harshly, as if unable to understand that he was alive. 'The other bombers have buggered off!'

Erskine was already making his way below to the roaring inferno of fire and black smoke. Around him men fought with hoses and extinguishers to control the feelers of flame, while others dealt with the menace beyond the glowing watertight doors. Messengers came and went, while Erskine passed his orders almost in a daze. He still did not know the full extent of the damage, but what he had seen was bad enough.

A petty officer and two seamen who had been pulped to a purple mess by the force of the explosion. An Oerlikon gun complete with gunner and magazine which had been torn from its mounting and hurled over the port rail with the ease of a child's toy. A nameless rating, stripped naked by blast, who had dashed past him screaming, his body flayed by foot-long wood splinters from the deck at the base of the turret.

The Chief Bosun's Mate said in his ear: 'We'll soon 'ave the fire in 'and, sir! Must get some of the wounded moved a bit sharpish afore they get roasted!'

Erskine shook himself. 'Yes. Very well, Buffer, you get your men on to it.' He broke off, coughing as more smoke funnelled its way through the avenue of shattered mess tables, shredded clothing and smashed crockery.

The Chief Bosun's Mate wiped his sweating face and gestured towards a pin-up which still remained seductively in position above a smouldering locker. 'I couldn't even manage 'er at the moment, sir!'

Erskine tried to smile, but his jaws felt fixed and taut. With a groan he began to retrace his steps as another messenger ran towards him through the smoke. I must report to the bridge. His brain rebelled, but he forced himself to concentrate, the effort making him sway.

There was so much to do. And there was still the mine-layer to be pinned down and sunk.

*   *   *   *   *

'Here, sir! Let me help you!'

Chesnaye felt Fox's hand beneath his elbow and staggered to his feet. His head felt as if it was splitting in half, and as the smoke billowed over the lip of the bridge he knew he was near to collapse. It was as if the bomb had been aimed at him. He had actually seen it, a dark smudge against the bright sky, before it struck the steel behind him and hurled him to the deck with its searing shock-wave. Everyone seemed to be shouting, and each voice-pipe and telephone was demanding attention.

'Bombers making off, sir!' Fox was still holding his arm, his dark face tight with concern. 'Damage reports coming in now.'

Chesnaye nodded vaguely and limped to the forward screen. Broken glass crunched beneath his shoes, and he felt a cold hand on his heart as he looked down at the deck below. The teak planking had been jack-knifed by the explosion, and from the jagged tear in the foot of the barbette he saw the unbroken spiral of black smoke. There were mixed cries and shouted orders, and he could see the stretcher bearers already groping their way towards the ship's wound.

He must not think of it. The others would do their job. He had to control the ship. To find the enemy.

He blinked his streaming eyes. 'Alter course two points to starboard.' Must get this damned smoke clear of the bridge.

He stared for several seconds at the raw scar on the edge of the steel left by the bomb. It must have missed me by inches, he thought. A few feet this way and the wheelhouse would have been knocked out. A bit further forward and the turret might have been wrecked.

Fox said, 'Eight of our people killed, sir. One missing.'

'Thank you.' Missing? That must have been the Oerlikon gunner.

Fox was holding a handset. 'The Gunnery Officer, sir.'

Chesnaye took the handset, his eyes still on the clouds of smoke. With the slight alteration of course the ship was being kept clear. 'Give me the target range, Guns.' He felt some of the tension draining from him. They had survived again. They had been attacked, but had hit back in spite of the enemy's determination.

'Range is ten thousand yards, sir.' McGowan sounded strained. 'I should like to clear the turret, sir.'

Chesnaye's mind snapped back to the immediate problems. 'Clear the turret? The Quarters Officer has reported no serious damage!'

McGowan said flatly : 'He has just reported to me, sir. The bomb passed through the working chamber below the turntable compartment and has sheared off a section of the lower roller path.'

Chesnaye tried to drive the sense of unreality from his brain. 'D'you mean the turret won't train?'

'That's right, sir. The guns are quite intact and fully operational. But the turret cannot be moved.'

Chesnaye felt as if the bridge was closing in on him. A strong eddy of wind cleared the smoke from the fo'c'sle, and for a few moments he was able to see the black silhouette of the Italian ship fine on the port bow. The minelayer's shape was already lengthening. She was sheering away.

Controlling his voice with an effort. Chesnaye said, 'If we can't use the training gear, what about operating the turret by hand?'

McGowan sounded almost gentle. 'No, sir. Until the shore artificers can fix the roller path the turret is fixed.'

'Very well. Keep me informed.' Blindly he handed the receiver to Fox and walked to the front of the bridge.

Like an additional mockery he heard a messenger repeat. 'Fire under control, sir! Damage Control report no damage to hull.'

The density of smoke faded, and Chesnaye lifted his glasses to stare again at the distant minelayer. He could see the ship quite clearly and the two trawler-type escorts which hovered on either beam. The Italian captain must be wondering what was happening. A powerful ship, its tall turret so easy to see with binoculars, had suddenly appeared in his path. Death and destruction must have seemed inevitable. Even the timely entrance of seven dive-bombers had failed to remove this new and threatening shape.

But now, as the Italian coaxed the last ounce of steam from the damaged engines and altered course away from the enemy, he must have become aware of something even stranger. Those great guns remained stiff and unmoving. As the bearing changed, the guns stayed pointing impotently at some point far astern.

Chesnaye said at length, 'Ask McGowan if we can try a sighting shot if I swing the ship by engines alone.'

He waited, aware that every man on the bridge was avoiding his eye.

Fox said quietly : 'Negative, sir. It could do the turret irreparable damage, and in any case it would be almost impossible to get a close shot under these circumstances.' Fox looked past Chesnaye and followed the enemy ship with hatred in his eyes. 'Goddamn, she was so near too !'

Chesnaye walked to his chair. Without looking, he knew that Erskine had joined the others behind him. At length he said : 'Fall out Action Stations. Resume course for Base.

He heard Fox swear, and then stiffened as McGowan joined him on the bridge. McGowan said, 'I'm sorry, sir.'

Chesnaye could not tear his eyes from the smudge of smoke which marked the place where the minelayer had dipped over the horizon. 'So am I, Guns.'

From far away he heard Erskine's voice, 'There will have to be a signal, sir.'

Damn you ! Chesnaye knew that Erskine was watching him, waiting for him to crack. To admit his mistakes.

Coldly he replied : 'Make a signal, then. We are returning to Base. Lost contact with enemy.'

Erskine persisted, his voice heavy, 'You could add that we have been damaged and require escort, sir?'

Chesnaye half turned, his eyes bitter. 'That's how you would do it, I suppose? Well, I don't need any damned excuses for my ship !'

A shutter fell across Erskine's troubled features. 'Very well, sir. I'll have the signal sent off now.'

Chesnaye stared ahead over the bows. Yes, you do that. Get ready to save yourself when I am being crucified !

Later in the charthouse McGowan said softly : 'Well, it was only a Wop minelayer. We were lucky to get away with the bloody bombing !'

Fox stared at him and then shrugged. 'It's not just a Wop minelayer to the Skipper. It was a chance for him and the old ship. In the eyes of your bloody admiral he's made a cock of it, an' that's all there is to it!'

McGowan frowned. 'I don't see it that way at all.'

'That's what is wrong with you regulars! You don't see anything beyond K.R.s and A.I.s. It explains why you're so bloody callous with each other!' With sudden rage Fox slammed down his ruler and stamped back on to the bridge.

Why should *I* care? he thought angrily. They're all the damned same! Why get involved with something which has always been the same, and probably always will?

He felt his eyes drawn to the Captain's shoulders and knew he was deceiving himself. Nothing could ever be quite the same in future.

6

Ann

'Ship secure, sir!' Erskine saluted formally and waited as Chesnaye stared down at the long, dusty jetty. Already parties of *Saracen*'s seamen were running out the long brows, watched incuriously by the drivers of the silent convoy of khaki ambulances which had been waiting for the ship to come alongside the wharf.

Alexandria was much the same as usual. Anchored ships, dust and the over-all heat haze. But it was Sunday morning, and in spite of the threatening news from the Western Desert, and the painful withdrawals from Greece, the vessels of the Mediterranean Fleet which were lucky enough to be in harbour were observing the ceremonial of the Day of Rest. Church pennants fluttered from ship's yards, and from a towering battleship which had once seen service at Jutland came the strains of a marine band. 'For those in peril on the sea . . .' Bared heads, best uniforms, and here and there the flutter of a sailor's collar, although there seemed to be no breeze.

Only the *Saracen* provided movement and an alien air of untidiness. Two tall cranes had squeaked along their miniature railway and now stood poised like ungainly herons as they inspected their prey. The ship's own derricks clattered into life and began to swing some of the more seriously wounded troops ashore, and Erskine could see Wickersley and his two sick-berth attendants conferring with some of the army medical orderlies on the jetty.

The engines had fallen silent, and groups of unemployed seamen were moving wearily around the upper deck as if seeing the scars and damage for the first time.

Erskine waited. He had nothing planned any more. He felt uneasy and unsure, as if he was on the brink of a new phase in his life. His orders might already be on their way to the ship. This time tomorrow he could be *en route* for

England. Involuntarily he glanced towards the white houses above the harbour and wondered if Ann was already watching the ship and waiting for him. This time there could be no excuses. He would have to try to explain to her. The ship would need a good deal of attention from the repair workers, and even with speed and priorities the work would take more than a week, perhaps longer. In that time he would have to make a decision.

Chesnaye said, 'Keep both watches at work until midday and then pipe Make-and-Mend.'

'Shore leave, too, sir?' Erskine turned to look at the Captain's tired, stubbled face and tried to keep his own mind from becoming involved with Chesnaye's problems.

'Yes. There'll be little done today if I know the authorities here. Just keep the duty part of the watch aboard. The rest have earned a breather. They've done well.'

Erskine said suddenly, 'I thought we might have a wardroom party while we're here, sir?' He was almost surprised to hear his own suggestion. Deep down he knew it was just another excuse. Surrounded by familiar faces it might be easier to explain to Ann. 'We could get a few friends from the Base, some of the nurses and so on?'

Chesnaye nodded, his thoughts far away. 'You arrange it if you want to.'

'Anything else, sir?'

'Yes. Get the hands out of working rig as soon as possible. There's no reason for the ship's company to look like a lot of pirates.'

Erskine sighed. Across the water on the battleship he could see the lines of white-clad seamen, the flash of sunlight on the band's polished instruments. By comparison the *Saracen* looked a wreck. Smoke-stained and battered, with her splintered deck and gashed turret adding to the appearance of shabbiness.

Chesnaye looked around the bridge and said, 'I'm going to my quarters to complete my reports.'

'I'll keep an eye on things.' Erskine hated this game with words. The Navy made it so easy. Question and answer. Challenge and password. In this manner you could speak to superior and subordinate for months and yet say nothing.

There was a slight cough, and Fox appeared at the head of the bridge ladder. 'Signal from Flag, sir.' He held out the pad, his eyes anxious.

Chesnaye did not take the pad. 'For the captain of *Saracen* to report on board the flagship forthwith?' He smiled briefly at Fox's discomfort. 'I was expecting it.' He seemed to square his shoulders. 'Tell my steward to lay out a clean uniform while I take a shave and shower. I expect the Admiral can wait a little longer!' There was no bitterness in his tone, in fact there was nothing at all.

Fox stood aside to let him pass and then said to Erskine, 'The signal requires a report from *you* too, Number One!'

Erskine started from his troubled thoughts. 'Me?' Fox's stare made him feel uneasy.

'The Admiral apparently requires your statement for some reason or other. It seems he was rather keen on catching that damned minelayer!'

Erskine looked away. So there was to be no escape, no easy way even from this. Beaushears wanted him to stab Chesnaye in the back. With sudden anger he kicked at the gratings. Well, Chesnaye had acted incorrectly. He should have kept clear of Tobruk once he had found that the original landing point was unusable. He had risked the ship to get rid of the stores, and by his bombardment had drawn attention to the ship's position. His action had cost the ship the chance of sinking the minelayer. It might cost Chesnaye much more.

Fox said quietly, 'What will you say?'

'That's my affair!' Erskine avoided Fox's hard eyes. 'It's unfair that I should be involved in this business at all!'

'So you intend to walk out on us, eh?' Fox stood his ground.

'What the hell are you talking about?'

'You think that getting promotion is suddenly so goddamned important that you can act like a bloody judge!' Fox's eyes were flashing dangerously. 'I know you can log me for speaking like this, but someone's got to tell you!'

Erskine felt the colour rushing to his face. 'What'd you know about it? After this war's over you'll run back to your damned banana boat! I'm in the Navy for a *career*!'

Fox threw the signal pad on to an ammunition locker.

'It may have escaped your notice, but we've not won the bloody war yet! And the way we're going, it now seems almost unlikely!' He stared at Erskine with calm distaste. 'When we *have* won you can throw men like Chesnaye back on the beach and men like me back to earning a living from the sea. Until that happy time just remember that it's the Chesnayes of this world who can save us, *if* they're given a chance!' He turned to leave. 'They're the only poor bastards who *don't* think of the future!'

Erskine knew he should have stopped Fox's outburst, but he had been incapable of doing anything. It had been like a scourge, a necessary punishment. Or perhaps it was because Fox was the most unlikely officer aboard to show such emotion.

He shook himself and moved to the rear of the bridge where Pike, the Master-at-Arms, was waiting with a little procession of defaulters. It never stopped, Erskine told himself wearily, peace or war, whatever you had to torment your inner self, routine must still be observed.

He straightened his cap. 'Very well, Master. Let's get it over with!'

* * * * *

Compared with the arctic brightness of the street outside the narrow window, the room seemed dim and somehow smaller than Erskine had remembered it. He sat heavily on the sagging sofa his hands hanging between his knees, his eyes on the girl's back as she stood silhouetted against the white-fronted building opposite.

Over her shoulder she said quietly, 'Well, that's it, then, isn't it?' Her voice was low and even, and it seemed to stir yet another memory in Erskine, like the return of an old pain.

'I thought I ought to tell you right away, Ann. It seemed only fair.' Already he was regretting that he was here, yet at the same time unable to stop his mind responding to her presence.

Ann Curzon was tall and slim, and Erskine noticed with another pang that she was barefoot on the tiled floor. She had remembered that he had once remarked about her being his own height. She had been waiting for him. Expecting him. Even the small, overcrowded room looked friendly and pleased with itself, as if Ann had taken special pains for his visit. She turned and looked down at him. She was wearing a plain white blouse and narrow green skirt which accentuated the perfect shape of her body.

Erskine could not see beyond the shadows which hid her eyes and said : 'I hope you'll be able to come aboard the *Saracen* this evening. It'll probably be the last time we'll all be together.'

The girl walked slowly to a small table and ran her fingers across the unopened wine which stood with its attendant glasses. Erskine noted the rich tan of her bare legs and the way the fringe of hair across her forehead had become bleached by the sun. The old yearning stirred inside him, and he added tightly, 'We knew this might happen, Ann.'

She sat down on a stool and picked up a packet of cigarettes. 'Did we?' Then she smiled, as if at some inner memory. 'I suppose *I* must have known.'

Erskine felt sick. Of this situation, of himself. Of what he had done.

As if reading his thoughts she said, 'Why did you have to tell that story about your captain?'

Erskine started. 'It was the truth as I saw it.' Being suddenly on the defensive made him confused.

'As *you* saw it !' She blew out a stream of smoke. 'I expect the Admiral was pleased with you.'

'I wish I'd not told you about it. I thought it might explain——'

She cut him short. 'You came because you thought it was your duty. Just as you felt you should inform the Admiral that in your opinion your captain is incapable of doing his job !' Her wide eyes flashed with anger. 'Result? Exit captain and enter John Erskine, the Admiral's friend !'

Erskine jumped to his feet. He felt betrayed, as if the ground had suddenly been dragged from beneath him. 'That's unfair ! I was asked what I thought. I told him !'

'I'll bet !' She was also on her feet, and as Erskine watched she walked quickly to the window. Across the street the carpet trader still sat outside his small shop surrounded by his dusty rugs, which hung from the flaking walls like battle flags.

Erskine tried again. 'Look, Ann, I didn't want it to be like this. I didn't want to talk about the ship, but about us.' He stood behind her and put his hands on her shoulders. 'I'll have to go to England, and after that I don't know what might happen.' He felt the moist warmth of her shoulders through the thin blouse and tried to pull her against him. He felt her stiffen, and saw the quick tilt of her head.

She slipped from his grasp and turned to face him. 'You've a short memory, John. It was here in this room, remember? Down there on the floor!'

He started to step back, but her voice held him. 'Don't you like to face it, John? Doesn't it fit in with your scheme of things?'

'I can only say that I'm sorry. I know it doesn't help.'

Her lips parted in a small smile. 'No, it doesn't.'

Then, in an almost matter-of-fact voice, she added, 'I'm leaving here, too.'

Erskine answered quickly, relieved to change the subject, 'Oh, where are you going?'

'To Malta.'

Erskine, who had been stealing a quick glance at his watch, stared at her with surprise. 'Malta? Like hell you are!'

'You have no control of my life any more, John. If you ever did. As you know, I've been some use at the hospital. I could do something over there too.'

'They'll never allow it!' Erskine was surprised to find out how much the news had unsettled him.

'They already have. The Red Cross can do any damn' thing!' She eyed him calmly. 'Even your admiral couldn't stop me!'

Erskine reached for his cap. 'Look, Ann, I must go back to the ship. There's a lot to do.' He knew he had to see her again, to make it right with her. 'I mean this, Ann. Could you come aboard tonight?'

Surprisingly she replied: 'I wouldn't miss it for the world. I think I shall get drunk!'

He reached out and held her arm. It was warm and very

253

smooth. All at once the old memories came crowding back. That evening ashore, the laughter and the friendly jibes from the others. Then being alone, here, with Ann. The quick, breathless movements, and the eager pressure of her flesh against his. He squeezed her arm. 'It doesn't have to be like this, Ann.'

She looked directly at his face. 'Perhaps we were lovers, John. But apparently we were not in love.' She withdrew her arm and touched it with her fingertips, her eyes distant. 'You want to go, John, but because of your code you want to go with my blessing.' She shrugged. 'Well, you've got it, now for God's sake leave me to think.'

He moved quickly to the door. An unnerving thought crossed his mind and he said, 'You'll be all right?'

Without looking up, she answered, 'I'll not cut my throat, if that's what you mean!'

Then he was out in the street and almost running towards the harbour. But the freedom he had anticipated still eluded him, and the guilt which he had tried to hold at bay enclosed like a sea-fog.

He slowed his pace, his face creased in thought. He had done the only thing possible, both with Ann and with the ship. Yet just being with her again had reopened the wound, and even as he walked away from the quiet street he could feel the old yearning and desire. How had she really taken this news? Did she even care? He was still deep in thought when he reached the jetty and the jagged outline of the *Saracen*.

* * * * *

Chesnaye left his littered desk and walked slowly to the open scuttle. The sun was already low and threw a dark shadow of the monitor's superstructure across the harbour's placid water. He loosened his jacket and peered down at a small harbour launch which was carrying a noisy party of libertymen from one of the anchored destroyers. He had always liked to watch the life of a busy port, but now it did not seem to matter. Behind him the desk waited with its pile of reports, requisitions and stores demands. The hundred and one things which every captain was expected to deal with the moment his ship nestled alongside. Normally Chesnaye enjoyed this task. From his aloof over-all position of command it brought him in regular contact with all the small details which made the ship a working machine. Even the pathetic signals about unfaithful wives, bombed-out homes and relatives killed in action helped to preserve his sense of humanity and understanding of the men who served him. Mere faces had become personalities, and abilities no longer had to be judged by record papers or the badges on a rating's sleeve.

Now that was soon to be finished. As a fresh wave of despair passed over him he began to move quickly and aimlessly about the wide, shabby stateroom, with its heavy furniture and frayed carpet. When Chesnaye had returned from his brief visit to the flagship he had thrown himself into the waiting correspondence as if by doing so he could blot out the misery which Beaushears had so coldly thrown at him. Now Paymaster Sub-Lieutenant Philpott and the Chief Writer had departed, and he was unable to keep his wretchedness at bay. The interview with the Admiral had been much as he had expected. After being kept waiting for the best part of an hour he had been ushered into Beaushears' quarters by the same elegant flag-lieutenant. But this time Beaushears had seen him alone, his face stiff and yet somehow eager as he slammed home one point after another.

'I warned you, Chesnaye.' Beaushears had started to pace, as if he had been working himself into a rage for some time. 'But you still think you know best! I've had a dozen reports to do concerning this minelayer business, and I'm about sick of it!'

Chesnaye had kept his voice under control with effort. 'My orders gave me a certain latitude, sir. I landed my stores and the Army were very grateful.'

Beaushears waved his hand impatiently. 'I've received a signal about that *and* the bombardment you took upon yourself to supply!' He seemed beside himself. 'Naturally the Army were pleased! What do they know about our situation? We're snowed under with work, and, in case you're interested, we're even shorter of ships and men than we were before!'

Chesnaye spoke carefully : 'The Greek campaign was a waste of time. I implied as much when I was here before!' He could feel his reserves of patience draining away. Days and nights on the bridge without sleep were taking their toll. In any case, Beaushears had obviously made up his mind without much goading. 'I understand we lost twenty-three ships in one day, and two hospital ships to boot. I'm not surprised the Admiralty are worried!'

Beaushears had stopped his pacing and had stared at him with sudden calm. 'Look, Chesnaye, you seem to mis-understand why you are here! I didn't call you to this ship to ask your opinions of world strategy or how to run my squadron. You were given a task, straightforward and un-complicated. Not to mince words, you made a complete muck of it. If it hadn't been for that stupid bombardment you would have been clear away and in a position to stop the minelayer. It's the convoy all over again. You just can-not bring yourself to understand that your job is not to decide policy but to obey orders, in this instance *my* orders!'

Outside the curtained doorway Chesnaye had heard the distant laughter of the flagship's officers as they gathered for their pre-lunch gins in the wardroom. Always after Sunday Divisions the occasion seemed gayer and more exuberant, like a first-night of a dramatic society where the players have brought off a performance without muffing their lines.

It had painfully reminded him of the day he had joined the *Saracen* for the first time in Portsmouth. A callow youth, nervous, but hiding behind a mask of impassive calm, as he was before Beaushears. At that far-off time the monitor's officers had also been recovering from Divisions. In his mind's eye Chesnaye recalled the scene like a picture from an old book. The heavy epaulettes and frock-coats, but otherwise the same Navy. The thought and realisation made him angry again. Of course, that was the fault with the Navy, with the whole fighting machine. The men who were the professionals were in fact only amateurs. They ignored experience, and carried on with their same out-worn ideas.

Coldly he had replied, 'The *Saracen*'s first task is to supply support for land forces——'

Beaushears' interruption had been loud and final. 'Not any more! She's little more than a store-ship as far as I'm concerned! With the enemy putting on the pressure throughout the Mediterranean it now seems even that role is unsuitable!' Beaushears had forced himself to sit down. 'Your orders will explain what you have to do. *Saracen* will sail when repairs are completed, probably within seven days, and proceed to Malta. The island is near collapse because of lack of supplies, and we are going to push a fast convoy from here in the hope that some of the ships get there. Force "H" will be faking a dummy run from Gibraltar to divide enemy forces, and everything will be done to get the ships through. *Saracen* will sail early, and our convoy should overtake you a day or so before you reach Malta. You can supply extra anti aircraft cover, and my squadron will screen the convoy from surface attack.' Beaushears had dropped his eyes. 'At Malta *Saracen* can continue to supply A.A. cover for the harbour and act as a base ship for personnel, etcetera. If she avoids being sunk she might still be of some use.'

Chesnaye could still feel the shock of those words. 'You mean she'll not be required for sea again, sir? Not *wanted*?'

'That is exactly what I mean. You have two hundred trained ratings aboard. Most of them will be needed for other ships as replacements. Your second-in-command has been offered a ship of his own, and most of your other officers will no doubt be willing to leave as early as they can.'

Chesnaye had a mental picture of the *Saracen* tied alongside the bombed shambles of Malta's dockyard as the island received one air raid after another. Destroyers and cruisers had already fallen to the attacks. The old monitor would survive for an even shorter period.

In a strangled voice he had asked, 'Will I be retained in command?'

Beaushears had regarded him directly for the first time. 'That will be up to your new flag officer. But I have stated in my report that I consider the maintenance of a full captain aboard to be unnecessary. The ship will be a floating gun battery. Any junior officer should be able to do that job! No, Chesnaye, your place is at home. Go back to training men for the Navy. Your ideas are out of touch. Perhaps later,' he had shrugged indifferently, 'but now we have an immediate job to do.'

It had taken every ounce of Chesnaye's control to stop from openly pleading. Looking back, it seemed as if that was what Beaushears had expected. There had been a long silence, and then Beaushears had said, 'You would have said the same if the roles were reversed.'

Chesnaye had stood up, his face pale. 'Your seniority gives you the right to express that opinion, sir. It still gives me the right to repudiate it!'

Chesnaye glanced at his watch. The interview had only taken place a few hours ago. The wounded troops had been landed just that morning. It all seemed so long past that Chesnaye felt confused. He needed sleep, and he had not found the time to eat, yet he knew that he could not give in or leave himself open to his despair. In a moment or two his steward would be fussing around him and getting his uniform ready for the wardroom party. The thought almost made him give in to the flood of emotion which pressed so hard on his reason.

No wonder Erskine had wanted a party. *He* had already known the outcome of the interview with Beaushears. To think that Beaushears could use his position to destroy him through a subordinate officer. It did not matter what Erskine had said. There was no open accusation of negligence, so, as usual, the Admiral had it all on his side.

Chesnaye thought of the pseudo-training establishments with their painted stones and pompous instructors. In a fit of anger he told himself he should have stayed in New Zealand, and then he looked again at the shabby stateroom and seemed to see beyond and through the length of the ship herself

Sailing day was still a week away. Anything might happen before that. But even as he tried to restore his belief he knew that he was deluding himself.

If he had been given command of any other ship this would never have happened. But he did not want another command. The *Saracen* was not just a ship, nor had she ever been.

He was staring at the open scuttle when the steward entered and began to lay out his uniform.

• • • • •

The *Saracen*'s wardroom had been cleared of unnecessary furniture and fittings for the party, but was nevertheless crammed to overflowing with noisy, perspiring visitors. Mostly officers and officials from the Base, with a sprinkling from other wardrooms of nearby ships. Older, more senior, officers looked unnaturally gay in their mess-jackets, whilst the reservists stood or slumped in white drill which was already crumpled and stained in the close, smoke-thickened atmosphere. There were women, too. Mostly nurses, with a handful of Wren officers, the wives of government officials and a few others who had merely arrived with their escorts.

Wickersley leaned back in a canvas chair, one arm resting on the side of the long makeshift bar, behind which the stewards ladled ice into pink gins and refilled glasses as fast as they were able. He glanced at his companions and swallowed some more gin. From his short experience of the Navy these parties all seemed the same. All you needed was a ship. There was always an unlimited number of people waiting to be invited. Mostly shore-based people who never turned their backs on a chance of getting hold of some duty-free booze. Wickersley laughed at the idea and groped vaguely for another glass.

Must be getting tight already, he thought. It was always the same. You drank too much to stave off the boredom of speaking to people you did not know and would not see again, and then you were too far gone to care. With one ear he could hear Fox speaking to Tregarth, the Chief Engineer. They had both been drinking steadily, their faces set and fixed with the grim determination of men who do not intend to give away their exact state of intoxication.

'Lot of bloody rot, Chief!' Fox sounded angry. 'It's as good as paying off the old ship!'

Tregarth grunted, 'Wouldn't last five minutes in the Union Castle!'

Wickersley wondered what would not last five minutes but he knew what Tregarth was angry about. Just before the first guests had arrived the Captain had met all the officers in the wardroom and told them of the new arrangements. Wickersley had watched him fixedly, looking for some sign of the man's inner feelings.

Only when Bouverie had said unexpectedly, 'Well, I

think it's a damned shame, sir!' had Chesnaye dropped his
guard. He had regarded the ex-barrister for several seconds
and then, 'It is, Sub.' Wickersley thought that was the end
of it, but something seemed to be driving Chesnaye on, as
if he could no longer bear the strain of his secret. 'As a matter of fact I love this ship. To some of you that may seem
strange.' He looked round the flag-decorated wardroom,
his eyes suddenly wretched. 'Given a chance we would have
done something worth while together.'

Wickersley still wondered about the use of 'we'. Did he
mean the whole ship's company, or just ship and captain?

Anyway, it was all decided. Wickersley tasted the neat
gin on his tongue and ran his finger around his tight collar.
But he knew what Chesnaye felt. From the moment
Wickersley had opened his letters from home he had under-
stood, perhaps for the first time, what loneliness meant, and
Chesnaye certainly knew that.

Wickersley's wife had written a neat, concise letter. She
always wrote like that, just as she lived. Neat, well thought
out, nothing wasted.

He felt the anger surging through his drink-clouded
mind. She had told him in the shortest possible style that
she had left him. Just like that. There was no hint of who
the other man was, except that 'he is a friend of yours'. So
that was that.

'Jesus!' Wickersley banged down the glass and the others
stared at him. Even Norris, who had been watching an
elderly officer dancing pressed against a slim nurse, looked
surprised.

Fox said : 'What's eating you, Doc? Been at the pills
again?'

Wickersley shrugged and signalled to a steward. 'Something like that!' What was the point of spreading it
around? It could not help him now. He caught sight of
Erskine approaching their small group with his hand resting lightly on the elbow of a tall, very attractive girl.

Erskine stood looking down at the others, his face smiling
but unsure. 'This is Ann Curzon.' He made the introduc-
tions as they got to their feet. 'They're the core of the wardroom!'

In spite of his anger and misery Wickersley's keen senses

told him that the atmosphere was strained. Fox was looking at Erskine as if he was a complete stranger, and the girl seemed too bright, too casual, like someone playing a part, he thought.

Rudely Wickersley interrupted the stilted conversation, 'Well, Ann, how about having a drink with the poor old doctor?'

She smiled, and it was then that he noticed the slight redness around her eyes. That bastard Erskine, he thought vaguely.

'Yes, I'd like that.'

She moved towards him, but Erskine said quickly, 'There are one or two more people you should meet, Ann.'

'Come with me.' Wickersley took her arm, an idea forming in his reeling mind.

He almost pushed the girl out of the small semicircle, and then Erskine tried to bar his path. 'I think you've had a bit too much to drink, Doc!'

Wickersley weighed up the facts with elaborate care. The girl was very willing to leave Erskine. She was not putting on an act now. He leaned across to Erskine and said in his ear, 'Go and get stuffed!' Then with a fixed smile on his streaming face he guided the girl through the swaying dancers and towards the quarterdeck ladder.

'It's cooler on deck,' he said. 'Much nicer.'

Erskine had mentioned this girl once or twice. Like a possession, he thought. Now, if half the rumours were right, he was getting rid of her too. 'I apologise for my haste, Ann. But, as you see, I've had a hard day.'

The quarterdeck was deserted but for an anonymous couple huddled right aft below the ensign staff. Side awnings had been rigged to protect any strollers from the cool harbour breeze and to contain the glare of light from the wardroom hatch. Wickersley led the girl to a gap in the awnings and pointed across the glittering water.

'A bit of air does the patient good, y'know!'

Her teeth gleamed in the purple half-light. 'Thank you for pulling me out of that crowd. I was beginning to wonder why I came at all!'

Wickersley fumbled for his cigarettes. We are all playing parts, he thought. Each hiding some inner worry from the next and thinking it doesn't show.

She took the proffered cigarette and waited as he clicked his lighter. 'I'm not usually like this,' he said after a moment, 'but things have been a bit hectic here lately.' And, by the way, my wife has run off with a good friend of mine, he wanted to add. 'It's like a calm *after* a storm.'

He felt her start and turn to the footsteps which thudded across the deck planking.

Erskine loomed out of the darkness, his mess-jacket gleaming like a ghost. 'Now what the *hell* are you playing at?'

Wickersley was not sure which one of them was being addressed, but the irritated rasp in Erskine's tone was the final straw. 'Go away!'

'You're drunk!' Erskine seemed twice his normal size in Wickersley's misty vision. 'D'you think this is the way to behave in front of my guest?'

The Doctor shrugged. 'I'm past caring what you think.'

The girl threw her cigarette over the rail. 'Really, John, don't be so stuffy! Anyway, I'm not your guest. I'm not your anything any more!'

Erskine seemed to recoil. 'So that's the way of it. Drop one, grab another!'

She turned her face away, and Wickersley said thickly, 'If you don't shove off I'm going to forget my oath and smash that arrogant face in!'

There was a quiet footfall by the hatch and Chesnaye stood motionless against the pale awning.

The other three stood like statues. Erskine with hands on his hips, jaw jutting forward, Wickersley, whose fists were already raised but frozen in mid-air. Only the girl seemed real. She had half turned and was watching Chesnaye's tall figure as if to gauge the power he seemed to hold over the others.

Chesnaye said evenly: 'There are guests below, Number One. There seems to be a preponderance of ship's officers up here.'

Erskine said, 'I was dealing with the Doctor, sir, he——'

Wickersley interrupted calmly, 'I was just going to knock his head off.'

There was a pause and Chesnaye continued, 'When I

was a midshipman I once knocked a senior officer to the deck!' Surprisingly he chuckled. 'It did me a power of good!' Then, as the other officers gaped at him : 'Now go below and behave yourselves. If anybody in this ship has a right to beat somebody brains out I think I have already proved myself eligible by my early example!'

Erskine sounded confused. 'Yes, sir.' Without another word he walked to the ladder.

Wickersley decided it was time for another drink. A large one. It had been a remarkably simple feat, really. Get the girl on deck *and* Erskine, and the Captain was bound to follow.

Chesnaye was completely alone, but unlike any other man aboard he could not share his emptiness. This Ann Curzon might make him forget, even for an evening. The near disaster had been worth it. Erskine needed a good hiding anyway.

Wickersley bowed to the girl and then said : 'Permission to fall out, sir? Perhaps you would take over my duties as escort?'

Chesnaye grinned. 'Go below before you fall over.'

They watched Wickersley stagger towards the ladder, neither aware of his inner misery, but on the deserted deck each suddenly conscious of one another.

'It's a beautiful view from here.'

＊　　　＊　　　＊　　　■　　　＊

The night air was almost cold as it fanned across the upper bridge, but the girl did not seem to notice it. She stood on the port gratings, her body pale against the grey steel, her arms wide as she rested them on the broken screen.

Chesnaye stood in the centre of the deserted bridge, his mind unable to associate this girl's presence with what had gone before. The ship was quite still and he could no longer hear the raucous beat of the wardroom gramophone, nor the almost hysterical gaiety from the remaining visitors. Overhead, the stars were large and very low, and it was quite impossible to imagine what had been enacted above this very place. The screaming bombers and the last desperate attack by that fanatical pilot.

Without even returning to the wardroom party Chesnaye and the girl had moved slowly along the deserted upper deck. Sometimes Chesnaye had talked, answered her questions, and other times they had both found a strange contentment in silence and looking across the darkened harbour.

She said, 'I still can't believe that the Germans may be here soon.' Her arm moved above the screen. 'Their ships where ours are now.'

'I don't think it will happen.' Chesnaye climbed on to the gratings, again conscious of her nearness, the scent of her body. 'Necessity makes our people achieve remarkable things.'

She shivered and he said quickly, 'Would you like to go down?'

'Not yet.' She half turned, and he sensed the sadness in her voice. 'I may not get another chance. It's been wonderful.'

Chesnaye asked, 'What made you come out here in the first place?'

She shrugged. 'I was in Malta when the war started. On holiday. I got sort of involved with things, and no one seemed to mind.' Some hair blew across her cheek as she said dreamily: 'I couldn't go back to England after that. My parents wanted me to, but I felt I belonged here.'

'Where is *home*?' Chesnaye felt that he wanted every last scrap of information about her. He could no longer explain his desire, nor the hopelessness of it.

She chuckled. 'Surbiton. Exotic, isn't it?'

'And now you want to go back to Malta?'

'I *am* going.' She touched the cold metal below her. 'I work with the Red Cross, although God knows how it happened. I'm really very squeamish!'

Somewhere below a pipe shrilled and a metallic voice intoned: 'Duty fire party fall in! Men under punishment to muster!'

She was facing him now, her eyes like dark pools in her face. 'You're not a bit as I imagined you would be. You're not even like the others.'

Chesnaye grinned. 'I haven't got two heads!'

'No, I'm not joking. Perhaps it's because you've been

away from the Navy for all that time. New Zealand, everything. Some of the others in your position are so—so pompous, does that sound silly?'

'It's a compliment.'

'And the way you are about this ship. I've been listening to you for hours. I could go on listening, and that's not like me at all! John is quite different. He always worries about something he can't even see.'

'He's a good officer.' Chesnaye no longer knew what to say.

She shrugged impatiently. 'So is Goering, I expect!'

'I think I know what you mean.' He looked past her at the flapping signal halyards. 'You must put every ounce of energy into a ship. Whatever ship it may be at the time. Otherwise it's just a pile of metal and spare parts!'

There was a movement of people on the deck below, and Chesnaye knew that the last of the visitors were leaving. He could feel another sensation of loss already, and he knew he was unable to prevent it.

She said quietly : 'I came here prepared to hate everything. But I don't remember when I've been so happy.' She laughed, but sounded unsure and suddenly nervous. 'That just proves what a weird creature I am !'

She turned to step from the gratings, but the heel of her shoe caught in one of the small holes and she fell heavily against him. For another long moment they stayed quite still, and Chesnaye could feel his heart pounding uncontrollably against her warm body.

In a breathless voice she said, 'If this was a film they would say I planned that fall !'

He felt her hair against his cheek and with sudden desperation pulled her tightly to him. She did not resist but stayed motionless, her breast pressed against his heart.

Her voice seemed to come from far away. 'Why didn't this happen earlier?'

Chesnaye held her bare arms and guided her across the bridge. There were so many things he wanted to say, so many fears to share. She was not for him. It was her natural reaction to Erskine's behaviour. In any case she was nearly twenty years younger. She was going away. He might never see her again, even if she wanted to after tonight.

But instead he said, 'Can I see you?'

She turned lightly in his hands, and he could see the brightness of her eyes. Like tears, he thought.

'I *want* to see you!' She tried to laugh. 'Do you think you can tear yourself from the ship for a while?'

If anyone else had said that Chesnaye knew he would have reacted differently. But they both stood on the empty bridge, smiling through the darkness like conspirators.

Quickly she said, 'I'll give you my address before I go.'

'If I'm delayed——'

She cut him short. 'I'll still be waiting.' She reached out and touched his hand. 'You just *get* there somehow!'

Below on the quarterdeck Wickersley watched them pass. He was near complete oblivion but not quite there. His eyes drooped, and when he opened them again the girl had vanished. The Captain was standing over him, and Wickersley realised for the first time that he must have fallen to the deck.

Through the mist he had built up to stave off the misery of that letter he nevertheless heard Chesnaye say quietly, 'You may be unconscious now, Doc, but you'll never know what you've done for me.' Then the Doctor felt strong hands under his armpits and allowed himself to be carried down to an all-enveloping darkness.

7

Convoy

Chesnaye finished tamping down his pipe and reached for his matches. The reflected glare from the shimmering sea was so intense in the noon sun that he was wearing sunglasses, and his white drill tunic, although freshly laundered, felt clammy against his skin. He drew in on the pipe and watched the blue smoke hover uncertainly across the baking bridge.

Lieutenant Norris, red-cheeked and perspiring freely, moved to the front of the bridge and saluted. 'Afternoon Watch closed up at Defence Stations, sir. Course two-seven-five, steady at six knots.'

'Very well.' Chesnaye eased his limbs more comfortably on the hard chair and stared absently at the empty horizon. Four and a half days out from Alexandria, six hundred miles of empty sea.

Norris sounded strained, he thought. It was strange how he changed once the ship was at sea again. In harbour he had been a different man. Whenever his duties permitted he had been ashore and usually returned on board slightly the worse for drink.

He heard Harbridge, the Gunner (T), say: 'Take the slack off them halyards, Bunts! Like a bloody Naafi boat!'

Chesnaye swung round in his chair and levelled his glasses astern. As he did so he saw the watchkeepers avert their eyes and become engrossed in their duties. It was all as usual.

His glasses settled on their one faithful companion. Squat, purposeful and seemingly out of place, H.M. Rescue Tug *Goliath* was keeping in perfect station about half a mile astern. Her bulky hull was garish in dazzle paint with the additional adornment of a giant bow wave which was as false as her appearance. Sometime tomorrow the fast convoy from Alexandria would overtake the *Saracen* and

267

her consort and consolidate in readiness for action. The rescue tug would be busy enough then. A friendly scavenger to remind every ship in the convoy of its constant peril.

On the fo'c'sle Chesnaye could see Mr. Joslin supervising a working party by the anchor cables, and other seamen were busy scraping and painting one of the capstans. Chesnaye bit on his pipe and refused to accept the everyday task as a waste of time. Whatever else happened, *Saracen* would not look uncared for when she entered Malta.

Erskine appeared with his usual quietness. 'We've just decoded that signal, sir. It's all over in Crete.'

Chesnaye did not look at him, but stared hard at the friendly water and the cloudless sky beyond the bows. 'I see.' So the British Army had pulled out of yet another impossible position. How was it that everything seemed so peaceful and quiet when only two hundred miles away that bloodied island would be the scene of so much suffering and despair? Where would the next blow fall?

Erskine had stepped back and was speaking quietly to Norris. He had given no sign or hint of his inner feelings, but Chesnaye guessed that he was watching him more closely than ever. Since that night of the mess party and the events which had followed so surprisingly quickly.

The *Saracen* had been in Alexandria exactly seven days. Each morning brought a flood of repair workers aboard until it seemed as if the monitor was the last ship they expected to work on. For the British at least.

Chesnaye could still remember Erskine's face on the first morning as the rivet guns began to crackle and stutter overhead. Chesnaye had signed a few letters and initialled several orders, and had then said : 'I am going ashore this afternoon. You can take control of the working parties for the moment.' A pause. 'Continue to give as much shore leave as possible to our people, and go easy on the libertymen when they come off.' There had been a long string of defaulters that morning for drunkenness and so forth. 'It does everyone good to let off steam once in a while.'

Erskine had said quickly, 'Where can you be reached in an emergency, sir?'

The two men had looked at each other in silence for a few seconds, and then Chesnaye had said, 'I'll leave the address with my writer.' But he knew that Erskine was well aware of his destination.

He had found the narrow street above the harbour easily enough. It was off the mainstream of wandering sailors and hurrying townfolk. Even the inevitable traders and hawkers were few, while the bustle of the harbour was forgotten. Only the Mediterranean itself showed between the buildings in a hard blue line.

He was not sure what he had expected to find. Surprise or embarrassment. A polite but awkward visit soon to be ended. Even when he reached the shaded door he felt on the edge of panic and uncertainty. There was nothing hesitant about her welcome, and he could still clearly remember the pleasure in her eyes as she guided him into the shady half-light of the small room.

'You *are* prompt!' She took his cap and then stood back with her hands on her hips. She was wearing a tan-coloured dress which seemed to accentuate her beauty and momentarily made Chesnaye marvel at Erskine's stupidity.

'This really *is* grand!' She was laughing again, like an exuberant child, he thought. 'Entertaining a full captain!' Chesnaye was sitting on the sagging sofa, and she stooped to touch the lace bars of his shoulder straps. 'But I simply can't call you Captain. Do you mind Dick? Or would you prefer Richard?'

He had forced a frown. 'Only my close friends are allowed Dick!'

She had jumped to her feet, her hands already reaching for the bottle of chilled wine. 'Watch out then, Dick! I may become more than a friend!'

And so it had continued. The small room had been full of laughter, quick changes of mood with each newly gained piece of understanding.

When the evening shadows had crossed the dusty street they had gone out. First to an overcrowded club where naval officers had outnumbered everyone else and many curious glances had been cast at the slim tanned girl and the tall captain. They had tried to dance on the stifling floor, and Chesnaye marvelled at the fact that his thigh no longer seemed to have any effect, as if a truce had been called.

After a while she said gravely, 'You hate it here, don't you?'

He had looked at her anxiously. 'Why d'you say that?'

'All these people. You must be tired of seeing them.'

So they had gone to the outskirts of the town, to a low-roofed café with a blaring radiogram. There were a few servicemen, mostly soldiers. But three seamen were about to leave as Chesnaye entered, his head ducking below the beams, and he stood aside as the white-clad trio lurched towards the street.

He suddenly realised that they were three of the *Saracen*'s men. They stared first at him, then at the girl. The sight of their captain in this sort of place seemed to un-nerve them.

One, an able seaman named Devlin, started to salute and then said, ''Evenin', sir; 'evenin', miss!' He had been unable to stop his huge grin. 'I thought the officers went to all the posh places, sir?'

Chesnaye felt sudden warmth for these three tipsy seamen. At sea they were little cogs he hardly saw. Names on a muster sheet, requestmen or defaulters perhaps. Now they were just men like himself.

One of the seamen said, 'No wonder we can't find any decent girls, sir!' and stared at Chesnaye's companion with open admiration.

Chesnaye coughed. 'One of the advantages of seniority, lads!' They had gone off laughing into the night, and Chesnaye had felt foolishly happy.

The far end of the café was lined with booths. The impassive-faced Turkish head waiter had guided them towards it with the air of a foreign ambassador, when suddenly, as Chesnaye had passed abreast of one of the booths, two soldiers had lurched upright and blocked his progress. For a moment he thought there was going to be trouble of some sort. He recognised the Australian bush hat and wondered if the soldiers took exception to his presence for some reason. Then he noticed that both men were wounded. One leaned on sticks, the other had his arm strapped across his chest. Behind them, still propped in the booth, was another soldier, whose bandaged eyes were turned towards the small group and whose hands were already reaching out in an unspoken question.

The biggest Australian, a corporal, said loudly, 'You'll not remember me?' He did not wait for a reply, but turned to the girl and took her hands in his big paws without further delay. 'I hope you have a very pleasant evening, miss. You happen to be with the best goddamned Pommie I have ever met!'

Chesnaye stared from one man to the other. 'I don't quite follow?'

The second soldier grinned and moved his strapped arm carefully. 'You brought us back from Tobruk, Cap'n. But for your bloody guts we'd be lying out there in the muck right this minute!' He held out his good hand. 'Here, take this, I want to be able to tell my folks I shook your hand!'

The blind soldier was now on his feet. 'We'll be off for home soon, Captain. I didn't see a thing after that ruddy mortar shell, but me mates told me what you did!' His voice shook. 'You didn't have to take us off, did you? You just bloody well did it!'

Chesnaye turned his face away with confusion. 'Thank you!'

The corporal waved his arm. 'Let's make a night of it!'

But the second soldier grinned and winked at the girl. 'Leave 'em be, you flamin' wombat! The Captain's got other things to attend to!'

They were still calling out cheerfully as Chesnaye almost pushed the girl into the end booth.

The waiter lit the candle on the table and went to get some wine. When Chesnaye had recovered sufficiently to meet her gaze he was astonished to see that her eyes were brimming with tears.

'What's the matter, Ann?'

But she reached across the small table and gripped his sleeve hard. 'Don't ask me, not yet!' Then she shook her head, smiling in spite of the tears across her cheeks. 'I know what those men meant. You really are a wonderful person!'

* * * * *

The small sea-cabin behind the bridge seemed stuffy and

271

humid, and after a quick glance at his desk Chesnaye unscrewed the dead-light and opened the scuttle. There was a good moon, and the black restless water came to life in its cold stare, and the horizon shone with a million tiny lights like some gay, uncaring shoreline.

He propped open the cabin door to encourage even the slightest breath of air, and half listened to Fox's voice from the compass platform as he patiently explained the mysteries of the stars to the two midshipmen. If anything, Fox seemed to be more interested in his duties now that leaving the ship was inevitable.

Chesnaye peeled off his jacket and allowed the air to explore his skin. Feet scraped on a ladder, and he could hear the faint strains of a mouth-organ from one of the four-inch gun positions below the bridge. The patient waiting, the sadness and the calm resignation of war.

He loosened his belt and lowered himself on to the bunk. It was peaceful, even relaxing. Automatically his hand moved to touch the scar on his thigh, but instead of pain the simple action reawakened another memory like the discovery of some precious souvenir.

Without closing his eyes he could see every yard of that walk home from the café with Ann, stepping across the bars of moonlight between the sleeping houses with serious concentration. They had not spoken much, and Chesnaye was again aware of the danger of words, and was almost afraid to break the strange spell which seemed to hold them together.

They had reached the house, and Chesnaye had half expected to find some urgent message waiting to jerk him back to reality, but there was nothing. The tiny room was quiet, and she had been humming softly as she lit the one small table lamp.

'I suppose I had better make my way to the ship?' Chesnaye had stared ruefully around him, as if rediscovering the birthplace of his new happiness. 'I don't know if I can go now.'

She did not answer, but left the room to return almost immediately with two glasses of brandy. 'The last,' she announced gravely.

They sat on the old sofa, their glasses untouched, their

eyes unseeing on the opposite wall and the shuttered window. Chesnaye felt lost, even desperate. Tomorrow the carpet trader would be squatting in the dust outside, while he would be cherishing a memory and sinking back into the endless and futureless routine.

She nestled her head against his shoulder and kicked off her sandals. For a moment she said nothing, then : 'It's been wonderful. It really has.'

'I know. I never believed it possible.'

'It's always possible. With the right person.' She twisted slightly so that he could feel her breath on his cheek. 'I'm so afraid.'

He encircled her shoulders in one quick movement, his eyes searching. 'Of what? Tell me, Ann !'

Her mouth quivered in a half-smile. 'Of smashing something. Of losing the only thing which really matters now.'

Chesnaye held her very tightly and smoothed the hair from her cheek. He could feel her quivering with each movement, and felt the forgotten pain returning to his heart.

'I don't want you to go, Dick. Not now. Not ever.' She had lowered her head against his chest as if unable to meet his eyes. 'There is so little time. We cannot waste it !' With sudden vehemence she said, 'You understand, don't you?'

A glass rolled unnoticed as Chesnaye pulled her to him. He could feel the desperate urgency of her kiss, and felt himself swimming in an uncontrolled desire.

With a jerk she freed herself and moved behind the sofa. Then with slow deliberation she pulled the dress over her head and threw her small shadows of underwear into the corner of the room. She walked across the room and knelt against Chesnaye's knees. He was still staring at her, wanting her, yet unwilling to break the spell.

'You see, you can't go now?' She looked up at him, her eyes misty.

Chesnaye could still feel the intensity of their love and the perfection of her body.

Afterwards, in an even smaller room, he had lain pressed beside her in the narrow bed below an open window. In the filtered moonlight he propped himself on one elbow to look down at her relaxed body and the deep shadows below her

273

breasts and across the silky smoothness of her thighs. It was
at that moment she had reached out and touched the scar
which he had carried through the years. Her eyes were still
closed, but he could see the quick movement of her breasts
as the contact reawakened desire.

Down, down . . . that other world which excluded all
else but the love of two persons. Once she cried out, but
their mouths found each other to stifle the delicious pain,
and her hands locked behind his back to complete their
bond.

When the first faint light of dawn cut through the narrow street Chesnaye prised himself away and knelt beside
the bed to look at her face. It was relaxed and still, like a
painting, and he wanted more than anything to hold her
just once more.

He passed through the other room and paused to pick
her clothes from the floor and switch off the lamp which
had been left unnoticed. Down the hill, through the gates
guarded by drowsy sentries, and out on to the long wide
jetty which had hardly changed since Roman soldiers had
mounted a similar watch. The fresh, early scent from the
sea, the querulous gulls nodding and grumbling on the
dockside sheds as the solitary figure passed. Then the *Saracen* and the startled Quartermaster springing to life at the
head of the gangway.

The decks felt damp and friendly, and in the pale light
the tired ship looked almost beautiful.

He thrust his hands behind his head and stared up at the
deckhead. How quickly those seven days had passed, and
how wretched had been the parting. *Saracen* had been required to slip and proceed to sea under cover of darkness.
On that last day he had spent only an hour with Ann
Curzon, an hour of brimming happiness verging on despair.

To leave her was bad enough, without the growing suspense of the convoy. It seemed as if she should still be in her
little room above the harbour and not at this moment lying
in some over-crowded cabin aboard a darkened, hurrying
ship.

Chesnaye was beginning to fret again, and with an impatient movement swung himself off the bunk. Slinging his
jacket across his bare shoulders like a cape, he walked

quietly on to the bridge his unlit pipe in his mouth.

The two midshipmen were just going below, their lesson completed. 'Learnt anything?' They both stopped startled as they recognised their captain half dressed and dishevelled.

Danebury said seriously, 'It's all very difficult, sir.'

Fox was standing by the compass, his hair ruffling slightly in the weak breeze. 'Too many classroom ideas in their heads, sir.'

'You'll soon put that right, eh, Pilot?' Chesnaye grinned. 'The Navy's never been very keen on matchbox navigation!'

'*Their* loss, sir!' Fox was unperturbed.

Chesnaye wandered around the bridge, his eyes slowly becoming accustomed to the distorted moonglow. The ship had little motion, and it did not need much imagination to conjure up a picture of Ann standing by the screen, her body poised like a statue. He touched the screen, smooth and unmarked from the repair yard.

In Malta they could pick up the threads again. They *must*.

She had wanted to walk with him to the harbour gates, but he had persuaded her against it.

'You'll soon be the Captain again!' She had held him at arm's length, her eyes bright and wistful. 'You're my life now, Dick. I need you so much.'

He had pulled her close so that she should not see the pain on his face. 'And I you.'

'I know. Just being together has been wonderful. But it's not enough. Not now. Not ever.'

A step grated behind him and he heard Fox handing over the watch. Midnight already. A shiver ran through him as he thought of what tomorrow would bring.

Sharply he said, 'Have you got the signal about the convoy decoded yet, Pilot?'

Fox sounded wary. 'In the charthouse, sir. The First Lieutenant has been working on the order of advance so that we can adjust the plot. There won't be much time after tomorrow, sir.'

'Right. I'll take a look.'

Back into the stuffiness, where the fresh charts and notebooks were lined up like surgical instruments. A new list of ships and their positions in convoy was pinned alongside the chart table. Quickly Chesnaye scanned the list. There was still a chance that Ann's ship might not have sailed for some reason. His gaze faltered. Third ship in the starboard column, *Cape Cod*, it *had* sailed. His finger was resting on the vessel's name, and Fox remarked casually, 'That one'll be just about on our beam if the Admiral sticks to his sailing orders.'

Chesnaye wondered briefly if Erskine knew the girl would be aboard that ship. If so he must have had bitter thoughts when he was decoding the signal.

Fox yawned. 'I'm going to turn in unless you need me for anything?'

'Nothing at the moment, Pilot.' Chesnaye sounded far away.

'We might get through without a scratch, sir.' Fox was watching him closely. 'I'm not too worried.'

Chesnaye gave a small smile. 'Well, you keep that way.' Bombers, submarines, even E-boats, might already be groping through the darkness.

Fox turned to leave. 'Radio room reports all quiet, sir. Might be a good sign.'

'When the jungle falls silent, Pilot, *that's* the time to watch out!'

Chesnaye walked back under the stars and watched the tug *Goliath* as she pushed her black bulk across the moon's silver path. If only a storm would blow up. Anything would be better than this. He could easily imagine a U-boat commander watching the *Saracen*'s shape in his cross-wires, or even the torpedoes skimming through the water at this very moment.

On one of the Oerlikon platforms a gunner laughed, and Chesnaye heard the rattle of cocoa mugs. Every man is my responsibility, he thought. But tomorrow I shall be helpless and have the agony of an onlooker. He gripped the screen and strained his eyes into the darkness. Oh, Ann, take care! I shall be so near to you tomorrow, yet so helpless!

In the deserted wardroom Fox paused to pick up a tattered copy of *Men Only* before going to his cabin. Then

276

he saw the Doctor dozing in one of the deep armchairs, a cup of cold coffee still by his elbow.

'Aren't you going to bed, Doc?'

Wickersley rubbed his eyes. 'I suppose so. What's it like up top?'

Fox looked round the wardroom. 'Quiet. I think the Skipper's worrying about tomorrow. But the way I see it this ship'll be the safest in the convoy. The bastards will be after the fat loaded merchantmen!'

Wickersley levered himself upright and peered at his watch. 'I think he's worried about losing something other than the ship,' he said quietly.

Fox watched him go and then gave a shrug. With his magazine under his arm he groped his way down the passage to his cabin. Poor, trusting merchant ships, he thought. In peacetime it was either depression or cut-throat competition. In war it was sheer bloody murder.

He was wondering what Wickersley had meant when he fell suddenly asleep, the magazine on his chest like a dead warrior's scroll.

＊　　　＊　　　■　　　◢　　　ᵣ

Chesnaye awoke with a start, aware that someone had touched his arm.

McGowan was waiting at a respectful distance. 'Convoy sighted, sir!' He watched as Chesnaye licked his dry lips and got slowly from his chair. 'Wing escort has just made the recognition signal.'

Chesnaye nodded vaguely and walked stiffly to the rear of the bridge. The sun was blazing hot, and seemed to strike up at him with every step. It almost brought physical pain to look seawards, to the tiny grey shape which had just lifted above the horizon. He steadied his glasses. The indistinct black crucifix of the newcomer's superstructure and the white slash of bow wave below. A powerful destroyer tearing ahead of the convoy, searching and listening for any lurking U-boat. A pinpoint of diamond-bright light flickered over the miles of shining water.

The Yeoman raised his telescope, his lips moving as his signalman wrote down each letter. He said a moment later:

'Signal from escort, sir. Convoy will take up station as ordered.'

'Very well.' What else was there to say? Others would call the tune. The convoy could only wait.

Like cautious and newly trained beasts the fourteen escorted merchantmen ponderously obeyed the impatient signal lamps and the jaunty hoists of bunting. It took half an hour to satisfy the flagship. Eventually there were two parallel lines of six supply ships, each line a mile apart. In the centre of the convoy the two most vulnerable vessels, an ammunition ship and a well-loaded oiler steamed ahead and astern of the *Saracen* to be given maximum protection by the monitor's anti-aircraft guns.

Far out on either beam of the columns four destroyers and two elderly sloops slowly fanned into their positions for the final drive towards Malta. Then at reduced speed the convoy settled down and awaited the Admiral's ultimate inspection. From right astern the cruiser *Aureus* steamed briskly through the length of the procession, her high bridge glittering with trained binoculars, her yards alive with soaring signal flags. She was a sleek-looking ship. A product of the early thirties, she was a craft to be proud of. Even her dazzle paint could not hide the outlines of power and speed. Her four twin turrets, as well as her secondary armament, were already manned and cocked skywards.

Chesnaye watched her pass, but lowered his glasses as Beaushears' sun-reddened face leapt into the lenses. Even at that distance he could see the searching, irritable expression beneath the multi-oak-leaved cap, and was not surprised to see the big signal lamp begin to stutter almost immediately.

The Yeoman said : 'From Flag, sir. Keep correct distance from *Corinth Star*.'

Chesnaye nodded. 'Thank you, Laidlaw.' Then to Fox, 'Fall back two inches from the ammunition ship, Pilot!'

Fox grinned. 'Aye, aye, sir!'

The flagship continued on its lordly way, and finally reduced speed with an impressive display of white froth when in position ahead of the convoy.

Sub-Lieutenant Bouverie sighed. 'Do you ever have the feeling you are being watched?'

A telephone buzzed, and Fox said, 'Screening squadron on station, sir.'

'Very well.' Chesnaye eased himself from the chair and walked quickly to the chart table which had been clipped in position on the bridge. Beaushears' four cruisers were steaming somewhere below the horizon, ready to give support and to head off any intrepid intrusions by enemy warships.

Chesnaye took a quick glance astern. Only occasionally visible beyond the rusty bulk of a Greek freighter he could see the squat outline of the rescue tug. She at least would probably escape any enemy attention.

McGowan hurried past on his way to the Director, a sheaf of papers under his arm. 'I've just been round the A.A. guns, sir. All cleared away and manned.'

'Good. You can use the crew of the fifteen-inch turret to relieve the gunners at regular intervals. I don't want them dropping off to sleep in this heat.'

McGowan tried not to look pained. 'I've attended to that, sir.'

Chesnaye walked back to the front of the bridge, but to the starboard side. Bouverie stepped aside to leave room for him, but watched curiously as his captain began to study the nearest freighter with apparent care.

The *Cape Cod* was a fairly new ship, her hull low in the water, and the wide upper decks also crammed with heavy crates and additional stores for the besieged island.

Bouverie said. 'She looks overloaded, sir. Wouldn't like to be in her if she gets a packet!'

'Be so good as to attend to your duties, Sub!' Chesnaye did not even notice the harshness in his own voice or the look of surprise on Bouverie's face. From the compass platform Fox glanced down at them and sensed the sudden tension.

Bouverie climbed up beside him and said in a bewildered tone, 'What's got into *him*?'

Fox felt suddenly uneasy, but answered unfeelingly : 'Do as he says! This isn't the bloody Old Bailey, y'know!'

Chesnaye moved his glasses carefully over the labouring freighter, across the upper bridge where a bearded captain was speaking to his mate and two seamen were fitting drums on a pair of Lewis guns. Then down past the black funnel and along the boatdeck. He stiffened. Beside one of the swan-necked davits he saw a small knot of figures. Two or three men in khaki and then four women. Three of the latter were nurses in uniform, but the fourth, in khaki slacks and grey shirt, whose hair rippled carelessly in the warm breeze was Ann.

She was shading her eyes with one hand and staring across the strip of surging water between the two ships, and seemed to be looking directly at him. He lowered the glasses to wipe one of the lens and felt a tinge of disappointment as the clear picture shrunk to the reality of distance. Forgetting the men behind him, he stepped up on to a locker and with his binoculars to his eyes began to wave his cap slowly above his head.

From the compass platform Fox took a quick look around the bridge to make sure that everyone was occupied, and then raised his own glasses. It did not take him long to find the small group of figures and the laughing girl who was pointing and waving towards the *Saracen*. So that was it, he thought. Chesnaye's sharpness earlier had made him suspect something else. He would not have blamed Chesnaye for being rattled and uncertain with Beaushears breathing down his neck, and knowing that whatever happened with this convoy his command was soon to be ended.

But this was something else again. He dropped his glasses hastily as Chesnaye stepped down from the locker. The girl; Chesnaye's complete change of manner while the ship had been undergoing repairs; it all added up. He caught Chesnaye's eye and wanted to share his inner happiness. But the Captain looked through him, his eyes distant and suddenly troubled. Fox sighed. So near and yet so far. He could guess what Chesnaye must be thinking.

Bouverie said suddenly : 'Signal, sir. One U-boat reported in vicinity.'

A string of bunting broke out from the flagship's yard, and Laidlaw said flatly, 'Alter course signal, sir.'

Slowly the signal was seen and acknowledged along the lines of ships. As the distant flags vanished, the slow-moving vessels wheeled heavily on to the new course. It didn't do much good because the enemy was probably well informed of both the convoy and its destination. But Beaushears obviously intended to play the game to its bitter end.

'Steady on two-seven-nine, sir.'

Chesnaye started to refill his pipe, the movements jerky and tense. 'Very good. Check the U-boat's alleged position, Pilot. There may be more soon.'

He jammed his pipe between his teeth and then forgot it. With the other ships all around the pace seemed even slower. Only the slosh of mingled bow waves and an occasional down-draught of funnel smoke gave any hint of movement.

Laidlaw interrupted his thoughts once more. 'Destroyer *Scimitar* reports aircraft bearing Green four-five, sir. Possibly a Focke-Wulf. Out of gun range and appears to be circling.'

Chesnaye forced himself to light his pipe. It needed all his concentration to stop his hand from shaking. So the enemy was showing his hand. As in the Atlantic, the big Focke-Wulf was merely a searcher and a shadower. He would already be reporting back, homing other forces on to the convoy. 'He may not see anything.' Chesnaye cursed himself for his empty words. Unlike the Atlantic, where weather was often the best ally, this flat, innocent sea was as ideal for a spotting aircraft as some giant plotting table.

He lifted his glasses. The destroyer which had made the signal was the leading escort on the starboard wing. It was almost lost in a bank of haze, but Chesnaye could see the tell-tale signal flags and the faint movement of her guns as they impotently tracked the invisible intruder.

Fox said imperturbably, 'Sunset in four hours, sir.'

'Good.' Was it really as late as that? It seemed incredible when each minute dragged with such painful slowness.

Erskine crossed the bridge, his eyes hidden by sun-glasses. 'I've checked with the supply officer, sir. He'll feed the men in four batches. Bag meals will be sent up to the guns first.'

'Good idea.' Chesnaye saw Erskine glance quickly towards the nearby freighter. 'You can relieve me for the night watches, John. I want to try to snatch a few hours' rest. I have a feeling it's going to be a busy day tomorrow.'

Erskine tore his eyes from the *Cape Cod*. 'She looks very vulnerable, sir.'

Chesnaye replied coldly, 'They all are.' For a moment he could find no words beyond the necessities of duty. 'But we'll give a warm reception to anyone who comes sniffing around!'

Erskine licked his lips. 'I'd like to see you privately, if I may, sir? There's something I'd like to get off my chest.' He removed his sun-glasses, and Chesnaye could see the deep shadows under his eyes. 'I want you to hear my side of the story!'

'I see.' Chesnaye looked at him calmly and found that it did not seem to matter what Erskine had said or done. 'It'll keep. But one day, John, when you understand the loneliness of command, I hope you can learn something from all this——'

He broke off as Fox said sharply : 'Urgent signal, sir. Intelligence reports heavy surface units at sea approx. one hundred and fifty miles east of Syracuse. No further details yet.'

Chesnaye climbed on to his chair and glanced towards the freighter. 'No further are necessary, I should think!'

So there were to be no slip-ups, after all. The enemy was ready and warned. Somehow, somewhere, there was to be a killing ground. He shifted his binoculars to the flagship. All at once she seemed to have become smaller and more vulnerable.

Over his shoulder he said, 'If you want to do something useful, John, go and tell the Chief Telegraphist to play some records over the tannoy!'

Erskine stared at him. '*Now*, sir? And our talk?'

'That can wait. I want our people to be relaxed when the time comes.'

So as the sun dipped towards the horizon haze, and the watchful escorts listened and watched for the hidden enemy, the *Saracen* ploughed steadily through the centre of the convoy, her speakers blaring music, the feet of her gunners tapping, as they were carried forward towards the prearranged settlement.

8

Don't look back!

In the comparative quiet of the Morning Watch the shock-wave of the torpedo explosion was magnified beyond reason.

Chesnaye slipped and fell from his bunk even as the dying echoes sighed against the monitor's hull, and for a moment he imagined that he had been allowed to over-sleep and that dawn was already upon the convoy. The sea-cabin door had been pushed open by the unseen hand of blast, and through it the upper bridge seemed to be shimmering in distorted sunlight.

Even as a bosun's mate crashed through the door, his voice calling for the Captain, Chesnaye realised with sudden chill that the light was that of a burning ship.

Voice-pipes were clamouring for attention, and Chesnaye could hear Fox barking instructions to the helmsman.

Erskine said hoarsely: 'There, sir! On the port quarter! It was the old Greek!'

Chesnaye shaded his eyes from the bright red glare and the tall curtain of spluttering sparks which mounted with every second above the ship's black shape. Already she had fallen out of station and had lost her identity.

A creaming white line cut across the dark water, above which Chesnaye could faintly see the rakish shape of a searching destroyer. There was a dull crack, followed in a few seconds by the snow-bright glare of a starshell.

Several voices cried as one: 'There it is!'

Chesnaye tore his night-glasses from the leather case and peered at the pencil-slim silhouette outlined beneath the motionless flare. He bit his lip and took a quick look at the other ships. The U-boat must have been temporarily mis-led by the convoy's alteration of course. To avoid losing a target altogether, its commander had chased after the convoy and made his attack on the surface. Even now the submarine was turning away, while the destroyer increased speed to engage.

A lookout called, 'Torpedo passing on the port beam!'

A faint, ruler-straight line lengthened across the *Saracen*'s bow wave and vanished into open water. Chesnaye breathed again. The U-boat must have fired a full salvo, but had found only one target.

'She's diving, sir!' Every eye watched as the shadowy hull hid itself in an upflung surge of foam and froth.

Fox said thickly : 'The Greek's capsizing! Poor bastards!'

In a smaller voice Bouverie asked, 'Can't we do something?'

Harshly Chesnaye snapped : 'Keep station! Tell the lookouts to watch the other ships. If the convoy breaks now they're done for!'

Inwardly he felt a kind of agony as he watched the dying ship. The tug *Goliath* was clearly outlined against the searing flames, but was held at bay by the force of the blaze. Chesnaye could even see the Greek's hull changing from black to glowing pink as the fire tore at her inside. Every ship in the convoy gleamed and shimmered in the reflected fires, like paintings come alive.

Then the blazing ship dipped her bows and with startling suddenness began to dive. The hissing roar of exploding boilers merged with the triumphant inrush of water and the tearing crash of steel as the engine tore itself free from its bed and smashed through the white-hot bulkheads. Like a candle extinguished she was gone, and only the drooping starshell showed the end of the drama.

Once more the *Saracen*'s hull boomed and reverberated to magnified explosions as the destroyer's depth-charges thundered down. Tall pyramids of spray marked each charge, and as the destroyer finished her attack, one patch of torn white water showed clearly the shining hull of the U-boat as it was blown to the surface. Like a beast gone mad the destroyer slewed round, every rivet and plate groaning as her forty thousand horsepower and a full rudder threw her over.

Above the crash of gunfire and hoarse bellow of orders they all heard the solid crunch of tearing steel as the destroyer's knife-like stem bit into the wallowing hull. Then she was through and over, while the broken U-boat writhed in a great bubbling cascade of black oil.

The victorious destroyer, her bows crumpled like cardboard, ploughed to a halt, her narrow shape rocking gently in the life blood of her victim.

Some of the *Saracen*'s men cheered. It was a cruel, desperate sound, and Chesnaye said sharply: 'Keep those men quiet! Tell them to watch their front!'

Someone else on the bridge started to say excitedly, 'That's one less of the bastards!'

But Fox added dourly: 'One less escort, too! She'll be no more use for a month or so!'

The escorts increased speed and dashed around the merchant ships like watchful dogs. As if for greater protection the two leading freighters had turned slightly inwards, and the milling vessels astern of them followed suit. It took over an hour to restore order and establish discipline. By that time the dawn had found the convoy once more, and when the sun climbed free of the brightening water it showed clearly the shortened line of ships, and of the destroyer there was no sign. She was already limping back to Alexandria. Beaushears could not spare another ship to accompany her, so she must make the lonely voyage unaided.

Chesnaye slumped in his chair, his mind still filled with the reddened picture of the burning ship. There were no survivors. But the other ships still headed westward and no one looked back. Close the ranks. Do not stop for anyone or anything. When it's your turn you must accept it.

Chesnaye swore aloud, and Fox looked across at him. 'Sir?'

'Nothing, Pilot!' Chesnaye watched the *Cape Cod*'s crew washing down the boatdeck with hoses. 'Not a damned thing!'

. . . . .

Just before noon the first bombers appeared high in the clear sky. This time they were not Stukas but twin-engined Italian aircraft which cruised in six neat arrowheads with such calm indifference that it almost seemed as if they would pass over and ignore the convoy completely.

The *Saracen* stirred into readiness, the gunners almost glad that the tension of waiting was over at last.

Chesnaye wiped his streaming eyes with the back of his hand and ran his gaze briefly over the monitor's defences. The four-inch guns were already tracking the tiny silver specks, and he could hear the clatter of the breech blocks as the first shells were slammed home.

'They're splitting up, sir!'

Chesnaye lifted his glasses again. Yes, the small flights of bombers were separating, and half of them seemed to be diving in a shallow sweep towards the escorts on the starboard wing of the slow-moving merchantmen. Chesnaye wondered briefly what would happen if the ammunition ship received the first salvo. Surely no one in the near vicinity could escape the blast? Her crew too must be thinking just that.

'Signal from Flag, sir! Retain station. Stand by for alteration of course.'

Fox said to Bouverie, 'Fat lot of good that'll do!'

'Three aircraft Green four-five! Angle of sight two-oh!'

Chesnaye kept his ear tuned to the flat, dispassionate voices from the voice-pipes, and watched the approaching aircraft with narrowed eyes. In spite of being prepared, he tensed automatically as two of the destroyers opened fire. The small brown shell-bursts mushroomed across the bright sky and seemed to drift past the purposeful intruders.

'Aircraft closing! Two hundred and fifty knots!'

A sudden burst of gunfire from astern of the convoy told Chesnaye that the other bombers were trying to draw the escort's firepower from the approaching trio. It was a good attack, he thought coldly. They would cross the convoy's line of advance at forty-five degrees, and would gain a bit of protection from the *Aureus*'s firepower by diving above the ammunition ship.

A gong jangled below the bridge, and in the momentary silence which followed Chesnaye heard McGowan's voice distorted by his microphone. 'Commence, commence, commence!'

The four-inch guns spat out orange flame and hurled themselves back on their mountings. Their ear-piercing cracks seemed to penetrate the innermost membranes of the men's ears, and more than one seaman cried out with pain. The guns swung like oiled rods and fired again. The barrage was thickening, and the air was already pock-marked with their mingled shell-bursts. Even some of the merchantmen had joined in with their ancient twelve-pounders.

Still the bombers came on, their cockpit covers glinting in the sunlight, their engines lost in the barrage.

Chesnaye watched the range falling away. Half a mile, and the three planes swept over the first zig-zagging escort. At last they were in range of the short-range weapons, and before the jangle of bells had died away the pompoms and Oerlikons clattered into life. Darker shell-bursts, long pale lines of tracer, it seemed impossible for anything to live in it.

One of the bombers swung out of line and dived whining over the flagship, a straight black smoke-trail marking its passing. The *Aureus*'s gunners pounced on the unexpected prize and followed it down, the savage tracers cutting away the fusilage like skin from bones, even as two small parachuts blossomed in the smoke-stained sky.

'Bombs falling, sir!'

Not a single one this time. As the leading aircraft swept over the convoy's centre Chesnaye saw the glittering stick fall with apparent carelessness from her belly.

The sound of the barrage changed, like thunder deflected by a sudden wind, as half of *Saracen*'s armament swung astern to cover the oiler from another attack from aft. Three bombers had side-stepped the screening barrage and were already large and stark in the madly vibrating gunsights.

Chesnaye felt his mouth go dry as the falling bombs gathered momentum and shrieked towards the ammunition ship. He felt his chest jar against the screen as the bombs exploded. The ammunition ship still steamed ahead, her stained hull neatly bracketed by the hundred-foot columns of water. But the remaining bomber was overhead and the next salvo was already falling.

'Alter course, sir!'

Chesnaye shook himself as the air split apart to the screeching roar of bombs. They had missed again, but he

287

could hear the whiplash crack of splinters as they slashed at the passing ships. Too damn' near.

Laidlaw reported calmly, 'Signal close up, sir!'

Chesnaye watched the ammunition ship ahead of the monitor's bows, and waited.

'Down, sir!' The small flag hoist disappeared from the flagship's yard, and obediently the convoy plodded round after her curving wake.

'Christ, a hit!' The words were torn from Bouverie's throat, and Chesnaye stared past him at the sternmost ship on the starboard column. In the middle of her turn the bomb had caught her right behind the bridge. Boats, mainmast and half of her superstructure flew skywards, and from the smoking crater Chesnaye could see the first licking tongues of flame. The freighter staggered like a wounded animal and began to swing inwards, her bows almost pointing at the oiler. A collision now would be fatal.

Chesnaye snapped, 'Signal her to keep station!'

Laidlow nodded, and seconds later the big projector began to clatter.

Three more aircraft were attacking from port, but Chesnaye ignored the fanatical clatter of automatic weapons and continued to watch the freighter. Her upper deck was well ablaze, and some of the crated deck cargo was also alight. But through the swirling smoke came an answering signal.

Laidlaw said in an awed tone, 'She says, "Mind your own bloody business", sir!'

Chesnaye smiled tightly as he saw the freighter's battered stem feel its way back on course. 'If they can talk like that they're all right!'

Fox said, 'That was close!' A long line of bomb-bursts churned the sea skywards in tall white waterspouts, and once more the air echoed to the whining splinters.

The four-inch gun immediately below the starboard wing of the bridge fell silent, and a voice yelled stridently: 'Still! Misfire!' A few moments later the voice came again, harsh with relief, 'Carry on!'

The whole convoy was now covered with drifting smoke, and all around men were coughing in the acrid fumes of burned paint and cordite.

Bouverie pointed over the screen as something surged sluggishly in the monitor's bow wave and grated along her fat reinforced bulge. 'Who bagged that?' It was a half-submerged bomber, its fire-blackened body already sinking out of sight. Pinned like some sort of insect, the pilot was still moving his arms and staring up at them as the hull thrust him down and back into the racing screws.

'The freighter's got the fire under control, sir!'

Chesnaye nodded and looked carefully down the line of ships. In the thick smoke it was hard to see anything, let alone the circling bombers.

There was a sullen roar from far astern, and moments later Fox said thickly: 'One of the escorts, sir. The sloop *Gorgon* has turned turtle. Direct hit.'

Another warship gone, and two hundred miles to go. Chesnaye mopped his face. His cheek muscles felt numb and his head ached from the constant gunfire.

The bombers had had a sharp reception. Four were shot down in twenty minutes, and the final flight of aircraft were apparently unwilling to press home their attack. Instead they climbed rapidly towards the sun and released their bombs at random.

The cunning and bravery of the other pilots were unrewarded but for the sinking of one poorly protected sloop. The bombs which fell from five thousand feet, with their bomb-aimers not even bothering to take note of the results, straddled the port column and cut deep into the heart of the leading freighter. Like some hideous steel flower the whole ship heaved and opened outwards, the sea and sky suddenly filled with flying wreckage. Chesnaye felt the hot breath of the explosions across his streaming face, and stared in horror as the big freighter began to career across the tightly bunched ships.

More inner explosions began to tear the ship apart, and derricks and bridge sagged together into the burning crater which had once been the foredeck.

'She's out of control, sir!' Fox sounded taut. 'She'll be up to us in a moment!'

Chesnaye watched, holding his breath as the burning ship floundered pathetically towards the ammunition ship.

The gap narrowed, until it was almost hidden by the eagerly licking tongues of flame.

'Missed her!' Fox changed his tone. 'Now it's our turn!'

Chesnaye watched the ship, feeling the sweat pouring down his neck and chest. The smoke stung his eyes, and he could no longer see the other leading ships.

'Starboard fifteen!' He tried to see some movement against the freighter's waterline, but smoke and fire hid it from view. It was not possible even to gauge her speed through the churned water. 'Midships!' Steady now, let her get nearer. God, she's almost on top of us!

Behind him he could hear someone whimpering like a child. Too much swing on her. 'Port ten!' The monitor's hull quivered and swung very slightly towards the other ship, to allow her room to brush past.

Faintly through the fog of smoke he could hear Erskine's strident voice, 'Stand by, fire parties!'

The men on the upper bridge fell back as the wall of fire drifted down the monitor's side, and there was a hurried clatter of metal while the Oerlikon gunners ripped off their loaded magazines and pulled them clear of the searing heat.

The freighter was an old three-island type with high poop and fo'c'sle. Her rusted bows and heavy anchors almost brushed the *Saracen*'s bridge as she moved past, but Chesnaye's eyes were fixed on the tiny group of figures which was poised directly on the fo'c'sle head. Four men, one already crumpled in the heat but held out of reach of the flames by his comrades, men without hope on a burning island. Already the ship was beginning to fall away, and Chesnaye could see the sea exploring the buckled remains of her afterdeck.

One of the stranded seamen reached out as if to touch the monitor's bulk, his face suddenly clear and stark to every watching man.

Bouverie cried: 'Can't we help, sir? Lower a boat?'

But Chesnaye did not answer. What was the use of words?

There was a tiny cry, and when Chesnaye looked again there were only three figures on the fo'c'sle head. One must have jumped. Chesnaye willed the others to follow suit. The *Goliath* might find them, even in this.

The two who were still standing seemed about to jump when one of them looked down at the man who lay helpless on the deck. As the *Saracen* pulled clear they were still standing like statues outlined against the advancing fire, and then they were lost, and mercifully hidden in the smoke.

Bouverie was biting his knuckles. 'Oh my God! Did you see that?'

'No damage, sir!' Erskine was on the bridge again, his eyes white in his smoke-blackened face. He seemed to notice Bouverie's attitude of misery and despair as a man will recognise some sort of enemy. 'Get a grip on yourself, Sub!'

Chesnaye watched Fox bringing the ship back on course. 'He's been doing well, Number One!' he said quietly.

'But it's had for the men, sir,' Erskine persisted, as if repeating an old lesson. 'Some of these reservists are sent to sea with nothing more than a brief idea of what's happening.'

Chesnaye dabbed his eyes and stared at him coldly. 'You must learn not to measure a man's worth by the amount of lace on his sleeve!'

The cease-fire gongs sounded cheerfully through the smoke, and he added, 'Go round the guns and tell them "Well done".'

He forgot Erskine as a stronger breeze pushed the smoke bank back across the convoy. Two merchantmen gone, and the escort depleted by an equal number. The enemy's wounds were unimportant. You could only gauge your loss against their successes.

When the smoke had rolled far astern the sky was again empty. There was even a slight breeze to fan the sweating faces of the men throughout the convoy. But the prowling Focke-Wulf was still nearby, and Chesnaye wondered what fresh hell lay in store across the deceptive horizon.

An hour later he was no longer in doubt.

He sat on his tall chair, an empty tea mug still grasped in his fingers, his eyes on the sun-dappled shape of the *Cape Cod*. Ann was somewhere within that overloaded hull. Sleeping perhaps after the fury of the air attack, or even watching him from some vantage point above the decks.

The big freighter was leading the starboard column now, and seemed desperately far away.

'Signal, sir.' Fox was there again. 'Priority.'

'Well, spit it out!'

Fox said evenly : 'Four heavy enemy units fifty miles to north-east of convoy. Appear to be shadowing.'

Chesnaye sat upright in his chair, his tiredness forgotten. 'Waiting for night, more likely!'

Fox stood by the chart, his hands almost gentle as he spanned the pencilled lines with his dividers.

Chesnaye looked across the port quarter, noticing as he did so the small, silver-edged splinter hole in the funnel. It must have been hit during the attack. He frowned and concentrated on the new threat. Four units. Cruisers most likely. He strained his aching mind and felt vaguely uneasy. There was something wrong, but he could not sort his ideas into order. He crossed to the chart and stared at Fox's calculations.

'Fifty miles, eh?' He rubbed his chin and felt the stubble against his palm.

'That's what it says, sir. But you know these Intelligence reports!'

'Hmm.' Chesnaye looked up as a signal lamp began to clatter on the flag deck. 'What's happening now?'

Fox shrugged as if unconcerned. 'I expect the Admiral has some ideas about all this.'

Chesnaye waited impatiently as the signalman finished his writing. He re-read the brief message twice before he understood what he had missed in his first summing-up. Beaushears intended to call up his own four cruisers which were screening the convoy and smash into the enemy ships without delay. He read the signal aloud and heard Fox say : 'Best bloody thing for them! They won't be expecting it!'

Chesnaye paced to the chart again. There was something wrong. What could it be? Beaushears was taking the correct action. And yet . . . 'Get me the first signals about that Italian force which was reported yesterday.' As Fox hurried into the charthouse Chesnaye said to Laidlaw : 'Make a signal to Flag, Yeoman! Reference yesterday's signal——' He broke off as Laidlaw's eyebrows lifted almost imperceptibly. 'I've not time to find the damned time of origin!'

He lifted his gaze to the distant flagship as he continued slowly, 'Enemy surface units may be different from those earlier reported.'

Fox was breathing heavily at his side, 'I don't quite understand, sir?'

Chesnaye made sure that Laidlaw was sending the signal and then walked back to the chart table. 'Yesterday's signal referred to a major enemy group one hundred and fifty miles east of Syracuse.' He tapped the chart in time to his words. 'Now we get a signal that they are fifty miles to the north-east of us.'

Fox sounded puzzled. 'They could do it, sir. Allowing for these positions being correct, and the fact that the Eye-tie ships can steam pretty fast. They *could* just do it.'

'Unlikely. The convoy had made umpteen alterations of course since leaving Alex. Tomorrow would be the earliest hope of making contact.'

'Well, what do you think, sir?' Fox stared at him. 'One of the signals is wrong?'

'No. I think there are two enemy groups, Pilot!' Chesnaye's voice was cold. 'And if the Admiral detaches the cruiser screen, the way will be open!'

Fox was still staring at him as the Yeoman called : 'Signal from Flag, sir. Disregard previous Intelligence sighting report. Inshore squadron will proceed immediately and engage!' The Yeoman cleared his throat and looked uncomfortable. '. . . and, sir, the signal adds : "Don't be frightened. *Aureus* will stay in company." End of signal, sir.'

Chesnaye clenched his fists as a wave of fury swept through him. Of all the bloody stupid fools!

'Quite a sense of humour, I don't think!' Fox sounded indignant.

Laidlaw was still standing unhappily on the gratings. He seemed to feel the Admiral's insulting signal as if it had been addressed to him. 'Any reply, sir?'

'No, Yeoman. Nothing.' Chesnaye had difficulty in keeping the anger from his voice. How Beaushears must be grinning on his bridge, and probably sharing the joke with Captain Colquhoun and the others. Practically every ship in the convoy must have read the signal.

Chesnaye forced himself to stand still for several minutes

293

until his mind cleared. It was easy to see Beaushears' point of view, of course, but then again how was it possible to question a senior officer's judgement without appearing to show insubordination?

Chesnaye stared round the convoy with despair. Even without seeing the shadowing cruisers of Beaushears' squadron it had been a comfort to know they were there. He banged his fists together. How typical of Beaushears to send them tearing away at the first hint of a prize. All he thought about was his own prestige. With the enemy ships driven off or sunk there would be no limit to his reward.

The worst of it was he was probably right in his assumption about the Intelligence reports. Nevertheless, his first duty was to the convoy. Nothing else mattered.

He stared half-blinded at the sun. Still eight hours before night hid the slow-moving ships. Even then it was never safe.

The afternoon dragged by, and as the sun moved with such painful slowness towards the horizon the next blow fell.

The first hint of danger was the shriek of a destroyer's siren on the starboard wing, followed by that ship's rapid alteration of course away from the convoy.

'Torpedoes running to starboard!' There could be no exact bearing from the tired lookouts, for the torpedoes, some seven or eight of them, swept across the line of advance in a widespread, many-fingered fan.

No doubt a U-boat had fired the salvo, all her bow tubes at once, after taking up a carefully planned position slightly ahead of the advancing ships.

Like tired troops the ships swung to starboard in response to the Admiral's urgent signal, and pointed their ragged lines at the glittering white tracks which sliced amongst them with breathtaking speed. Two torpedoes struck home, the rest passed between the ships and flashed harmlessly to the open waters beyond.

One old freighter was loaded with steel frames and building materials for the Malta defences. She received the death blow deep in the boiler room, and lifted only slightly with a muffled bellow of pain. She broke in two and sank out of sight almost before her consorts had completed the turn. Only a few pieces of flotsam littered the spreading oil-slick, but not a single survivor.

The second victim was luckier. The torpedo exploded twenty feet from her stem and sheared off the bows like a butcher carving meat. She too was well-laden, but before the forward bulkhead collapsed her master had time to stop engines and call away the boats. But even she went to the bottom in only seven minutes.

The three destroyers dropped depth-charges and searched the placid water without result. They did not even make a contact with their probing Asdics, and after an hour the Admiral called them back and re-formed the convoy.

Goliath signalled briefly, 'Have twenty survivors aboard' and then fell silent.

As darkness mercifully closed over the ten remaining merchantmen and their depleted escort, the crews no longer felt like rest. Like Chesnaye they seemed to sense that their ordeal had only been a beginning, a casual probe by an enemy who was prepared to wait.

Chesnaye watched the bosun's mates going their rounds of the guns with their massive fannys of cocoa and enamel mugs. Corned-beef sandwiches of stale bread, and meat which had been tinned many years ago.

The cruel injustice seemed the more bitter when Chesnaye compared the convoy's planning and management with that other war of so long ago. Then the generals had used their infantry just as today's strategists used these ships. No one even expected half of the convoy to survive. They might have allowed for only two ships to reach Malta. The others were the justifiable odds, the expendable fodder of war.

Chesnaye recalled with sickening clarity the soldiers at Gallipoli, their shoulders hunched beneath packs and equipment, walking, some just staggering, into the wire and the stammering machine-guns. Far away from such madness the planners moved their coloured flags and markers, and played soldiers with reality and blood.

His head suddenly touched the vibrating screen, and he jerked himself awake with almost vicious determination. 'What time is sun-up?' His question fell across the bridge like a rebuke.

Fox answered slowly, 'Well, with this visibility it'll be light at eight bells, sir.'

'Very well.' Chesnaye settled himself more comfortably in the chair. We'll see who's right when daylight comes. He stared ahead at the cruiser's graceful upperworks. Suddenly he found himself dreading the dawn, and all that it might hold.

9

Make this Signal

Lieutenant Fox bent over the bridge chart table and carefully blew some funnel soot from his pencilled calculations. When he straightened his back he looked again at the blood-red curve of the sun as it lifted slowly above the horizon astern. The forward part of the monitor was still in black shadow, but like the other ships in convoy and the surrounding water itself, the *Saracen*'s superstructure and guns were shining like dull and unused bronze.

I've rarely seen a dawn like this, he thought. Fiery, menacing. Aloud he said casually, 'Looks like another scorcher today!'

A messenger paused in his task of gathering the night's enamel mugs and battered plates to stare with open amazement at his captain. Chesnaye was standing just outside the charthouse, stripped to the waist, apparently wholly intent on shaving. He was using a tiny mirror and was busily scraping away several days of stubble as if it were the most natural thing in the world. The messenger caught the eye of a bosun's mate, who merely shrugged. It seemed to sum up the complete uncertainty of officers in general.

Sub-Lieutenant Bouverie stepped down from the compass and said flatly, 'All ships on station, sir.'

Fox watched the young officer with narrowed eyes. It was quite obvious that Bouverie had still not recovered from yesterday's impartial slaughter. He looked and sounded completely exhausted.

Whereas the ship's company were relieved in batches from their posts, the officers remained at their Action Stations. The lucky ones snatched an odd hour's rest from time to time, others used every ounce of cunning and will-power to restrain their drooping eyelids and sagging bodies.

Fox wondered how long they could all stand it. Another hot day ahead. And probably it was all for nothing. He had sensed the mood of resentment which had passed through the ship when at sunset they had all heard the distant bugle from the flagship. *Aureus*'s men were even now still at Defence Stations. Half the men on watch, the others sleeping like dead men. While we . . . he shook his head angrily, shutting out his dulled thoughts.

Instead he looked at Chesnaye. In the bold red-gold light his lean, hard body looked youthful and alert. Perhaps that was why he was taking the trouble to shave instead of sleeping in his chair? He must be dead on his feet. Held together with sheer determination.

Erskine walked across the bridge carrying his cap. He glanced first at the chart and then at the compass. To no one in particular he remarked, 'We might get a clear run today.'

Nobody answered. Fox felt almost sorry for Erskine. It was amazing the way he had changed. Perhaps we all have?

High above the monitor's outmoded superstructure Lieutenant Norris tried to ease the cramp which repeatedly returned to his legs. The confined shell of the Control Top was filled with the strange glare, and being the highest vantage point in the ship, and for that matter throughout the convoy, Norris had been aware of the dawn for some time. Close at his side but on a slightly higher stool sat McGowan in his position as Control Officer. His neat, plain features were completely relaxed in sleep, and his fingers were laced together in his lap.

At regular intervals the small tower revolved, first on one beam and then in a full one hundred and eighty degrees to the other, as the rating at the training controls rotated their little eyrie to allow the giant telescopes and range-finder to peer to and beyond the horizon. Of course, the sea was empty. It was just as Norris had expected, and the constant image of his comfortable bunk reawakened the irritation in him like a bad tooth.

The training mechanism squeaked and began to move again. The slight motion and the smell of sweat and oil all around made Norris swallow hard. Even with all the observation shutters pinned back it was a foul place, he thought. His stool was now pointing across the starboard beam, and through an open slit he could feel the hint of

298

warmth on his right cheek. God! Another day in here. The fans were useless, and soon it would be like an oven.

He leaned his elbows on the telephone rest and peered down at the nearest merchantman. She seemed far below, her decks still deserted. Lucky bastards, he thought savagely. Once when he had first joined the ship, watch-keeping had been almost enjoyable. With Fox to cover his mistakes he had been able to lose himself in his imagination. He often saw himself as in a film, and thought of what those dowdy creatures in the school staff room would think if they had been lucky enough to see him too.

'Ship, sir!' He realised with a start that the Control Top was motionless and the rating at the big telescope by his knees was stiff in his stool like a gun-dog.

Norris released the catch on his own spotting telescope and pressed his eyes to the sight. High above the monitor's decks, in the centre of the quiet convoy, Norris and the seamen watched the tiny black flaw on the gleaming horizon line.

He felt a sharp movement at his side, and McGowan was as wide awake as he had been fast asleep a second before. He too crouched to look, his fingers moving deftly on his sighting controls.

Norris knew what McGowan was doing without pausing to look at him. As the light hardened across his lenses he stared with fixed concentration at the far off ship. He heard McGowan say sharply : 'Two more ships. One on either side of the first.' Then in a more normal tone. 'Disregard those. Concentrate on the centre one.'

How typical of McGowan's sort, thought Norris. He could see the second pair of ships as indistinct smudges in the morning haze, but they could very likely be cruisers. The centre vessel was much smaller. Surely he was wasting valuable time? Querulously he said, 'She's a small cruiser, Guns, or even just a destroyer, don't you think?'

There was a faint smudge of smoke, too, which seemed to link the three strangers together in a flimsy canopy made golden in the sunlight.

McGowan ignored him and snatched the handset. 'Director . . . Forebridge!' Then a second later, 'Call the Captain to the phone!' Over his shoulder he said with a

299

faint grin : 'Keep watching, my friend. Just watch your *destroyer* grow!'

Norris flushed, aware of the stiff backs of the ratings sitting below his legs. Damn McGowan!

He peered again through his sights, and then as he watched felt his heart falter, as if it would stop altogether. McGowan was speaking in terse, short sentences, but in Norris's curdled brain the words meant nothing.

The centre ship, at first so small and delicate in the lenses, had indeed grown. Even as he stared it seemed to heighten with every passing second. What he had taken for a destroyer's bridge was merely an armoured fire-control position, and as the ships moved to meet the convoy more and more of the central warship crawled up and over the horizon, as if it was rising out of the sea itself. Bridge upon bridge, and even the massive triple turrets could not be masked by distance. Norris bit back a gasp of terror. It was a battleship!

He had seen battleships before. Usually in harbour, or at naval reviews. They always appeared so safe, so impressively permanent like the legend of the Royal Navy and all it stood for. But they had never seemed as warlike or as real as other ships, and now . . . He dashed the sweat from his eyes as McGowan's voice broke into his jumbled thoughts.

'Yes, sir. Battleship and two cruisers.' He broke off as a rating said abruptly, 'Two more ships astern of the cruisers, sir.' McGowan nodded and continued evenly : 'Two more cruisers, sir. The whole squadron is on the same bearing of Green eight-five. Still at extreme distance of thirty thousand yards. I'll start reading the ranges in five minutes.' He slammed down the handset and reached for his headphones and mouthpiece. Catching Norris's wide-eyed stare he said, 'I think the Captain was *expecting* visitors!'

＊　　＊　　＊　　＊　　＊

Surgeon-Lieutenant Wickersley rubbed his eyes and stared at the nearest freighter. It looked as if it was covered in a skin of fine gold, he thought, and in the dawn light the old merchantman took on a kind of majesty. Wickersley swallowed hard to clear the stale taste from his throat. He had been asleep in the Sick Bay but had decided to get up and take a breath of fresh air. His sick-berth attendants were still snoring. They were like himself in that their lack of duties made them the most envied men aboard. Apart from the Captain's steward that is. He was answerable to nobody but the Captain, and was known to drink heavily from anything which took his fancy.

Wickersley climbed the cool steel ladders to the upper bridge and felt some of the night's muzziness clearing from his dull brain. He was almost ashamed of the amount of gin he had consumed in the privacy of his quarters. It was odd to think of the advice and warnings he had given to others, the sad contempt he had felt for them. Because of that letter he had almost joined their ranks. Almost. He reached the bridge and was instantly aware of its alien and tense atmosphere.

Chesnaye was standing by the voice-pipes and speaking rapidly into a handset. Fox was watching the flagship through his glasses, and Bouverie leant across the chart, watched by Erskine.

Chesnaye dropped the handset and saw Wickersley for the first time. His drill-jacket was open to the waist and his hair was dishevelled. By contrast his smooth cheeks and cold, alert eyes seemed to belong to someone else. 'Hello, Doc. Come to referee?'

He turned away as a voice-pipe squeaked, 'Main armament closed up!'

Wickersley's brain was completely clear now. Main armament? He joined the Yeoman who was looking at his young signalman on the flag deck below. 'What's up, Yeo?'

Laidlaw plucked at his beard. 'Battleship and four Eyetie cruisers on the starboard beam. They're heading this way it seems!'

Wickersley peered towards the open water beyond one of the wallowing freighters as if he expected to see the enemy for himself.

The Yeoman added, 'They're about fourteen miles off at present, sir.'

As if to back up his words they heard the magnified voice of the range-taker. 'Range two-eight-five!'

Bouverie looked up. 'Flagship's signalling, sir!'

A shaded lamp flickered along the lines of ships. 'Alter course, sir! Steer two-two-five!'

Chesnaye sounded cool. 'Follow the next ahead, Pilot.'

'We might miss them, d'you think?' Wickersley found he was whispering.

Fox lowered his glasses and grinned. 'If we take our shoes off!'

Lifting a spare pair of glasses from their rack, Wickersley climbed on to a grating and peered vaguely across the lightening water. It was all glare, and gold mirrors. The sea was flat, yet alive with a million tiny movements and reflections. As far as he could see the convoy had the sea to itself. He felt suddenly frustrated and out of place. 'Seems quiet enough!'

Chesnaye was crossing the bridge and paused at his side. 'The Admiral intends to steer away from the enemy. There's always a chance, of course.' He did not sound as if he believed it. 'It's a *Littorio*-class battleship. One of the new ones. Nine fifteen-inch guns, thirty knots.'

'*Aureus*'s turning, sir.'

They watched the sleek cruiser fall away and begin to steam slowly round the convoy to place herself between the ships and the invisible enemy.

'How far can they shoot, sir?' Wickersley was watching Chesnaye's calm, unblinking eyes.

'They'll be in range at twenty thousand. Effective shooting at ten thousand yards in this early haze.' He shrugged. 'After that it's anyone's guess.'

'Range two-eight-oh!'

Wickersley half listened to the regular, patient reports and the repeated orders. It was unreal and unnerving. Everything was just the same. The columns of ships, the monitor's steady engine beat, the bright, empty sky. Yet somewhere over the horizon, steaming at full speed, was a terrible force which his mind could not contemplate. A battleship, a floating steel town of guns and armour, as well as four cruisers. Against them would be one cruiser, three destroyers and a sloop. And the *Saracen*. He stared round with sudden despair. The *Saracen*. Even at the mention of the battleship's speed his heart had sunk. Thirty knots against six and a half. The monitor would not even be able to join battle. With the merchantmen she would be made to wait like a patient animal outside the slaughterhouse.

All at once Wickersley felt the anger boiling inside him, driving out the misery and self-pity which had been his companions for so many days. 'Have we just got to damned well sit here and take it?'

Chesnaye eyed him calmly. 'We'll have to wait and see.'

'Range two-seven-oh!'

Fox crossed the bridge. 'The bearing's changed, sir. They're after us.'

Chesnaye nodded as if his mind was elsewhere. 'Yes.'

Fox glanced at the Doctor and shrugged. He knew that he had wanted the Captain to produce some miracle, to reassure him. Just as he was certain that there was no miracle now.

Chesnaye turned his back on all of them and watched the *Aureus* as she swung round in a tight turn to take up station on the convoy's starboard flank. Her four turrets were already trained on her quarter, and he could see the tiny figures filling her bridge. He wondered briefly what Beaushears was thinking at this very moment. As far as he was concerned he was alone. The trap was sprung. There was no time for the 'if onlys' and the 'perhapses', this was now.

He heard a lookout say involuntarily, 'Christ it's gettin' bright!' as if the man was willing back the sun.

'Range two-six-oh!'

Twenty-six thousand yards. Thirteen miles. Chesnaye levelled his glasses and stared for several seconds at the faint black shapes which were already lifting above the blue and gold line.

Chesnaye felt his fingers buttoning his jacket, as if the agonising wait was too much for them. He had to control and regularise his breathing to stop his anxiety joining the white-hot anger which he felt for Beaushears and everything which he had known was going to happen. He could even foretell Beaushears' next move. He would wait until the enemy was within range and then go in to the attack. A brave, useless gesture. The battleship would pound him to pieces before his little six-inch guns could even splash her paintwork. There was no hope of air cover, and the sup-

porting cruisers of Beaushears' squadron would take a day
to find the convoy. By that time . . .

'Signal from Flag, sir. Maintain courses and speed!'

Chesnaye did not turn round. The signal made him feel
sick. It was as if Beaushears was issuing signals merely for
something to do. Perhaps his nerve had gone and he was
unable to think beyond his normal routine.

Chesnaye concentrated on adjusting his mind yet again.
It was just possible that *Aureus* could hold off the attacking
ships long enough. The merchantmen still had the destroyers and one sloop. If they could hold out for another
day, and increase speed, there might be time to get help
from Malta. Submarines perhaps?

'Range two-double-oh!'

A ripple of orange flashes mingled with the sunlight, and
Chesnaye found himself gripping the screen with sudden
doubt.

'The enemy's opened fire, sir!'

Every eye on the bridge watched the flagship, a slender
outline above her glittering reflection.

With the sound of tearing silk the first salvo came
screaming down from above. It seemed to take minutes; to
some the wait was like an hour, but there were cries of surprise and horror as the first six waterspouts rose with mag-
nificent and terrible splendour not around the flagship, but
across the starboard line of merchantmen.

Chesnaye could only stare with disbelief as the nearest
merchantman received a direct hit from one of the great
fifteen-inch shells full on her maindeck. The blast was like
a thunderclap, and the great searing tongue of flame
seemed to cut the ship in two.

The battleship had turned on an almost parallel course,
so that her third turret could be brought to bear, and within seconds the next salvo was on its way. The stricken
freighter seemed to topple over as some internal explosion
rocked the hull and brought the bridge tottering into the
great flaming crater left by the shell.

The flagship turned towards the enemy, the froth mounting beneath her counter as she increased to maximum
speed. Beaushears had expected to be the target, to die
doing his duty. But the Italian commander had no inten-

tion of being side-tracked by any noble gestures. He was after the convoy. The convoy would go first.

The Yeoman ducked as a tall column of water rose less than half a cable from the *Saracen*'s bows. 'Signal from Flag, sir! *Scatter!*'

Chesnaye tasted the salty spray hurled by the explosion, and stared at the signal flags on the *Aureus*'s yard. *Scatter*. Beaushears had taken the only solution he knew. Every ship for itself. Instead of being destroyed together, they would be sunk one at a time by the speedy cruisers.

Fox said sharply, 'The *Cape Cod*'s been hit!'

Chesnaye spun round as if he had been struck. The big freighter had never faltered, had never lost station even under attack. Now as he watched he saw the smoke pouring uncontrollably from her foredeck, and realised with sudden shock that the front of her tall bridge had gone completely. *Cape Cod* was momentarily hidden by another three tall columns of water. Each falling shell threw up a waterspout some hundred feet in the air. Even the noise of their falling made his ears sing.

Fox said: 'Their steering's gone, sir. They're trying to steer from aft!'

A lookout called, 'Direct hit on the destroyer *Brigadier*, sir!'

Chesnaye tore his eyes from the burning freighter and the tiny figures which were running aft to the emergency steering position. One of the escorts was already sinking, her stern high in the water like the arm of a drowning man.

Through his teeth he barked: 'Request to re-form convoy! Make that signal to Flag, Yeoman!'

They must keep together. It was their only chance.

Fox threw up his hands to shade his eyes as the flagship's upperworks burst apart with one deafening roar. Her control top and upper bridge seemed to slide sideways, and even the main topmast, with Beaushears' own flag still flying, staggered over the great pall of black and yellow smoke which surged to meet it.

Laidlaw, who had been about to flash the signal himself, lowered the lamp and stared at the cruiser, which in a second had changed its shape and form to a blazing hulk. The *Aureus* slewed round, the smoke blown across her impotent guns which had still not fired.

Fox lowered his hands. 'My God!' He seemed at a complete loss. 'God all-bloody Mighty!'

Chesnaye stepped to the centre of the bridge, the *Cape Cod* was burning fiercely, the flames glittering across the water like the dawn sun. But she was afloat. If only they had more time. Like a stranger he stared round his shocked bridge. Laidlaw with the signal lamp hanging from his fingers. Fox, who could not drag his eyes from the battered cruiser, and Bouverie, who seemed like a man under drugs.

In a strained voice Chesnaye heard himself say: 'Make a signal to escorts. Reassemble convoy forthwith and proceed on course at maximum speed.'

He felt his legs shake as he crossed to the front of the bridge. Dear God, let Ann be safe. She *has* to be safe!

He closed his mind again. 'Starboard twenty!' It was a second or two before Fox repeated the order or realised what it implied.

Then as the wheel went down and the bows began to swing, Chesnaye said sharply: 'Tell the Chief I want maximum revolutions! I want this ship to go as she did at Gallipoli!'

Laidlaw returned, shaking his head like a dog. 'Signal executed, sir!'

'Good. Now, Yeoman, you can do one more thing this morning.'

'Sir?' Laidlaw's tired eyes were watching the merchantmen careering across the monitor's bows as the *Saracen* continued to turn.

Chesnaye paused, his glasses levelled on the far off shapes. 'Midships! Steady!' He glanced briefly at Laidlaw again. 'Hoist battle ensigns!'

Above and below the bridge, gunners, signalmen and lookouts watched with awe and shock as the big ensigns broke out from gaff and yard. Even down in the engine room Lieutenant-Commander (E) Tregarth and his assistant sensed the new flood of power which pulsated through the old ship like fire. Tregarth watched the dials and wiped his hands across his white overalls. 'Glad I'm down here,' was his only comment, and that was lost in the roar of *Saracen*'s machinery.

Vice-Admiral Sir Mark Beaushears clenched his teeth and bit back the agonising pain. He shook his head from side to side, still unable to speak lest the waiting scream escaped from his lips. The arm behind his shoulders lowered him again to the deck, and Beaushears stared fixedly at the bright star-shaped area of blue sky which shone through the jagged hole above him. The bridge was a shambles, and above all there was an ear-splitting hiss of escaping steam. If he closed his eyes Beaushears imagined he could see himself as a young midshipman beside his tearful mother at Waterloo station. He had hated her coming with him to the train. There were other midshipmen all around him, watching, and passing knowing smiles. Over all there had been that nerve-shaking sound of steam from the engines in the station, which had made the parting even more difficult.

A shadow crossed the patch of sky, and he stared vaguely at Captain Colquhoun, who was watching him as if from far away. Beaushears tried to move again. 'Harmsworth! Where the devil's my flag-lieutenant?'

Colquhoun looked at the ship's surgeon, who was still trying to support the Admiral's shoulders as he struggled weakly on the littered bridge. The surgeon shook his head briefly, and the Captain guessed that nothing could be done.

Around and below the bridge the air was filled with shouts and the clatter of running feet. Colquhoun wanted to dash out into the smoke and sunlight. His ship, his precious *Aureus*, was listing badly, and a thousand things were needed. He glanced unwillingly at the pulped corpse below the voice-pipes. Harmsworth was still grinning, his teeth white against the flayed skin.

Beaushears said thickly, 'What's happening, Colquhoun?'

The Captain listened to the steam and felt the wretched shuddering of the ship beneath him. 'Direct hit, sir. Steering's gone. I'm going to try to——'

He broke off as an officer, his cheek torn apart in a long gash, staggered into the bridge and shouted: 'Sir! The *Saracen*'s going past!' He reeled against the torn plates as if shocked by his own words. 'The old girl's closing the enemy!'

307

Colquhoun stood up and walked quickly to the screen. Flotsam from his own ship floated around in the calm water, and he could see the smoke from the *Aureus*'s wounds streaming astern towards the scattered convoy. But for a few moments longer he forgot his own duties and stared fixedly at the monitor.

She was less than a quarter of a mile away, and seemed to be leaning forward as she thrust her blunt bows deep into the blue water, the plume of funnel smoke adding to the impression of desperate effort and urgency. He saw the great battle ensigns, and the two massive guns swinging slowly on their barbettes, their muzzles pointing protectively across his own stricken ship.

Behind him he heard Beaushears croak: 'What *is* it? What is that madman doing?'

Colquhoun said: 'It *is* the *Saracen*. She's going to tackle the bastards alone!'

Beaushears contracted his muscles against the pain. It was almost as if the shell splinters were gouging his chest wide open. 'Tell me, Colquhoun! Describe it!' Each word was agony.

The Captain winced as three waterspouts rose alongside the monitor. 'The enemy have found her!' He banged the screen with mounting excitement. 'By God, she's going to open fire!' As he spoke the two long guns belched fire and brown smoke, and the air seemed to shiver from the force of the twin detonations.

Beaushears fell back, suddenly quiet. So Chesnaye had been right, after all. He had thought it all out, just as he did at the Dardanelles. He closed his eyes and saw with sudden clarity the boats crammed with marines and Major De L'Isle waving his walking stick. The *Saracen*'s spotting officer falling dead on the beach, and Chesnaye saying '*I'll* go!' Now he was steaming past. The pictures were becoming mixed and disjointed. He could see the trim, clean-painted monitor with ensigns streaming, but Royston-Jones was the officer in command. Faintly he muttered: 'Chesnaye'll do something today! He's mad enough for anything!' Then in a stronger voice he called. 'Helen! For God's sake!'

The Doctor stood up. 'He's dead, sir.'

'Come over here, Doc!' Colquhoun seemed to have forgotten his admiral. 'Take a good look. You'll never see the like again in a lifetime!'

The Doctor clung to the screen as the monitor's guns lurched back once again. The flagship had swung slightly in the gentle swell, so that he could see the *Saracen* steaming away at right angles. Over and beyond her queer tripod mast he saw the battleship for the first time. It seemed to fill the horizon, flanked on either beam by two cruisers. Every gun on the battleship was firing, and the water ahead and on either side of the monitor was pitted with rising waterspouts or torn curtains of falling spray. The enemy cruisers were silent, and Colquhoun said: 'They can't reach the *Saracen* yet. The battleship is sharing the kill with nobody!' Then, as if the strain was too much for him, he took off his cap and waved it wildly in the air. 'What d'you think of *that*!' When he tore himself away to tend to his own ship, the Doctor saw that the Captain's eyes were streaming.

Lieutenant Norris drew his head into his shoulders as the monitor opened fire. He wanted to tear his eyes from his telescopic sight, but the sight of the battleship held him as if paralysed. He saw the two pinnacles of silver water leap across the great ship's outline and had to lick his parched lips before he could speak. 'Short! Up eight hundred!' The lights flickered and a small bell rang in the fume-filled Control Top.

McGowan sat hunched on his stool his eyes on his own sight, his lips moving as he spoke into his microphone. At the other end of the communicating wires, hidden within the swivelling turret, Lloyd, the Quarters Officer, and his crew of fifty men sweated and fed the smoking breeches.

'Sights on!'

'Shoot!'

As the switches were made yet again the whole ship seemed to lurch with the recoil. The Control Top felt as if it would tear itself from the tripod mast and hurl itself into the sea.

Norris gulped as his vision momentarily misted with spray. He felt the sudden shock-wave like a body blow and ducked away from the sights as a sheet of flame rose from the monitor's bows.

McGowan pushed his arm and snarled: 'Keep watch! Report the fall!'

Shaking and sick, Norris pressed his forehead to the rubber pad. He was just in time to see the small white feathers rise beyond the other terrifying ship. He could hardly speak at all now. 'Over! Down two hundred!'

McGowan was shouting orders with wild excitement. He seemed completely absorbed, almost unaware of the danger and the fact that an enemy shell had exploded within feet of the *Saracen*'s stem. At last the old monitor had made herself felt. The next salvo might make an impression. Victory was impossible. But they would show the bastards.

At that very instant the air was sucked from the Control Top, and Norris jack-knifed in a fit of coughing. He felt the shudder of a hit on the monitor's hull, and with his eyes closed against the hot smoke he pushed open one of the steel shutters, retching and moaning as he sucked at the fresh air from that other world.

The rating with the headset shouted wildly, his eyes red-rimmed with smoke, 'Sight set, sir!'

A bell rang urgently, but Norris could not stop himself from coughing.

He half turned to see what had happened to McGowan's control, but stared instead at the Gunnery Officer's bent frame and the long, unending stream of blood which coursed down the back of his stool. His telescopic sight was fractured and must have deflected a flying splinter from the last shell. Sobbing hysterically, Norris reached over and seized McGowan's jacket. 'For Christ's sake speak to me!'

The bell rang again, and the rating said sharply, 'He's had it, sir!' As if to emphasise the horror he gestured to the flecks of scarlet which had sprayed across the switches. 'Straight through the guts!'

'Oh my God!' Norris rocked back on his stool as the ship quivered yet again. The mast vibrated to the fall of broken plating, and in the far distance he heard the crackle of flames.

A telephone buzzed and the rating said urgently: 'Sir! It's the Captain!'

Norris took the handset, his eyes still fixed on McGowan's pale, piercing stare. It was over. He was alone. He felt as if he was already dead himself, instead of McGowan. All four of the seamen who completed the control-team had turned in their seats to watch him. Even McGowan was watching him.

He felt an all-consuming madness hovering in the corner of his mind, so that the tiny steel space seemed to be closing in, crushing him.

Suddenly, out of the horror and mounting insanity came a voice. Norris clutched the handset and stared at it, his face changing to an expression of pathetic submission. Almost gratefully he listened to Chesnaye's calm, even caressing, voice. After a while he nodded, oblivious of the watching seamen, even of McGowan.

'Yes, sir,' he said. 'I shall do my best.'

He dropped the handset and lowered his head to the sights. In a strange, robot-like tone he murmured : 'Continue tracking ! Stand by !'

. . . . .

Lieutenant-Commander John Erskine stood loosely in the centre of the damage-control base, a small enclosed compartment below the aft shelter deck. On one bulkhead was a plan of the ship showing every watertight compartment, magazine, store-space and the thousand smaller corners which had been crammed into the monitor's hull. Four ratings sat at the switchboard, their lips moving into chest-mouthpieces as they answered calls from other parts of the ship.

Craig, the Chief Bosun's Mate, said unhurriedly, 'Fire in the starboard four-inch battery, sir !'

Erskine forced his mind to concentrate on the plan, and tried to imagine his small parties of stokers and seamen who were already dealing with the first shell damage.

Craig nodded to one of the telephonists. 'Send Benson's party at the double !'

The deck bounced beneath their feet like a steel springboard. From the cracks around the sealed door came small wisps of smoke, like steam being forced from an overheated engine.

'Direct hit aft, sir!' The rating sounded hoarse. 'Tiller flat flooded!'

Erskine ran his fingers through his hair. 'Very well. Report any other damage!' He wanted to leave this enclosed prison, to help the damage-control parties, anything but stand here and supervise the ship's funeral rites.

Craig said, 'Must be hell up top, sir?'

How true, Erskine thought wildly. The monitor would be destroyed piecemeal. The great fifteen-inch shells from a modern, fast-moving battleship could gnaw away even the heaviest armoured ship in minutes once the range had been found. He staggered as the deck canted suddenly beneath him. The wheel was going over again. Chesnaye must be doing everything possible to avoid those terrible waterspouts. Erskine remembered the numbing shock he had endured when he had seen the flagship struck by just one shell. And every dragging minute brought the two antagonists closer together.

Midshipman Gayler pushed open the door, a grubby rag pressed to his mouth. He was covered in dirt and his uniform was dripping with water. 'Four-inch battery well alight, sir!' He seemed calm enough, Erskine thought, but his youth probably saved him from the agony of experience. 'Mister Joslin wants to flood the battery's magazine!' Gayler blinked rapidly as two more thunderous explosions shook the compartment and brought the paint flakes cascading over their heads.

Erskine swallowed hard. Flood the magazine? It would take all of twenty minutes. But if they waited? He snatched up the bridge telephone.

Far away, his voice punctuated by explosions and the tearing roar of passing shells, Fox answered his questions. 'Range down to twelve thousand yards! Still closing!'

Erskine said: 'Permission to flood starboard magazine? We've a bad fire there!'

A fit of coughing. 'I can bloody well see it!' A pause, complete silence as Fox covered the telephone with his hand, and then, 'The Captain says flood!' Click. Erskine stared at the dead handset, then nodded to Craig.

'Have the valves opened. Watch the table and get ready to order a counter-flooding to port. We must keep her at correct trim. Guns will need that at least for his fire-control!'

Gayler looked up from wiping his face. 'Lieutenant Mc-Gowan's dead, sir.'

Erskine turned away. My God! Outside this prison friends and familiar faces were being wiped away as if from a slate. Tightly: 'I'm going aft to supervise the quarterdeck party. Report any major damage to the bridge!' Then he was through the door, blundering through the mad world of tearing noise and billowing, blinding smoke. Voices called all around him, and he could hear the ring of axes, the desperate voices of men working in semi-darkness. A man yelled, 'Stretcher party *here*!' And there was an inhuman sound of groaning and bubbling.

Another voice: 'Keep still, Fred! I'll get help!'

A great explosion almost alongside and a tidal wave of shredded water which tasted of cordite swept across the decks.

A petty officer cannoned into Erskine and stared at him wild-eyed. 'Lost three men, sir. There are seven more right aft. Smashed ter bits.' He peered through the smoke. 'It won't be long now, sir!'

Erskine pushed past him and felt his way further aft. There were several bodies scattered amongst the wreckage, their limbs and entrails mingling with the fire party's hoses. In the middle of the carnage Wickersley was squatting beside a wounded seaman, his face grimy but intent as he forced morphia into the man's arm. He glanced up. 'Busy day!'

Erskine felt suddenly ashamed. Even the Doctor seemed to have forgotten everything else but the immediate present. His own hopes for the future, a command, a fresh start, meant nothing now. He had misjudged everything, just as he had lost his real opportunity with Ann. She had died already without a doubt. Carried down in a blazing ship, as he would be too. He felt his limbs beginning to shake in sharp, uncontrollable spasms.

Wickersley was on his feet, waving impatiently to two cowering stretcher bearers. 'I wish I felt as cool as you look, Number One!' Wickersley wiped his mouth with the back of his hand. 'No wonder you're always carping about we reservists!' He laughed and picked up his satchel. 'Well, see you around!' Then he was gone, swallowed up by the smoke.

Erskine stared after him and wondered. The Doctor's words seemed to steady him, to sober his wretched thoughts.

A messenger skidded to a halt beside him. 'Can you come, sir? Control report damage and casualties in the T/S!'

He started to run, but Erskine said: 'Walk, lad! We don't want to start a panic.'

The seaman saw his smile and felt reassured. There might still be hope.

Together they walked towards the bank of smoke with its depraved scarlet centre.

. . . . .

Chesnaye ducked as the blasted water spattered over the bridge screen. Each shell-burst seemed to punch his body like a steel fist, and every direct hit drove him to a kind of inner frenzy. The water boiled and seethed on either beam, like devils' whirlpools.

That last salvo had been a perfect straddle. 'Port twenty!' He prayed that the armoured wheelhouse was still unscathed. He felt the ship beginning to swing, and saw the big turret turn slightly to compensate for the alteration of course. Thank God he had been able to calm Norris after that first hit. He watched narrowly as more shells whimpered overhead. Not so heavy this time?

Fox said sharply, 'The cruisers have opened fire, sir!'

Chesnaye felt his heart plunge. They had to hit the battleship before the combined gunfire of the enemy blasted the *Saracen* bodily out of the water. They *had* to! Dazedly he ordered, 'Midships!'

The turret shivered as another two shells roared away into the smoke. He steadied his shaking body against the screen and tried to clear his thoughts. All around him men were shouting and passing orders. Occasionally a voice-pipe fell silent, only to be reopened by some different, frightened voice as a man stepped into the place left by killed and wounded. It could not last. Then the enemy would still destroy the convoy after all.

Another salvo. More spray, and at least two thudding blows into the monitor's battered hull. 'Starboard ten!'

At the back of his mind Chesnaye could still feel the agony he had endured when Laidlaw had reported: '*Cape God*'s gone, sir! She's rolled over!'

Even the overpowering menace of the battleship's winking guns could not lessen that final anguish.

There was a sharp crack behind him as more splinters whined over the bridge. As he turned he saw Fox stagger and fall beside the compass, his teeth bared in pain.

Bouverie fell on his knees beside him, his eyes searching but helpless. Fox spoke between his teeth, his agonised gaze fixed on Bouverie's face. 'Get away from me, you maniac!' He moved his hands across his waist where the scarlet stain was spreading with each painful breath. 'Get up on that compass, you bloody lawyer! And try to remember what I've taught you!'

He even grinned as Bouverie staggered to his feet and climbed on to the compass platform. Then he looked up at Chesnaye who had knelt beside him. 'He'll do, sir! He won't let you down!' His hard, uncompromising features seemed to soften, and he lowered his forehead against Chesnaye's shoulder. 'Don't reproach yourself, Skipper! You were right!' Then his head lolled to one side.

Chesnaye stood up, his face ashen. 'Report damage!'

They were all dying. And for what?

He crossed to the bridge sight and pressed his head against the worn pad. The careering battleship leapt into life in the lenses, her three turrets smoking as the gunners reloaded. His feet tingled as another shell ploughed along the *Saracen*'s deck and exploded below an Oerlikon mounting, blasting the gunners to oblivion. The enemy cruisers were increasing speed, dashing in to complete the kill.

Chesnaye stared with dull disbelief as the battleship's forward turret opened skywards in one long orange flash.

Chesnaye snatched the control handset, only to hear Norris screaming like a maniac: 'A hit! Jesus Christ, a bloody *hit*!'

One of the monitor's shells, dropping with the speed of hundreds of feet a second, had found a target. The great, armour-piercing mass of screaming explosive had punctured the flat surface of the ship's 'A' turret even as the gunners had been reloading. Three fifteen-inch shells had been about to enter three smoking breeches. The Italian gunnery officer had been confident that they would be the final death blow to the shell-blasted wreck which had been crawling and staggering towards the ship, and which had defied every explosion.

The *Saracen*'s shell and the three Italian ones joined together in one mighty chorus, which was heard in the convoy and by the trapped and dying men in the *Saracen*'s hull. The battleship's turret was lifted bodily from its barbette, and in going severely buckled the neighbouring 'B' turret, so that it too was rendered harmless.

The cruisers continued to fire. The nearest one was already sweeping round in a tight arc to cut its way past the maddened *Saracen*.

Chesnaye lowered his glasses and heard the puny cracks from the port four-inch battery. Pin-pricks against the cruiser. But whatever else happened now, his ship, his *Saracen*, had struck home.

He thought distantly of Royston-Jones' small monkey face. His grave, unwavering pride in the ship. 'With courage and integrity, press on!'

Bouverie called. 'Fire gaining hold aft, sir! They want to flood the compartment!'

Chesnaye answered wearily, 'Very well.'

The monitor was already sluggish and hardly answering his constant wheel orders. As soon as the battleship had recovered its wits the other big turret would be brought to bear again. There would be no mercy now.

Chesnaye turned his back on the enemy and looked back at his ship. The tripod mast was only supported by its stays, the whole structure sagging against the rear of the bridge. The funnel leaked smoke from hundreds of splinter holes, and through the fog of battle Chesnaye caught glimpses of the upper deck. It was pitted with massive craters, some of which glittered with black water. The ship was slowly being torn apart. Dead and dying men lay everywhere. Even his own uniform was spattered with blood from a cut across his scalp.

Yet the old girl was hanging on. With a schoolmaster,

half crazy with terror, gauging each shot and guiding the monitor's guns on to their target. A barrister at the compass, white-faced, but strangely determined as his legs still straddled Fox's crumpled body.

And what of me? He ran his eye across the smashed and torn ship. I brought them all to *this*.

The bridge shook, and a signalman screamed as a splinter tore away his arm. Chesnaye heard Wickersley's voice through the bedlam, and watched as the first-aid party clambered over the buckled metal to get at the victims.

The cruisers were on either beam, but Norris still obeyed Chesnaye's last order. Keep firing at the battleship. Keep hitting her no matter what else happens.

A seaman was staggering down the port waist carrying a limp, spread-eagled figure. Chesnaye watched the man's groping foot-steps with chilled fascination. He was carrying Danebury, the small midshipman. The man passed into safety behind the bridge, and Chesnaye had to shake himself to clear away the nightmare. The dead midshipman. Back across the years. It was like an additional, cruel taunt.

Bouverie was sobbing : 'Sir ! Sir !'

Chesnaye turned slowly, afraid of what he might see.

Bouverie half fell as he groped his way towards him. He held Chesnaye's hands, all else forgotten but what he had just seen.

'Sir ! They're pulling *away* ! They've had enough !'

Dazed, Chesnaye lifted his glasses for the hundredth time. The battleship's shape looked quite different. She was end on, a mounting froth at her stern. Like unwilling hounds the cruisers fired their last shots and then closed protectively around their leader. They too would have a difficult passage home now.

He nodded vaguely and touched Bouverie's arm. He could find no words. They were all round him. Wickersley, quiet and concerned, Bouverie, grinning like a schoolboy. Even Fox looked as if he was smiling.

Below he could hear cheering. Faint at first, then stronger, unquenchable, like the old ship herself.

Chesnaye saw Erskine too. He looked older. Changed. He felt his hand in his and heard him say, 'I'm *sorry*, sir !'

Sorry? For what? For Ann perhaps. For the poor, battered ship, or for himself? It did not matter which any more.

'Signal from destroyer escort, sir!' Laidlaw's beard was singed but still jaunty. 'Request instructions?'

Chesnaye felt his way to the front of the bridge. Through the mist across his eyes he could still see the fast-disappearing shapes of the enemy ships. He felt the heat-blistered steel. We did it.

The Yeoman added excitedly, 'Escort reports return of our cruiser squadron, sir!' The lights still stammered. 'They request instructions?'

Chesnaye said in a tired voice, 'Tell the Senior Officer!'

Laidlaw said thickly, '*You* are the Senior Officer now, sir!'

Chesnaye nodded. 'Very well.' They were all looking at him.

Laidlaw unconsciously left the most important item till last. 'Tug *Goliath* reports all survivors of *Cape Cod* safe on board.' He sounded puzzled. 'They keep repeating, sir. *All* survivors safe?'

Chesnaye turned away from them, and Erskine said, 'Thank you, Yeoman.' Then in a loud, clear voice he continued: 'Make this signal. To Commander-in-Chief, repeated Inshore Squadron.' He paused, his eyes fixed on Chesnaye's bowed shoulders. Then he looked across at Wickersley, and together they stood behind him.

The Captain was resting his head on the screen, as if he was speaking with the ship.

Erskine continued, 'His Majesty's Ship *Saracen* and convoy will enter harbour as ordered.'

Epilogue

Dr. Robert Wickersley walked slowly from the club dining room and crossed to the library. It was cool in the club after the exhaust-filled streets, and the London traffic was entirely cut off by the stout old walls and ancient furniture.

The library was fortunately empty, but for one of the brass-buttoned servants who immediately crossed to a corner chair and pulled a small table beside it.

'Good evenin', sir. Your usual?'

'Yes, thank you, Arthur.' Wickersley sank down in the chair and reached again for the evening paper. He no longer felt the weariness of a long day in his surgery, nor the irritation of delving into the case histories of people who had too much time and too much money to know the meaning of real illness.

With something like shock he noticed that his hand was shaking as he opened the paper at the middle page where his efficient secretary had ringed a small item near the bottom.

He had read it several times already, even in the heavy traffic as Matthews had guided the powerful Bentley skilfully towards the club. All through dinner he had thought of nothing else, yet he had been afraid to allow his mind to explore its full impact, as a surgeon falters before the moment to begin an operation.

Now he was alone. He read the item of news very slowly.

The death was reported last night of Captain Richard Chesnaye, Victoria Cross, Royal Navy(Retired), who died at his Hampshire home of a heart attack whilst watching television. Captain Chesnaye won his V.C. during the last war when defending a convoy to Malta against superior enemy forces. He leaves a widow and one son.

Wickersley folded the paper across his lap and stared unseeingly at the glass which had quietly appeared at his elbow. Twenty-three years ago. Yet in the cool silence of the library it seemed like yesterday. Like now.

Were we really like that? One figure remained fixed in his drifting thoughts. He could see Chesnaye's face outlined against the smoke and flames, and seemed to hear his voice.

Suddenly Wickersley was on his feet and groping through the neatly laid lines of papers and magazines. He found the *Radio Times* and thumbed back to the previous night's programmes. His heart was thumping painfully, but he knew somehow that he would find the answer there.

There it was, another small item near the bottom of the page.

Tonight viewers will see a short film from the Pacific of Britain's latest air-to-surface nuclear missile. The film, presented with the co-operation of the United States Navy, will show the missile being homed on to a moored target ship. The vessel used was an old British hulk, once named Saracen.

Wickersley sat down in his chair and stared emptily at the shadows.

So, even at the end, they had been together.